YOUNG LADIES JUST WANT TO HAVE FUN . . .

Unfortunately Eleanor Griffin has three strapping brothers to frighten away any beau they deem unsuitable. She knows she's expected to marry eventually—probably some staid, crusty old lord—but until that dark day dawns, Nell intends to enjoy herself. However, the Duke of Melbourne isn't about to let his sister run completely wild, and asks his best friend, the Marquis of Deverill, to keep a close eye on the spirited lovely.

Could any chaperone be less qualified—yet more appreciated—than Valentine Corbett? Here is a man as sinful as he is attractive; a notorious rake, gambler, and pursuer of women, whom Nell has fancied since girlhood. Alas, the irresistible rogue seems uncharacteristically determined to be honorable, despite the passionate longing in his gaze. And Nell must tread carefully, for she has promised to immediately wed whomever her siblings choose should so much as a *hint* of scandal arise . . .

By Suzanne Enoch

SIN AND SENSIBILITY • ENGLAND'S PERFECT HERO
LONDON'S PERFECT SCOUNDREL • THE RAKE
A MATTER OF SCANDAL • MEET ME AT MIDNIGHT
TAMING RAFE • BY LOVE UNDONE
STOLEN KISSES • LADY ROGUE

And Coming Soon the Contemporary Romance

FLIRTING WITH DANGER

If You've Enjoyed This Book,
Be Sure to Read These Other
AVON ROMANTIC TREASURES

DUKE OF SIN *by Adele Ashworth*
HIS EVERY KISS *by Laura Lee Guhrke*
MY OWN PRIVATE HERO *by Julianne MacLean*
A SCANDAL TO REMEMBER *by Linda Needham*
A WANTED MAN *by Susan Kay Law*

Coming Soon

SOMETHING ABOUT EMMALINE *by Elizabeth Boyle*

Suzanne Enoch

Sin and Sensibility

An Avon Romantic Treasure

AVON BOOKS
An Imprint of HarperCollinsPublishers

This is a work of fiction. Names, characters, places, and incidents are products of the author's imagination or are used fictitiously and are not to be construed as real. Any resemblance to actual events, locales, organizations, or persons, living or dead, is entirely coincidental.

AVON BOOKS
An Imprint of HarperCollins*Publishers*
10 East 53rd Street
New York, New York 10022-5299

Copyright © 2005 by Suzanne Enoch
Excerpt from *Flirting With Danger* copyright © 2005 by Suzanne Enoch
ISBN: 0-06-054325-6
www.avonromance.com

First Avon Books paperback printing: January 2005

Avon Trademark Reg. U.S. Pat. Off. and in Other Countries, Marca Registrada, Hecho en U.S.A.
HarperCollins® is a registered trademark of HarperCollins Publishers Inc.

Printed in the U.S.A.

10 9 8 7 6 5 4 3 2 1

For my sister, Cheryl,
who despite an unbelievably tough year
has still managed to be both
supportive and silly.
I love you, 'lil Bub.

Chapter 1

Valentine Corbett, the Marquis of Deverill, lifted his glass. "I see trouble," he murmured, taking a swallow of whiskey.

"Not my husband," Lydia, Lady Franch said, lifting her head.

"No, he's still ogling Genevieve DuMer." Shifting a little, Valentine could make out Lord Franch's profile near the entrance to the gaming room. The elderly Franch's attention remained steadily on young Miss DuMer's ample bosom as they chatted.

"The oaf." Lydia lowered her head again.

Half closing his eyes, Valentine cupped the back of the viscountess's neck, encouraging her ministrations. His gaze, though, returned to the more significant little drama unfolding beyond the gauze of curtains.

Lydia paused again. "What trouble do you see, then?" she asked.

"John Priestley is offering Lady Eleanor Griffin a bracelet of pearls, and she's allowing him to fasten them around her wrist."

Lady Franch's next comment was muffled and tickled a little, but Valentine assumed it to be a request for more information. Setting aside the whiskey, he slid his fingers along the edge of the curtain.

"The two of them are standing in plain view of everyone," he continued, "including all three of her brothers." He sighed, firming his grip on Lydia's head as her bobbing became more enthusiastic. "I very much doubt that the Duke of Melbourne, at the least, approves of his sister accepting gifts from a gentleman—especially in public, and especially from an idiot not deemed worthy to be a suitor."

He tilted his own head back, the antics of his fellows becoming less interesting as the motions of Lydia's mouth upon his cock began to produce results. Even as he allowed himself to go over the edge, though, Valentine kept his eyes open and his attention on the crowded ballroom beyond their cozy little hideaway. He never closed his eyes; with the games he enjoyed playing, that would be both stupid and suicidal.

As Lydia straightened again, he handed her the glass of whiskey. "I do enjoy waltzing with you, my dear," he said, standing and helping her off her knees.

"Yes, but you enjoy dancing with everyone, Valentine," she returned, finishing off the whiskey as he buttoned his trousers.

"A fact about which I have always been honest."

"One of your few positive qualities."

Valentine returned his attention from the room long enough to lift an eyebrow. "I have at least two positive qualities. And the bosom has found a dance partner, which, I believe, means Franch will be looking for his wife."

"Yes, with his poor eyesight he likes to have something close by to ogle." She adjusted the barely covered objects of her husband's adoration. "I'll be at the Beckwith soiree on Thursday," Lydia continued, smoothing the front of her gown. "They do have that lovely tropical garden."

"And with insufficient illumination, I hear. Perhaps I should try archery."

"Shall I paint a target on myself?"

"I believe I can hit the mark." Stepping sideways, Valentine allowed Lady Franch to reenter the ballroom first.

He leaned against the wall for a moment, looking out at the drama that had originally caught his attention. Lady Eleanor Griffin was being a foolish chit. Not only had she permitted Priestley to place the bracelet on her wrist, but now she appeared to be encouraging him to parade her about in a waltz. Emerging into the large, mirrored ballroom, Valentine glanced at Eleanor's eldest brother. Sebastian, the Duke of Melbourne, continued his conversation with Lord Tomlin, but Valentine knew him well enough to see that he wasn't pleased. *Hm.* Perhaps the evening still had a few moments of interest left in it.

"He's insane."

Valentine glanced to his left, though he'd already recognized the voice. "I assume you're referring to Priestley?"

"He's already been warned." Standing against the back wall of the ballroom, Lord Charlemagne Griffin followed the meanderings of his younger sister and John Priestley with pale gray eyes.

"Then you have to give him a point or two for bravery." Valentine gestured for another glass of whiskey.

The gray gaze flicked in his direction and back again. "For abject stupidity."

"It's just a bracelet, Shay. At a soiree hardly worth a footnote in the society pages."

"A bracelet on my sister's wrist." Charlemagne straightened. "And I don't care where in damnation we are. I booted him off the front walk last week, and Melbourne's already bared his teeth at the fortune-hunting idiot. Eleanor knows all of that, as well."

Valentine looked at the pair of dancers again. Honeyed brunette hair coiled into an artistic knot at the top of her head and pale green gown swirling about her legs, graceful Lady Eleanor Griffin actually looked more composed than her dance partner. Her brothers weren't likely to kill *her*, however. Priestley might not be so lucky. "Perhaps your sister is staging a little rebellion."

"If she is, it's going to be a short-lived one."

Chuckling, Valentine finished off his new glass of whiskey. "Complications. They are one of the reasons I'm happy not to have siblings. I'll see you tomorrow, yes?"

Charlemagne nodded. "Melbourne said he'd asked you by."

With a last glance at Eleanor and Priestley, Valentine headed for the door. He might be friends with the male members of the Griffin family, but becoming involved in their domestic troubles not only didn't interest him, but left him with a keen desire to be elsewhere. Especially when he'd heard rumors of a rich game of loo beginning at the Society Club.

As he left, he glimpsed several young ladies following him with their eyes. It was something he was used to, and offering the chits a slight smile, he memorized the faces for future reference. One never knew when one might become bored with cards.

Eleanor Griffin had lately begun to notice a pattern in her life. Whenever she had an evening she would loosely label as "fun" or "amusing," the next morning would feature a lecture from one, or perhaps two, or occasionally even all three of her brothers on what she'd done incorrectly and how she should endeavor never to do it again. As if she didn't already know both the rules and the consequences of breaking them—even if she'd never dare to do more than bend them a little.

"I'm not going to waste my time lecturing if you're not going to pay attention," brother number one said, tapping his fingers on the smooth surface of his mahogany desk.

She supposed authority came naturally to Sebastian Griffin; he'd been elevated to the position of the Duke of Melbourne, and the patriarch of their family, at the age of seventeen. If the ensuing fifteen years had done anything at all, they'd made him even more blasted arrogant and sure of himself than when he'd begun.

It seemed her duty to take him down a notch or two, or at least remind him that he was human, whenever possible. Eleanor straightened. "Good. I'll be in the music room, then."

"The point being, *pay attention.* If I meant to talk merely for the purpose of hearing my own voice, I'd deliver an address to Parliament."

"Has anyone told you that you're insufferable, Sebastian?"

Dark gray eyes gazed at her. "Someone has to demonstrate a little dignity and restraint in this family. You don't seem capable of doing it."

She blew out her breath. "Don't you ever tire of proclaiming us the perfect and almighty Griffin clan? Society already looks upon us in awe and despair."

"You wouldn't find it so tiresome from the outside looking in." The Duke of Melbourne resumed drumming his fingers. "Men wouldn't be trying to give you jewelry if you were a shopkeeper's sister."

"The jewelry, Sebastian, is not important. All three of you seem to delight in chasing men away from me before they can even say hello."

"We only chase the wrong men away." He leaned forward. "And today, jewelry *is* important."

"No, it's—"

"Shall we focus on your behavior, then? Though if you wanted to demonstrate that your actions can cause damage, I'm already aware of that."

"For heaven's sake, Sebastian, you have no idea—"

"Perhaps then it was about you intentionally making trouble for me. Whatever the reasons, Eleanor, today we will focus on what you did. You will tell me—promise me—that you will no longer accept sparkling baubles from gentlemen while in public places. Especially not from fortune-hunting gentlemen making poor attempts to look as though they aren't after your dowry."

Sometimes Eleanor wanted to scream—even when her brother was correct, which happened surprisingly often considering that he usually didn't deign to look beyond her actions to try to understand *why* she did things. But right or wrong, he didn't need to talk to her as if she were a half-wit child. "I agree. I will only accept sparkly things from gentlemen, fortune-hunting or otherwise, in private."

The expression on the tanned face beneath his dark, wavy hair didn't change. Only his eyes grew cooler, but it was enough. Sebastian had a long fuse to his temper, but she was nearing the end of it—again.

Slowly he stood, forcing her to look up to continue meeting his gaze. "The Griffin name and reputation has been beyond reproach for eight hundred years. That fact will not alter while it is in my charge."

"I know that, Seb—"

"If you don't wish to spend the Season in London, I can arrange for Charlemagne to escort you back to Melbourne Park."

She lurched less gracefully to her own feet, her heartbeat accelerating at the threat. For heaven's sake, the Season had just begun, and Melbourne was half the island away in Devon. "Shay wouldn't do it."

One eyebrow lifted. "Yes, he would." The duke leaned forward, setting his knuckles against the desktop. "I wouldn't choose to play this game if I were you, Eleanor. You will lose."

With a growl she yanked the pearl bracelet out of her pocket. She didn't even particularly like pearls, but it had felt romantic when Viscount Priestley had placed them around her wrist, particularly when he'd been banned from anything more than the occasional dance with her. She had to admire John's bravery, whatever his motives. "Fine. Send it back, then. Heaven forbid that some gentleman should like me enough to actually give me a gift." She slammed the bauble onto the desk.

At least she'd managed the last word. Lips clamped together, Eleanor stalked to the office door. With a disdainful sniff she pulled it open.

"A true gentleman wouldn't risk causing a scandal by

giving you a gift in the middle of a crowded ballroom. He would come to me and ask permission to call on you." She heard the bracelet slide across the desk and fall into a drawer. "Lord Priestley," Sebastian continued, "will not be receiving that permission."

Gripping the door handle, Eleanor forced in a deep breath. "You already told him that."

"Then he had no business giving you anything."

That settled it. She was simply going to have to take up drinking. "I'm going to a nunnery," she said, "so at least I won't expect to find gentlemen calling on me."

"Don't tempt me, Nell."

Ha. She'd like to see him try it. "Good day, Your Grace. Shall I send in a peasant for you to behead?"

"No, thank you."

One day she intended to knock the wind out of his arrogant, condescending sails. The only thing worse than Sebastian treating her like a child was that he made her *feel* like a child. Of course she knew accepting baubles in public was improper; if her brothers hadn't preemptively turned Lord Priestley away on four previous occasions, she never would have felt sorry enough for the viscount to allow him to fasten the bracelet around her wrist. Last night, though, it had seemed the only way to show the tyrants that they couldn't completely control every aspect of her life.

Except that apparently they could. And turning away suitors they found unacceptable was one thing; now that she'd past her twenty-first birthday she'd begun to worry what would happen when they decided to find her an acceptable one. For all she knew, they already had several dull, thin-blooded prospects in mind. Prospects who would, of course, acknowledge the superiority and authority of the Griffin males. Someone who wouldn't challenge their leadership and who therefore would never be a match—or a challenge—for her.

Zachary and Charlemagne, Shay for short, were upstairs playing billiards, and it annoyed her that they could be having fun while she was being lectured and while she'd begun worrying about what they might have planned for her future. Heaven help them if they decided she needed further chastisement today. With the way Sebastian had a counter for every argument, her blood boiled for a fight she could win. And each loss only made the determination stronger. This morning she felt like Mount Vesuvius. Eleanor stalked up the wide, curving staircase, her blue muslin skirt gathered in one hand as she stomped to the second floor.

At the open door to the billiards room, though, she stopped. Inside her brothers conversed, their voices joined by a third who spoke in a low, sardonic drawl. For a moment she listened, enjoying the smooth, cultured tone. She knew the rules as well as any Griffin—no family rows in public. Thankfully this guest didn't count as public.

"You two are cowards," she announced, entering the room.

A ball thudded onto the carpeted floor. Shay, the taller of the two, straightened from the table. "Damnation, Nell," he cursed, standing his cue upright. "You just cost me five quid."

"Good. I thought it was your duty to protect me."

"Not from Sebastian."

"Besides," Zachary broke in, leaning on his own cue, "Melbourne's correct. We don't want a member of the family giving the impression that she can be bought for a short string of pearls."

"He wasn't buying me!" she retorted. "And apparently he tried to give me the bracelet in a more discreet setting, and on more than one occasion. Someone—several someones—made it impossible for him to do so."

Zachary, the youngest of the three brothers, made a face. "Then he should have acted like a gentleman and desisted."

Eleanor folded her arms, turning her attention to the tall, black-haired man pouring himself a whiskey at the liquor table. "Humph. And what do you think, Lord Deverill?"

"Actually," Valentine Corbett, the Marquis of Deverill, returned, "your brothers are completely correct."

"What?"

"See? You may not listen to—"

"Shut up, Zachary," she snapped, otherwise ignoring her brothers in favor of the lean face and half-lidded green eyes of the man she'd always considered not her champion, but her best example of how she wished she could behave but knew she wouldn't ever, ever dare to emulate. "Explain yourself, Deverill."

He inclined his head. "Little as I like to give the Griffin brethren credit for anything, any male knows not to show favor in public to the female he pursues. Causes all sorts of difficulties."

"I'm not speaking of your clandestine relationships with married ladies and opera singers," she retorted. "I'm discussing a true gentleman with a genuine regard for a lady, one who wanted to demonstrate his honest interest by giving her a small gift."

A slight smile touched that famously capable mouth

and vanished again. "You should have been more specific, then. I don't know anything about that sort of nonsense. 'Honest' interest?"

"You see?" she exclaimed, flinging out her arms in her brothers' direction. "Not even Deverill knows what you're talking ab—"

"On the other hand," Lord Deverill interrupted, "in the case of an 'honest' regard, Priestley should have joined the bracelet with a necklace and ear bobs. Then at least we could be assured that he didn't just nick the trinket from his mother's jewelry box. Which he likely did, considering that he has no money of his own and is after yours."

While Shay and Zachary laughed, Eleanor looked into those deceptively lazy green eyes, one of them obscured by a falling lock of coal black hair. Some mamas with impressionable daughters claimed that if the devil could choose a countenance with which to lure young ladies into sin, he would look precisely like Valentine, Lord Deverill. Thank God she knew how charming he could be. Of course it wasn't much of a challenge to resist him when he never even looked at her askance. Her lips twisted. "Now I've determined to keep you off my side in this argument."

"I can understand that. I wouldn't want me on my side either. You should be ashamed of yourself, anyway, allowing Priestley to approach and speak to you in public. Next you'll tell me you were just standing there and he accosted you."

"That's not the point, Deverill," Zachary interrupted. "She didn't have to accept the bracelet, regardless."

"Bravely said by a brother who should have done a better job of warning Priestley away from her in the first place," the marquis said, his easy drawl deepening, "before the fellow could tempt her with a pretty trinket. Not that I'm taking sides, but it does seem to me that you three are the ones who made the error."

Shay's complexion darkened. "We can't be expected to—"

"And you continue to err," Deverill broke in, leaning across the billiards table to take his shot. "For instance, if you're concerned over Lady Eleanor's maidenly virtue, why the devil did you let me into the house yet again?"

"I was just about to ask myself the same question," Sebastian's dry voice came from the doorway.

"I think you should *all* leave," Eleanor muttered, folding her arms across her bosom.

At the beginning she thought Lord Deverill had been at least partly on her side, but declaring her brothers responsible for *her* actions didn't precisely leave her feeling any better. In fact, it was almost more insulting than her brothers' original argument. She could easily have turned Lord Priestley away if she'd wanted to, after all.

It was far more likely that Deverill wasn't on anyone's side, and didn't give a whit about the outcome. He did have a penchant for arguing simply because he enjoyed it. Which of course meant he was frightfully good at it, as he was at everything he attempted.

"I was invited," the marquis returned, unflappable as always.

"So you were," Sebastian admitted. "Care to join me in the stable?"

Deverill tossed his cue to Charlemagne. "You still want my opinion of your new mount, then?" he asked, making for the doorway.

The duke nodded, stepping aside to let Valentine pass.

"I actually thought you might want to take him off my hands. The beast tried to nip Peep yesterday."

Eleanor stood there for a moment, her mouth hanging open. "Of all the nerve," she finally blurted. "That is *my* horse, and Peep already said she was teasing him with an apple."

Valentine stopped in the doorway to look from her to Sebastian. "I won't deprive a lady of her mount," he said, and his lips curved in a sly smile. "Not without offering a suitable replacement, at any rate."

"Valentine," the Duke of Melbourne said, his tone clipped.

"I'm damned well not going to be pulled into the middle of a family feud. I canceled luncheon with L— with a very nice young lady to answer your summons."

"Lydia Franch, perhaps?" Shay suggested, rolling the "L" on his tongue.

"Or Laurene Manchester?" Zachary put in.

The marquis chuckled. "I never kiss and tell."

Oh, this was too much. "Excuse me, but I believe we were discussing my horse," Eleanor interrupted. "Ask Peep if you don't believe me. She promised to be more cautious."

Sebastian gazed at her with an expression in his eyes that could allegedly make grown men quake in their boots. Even though she'd grown up under his command, it made her want to either punch him or flee. The Lord knew she'd never asked to have a duke for an eldest brother. Lately that circumstance had been gnawing her insides raw.

"Eleanor," he said in the cool, patient voice that belied the glint in his eyes, "my daughter is six years of age. I trust my opinion over hers."

"You trust your opinion over everyone's, Sebastian. And you are not taking my horse."

"No, I'm not. Deverill is."

"I haven't even seen it yet," the marquis cut in, "though I do have to wonder why you think I would want a lady's animal."

"He's not a lady's animal," Sebastian returned. "Eleanor's been training him to tolerate the sidesaddle."

"I *have* trained him to do so." She put her hands on her hips. "Don't you dare take my Helios, Valentine Corbett."

"That is enough, Eleanor," Sebastian snapped, the remaining humor leaving his voice.

"Yes, it is," Deverill seconded. Inclining his head in Eleanor's direction, he headed past Sebastian out the door. "If you'll excuse me, I may still be able to salvage my luncheon engagement."

As the marquis descended the stairs, Eleanor's brothers stood glaring at her. "Scowl all you want," she said, turning her back on the lot of them. "You may take my bracelet, and you may attempt to steal my horse, but that doesn't make you right. It only makes you bullies." She strode into the hallway.

"Where do you think you're going?" Sebastian's even, controlled voice came.

"I think I'm going shopping," she returned over her shoulder as she stalked to her bedchamber. It would have been more effective if she'd had something stronger with which to retort. "I'm going off to sea" or "I'm joining the army" would have sounded so much more defiant. Still, even shopping was something, and it did show the brothers Griffin that they didn't rule her or her schedule entirely, as much as they might like to think so.

Eleanor stifled a frustrated sigh. No, a declaration of

shopping didn't prove much of anything. And no distraction was as effective as it used to be at calming her desire to do something outrageous, something completely . . . wicked, something that wouldn't show her brothers as much as it would show *her* that she could be free.

She paused in her search for a pair of gloves to look out her bedchamber window. Below her, Valentine took his horse's reins from a groom and swung into his saddle. Blast it, she envied the Marquis of Deverill, able to do whatever he wanted whenever he wanted and with whomever he wanted. No one told him it wasn't proper, or correct, or threatened to withhold his allowance, or even frowned at him—well, some of the old, tight-laced patronesses might frown, but he certainly didn't care what they might think. He didn't care what anyone thought.

Drawing a deep breath, Eleanor pulled on her gloves. *Hm.* She did care about the Griffin name and reputation, whatever Sebastian might think. She therefore might not be able to gamble or smoke cigars or go about . . . fornicating with whomever she chose, but her brothers hadn't won, yet. Eventually they would, when they decided they were tired of her rebellions and forced her to marry. She had no illusions about that. It would happen, and Sebastian had such complete control over her finances that realistically she would be unable to refuse his orders.

That was then, however, and this was now. And tonight she meant to make a stand.

Chapter 2

By the time Eleanor arrived downstairs for dinner, Zachary, Shay, and Melbourne were already seated, as was Sebastian's daughter, Penelope. Peep's presence might be a problem to her plans, but once the drama began Eleanor was fairly certain Sebastian would see to it that the six-year-old exited before any blood could be shed.

"Good evening," she said, relieved that she sounded calm. No hysterics, no shouting, nothing but calm and logic. That was how she would succeed tonight.

"I believe I had your maid notified that dinner would begin at seven this evening," Sebastian returned. "Do I need to have her dismissed for failing to pass on that information?"

Calm. "Helen informed me. The fault is mine, not hers."

"I don't doubt that. Take your place, if you please. Stanton, you may begin serving."

The butler bowed. "Thank you, Your Grace."

"A moment, if you please, Stanton," Eleanor countered, drawing the folded paper she held from behind her back. It had been so difficult not to clench it in her fingers, but wrinkles or sweat marks on the paper would have lost her the game before it began.

Sebastian glanced toward her hand and returned his gaze to her face again. "What do you have there, Nell?"

If he was using her nickname, he'd already realized something was afoot. Damnation. He knew "Nell" made her feel like a child. "It's a declaration," she said, moving forward to hand it to her eldest brother.

"A declaration of what?" Zachary asked, as she reversed direction to take her seat farther down the table.

She'd considered standing defiantly beside Sebastian while he read her missive, but putting a little distance between them had seemed wiser. "Of independence. *My* independence, in case that was your next question." She'd come to the table prepared for a battle of wits and wills, so they might as well get on with it.

Peep, sitting beside her, leaned closer. "Aunt Nell, the Colonies got in trouble for having one of those."

"Yes, I know," she whispered back. "I'm likely to have the same difficulty."

"Oh, dear," Peep whispered, shaking her head so that her hair bounced in dark, curling ringlets.

Sebastian hadn't opened the paper. He hadn't even looked at it again, but instead kept his gaze steady on Eleanor while she gazed back at him. This was serious, and the sooner he understood that, the better.

"Stanton," he said quietly, "please escort Lady Penelope upstairs to Mrs. Bevins, and then inform Cook that dinner will be slightly delayed."

The Duke of Melbourne understood.

"At once, Your Grace."

"I don't want to go," Peep protested, even as the butler moved around to pull her chair out from the table. "I want to help Aunt Nell."

"No, you don't," her father replied. "Upstairs. I'll have your dinner sent to the playroom."

The butler and his charge exited, and after one look from Melbourne, the two footmen who'd remained behind also made themselves scarce. It would have been more fair if Sebastian made Zachary and Shay leave, as well, but of course they'd all hate to miss an opportunity to gang up on her. Eleanor folded her hands in her lap and waited, and tried to ignore the sick flutter of butterflies in her stomach. She'd thought this out; she could do it.

Once the door closed, Sebastian turned his attention to the folded paper in his hand. He opened it, read perhaps a line, and looked up at her again. "This is ridiculous."

"It is perfectly serious, I assure you. As am I."

Shay reached for the paper. "What does it—"

The duke avoided his brother's grasp. "In the interest of saving time, allow me. 'I, Eleanor Elizabeth Griffin,' " he read aloud, " 'being of sound mind and body, do hereby declare the following. I—' "

"Sounds like a bloody last will and testament," Zachary muttered, sending a look in Eleanor's direction. "Hope it's not prophetic."

"Don't interrupt me," Melbourne said, his clipped voice the only indication that he was less than tranquil. " 'I am of legal age to make my own decisions. I am competent to make my own decisions. I am aware of the consequences of poor decisions, and I am capable of taking responsibility for any and all of my decisions, poor or otherwise.

" 'Further to this point,' " he continued, " 'I hereby request—no, insist—on being permitted to make my own decisions without restriction, up to and including the selection of a husband. No further tyranny or bullying will be tolerated, or I shall be forced to note in public my dissatisfaction with my treatment in this household.' "

Eleanor thought Sebastian's voice shook a little as he read that part, but her own nerves were unsteady enough that she couldn't be sure. At any rate, he didn't hesitate to continue. " 'In consequence, I hereby absolve my brothers, Sebastian, Duke of Melbourne; Lord Charlemagne Griffin; and Lord Zachary Griffin of any responsibilities for my life from hereon, and in the event of any untoward circumstance, shall make clear to anyone necessary that the other members of the Griffin family are not to be held at fault in any way, form, or manner for my actions.' We then have the signature, dated 23 May, 1811."

For a long moment no one spoke. From his overall tone Eleanor couldn't tell whether Melbourne was reading a list of laundry items or a declaration of war with France. Her brothers were easier to decipher, though she almost wished she couldn't do so. Zachary, the closest to her in age and temperament, looked aghast, while Shay's jaw was clenched tight with obvious anger. Well, she'd thrown down the gauntlet. The only question was who would take it up first.

Finally Sebastian's dark gray eyes lifted again to meet hers. " 'Tyranny'?" he repeated slowly, curling the word into something that made her flinch.

"When you refuse to listen to my side of a story, or to take into account my feelings or wishes, and instead make sweeping declarations which are counter to any hope of happiness on my part, then yes, I call that tyranny." She sat forward. Vesuvius was erupting; look out, Pompeii. "What would you call it, Your Grace?"

"We're your older siblings," Shay bit out. "It is our obligation, our duty, to offer guidance and to—"

"*Offer*? I hardly th—"

"I would assume that in addition to your absolute freedom you would require a continuance of your monthly allowance?" the duke interrupted, as though she and he were the room's only two occupants.

Ah, the threats. "I'm not removing myself from reality," she responded. "This is not some flight of fancy. I will merely be making decisions on my own behalf. I have no wish to estrange myself from my family." She'd known this would be the stickiest point, and she'd spent hours considering her response. "I insist that my choices be independent and free from your interference."

"Interfe—" Shay started to say.

"Done," Sebastian stated.

Charlemagne snapped his mouth closed. "What?" he blurted, his face darkening. "Melbourne, you can't be serious."

"I'm very serious." The duke tucked her letter into his pocket. "Your independence is granted—under one condition."

Ha. She knew there would be a catch. "And what might that be?"

"I have no intention of letting your 'declaration' be bandied about in public, any more than I would permit you to publicly air your grievances with this household. And whatever you put in writing, you cannot absolve this family from a scandal of your making. Therefore, if a scandal involving you comes to public attention, this agreement ends."

Eleanor took only a moment to consider that. She'd actually thought he'd have something much more heinous in mind. "Done."

"I'm not finished. Not only will this agreement end, but once I've dealt with whatever trouble you've caused, you will agree to marry the gentleman of my choosing, without—"

"*What?*"

"Without delay, and without protest." Sebastian picked up the bell sitting at his elbow and rang it. Immediately footmen appeared to begin placing dinner on the table. "Did you think there wouldn't be consequences?" he continued in the same even tone.

"You are . . . evil," she sputtered, images of a dozen dull gentlemen crashing about in her skull.

"I am a tyrant, I believe," he returned. "There's always a price for freedom. If you wish to play, you must be prepared to pay. Are we in agreement?"

If she refused, he would use both her declaration and her cowardice against her at every opportunity. And he would probably force her to marry the first insipid man he encountered just to prove his point, anyway. Eleanor took a breath. The greatest difficulty in this was deciding to fight a battle when the outcome of the war was already a given. She was a Griffin, and she would never forsake her family. Any husband she selected would have to be at least marginally acceptable to Melbourne. But it was the moments before she made that decision—or before it could be made for her—that would count.

She at least had forced open a door. She only needed to go through it, and she could have a moment of freedom, and a voice in deciding her own matrimonial future. "We are in agreement," she said slowly.

"No we are not," Shay growled. "This is ridiculous, Melbourne."

Blinking as though he'd forgotten his brothers' presence, the duke turned his attention to the other side of the table. "Eleanor and I have made an agreement. You will honor it. Is that clear?"

For a moment she thought Shay might have an apoplexy, but with a strangled growl the next-oldest brother nodded. Zachary, looking as if he was torn between horror and laughter, followed suit. "By God, Nell, you've got a pair," he murmured.

"A pair of what?" she asked sweetly, though she knew perfectly well what he was referring to. One didn't grow up with three older brothers without hearing the occasional vulgarity, most of it involving the male—or female—anatomy.

Zachary only shook his head. "Jesus. Just be careful."

"That's the thing, Zachary," she returned, "I'm free. I may do whatever I please"—she glanced at Melbourne—"as long as it doesn't cause a scandal."

"And heaven help us all," Shay muttered.

"No," Sebastian put in, as he calmly selected a prime cut of beef from a footman's tray, "heaven help Eleanor. Because we won't."

It was nearly one o'clock in the afternoon when Valentine dragged himself upright among the tumble of his down pillows and silk sheets. The Griffin clan and their squabble had indeed ruined what he'd hoped would be a private, decadent luncheon yesterday, but because of that he'd run across Lord Whitton and Peter Burnsey and a high-stakes game of faro at White's. Fifteen hours later and nearly a thousand quid richer, he'd returned home and to bed after sunrise.

"Matthews!" he bellowed, shedding bedsheets and reaching for a pair of buckskin trousers while clutching at his skull with his free hand to keep it from exploding.

His bedchamber door opened so quickly that his valet had likely been leaning against it. "Yes, my lord? Shall I have breakfast set out?"

"No. Get me a clean shirt."

The trim valet nodded, diving into the nearest wardrobe. "You should eat something, my lord," his muffled voice came.

Valentine scowled. "If you mention food or eating again today, I will have to shoot you," he grumbled. Entertaining and profitable as the evening had been, Burnsey was one of the few men who could match him drink for drink. The fact that Peter outweighed him by two stone probably helped, but he'd never been one to pass up a challenge.

"Yes, my lord. But Mrs. Beacon will want to know—"

"I'll have luncheon at the Society. Now fetch my pistol."

The valet emerged from the wardrobe. "My lord?"

"You heard me. I warned you, and now I have to shoot you, or everyone will think I'm not a man of my word."

"But you're not, my lord. A man of your word, I mean."

"What?" Valentine downed the remains of the stale brandy left at his bedside. "Yes, I suppose you're right. Where's my damned shirt?"

"Here you are, my lord."

Valentine donned the shirt and sat at his dressing table to shave while Matthews laid out a dark gray jacket and a cream waistcoat, then threw open the heavy, dark curtains.

"Very nice, Matthews," he complimented the selection of wardrobe, squinting in the reflected light as he lifted the razor to his chin.

"Thank you, my lord. And I sharpened your razor last evening."

At times Valentine wasn't sure whether he kept Matthews about because of his supreme unctuousness or because he had half a suspicion the valet was trying to kill him. Readjusting his grip, he slid the razor along his face. "Any news?"

"Well, Lord and Lady Arthorpe's housekeeper has rather abruptly been relocated to the estate in Sussex."

"Good God. I hope the infant won't have Arthorpe's nose."

"We all hope so, my lord. And as you usually ask, I made a point of discovering that Lady Arthorpe and the earl are not at this moment on speaking terms."

Valentine made a face. "Mary Arthorpe hasn't bathed since last Christmas, I'd wager. I prefer less aromatic bedmates. Anything else?"

"Oh, yes. Mr. Peter Burnsey has closed the east wing of Burnsey House and dismissed nearly half his staff."

"That explains why the idiot wouldn't leave the game last night. I probably won his last twenty quid."

"He should have known better than to wager against you, my lord."

"Yes, he should have."

That explained both Burnsey's exceptionally heavy drinking and his own pounding skull, but not why the usually pragmatic gentleman had decided to wager what amounted to the remainder of his estate in a card game. Valentine shrugged. God help the world if he ever became that desperate. All things considered, if armed robbery failed, a ball through the brain seemed both more decisive and less painful than the path Burnsey had chosen for himself.

Shrugging off Burnsey's troubles, Valentine finished his morning—afternoon—ablutions and had Iago saddled. The big bay stallion was used to irregular hours, and he barely batted an ear as they trotted off in the direction of the Society Club.

He chose a path that took him along Bond Street, nodding at various acquaintances spending the afternoon shopping. A glimpse of bright material caught his attention down one of the narrow, less-populated side streets, and he turned his head to look down the lane. And pulled Iago to a halt.

"Lady Eleanor?"

Eleanor froze halfway out of the small dress shop she'd obviously been visiting. With a breath she faced him, then visibly relaxed. "Deverill. Thank goodness."

"That's the first time goodness and I have ever been mentioned in the same breath," he returned, urging Iago toward her down the narrow street. He glanced at the rear door of the shop from which Lady Eleanor had just emerged, and at the deep, rich burgundy material half hidden beneath her bundled shawl. "Madame Costanza's?" he murmured, lifting an eyebrow.

The fine rose blush of her cheeks deepened. "I needed a few new gowns."

Valentine nodded, deciding to keep to himself the information that some of London's finest—and most daring—actresses and high-flyers hired Madame Costanza to make their gowns. From Eleanor's high color, she already knew that, anyway. "I'm certain they'll be stunning."

Before he could take his leave she approached, clasping

the toe of his Hessian boot in one hand. "Don't say anything, Deverill. I want it to be a surprise."

He couldn't help grinning. "No worries. I'm all for creating a ruckus, but it doesn't seem quite in your character."

The color fled from her cheeks. "It is not in my brothers' character. I doubt anyone knows *my* character. Yet."

That sounded intriguing. At the same time his stomach rumbled, reminding him that he hadn't eaten in twelve hours. "I hope I'm there for the unveiling, then."

"Do you attend the Beckwith soiree tonight?"

"I do."

"Then you will be."

A small, secret smile touched her mouth, the expression lighting her eyes with a breathless, indescribable excitement. Valentine realized he was staring, and shook himself. He'd known Eleanor Griffin since she was five, and she fell into one of two well-defined categories he had for females. She was in the *do not touch* section, along with nuns and grandmothers and very ugly chits. She was the younger sister of a good friend, and therefore not actually a female as much as she was a . . . puppy dog.

Except that puppy dogs didn't have that sly smile or those fine gray eyes. Valentine cleared his throat. "I'll see you then."

Her smile deepened. "Unless you're distracted elsewhere, of course."

Hm. "I think it's fair to say I won't be."

Chapter 3

~~~~~~~~~~~

"My lady, are you certain you wish to wear this . . . particular gown this evening?"

Eleanor pretended to ignore both Helen's carefully worded commentary and the way her maid kept wringing her hands in obvious dismay. Of course she knew what a risk she was taking, but tonight she had a definite purpose. This was a test, both of her resolve and of her brothers' willingness to abide by their agreement.

"Yes, I'm certain," she returned, facing herself in the full-length dressing mirror. Burgundy silk stitched with fine gold thread complemented her dark hair and gray eyes, and while the close-fitting bodice left little room for disguising flaws. The skirt hugged her hips and then flowed into a beaded, glittering swirl of the same-colored material.

"But your brothers, my lady. Won't they dis—"

"Disapprove? I'm sure they will. It's not a hair shirt or a nun's habit." She smiled at her reflection, and was surprised at the excited, seductive female gazing coyly back at her. "I, however, don't care what they might think."

"You don't?"

"No, I don't. All the parts which should be covered, are. Perhaps with a little less material than usual, but there are other perfectly respectable females who dress in a similar style." Not many, but a few. "Now help me on with my cloak, if you please."

"But if you don't care—"

"I'm not an idiot, either."

The gray cloak, which covered all but the very bottom of her new gown, was only for effect—or so she told herself. Her brothers and the rest of the guests at the Beckwith soiree would all see her at the same moment. It was just a happy coincidence that by the time she unveiled the new creation it would be too late for Melbourne to do anything about her appearance.

The cloak did its job well, and when she reached the foyer downstairs the only suspicious looks were at her hair, which she'd had Helen pin in a confusion of burgundy ribbons and curling brown hair cascading down to her shoulders.

Melbourne's gaze, however, was on her face. "Remember what I said about scandal, Eleanor," he said as he shrugged into his caped greatcoat.

"And you remember that scandal and conversation are two different things," she countered, stepping outside as Stanton pulled open the front door.

"They can be two different things," the duke replied, following her out and handing her up into the coach. "Push the boundaries of one too far, and it becomes the other."

"I should have started drinking earlier," Zachary muttered, climbing up behind her. "Be cautious, Nell, will you?"

She straightened her gloves. "No, Zachary. I'm not doing anything wrong, and I'm not going to be cautious."

"Then this will be a short-lived experiment," Charlemagne put in, "and you can forget that nonsense about finding your own husband."

Eleanor hoped with all her heart that Shay was wrong about that. "I wouldn't wager against me, if I were you," she declared, hoping she sounded more confident than she felt.

Beckwith House was only five blocks away, but she couldn't recall a coach ride that had ever taken so long. She fairly vibrated with tension, and it didn't help that the cloak, fastened all the way up to her chin, was stifling in the closed carriage. In addition, Sebastian sat gazing at her for the entire duration of the ride. She'd always half thought he could read minds, but the fact that he didn't stop the coach and make them turn around proved that suspicion false.

It wasn't as though she intended to do anything bad, but she was quite aware of how seriously her eldest brother guarded and protected the Griffin name. She had chosen to walk a very narrow path, with scandal on one side and his constraints on the other. Eleanor only hoped that her road led somewhere other than to a dead end.

At twenty-four and twenty-eight respectively, Zachary and Charlemagne had certainly had lovers and mistresses, but that was perfectly fine with Society as long as it was done discreetly. The rules for females were much stricter, and the possibility of downfall much greater. But she didn't want a lover or anything so blatantly wicked. If she didn't take this chance to explore life, she might as well shrivel up and die.

At the crowded drive of Beckwith House they disembarked. Traditionally when the Griffins attended an event as a family they entered in ranks, with her on Melbourne's arm and Shay and Zachary bringing up the rear. Tonight, though, once they'd navigated the last of the trampled mud and horse manure and reached the marble and stone of the front portico, Sebastian released her.

"After you," he said, gesturing her to lead the way.

She nodded, pretending she'd expected the move, and entered the grand house. Since she'd handed over her declaration she'd sensed that Melbourne had been angry with her, not so much because of the paper as because of the idea behind it—that she'd been dissatisfied enough with his patriarchy that she'd staged a rebellion. Well, she'd meant to shake him. Perhaps they would both learn something from the exercise. At the least he might realize that other people had thoughts and feelings that didn't necessarily equate with his—and that those thoughts wouldn't necessarily lead to the downfall of their family.

At the coatroom she hesitated, but they were already in view of at least two dozen guests, several of them notorious gossips. Eleanor took a deep breath and unfastened the button that held her cloak closed. Whatever she'd said on paper, her declaration began now.

As a footman helped pull the cloak from her shoulders, Zachary at the rear of the group made a choking sound, while the silence from her other two brothers spoke at least as loudly. *Ha. Wait until I turn around.*

She turned around. The gaze of all three brothers dropped to her bosom and then slid back to her face again.

"Holy mother of God," Shay whispered, his tanned face growing pale.

She hoped he meant that in a good way. With another breath Eleanor faced the open ballroom doors and started forward. "Shall we?" she asked with a smile, stopping beside the butler just inside the doorway.

The Beckwith butler didn't need their invitation to make the announcement of their arrival. Most servants of good households were aware of the Griffin clan. "Ladies and gentlemen, the Duke of Melbourne, Lord Charlemagne Griffin, Lord Zachary Griffin, and Lady Eleanor Griffin."

The room stirred as she stepped forward. She could hear her brothers walking behind her, practically feel the hostility they directed toward the room at large as they silently dared anyone to say a word about her choice of wardrobe.

With the ease of long practice, Eleanor hid a scowl. Though their silent intimidation might make the evening progress more smoothly, it also meant that she was still under their protection—and their watchful eyes. She spun around, feeling the silk material of her gown swirling deliciously about her legs.

"Stop it," she muttered.

"Stop what?" Charlemagne returned in the same tone, his gaze over her shoulder at the crowded room beyond.

"Trying to intimidate everyone in sight. As long as we're here, you don't know me, and I don't know you."

Shay opened his mouth to protest again, but abruptly Melbourne stepped between them. "I think it's time we began that drinking Zachary mentioned."

In a moment Eleanor stood alone inside the ballroom. Remaining there too long would make it obvious that something was afoot with the Griffin clan, so as soon as she spied her friend Lady Barbara Howsen, she made her way toward the refreshment table.

As she neared, though, her eyes found another acquaintance. He stood beside the doors that led to the Beckwiths' substantial tropical gardens. Lord Deverill gazed at her, plainly ignoring Lady Franch as the countess overtly flirted at him from the far side of the door.

For the first time she realized how other females must feel when the green-eyed god gazed at them. The sensation of heat running down her spine as she met that deceptively lazy gaze made her feel . . . wicked. Thank goodness they were friends, and she'd only caught him by surprise. And thank goodness she knew what a scoundrel he was.

Shaking herself, she turned toward Barbara at the refreshment table. "Good evening, my love," she said, kissing the Marquis of Pelton's second daughter on one cheek. "You look wonderful."

Barbara returned the gesture, her expression one of undisguised delight. "I told you to try Madame Costanza," she whispered. "I'm surprised Melbourne didn't have an apoplexy when he saw you. How did you talk him into letting you out of your bedchamber?"

"He didn't see the gown until you did," Eleanor returned in a low voice. It wouldn't do any good for anyone else to overhear where she'd begun shopping for dresses—not with Melbourne's clause about scandal. "And besides, we made an agreement. I, my dear, may do as I please."

"It does appear that way," Barbara admitted with a chuckle. "And you look absolutely stunning, by the by. I think Wendell DuMer was drooling."

Eleanor grinned. "I don't think that has anything to do with me, Bar. In fact, I—"

"Lady Eleanor," a masculine voice came from behind her.

She turned around. "Mr. Cobb-Harding," she said, not having to feign her surprise. "I thought you still in Paris."

"I returned a few days ago. The first dance of the evening is about to begin, and I notice you haven't used your dance card. Will you do me the honor of joining me for the waltz?"

Not even five minutes into her adventure, and already she'd been asked to dance by someone Melbourne would have rejected. As if it was Stephen Cobb-Harding's fault that his father was only a baronet, and that his mother's family, the Cobbs, had had the money—hence the hyphenated surname.

"I would be delighted," she answered, taking his outstretched hand.

The orchestra began the waltz just as they reached the cleared area of floor in the center of the ballroom. Mr. Cobb-Harding slid a hand about her waist and drew them into the dance.

"I've been trying to find a way to do this for a year," he said, his light blue gaze focused somewhere below her neck.

Well, she hadn't worn a low-cut gown by accident. In a way, it was refreshing to be seen as something—someone—other than a member of the almighty Griffins, even if it was only her bosom being noticed. "Then why have you waited until now?"

Finally his gaze beneath wavy blond hair lifted to her face again. "I'll give you three guesses, my lady."

Three, indeed. "Ah. Well, my brothers and I have recently come to an understanding. And so you and I may dance whenever we wish to do so."

He smiled. "That is the best news I've heard in weeks."

"I don't know about that, but thank—"

"I do. And thank *you*."

Hm. She'd always thought of Stephen Cobb-Harding as handsome, and though she'd never experienced it first-hand, she'd heard of his reputation for wit and charm. Apparently wit, relative poverty, and a low social standing among the nobility made him too . . . dangerous for her. For heaven's sake, she had a brain. Dancing with a man didn't mean she intended to marry him. Yes, here she was, seeking out her own husband and her own adventure, but some mild, harmless fun could fit in quite nicely. "You are quite welcome, Mr. Cobb-Harding."

"Stephen, please. Sometimes I think people forget what they're about to tell me by the time they've finished saying my name."

Eleanor chuckled. "I think it has an air of distinction about it, myself."

"In light of that compliment, Lady Eleanor, allow me to confide that I've heard some rather off-putting tales about men who don't meet your brothers' approval. Just how many limbs am I risking?"

"None. That, I promise you. In fact, if they even scowl at you, please let me know, Stephen."

His deep laugh made her smile in return. "I would like to think I can call on you without having to hide behind your skirts." He paused. "Though your skirts are exceptional."

Perhaps this could be more than mild fun. Stephen was a member of the nobility, after all, and didn't have any scandal attached to his name. "Thank you. It's something of a new style I'm trying."

"Please continue with the effort." He gazed at her, admiration clear in his light blue eyes. "By God, you are lovely. And that is another thing I've been wanting to tell you for the past year."

She had the abrupt desire to punch each of her brothers in their arrogant noses. Already tonight she'd managed to have more fun and excitement than her brothers had allowed her since she'd turned fifteen—which was when Melbourne had decided it was time she stopped behaving like a child. In an instant he'd put a stop to her racing about barefoot and practicing her fencing with Zachary, and so many other things that it made her want to cry when she thought about them. Six years later, and she'd finally won her freedom again. Now, thanks to Stephen Cobb-Harding, she had a direction to go with it.

"Perhaps you would care to escort me to Hyde Park tomorrow, then, Stephen?"

His charming smile deepened. "Might eleven o'clock be acceptable?"

"Eleven o'clock would be perfect."

"Valentine!"

At the strident feminine hiss, the Marquis of Deverill looked away from the ballroom floor. "Lady Franch?"

"Lord Franch isn't feeling well, and he'll want to leave early," Lydia said, from her tone not for the first time.

"Gout?"

She edged closer. "I have no idea. Probably. So we must hurry."

A burgundy gown swirled by and vanished into the crowd of dancers again. "Hurry?" he repeated, shifting his gaze to the Griffin brethren. None of them were dancing, and none of them were looking at their sister. Eleanor had been right. Something significant had happened. Something that had allowed her to pour herself into one of Madame Costanza's famously decadent creations. And considering the results, he could only applaud the change in the Griffin weather.

Lady Franch moved closer still, so that he could feel her breath warm on his cheek. "Hurry to give me your cock," she whispered.

"Apologies, Lydia, but I need it elsewhere this evening."

He could practically feel the vibration of her abrupt annoyance as she turned to follow his gaze. "Lady Eleanor? Simply because she's wearing that rag? You've never even looked at her before."

"I've never seen her before," he returned absently.

It was so odd. Though he'd known Eleanor Griffin for years, most of their encounters had consisted of light bantering and the occasional bit of frivolous nonbrotherly advice, generally concerning how to avoid entanglements with blackguards such as himself. He didn't consider her a sister, mainly because he didn't have siblings and didn't care to acquire any through social adoption. Far too much of an obligation and a burden, family members were. Since this afternoon, though, Eleanor had abruptly become . . . interesting.

"I don't suppose I can do anything to distract you from the little upstart?" Lady Franch queried, her tone edged with frustration. Lord Franch would owe him a vote of thanks for tonight, no doubt. The old fool's birthday had just come early.

"I'd hardly call the Duke of Melbourne's sister an 'upstart,' but actually I'm merely curious about her presence and appearance," he returned. "What would cause Melbourne to escort her here, and then not pay any attention to what she does?"

Except that the brothers, or the duke, at least, *were* paying attention. He'd lay a wager on that fact. They simply weren't taking any action about it. And that intrigued him.

"I have no idea. Is figuring it out worth missing a fuck with me?"

"Apparently it is. And there's your husband, anyway." He inclined his head in her direction. "Good evening, my dear."

As soon as Lady Franch left his side, he returned his attention to Eleanor. The waltz had ended, and the group of young men surrounding her, claiming spots on her dance card, were for the most part so-called gentlemen that her brothers would normally never have let bow in her direction—gamblers, fortune hunters, and general idiots, mostly. Well, they were bowing now, and practically falling over one another to get close to her. It never took long for the wolves to recognize new prey—even prey that had until yesterday been under the protection of a great, large lion and his two brothers.

He kept his distance himself, but obviously Eleanor Griffin had had an effect on him as well. After all, he'd chosen to stand gazing at her from across the room rather than put Lydia Franch on her back.

Something was out of balance—and quite interesting as a consequence. He looked at Eleanor again. Quite interesting.

One consequence of a relatively early evening was that Valentine was actually downstairs eating breakfast when the knock came at the front door. If he'd known what would transpire next, however, he would have stayed in bed.

As it was, he continued with his roasted ham and biscuits; he daily updated his butler regarding which guests he was or wasn't home to receive. Hobbes would see to it that no unapproved persons, especially of the female variety, entered the house. And this morning the list included Lydia, as well—in the space of an evening and through no real fault of her own, she'd gone from being a pleasant diversion to something of an annoyance. And she knew something—or rather, someone—had caught his attention before he'd acted on it, which he intensely disliked.

Hobbes appeared in the breakfast room doorway. "My lord, His Grace, the Duke of Mel—"

"Valentine," the Duke of Melbourne interrupted, sweeping past the offended butler. "I need to speak with you."

"So I immediately surmised," the marquis returned dryly. "It wouldn't be concerning a particular female in a burgundy gown, would it?"

"It's private," the duke said, striding to the window and back again, sending a glare at the attending servants as he repeated the motion.

Chewing a mouthful of ham, Valentine eyed his uninvited guest. For as long as he'd known Sebastian, he didn't think he'd ever seen the duke quite so . . . agitated. He jerked his head at Hobbes, and without a word the butler and his two footmen vanished, closing the door behind them.

"Have some breakfast," he offered, indicating the laden sideboard.

"I've eaten."

"Then for God's sake stop pacing and let *me* finish eating. I've already got an aching head this morning, and you're making me ill."

With a frown the duke seated himself at Valentine's elbow. "You saw Eleanor last evening."

"Couldn't help it, really. Why? Are you calling out every gentleman who ogled her?" He snorted. "That would take a week."

"Oh, shut up. And this stays between us, Valentine."

"I don't gossip, Seb. You know that."

Melbourne let out a breath. "Yes, I do. And that's partly why I'm here. The evening before last," he continued, pulling a folded paper from his breast pocket, "Eleanor gave me this."

The marquis wiped jam from his fingers and took the paper. As he read through it, he was conscious once again of being extremely grateful to have been born without brothers and sisters. "And why are you showing me this?" he asked, handing it back. "Other than to allow me to admire the fine penmanship, of course."

"Last night was her first evening of playing this . . . game," Melbourne muttered, tucking the letter away again. "And this morning she left with that damned Cobb-Harding for some outing in Hyde Park."

For a moment Valentine gazed at his friend. One of his few friends, when he considered it, for he was more choosey than most people might think. Something he'd learned from his father, he supposed; sleep with any chit you like, but choose your friends with care. "Her behavior obviously annoys, you, Melbourne, so put a stop to it. You control her purse, don't you? But you don't need me to tell you that."

"It's not that simple. I . . . agreed to her terms, as long as she doesn't become embroiled in a scandal."

"You agreed?" Valentine repeated, lifting an eyebrow and truly surprised. "*You*?"

"Yes, I agreed, damn it all. She made me angry."

"Then you have to let her be, don't you? I'm sure Madame Costanza will appreciate the business."

"So that's where she got that bloody gown." Hard gray eyes met his and slid away again. "It's more complicated than that, Valentine. Whatever she's up to, she still bears the Griffin name. And the Griffin reputation. I tried to warn her again this morning that if it was a spouse she wanted, she needed to stay out of trouble and not waste her time with fortune-hunting fools like Cobb-Harding, but trouble and fools seem to be precisely her goal. And the more it irritates me, the further she goes in that direction."

With a short smile, Valentine finished off his tea. "Then let her go. She'd never marry Cobb-Harding. Seems Nell just wants some fun—take a look at the herd before she chooses her stallion."

"I can't let her go—and please desist from the allusions. She's not you, Valentine. Scandal will affect her. It could ruin her."

"And the Griffin reputation."

"Precisely. However bright she is, she's never stepped outside our circle before. She wants fun without scandal, but she has no idea how to accomplish that—or how badly it could turn out."

"I still don't see how you can dissuade her, if you agreed to this," Valentine continued, "you being a man of your word and all. The harder you pull on her tether, the harder she'll pull against it."

The duke slammed his fist against the table. "Correct once again. And that is why I'm here."

Valentine had the queasy feeling he'd just stumbled into some sort of trap. "I don't suppose you'd care to explain that?"

"You're the most hedonistic man I know."

"Well, thank you."

Melbourne snorted. "That wasn't a compliment."

"Yes, I had that suspicion. What's your point?"

"That you come from the opposite place I do, propriety-wise. And Eleanor knows that. So where she won't take advice or guidance from me, she will very likely do so from you."

Valentine pushed to his feet, an uncomfortable heaviness thudding into his gut. And he didn't think it was the ham. "What? You want me to mentor Eleanor? In sin?"

"Good God, no. But as you observed so astutely, all my interference will do is push her further into this insanity. You're already more immersed in decadence than she could ever hope to become. She'll listen to you. She even respects you, I think. Therefore you, Valentine, can keep her out of serious trouble."

"I need a drink," Valentine said, exiting the breakfast room in favor of the library and its well-stocked liquor cabinet.

"I've put a great deal of thought into this," Melbourne continued, following him. "You can keep an eye on her, keep her out of trouble, where Shay, Zachary, or I would only push her to do worse."

Suppressing a shudder, Valentine poured himself a whiskey. "What in the devil's name makes you think I'd want to have anything to do with this?" That, in addition to the fact that over the past day he'd been having distinctly impure thoughts about Eleanor Griffin. "Go away, Melbourne."

To his growing dismay, the duke smiled. "I thought you might be reluctant to participate, which is why I also brought this." From another pocket he produced a yellowing, much-folded scrap of paper.

Valentine stared at the paper, wishing he could cause it to burst into flames by power of thought alone. "That is not fair, Melbourne," he grunted when the missive didn't combust. "I was drunk when I wrote that." Swearing, he downed half his whiskey. "Damnation."

"And I was drunk when I accepted it. We were equally inebriated, so you can't possibly claim that I took some sort of advantage of you."

"You should have been a bloody solicitor, Sebastian."

The duke only smiled again. "Insulting me is not going to help your cause." Dangling the paper in his fingers, he sank into one of the ill-used reading chairs by the fireplace. "I could read it to you, though I actually have it memorized."

"Spare me. It's bad form to remind someone of their one moment of weakness."

"One? Ahem. 'In exchange for services rendered in regards to turning away a certain persistent female,'" His Grace recited, "'I hereby owe the bearer of this note one favor of his choosing. Signed, Valentine Eugene Corbett, Marquis of Deverill.'"

Valentine dropped into the opposing chair. "For God's sake, all right. You win, you bastard. Just never repeat my full name to anyone ever again, myself included."

"Splendid." The Duke of Melbourne rose again, tucking the damned scrap away. "She should be somewhere in Hyde Park by now. I suggest you not delay."

"You want me to go now?"

"Cobb-Harding came for her in a high-perch phaeton. That should make your search a bit easier."

"Melbourne—"

At the doorway the duke faced into the depths of the library again. "Keep her out of trouble, Valentine. That's all

I ask. I'm putting my trust in you. I'm putting my family's honor in your hands."

Valentine favored Sebastian with a two-fingered salute as the duke left, and then sank back to polish off his whiskey. That hadn't gone well by any stretch of the imagination. Because of that damned note, he'd just become embroiled in a family dispute, something he'd managed to avoid since he'd been eighteen and his father had finally succumbed to oblivion.

Sebastian had to be desperate, to come to him. Even so, and even with the qualifications the duke had listed, he was fairly certain that he wasn't the wisest choice to become anyone's chaperone. And although a week ago he would have considered the favor vaguely annoying, since yesterday it had become much more troubling than that. "Talk about sending a fox to guard the henhouse," he muttered, rising to have his horse saddled.

The problem was, this fox now had a prestigious family's honor, a friend's honor, in his hands. And so Eleanor Griffin would have to remain safely out of his reach, no matter what he might be considering in private.

Chapter 4

"I still don't understand how you managed it," Stephen Cobb-Harding said, as he angled the sporty, high-perch racing phaeton into the shade of some oak trees.

Across the driving path a group of mamas had gathered, likely to discuss marriage matches for their sons and daughters. Eleanor couldn't imagine her austere brother Melbourne in such a gaggle, but neither did she think he'd never discussed her matrimonial future with anyone. "As I said, His Grace and I have an understanding. I prefer not to discuss the details of it."

"Very well. Far be it from me to ruin the day with sticky questions."

His charming grin made her smile in return. "That's very diplomatic of you, Stephen."

He shrugged. "I have the feeling that a lack of strife might be a pleasant change for you."

Her smile deepened. Shame on her brothers for keep-

44

ing her from such pleasant exchanges—for heaven's sake, speaking with Mr. Cobb-Harding didn't mean she'd end up married to him. It only meant she could laugh and feel carefree and have a bit of fun for a few hours. Of course, she could consider the matrimonial portion of her declaration if she wanted to. "Diplomatic and perceptive. My goodness."

"And in need of something cool. Would you care for a lemon ice?"

"That sounds delightful."

Under the circumstances it also sounded impossible, though she didn't say so. Free or not, she wouldn't have joined Stephen without a chaperone if he'd arrived for her in anything but a high-perch phaeton. As the saying went, a racing phaeton was the friend of a girl's good name—mostly because once a driver took the ribbons, he couldn't let them go unless a groom was present to hold the team, and there was no room for a groom on board. It did ensure his female companion's virtue, but at the same time made it impossible for the driver to disembark for the purpose of procuring lemon ices, for example.

Mr. Cobb-Harding glanced at the ribbons in his hands, then over at the ice vendor. "You seem like a lady who enjoys new experiences," he said, facing her again. "Have you ever held a phaeton?"

"Really?" A delighted giggle escaped her lips before she could stop it. "Not since I was fifteen. Are you certain?"

He handed her the reins. "They'll try to pull forward. Hold them hard."

"I will."

He jumped to the ground. The bay pair immediately took a step forward, pulling so hard that Eleanor slid forward on the narrow seat. She leaned back, hauling against them, and they settled down again.

"First that dress, and now horses," a low drawl came from her left. "You're becoming a Gypsy, aren't you?"

A low flutter of amused excitement started low in her chest. "Lord Deverill. Whatever are you doing out and about before noontime?"

The marquis, mounted on his prime and infamously bad-tempered stallion Iago, tilted his beaver hat at her. "Good God, is it that early? I must be ill."

"The daylight will do you good."

"That remains to be seen." He sent a glance toward the shaved ice vendor. "Stephen Cobb-Harding," he murmured. "Interesting choice of companion."

Eleanor frowned, her pleasure at seeing the marquis dissipating. "Don't tell me *you've* become stodgy."

Both dark eyebrows lifted. " 'Stodgy'?" he repeated. "You wound me. My only complaint is against his poor choice of coat color. What is that, puce?"

"Ah. His coat color. Very likely."

The marquis chuckled. "I suppose his dress is tolerable. I was just surprised to see you here in his company, and without a Griffin brother in sight."

"I told you yesterday that things would change."

"So they have. And for—"

"Here you are, Lady Eleanor," Stephen interrupted, setting a pair of ices on the seat and clambering up beside them. "You did well. I think driving lessons may be next."

"I'd love to," she blurted.

Her escort's attention, though, had already turned to Deverill. "Good morning, my lord."

"Cobb-Harding. That's a fine-looking pair."

"Yes. Thank you. If you'll excuse us?"

The marquis touched the brim of his hat again. "Of course. Good day to both of you."

Eleanor watched Lord Deverill ride off toward the north part of the park. She didn't know anyone who rode as well as Valentine Corbett—or any man who looked as fine in a rust-colored coat and tight buckskin breeches.

"I've always been surprised," Stephen said into the silence, "that your brothers could be so protective of you and still allow Deverill into Griffin House."

"Deverill and Melbourne attended Oxford together, and they inherited at nearly the same age. They've always been quite close—well, as close as Deverill gets to anyone. And the marquis has never been anything less than respectful toward me."

"I meant no offense, Lady Eleanor."

She smiled at him. "None taken."

It was a question she'd asked herself from time to time anyway, considering how differently Melbourne and Deverill viewed the world. Mostly, though, she was just thankful for the marquis's occasional visits. He always felt like a breath of fresh air, a contrary breeze in the face of her brothers' harsh north wind. She'd even conjured his image when she'd written her declaration. There were certainly a few things about his style of living that she wanted to emulate, though the majority of them would see her married or in a convent.

There were other things she'd imagined about him too, about what she would do if those deep green eyes turned in her direction with more than mild amusement. And she'd imagined kisses, and warm hands, and pleasures she couldn't put a name to, but could only guess about.

And the odd thing was, since he'd run into her outside Madame Costanza's shop yesterday, she'd sensed a change in those eyes. A change that made her heart thud, and that made her recall her young girl's fantasies all over again.

"How's your ice?"

She shook herself. "Very refreshing. Thank you."

"You know, my lady, I would very much like to escort you to the Hampton Ball tomorrow evening, if you would permit me."

Oh, Melbourne would have an apoplexy if the same man escorted her twice in two days. "If you will come by at eight o'clock, I will be happy to have you escort me."

Stephen nodded. "Splendid."

As they passed between two rows of hedges, he leaned closer. Before she could move, he flicked the tip of his tongue along the left corner of her mouth. "What are you—" she stammered, shocked at the startling intimacy.

"Lemon ice," he said easily. "Even sweeter, melted upon your lips."

Eleanor spooned up another mouthful of lemon ice and tried to regain her breath. No man had ever dared to be so forward with her before now, and for a brief moment she'd been offended. This was what she'd wanted, in a manner of speaking—not some man she barely knew licking her mouth, but the freedom to have something out of the ordinary happen, with no one to chastise her for it later.

"You're being very quiet. I haven't offended you, I hope."

"No! No. You only surprised me."

One fine eyebrow lifted. "And you don't like surprises, Lady Eleanor? I'm sorry if I've erred in my assessment of your charac—"

"You haven't, Stephen," she said quickly, frowning. Heavens, the last thing she wanted was for Mr. Cobb-Harding to think her timid or prudish. Not after she'd finally won the opportunity to be anything but. "I love surprises. And you may call me Eleanor." If he kept calling her Lady Eleanor, neither of them would be able to forget her family's large shadow.

The smile touched his mouth again. "I am very glad to hear you say that, Eleanor."

After another pleasant hour spent chatting as they meandered about the park, Stephen returned her to Griffin House. As they turned up the drive, she could practically feel three pairs of frowning eyes glaring at her from the upstairs windows, and she sent a frown back in that direction just for good measure.

"Good afternoon, Lady Eleanor," Stanton greeted, as he opened the front door for her.

"Stanton. Where might my brothers be?" She supposed she might as well get the argument over with.

"His Grace has gone to the House of Lords for a meeting. Lord Shay and Lord Zachary were to have luncheon at the Society Club, and they haven't yet returned."

"They—oh. Thank you. I'll be attending to some correspondence in the morning room."

"Very good, my lady. Shall I send in some tea?"

"Yes, that would be lovely."

Her brothers weren't even there? That didn't make any sense at all. Melbourne had hounded her for better than twenty minutes before Stephen had arrived this morning, questioning the soundness of her mind and demanding to know what she hoped to gain from spending time with a fortune hunter—as if every single gentleman with a limited income was a fortune hunter. And yet now they couldn't even be bothered to see whether she arrived home safely or not.

She seated herself at the writing desk, and with a sigh pulled a sheet of paper from the drawer. So they weren't home. She hoped that meant they were finally taking her declaration seriously, and had realized that she wasn't to be trifled with.

The morning room door flew open and she jumped, immediately steeling herself for a fight. "You might at least knock," she said, wishing she'd begun her letter so she could protest being interrupted.

"I forgot," Penelope's small, sweet voice came.

Eleanor scowled. *Wonderful.* Now she was scolding little girls. "I'm sorry, Peep. I didn't realize it was you." She turned in her chair to face the doorway. "What might I do for you?"

"Mrs. Bevins said I may have a tea party," the girl replied, prancing up to stand beside Eleanor. "I wish to invite you to attend."

From her careful diction she'd memorized that last bit. "Well said, Peep. And I would be delighted to join you."

"Thank you." Peep took her hand to pull her to her feet. "Uncle Zachary was going to attend, but Uncle Shay made him leave for luncheon."

" 'Made him?' " Eleanor repeated. Now *that* sounded interesting.

"Yes. Uncle Shay said Papa told them to vacate. What does that mean, anyway?"

It meant several things, and mostly that Sebastian was up to something. "It just means he wanted them to leave the house for a little while," she explained.

"Oh, good. I thought it might be something worse, because Uncle Zachary said some bad words before he left."

"Well, that's Uncle Zachary for you." Eleanor held on to her young niece's hand as they climbed the stairs to the nursery. "Should I wear my bonnet to tea?"

Peep gave a dismissive wave of her free hand. "Miss Hooligan and Buttercup don't have their bonnets on, so you don't have to either. Besides, I don't like to wear bonnets. The ribbons scratch my chin."

"Mine too. I hadn't realized your doll and your pony were attending as well. Am I dressed appropriately?"

"Everyone wears whatever they want to my tea parties," Peep declared. "I'm not stuffy."

Heavens, Eleanor could remember those days, when she'd been six and hosted tea parties for her brothers and ridden horses astride and jumped into the estate's lake wearing only her shift. It hadn't even occurred to her then that in a few short years all of that would be taken away. She squeezed Penelope's hand. "This will be a very nice tea party."

"A *splendid* tea party," Peep amended.

Eleanor smiled. "Yes, a *splendid* tea party."

If Melbourne expected Valentine to render twenty-four hours of constant surveillance on his sister, the duke was going to be sorely disappointed. The marquis leaned forward in the saddle, hands crossed over the pommel, and watched as Eleanor left Cobb-Harding on the front drive and vanished into the depths of Griffin House.

He counted to ten, then decided he'd done his duty for the day and turned Iago toward Jezebel's. If he could get some light wagering done, at least the outing wouldn't be completely wasted.

Obligations. He hated them, and rarely found himself on the paying end—with one glaring exception. In truth, though, he'd thought if Melbourne had ever intended on calling in his favor, it would be for something more . . . nefarious than keeping an eye on a virtuous female.

Or perhaps Eleanor was a bit less virtuous than he'd previously thought. From his vantage point along one of Hyde Park's riding trails, he'd seen Cobb-Harding kiss her. She hadn't fainted or screamed or fled, but instead had taken another bite of her lemon ice. Calm and collected or not, though, Nell had best be careful if she wanted to avoid ending up in some gossip sheet.

Whatever seduction Cobb-Harding had intended, it obviously hadn't gone well. While Valentine could give the buffoon some credit for his boldness, he wasn't certain he would have used the same strategy himself. Angering the Griffin brothers was a sure way to ruination—or worse. Aside from that, a kiss—a first kiss—between two potential lovers should never have to be squeezed in between hedge rows. And Eleanor's renewed interest in her ice was *not* good news for Cobb-Harding.

Valentine sighed. Ordinarily one man's misfortune with a chit could be his own good luck. Not this chit, however. No matter how attractive she looked in her light green sprigged muslin gown. It hadn't even been one of Madame Costanza's creations, and in fact he was fairly certain he'd seen her in it before. But the light in her eyes, the defiant delight in her smile—that was new. And absurdly disturbing.

"Show a bit of control, Deverill," he muttered at himself. Hell, if nothing else it would be a good exercise for him. The devil knew he didn't ordinarily use the muscles, physical or mental, designed to aid in restraint.

By the time he left Jezebel's he'd won enough to pay for a late luncheon and a bottle of fine claret, and feeling fairly satisfied with himself, he rode home to change for dinner.

"Any news?" he asked as the butler followed him down the hallway.

"You received a letter by private messenger, my lord," Hobbes said, offering the missive on a silver salver.

Valentine took it. The edges looked only a little warped, so the butler hadn't had much luck reading the contents. "Probably Lady Marie Quenton," he speculated, holding it up to his nose and inhaling. Nothing. "Hm. Lydia, perhaps."

"I couldn't wager a guess, my lord," the butler offered. "Do you wish some tea?"

As Valentine unfolded the letter, he tossed the bottle of claret to Hobbes with his free hand. "Open this for me, will you?" he said, heading into his office to read in private.

The opening, written as was the rest of the letter in a spare, neat hand, was brief and to the point.

Deverill,

According to Eleanor's calendar she has accepted invitations to the following.

He looked up and reached for a cigar. "You must be joking, Melbourne," he muttered, sinking back into his chair. From the short, detailed list of places, dates, and times, the duke was extremely serious. Valentine skipped down past "Lady Delmond's—Embroidery" to the bottom of the note.

Most of these outings won't require your participation, but as you can see, there is a great deal of unaccounted-for time in between. That is where you will have to be.

Melbourne

Valentine's first thought was to tear the note into small pieces and toss it into the fire. At the very bottom of the page in large letters, however, Sebastian had scrawled "YOU OWE ME."

Thankfully Hobbes picked that moment to scratch on the library door and enter with the glass of claret on a tray. "Anything else, my lord?"

"Yes. Bring me the bottle." As the butler exited, Valentine skimmed through the list of Eleanor's outings again. "You'd damned well better tear up my paper after this, Melbourne," he growled, taking a swallow of the claret.

The gaps in her schedule would take all his free time, and then some. In addition, he would have to keep track of her without appearing to do so; if she realized that he was acting as her rather tarnished guardian angel, she'd never forgive him—and for some reason, that mattered.

Since according to her calendar the scheduled event for that evening was dinner with Lady Barbara Howsen and her family, he had until the Hampton Ball to decide what he meant to do. And of course attending that relatively tame affair meant he would miss the decadence and sin going on at Lord Belmont's more private soiree that same evening.

An abrupt thought occurred to him, and he smiled. Eleanor would undoubtedly unveil another of Madame Costanza's creations tomorrow evening. He hoped it would be something in red.

"Nell, it's nearly eight o'clock!" Zachary's voice came from the other side of her bedchamber door. "Are you ready yet?"

Eleanor turned in front of the mirror again. The gown had arrived only an hour ago, and it would take at least ten times that long for her to get used to seeing herself in it. "Goodness," she murmured, running her fingers along the low crimson neckline that just barely concealed her bosom. "I feel practically naked."

"You won't hear an argument from me, my lady," Helen put in, fitting a silver shawl across her shoulders. "What will your brothers say?"

She'd thought about that. Agreement or not, she'd never make it out the front door without them demanding to see what she was wearing. And it would be even worse if she told them that they weren't escorting her to the ball.

"It's time, I suppose. Please inform Zachary that we've tried cool compresses and violet nosegays, but I still have a terrible head, and so I won't be attending tonight."

"You want *me* to tell him that?" Helen squeaked.

"I can't do it," Eleanor whispered back. "At once, if you please, before he breaks down the door."

She hid out of view of the doorway while Helen did as she was bid. With the agreement in place, she should have been able to waltz out the front door wearing anything she chose and climb into anyone's carriage without a word of explanation, as long as she was willing to face the consequences. In truth, though, she was quite aware that her agreement was only a piece of paper, and that her brothers had twenty-one years each of overprotective, arrogant behavior burned into their thick skulls. Better, then, to avoid tempting them to act.

Helen closed the door and turned around to lean back against it. "Saints preserve me, I'm going to the devil for this," she muttered.

Eleanor came out of hiding. "Nonsense. When I arrive at the ball they'll know I put you up to it. I'm just attempting to avoid any unnecessary stickiness, is all."

"Yes, my lady. But what do we do now?"

"We watch out the window until they're gone, and then we go downstairs to await my escort."

She actually made Helen watch out the window, because it would never do for one of her brothers to catch sight either of her or of her loose hair woven through with crimson ribbons. They'd see her soon enough at the ball—where they wouldn't be able to do anything about either her hair or her gown. *She* knew that while her clothes might cause conversation, they couldn't truthfully cause a scandal—whatever her brothers might choose to think.

"They've gone, my lady," Helen said after a few moments. "I swear His Grace looked right at me."

"Even if he did, it doesn't signify." A nervous flutter went down her spine. She was going to do this, in complete defiance of anything Melbourne might wish. *This* was freedom, and romance—and it was exhilarating, if exceedingly nerve-racking. She wondered briefly how

Deverill could so constantly maintain such a level of excessive behavior without suffering an apoplexy.

They hurried downstairs. Stanton looked as though he wanted to drop dead rather than be responsible for letting her out of the house, but she gave him her version of the Griffin glare, and he swallowed whatever it was he'd been about to say. As a coach rattled up outside, he silently pulled open the door.

Not a coach, she amended as she stepped out to the front portico. The racing phaeton again.

"No need for chaperones," Stephen said, evidently reading the question in her expression. He extended a hand to help her into the high seat. "And we can make a quick getaway, if need be."

Eleanor laughed. "I hope we won't need to flee into the night," she returned. "Helen, you're excused for the evening, it seems."

The maid looked at her, concern plain on her upturned face. "But my lady, you—"

"Good evening," she said firmly, facing forward again. "Shall we?"

"As you wish." With a cluck Stephen Cobb-Harding sent the team into a smart trot. "And may I say you look . . . beyond stunning this evening?"

She'd noticed that several times his gaze had focused on her breasts. The attention made her feel both desirable and surprisingly uncomfortable, and she pulled the shawl closer around her shoulders. Eleanor shook herself. She simply wasn't used to that sort of attention. "Thank you, Stephen."

"And your brothers didn't give you any trouble when you said you'd be attending with me tonight?"

"No." She frowned. Dishonesty hadn't been part of her plan, but she seemed to be doing more than her share of lying. "I . . . didn't actually tell them."

"You didn't? Did you say you'd be arriving with someone more acceptable, then? Eleanor, I don't—"

"I told them I had an aching head and wouldn't be attending at all," she cut in. "One complete surprise and ensuing argument seemed better than several smaller ones."

He sat beside her in silence for a minute. She hadn't meant to offend him, but he already knew that he wasn't on her brothers' list of acceptable suitors, or he wouldn't have made those comments the other night about having wanted to talk to her for the past year. To her surprise, Stephen Cobb-Harding seemed to understand her need for freedom and excitement and romance better than any other male she knew, including the Marquis of Deverill. And though he occasionally made her feel a tad uncomfortable, that was only because she wasn't yet used to spreading her wings. Yes, that was it.

"I have an idea," Stephen said abruptly.

"What sort of idea?"

A slow, attractive smile touched his mouth. "Do you want to go to the Hampton Ball, or do you wish a real, genuine taste of freedom and adventure?"

The ball, her sensible voice shouted. She'd make quite the stir there. But would that be real, genuine freedom? Or was she merely making a spectacle of herself for the sake of unsettling her brothers? "What would I be tasting?" she hedged.

"It's another soiree, at a perfectly respectable house, but the ladies are permitted to wager and to drink and to ask gentlemen to dance."

This sounded like trouble. "I don't—"

"And everyone wears masks, so you won't have to worry about any kind of scandal. We could leave if you feel the least bit uncomfortable, of course. But I thought freedom was—"

"Yes," she blurted. "Let's go."

With a mask, she could attend. In a crimson gown and a mask, no one but Stephen would know she was Lady Eleanor. She could at least look about and decide if she wanted to stay. Her brothers thought her at home in bed, anyway, so they wouldn't cause a stir when she didn't arrive at the Hampton Ball.

"Are you certain?" Stephen asked.

"Yes. I want to go."

His smile deepened. "Good. We'll have fun. You'll see." Stephen chuckled, obviously reading her uncertain expression. "And it will be exciting and romantic. Everything you want."

She dearly hoped so, because the sensible voice in her head was still yelling at her to change her mind.

Chapter 5

~~~~~⌇⌇⌇~~~~~

Valentine arrived at the Hampton Ball at precisely seven thirty-five in the evening. According to the invitation the soiree began five minutes before that, and indeed, he was the third guest to arrive. Certainly no gray-eyed chit in a daring gown of red, or any other color, had yet made an appearance.

It was ridiculous. He made a point of not being early—or even on time—anywhere, and even after Eleanor arrived nothing interesting was likely to happen tonight. At two hours or more before his usual arrival time, he'd be lucky not to die of boredom before she did put in an appearance.

He was on the verge of striking up a conversation with a footman when the next group of guests came through the door. The butler announced each one, though he certainly wasn't impressed, and the other couple there were too deaf to hear anything short of a cannon shot. After the fifth round of introductions, he was ready to gouge out his own ears and join them.

"Deverill?" a surprised voice came from the edge of the ballroom.

With a sigh Valentine turned around. "Francis Henning," he acknowledged, shaking the rotund young man's hand.

"What the devil are you doing here already?" Henning cast his gaze about the slowly filling room. "I say, which game are you stalking tonight?"

"None," he answered. "I'm here for the roast duck."

Henning's open face folded into bafflement. "Duck? You mean there's no chit?"

Valentine smiled. "There's always a chit."

"So who is—"

"I haven't decided yet."

After a moment, Henning burst into uncertain laughter. "Oh, I understand. Very good, Deverill. Ha ha."

Luckily for Henning the butler took that moment to bellow Melbourne's name, and Valentine looked up. "Ah. There he is. If you'll excuse me, Henning, I'll have to stop toying with you now."

He made his way over to the doorway where Sebastian, Shay, and Zachary lingered, accepting greetings from the host and hostess. Halfway there, he frowned. Where was Eleanor? Under normal circumstances she was at least as easy to spot as her powerful brothers, but tonight she should have stood out like a dove among crows. *Wonderful*. Now he was paraphrasing Shakespeare.

"Deverill," Zachary greeted, clapping him on the shoulder. "You just won me twenty quid. Shay said you'd never be here when we arrived."

"Well, I *am* here," he returned, scowling at the duke. "Where is she? I'm definitely not doing this for my health, you know."

The duke had the bad manners to chuckle at him. "You, my friend, are off the hook tonight."

Valentine glared at him. "Beg pardon?"

"She had an aching head, and is home in bed. You're free to go off and damage your health to your heart's content tonight."

To his surprise, Valentine felt . . . disappointed. He wouldn't be able to see the gown she'd chosen for this evening. "You might have sent over a damned note."

"We didn't know until the last moment," Zachary protested. "She wanted to come; I think she might even have dressed. It's not our fault."

Now that was interesting. "She 'might' have dressed?" he repeated. "You didn't see her tucked into bed?"

Melbourne pushed in front of the youngest Griffin brother. "Are you implying that she waited for us to leave and then snuck out somewhere?"

Valentine shrugged. "I don't know. She's not my sister. But the fact that it didn't occur to you until now makes me ashamed to know you."

The duke looked at him for a moment, his expression thoughtful. Finally he began to swear, quietly and vehemently. "Her maid watched out the window for us to leave," he muttered. "I saw her, and I didn't think anything of it."

"But Nell has an agreement with us," Zachary protested. "She doesn't need to sneak about."

"That, my friend, would probably depend on what she's up to." Valentine stifled the urge to smile. A chit had outsmarted the Griffin brethren; that didn't happen every day. "I could be wrong, you know. She could be at home, asleep."

"Shay, go and see," Melbourne ordered.

Without another word Charlemagne turned on his heel and slipped back down the hallway. Zachary, on the other hand, backed away and headed into the depths of the room.

"I'll see which of her friends are here," he said as he vanished.

"Most of them," Valentine supplied.

"Deverill, you—"

"Oh, no, you don't. *You* lost her. I've been granted the evening off. I'll be lurking in your damned shrubbery in the morning. But if you find out where she might be going tomorrow, *send me a bloody note.*"

Melbourne gave a short grin. "Have a good evening."

"I intend to."

"So, my lady swan, are you enjoying yourself?"

Eleanor blinked. She'd never seen chandelier light glow so brightly, and she kept catching herself staring at the massive wrought-silver piece hanging above the center of the ballroom. "I think I've been too liberal with the brandy and . . . whatever else that is."

"Rum," the man in the black fox half mask replied. "And you've had less than most of the other females here."

With a grin that didn't feel quite centered, Eleanor gestured for one of the footmen, who were all dressed as white doormice. "Another rum if you please, my good mouse."

In the corner a bear and another swan swooned across a chair, masks bumping as their mouths locked. Quietly in the background an orchestra of pan flutes and sitars played something that sounded Eastern and erotic, while a pair of wolves, male and female, emerged from one of the many closeted alcoves along the far side of the room. The male wolf's hand was firmly attached to the female's left breast, which barely had enough material over it to call it covered, anyway.

Other muted sounds of women moaning and men's lower-pitched grunts were even more unsettling. She pretended to ignore them. The liquor helped her accept the idea of staying, but it also seemed to attune her to the illicit activities going on all over the house. Eleanor took another long swallow of rum and swayed.

The fox cupped her elbow, his voice soft in her ear. "Perhaps you should sit down for a moment, my lady swan."

Exotic perfumes mingled with the smell of liquor and heated bodies. With her third snifter of brandy the sensible voice in her head had become slurred and unintelligible, but even the part of her that acknowledged that she'd never been anywhere as decadent and wild in her life knew she should be elsewhere. Every time she thought to suggest that she and Stephen leave, however, another glass appeared in her hand, and another slightly condescending taunt came softly regarding her courage and her resolve.

"Yes," she returned, hearing the slur in her own voice, "I think I would like to sit down for a moment."

She took a step toward a free chair, but the floor was lower under her feet than she expected. Stumbling, she would have fallen flat on her swan mask if Stephen hadn't caught her.

"Steady there," he said, amusement dripping from his

voice. "This way. There's somewhere private where we can relax a little."

"I really think I should go home," she managed, casting one hand out for balance. She'd had a little too much wine before, though rarely, but she couldn't remember ever feeling so . . . thick, and dreamy. "We've been here for a very long time."

"We'll go shortly," Stephen agreed. "After you've recovered yourself a little. We can't have Melbourne seeing you like this, now can we?"

"Oh, no." Eleanor put a finger to her lips. "Shh. Don't say his name. I don't want anyone to know who I am."

"Right." Stephen pulled aside a heavy curtain and helped her into a small room with only a couch and a small table bearing one candle. "There you go. Have a seat, lady swan."

She sank gratefully onto the soft couch, so weary she could have fallen asleep then and there. Stephen sat beside her and reached over to pull the mask from her face. "Better?" he asked.

Her eyes closed dreamily, and she forced them open again. "Yes, thank you."

He stroked a finger along her cheek. "Good. Just relax for a few minutes. Close your eyes if you like. I'll keep watch."

A helpless giggle crossed her lips as her eyelids sank down again. "So gallant, you are."

The finger stroked her cheek again, then glided down the length of her throat. It lingered there for a moment while Eleanor tried to muster enough of a thought to tell him to please stop that and take her home. Then the fingers sank lower again, drawing across her chest along her low neckline.

"You are so lovely, Eleanor," Mr. Cobb-Harding murmured, and lips covered hers, sucking and pulling so that she could barely breathe. The material on one shoulder slid down her arm, lowering the front of her dress, and a hand abruptly covered her bare right breast, cupping and tugging and kneading.

"*Stop!*" she shouted, except that only an unintelligible whimper escaped her. Forcing open her eyes, she could see nothing but the black fox half mask looming over her and smell only harsh, liquor-tinged breath in her face. "No."

"I know you like this," he whispered, shifting to slide the gown off her other shoulder. "All females d—"

Abruptly a black-clothed arm and attached fist darted into her vision and connected with the fox's pointed nose. In great detail she saw the nose cave in, then Stephen lurched backward.

"What—"

"Stay down if you want to keep breathing," a low voice growled. A heartbeat later a black panther's half mask with glittering green eyes entered her vision.

"Deverill," she muttered, trying to sit up.

"At your service," he returned in a tight voice she'd never heard from him before. It chilled her to the bone, and she was grateful it wasn't directed at her.

At least she didn't think it was. "I tried—"

"No worries. Are you hurt?"

"No. Very fuzzy."

He moved closer, and she felt the warm silk of her dress slide back up over her shoulder. Abruptly she remembered that at least one of her breasts had been bare, and that he'd seen it. "Deverill?"

"Shh. Here. You have to put this on again." He held up the mask, watched her try to reach for it, then gently placed it over her face himself.

"I want to go home, Valentine."

"We're going. In just a moment." He shifted, and in a second she heard flesh hitting flesh again. "If you breathe a word about tonight to anyone," the quiet, black voice came again, "I will destroy you. Is that clear?"

"Y . . . yes."

Though he didn't want to settle for delivering a warning, Valentine clearly had more urgent matters to deal with. He returned to Eleanor, who just moments before had had the shimmering folds of her crimson skirt pushed up past her knees, and one breast bared like an Amazon princess. Now she half lay limply on the couch, barely able to keep her eyes open. Cobb-Harding was a damned, bloody bastard.

Taking both of her hands, Valentine pulled Eleanor to her feet. With a sigh she collapsed against his chest. Walking wasn't going to work. With another glare at the prone, bloody-faced Cobb-Harding through the slits of his panther eyes, he lifted her into his arms. Ducking through the heavy curtains, he carried her through the main room, ignoring the hidden faces and sly smiles from the guests who hadn't already vanished into private rooms. Most of them knew who he was, but they would have no idea who the black swan in the crimson gown—one hand coiled into his lapel and her face tucked against his shoulder—could possibly be.

Thank Lucifer he'd taken his coach to his second outing of this evening, though he'd done so with a less innocent conclusion in mind. As he emerged from Belmont House he whistled for his driver, and a moment later the large black vehicle with the yellow crest on the door pulled into the drive.

"Drive around Hyde Park," Valentine instructed as he lifted Eleanor into the vehicle and settled her onto the cushioned seat.

The coach rocked into motion, and he pushed up both windows to allow in the damp night air, then settled into the opposite seat to pull off his panther mask, flinging the thing to the floor. He'd never thought particularly much of Stephen Cobb-Harding, if he'd thought anything at all, but this was beyond what even he might have expected.

"Deverill," Eleanor's weak, dreamy voice came.

"Relax, love. You're safe."

"I feel very strange."

He leaned forward, gently lifting the swan mask from her face. "You've been drugged. Laudanum in your rum, I would wager."

"Why . . . why would he do that?"

"So you wouldn't protest overly much, I should imagine."

With obvious effort she grabbed one of the wall straps and pulled herself more upright. For a long moment she looked at him, her face pale and her pupils enormous. "Do you—"

Valentine scowled. "I don't drug chits," he growled. "She either wants to be with me, or she doesn't."

"But you were there. At Belmont's."

"Only for consensual sin." He sat back, twirling her mask in his fingers. "Why did you think you were there?"

Eleanor closed her eyes for a moment, color tinging her cheeks. "I don't know. He was supposed to take me to the

Hampton Ball, but then he suggested another soiree, and it sounded . . . it sounded like something Melbourne would never have allowed me to attend."

"So you knew there would be sin."

A lone tear ran down her face. "I don't know. I wanted . . . I wanted to feel free. Like you."

Valentine gazed at her in the lantern-lit darkness for a long moment. The fright and the cool night air seemed to be rousing her physically, but obviously her mind remained murky. Women might wish to sleep with him, but they didn't want to emulate him. That was insane. And extremely unnerving. "Being like me would ruin you, darling."

"But I—" She stopped, her face going white again. "I'm going to be ill," she rasped, clutching one hand to her stomach and the other to her mouth.

Flinging open the coach door, Valentine leaned out. "Stop the coach, Dawson!"

The driver complied, and Valentine pulled Eleanor back out the door, half carrying her to the shelter of some bushes, where she bent over and vomited. He wouldn't recommend it for fun, but casting up her accounts would at least help her clear her head.

"My goodness," she said weakly, straightening.

Wordlessly Valentine handed over his handkerchief and offered an arm to help her back to the waiting coach. At the foot of the steps she hesitated, looking around.

"We're not anywhere near home," she said, shifting a little away from him.

"I don't kidnap chits, either," he grunted. "If you appeared back at home half unconscious, Melbourne would h—"

"No!" she interrupted, shuddering. "They think I'm at

home, asleep. They can't know anything about this!" She clutched his sleeve. "Deverill, if I cause a scandal Sebastian will marry me off immediately, and to whomever he pleases. I have to get home without them ever knowing I left."

Hm. And if Melbourne learned what had transpired and Valentine's part in extracting Eleanor from harm, both the obligation and the debt would be wiped clean. "We'll worry about all of that later," he hedged, helping her back inside and climbing in after her.

"No, we can't. Please promise me, Deverill—Valentine—that you won't tell anyone about where I was or what Stephen . . . what he did."

"I'm not sure my silence would do you any good, Eleanor. Cobb-Harding has a great deal to gain, and almost nothing to lose, by spreading the rumor that he ruined you."

Her eyes narrowed. "If he thinks this will force me to marry him, he's sadly mistaken."

Valentine shrugged. "Stranger things have happened, and for less reason."

Gray eyes absorbed that. He could see exactly when she realized just how much trouble she was in, and that tonight being a Griffin meant nothing—unless she admitted everything to her brothers. "Oh, no," she whispered, bowing her head. "Oh, no."

"And I hate to add to your troubles, but shortly before I left the Hampton Ball, Melbourne sent Shay back to Griffin House to look in on you. That would have been some time ago."

Her shoulders heaved, curling dark hair in its dishevelment of crimson ribbons curtaining her face. Christ, he'd experienced it all before—the weeping, the begging, the feigned helplessness to change his mind or gain his mercy. He studied her bowed head. Cynical as he was, he knew honest despair when he saw it. And for the first time it touched him.

"Vauxhall," he said into the silence.

"What?" She sniffed in a poor attempt to stifle tears.

"There were to be acrobats there tonight. Tumblers, tightrope walkers, men on wooden stilts."

"What do I care about that?" she whispered unsteadily.

"You care about it a great deal, because you knew Melbourne would want to attend the ball, and you wanted to see the acrobats. So you waited until they left the house, and then you slipped out yourself, hired a hack, and went to Vauxhall."

She lifted her head, hope sparking in her gray eyes. "Melbourne would be furious."

"Yes, but there would be no scandal."

Her face folded again. "Not until Stephen talked, you mean."

Valentine gave a slow, humorless smile. "Leave Mr. Cobb-Harding to me. By the time I'm finished, he won't ever mention your name again, except in the most polite of terms." Agreement or not, dislike for entanglements or not, this infuriated him on the most basic of levels. Cobb-Harding was a damned, bloody, lazy bastard who couldn't be bothered to make the effort of a proper seduction.

Eleanor reached across the coach and grabbed his hand. "I will owe you so much, Deverill, and I will never forget this. You are a good friend—and a good man."

He pressed her fingers and then released her, abruptly uncomfortable. "I'm taking an opportunity to engage in some mayhem," he muttered. "I should thank *you*." Not wanting to wait for her to argue in favor of his lack of self-interest, he leaned his head out the coach window again. "Dawson, hail a hack and have it follow us, then head for the corner of Avery Row and Brook's Mew."

"Yes, my lord."

That would put them two blocks from Griffin House, far enough away that her vigilant brothers wouldn't see anything, and close enough that he could place her into the hired carriage without worrying that something else might happen to her before she reached home. If Eleanor deserved one thing, it was to arrive home safely and without another fright for the evening.

"Deverill, I don't know what to say."

"Firstly, say you'll never be caught in that situation again."

"Oh, I promise that," Eleanor said vehemently.

"And secondly, you can never wear that gown again. It's a damned shame, because you looked like the goddess of fire in it, but someone who attended Belmont's might recognize it—and therefore, you. Especially since you arrived with Cobb-Harding and left with me."

She nodded, looking down at the exquisite creation. "I don't think I ever want to wear it again, anyway." Her fine cheeks darkened again. "And you saw—"

Yes, he had, and he wasn't likely to forget it. Melbourne's sister wasn't a puppy dog any longer. She was a magnificent specimen of feminine beauty. "Nothing I haven't seen before, Nell," he drawled. "Many times."

"And you won't tell anyone? I know how close you and Sebastian are, but please, Deverill, *please* don't say anything."

"Say anything about what?" he returned, standing as the coach stopped again. "And for God's sake, call me

Valentine." He forced a grin, hoping it looked easy and natural. "I did rescue you, after all."

She only nodded, her fingers gripping his tightly as he handed her to the ground and led her to the second coach.

"Remember, Eleanor, all you did was slip away to see some acrobats."

"Acrobats. And men on stilts."

He could see her pulling her thoughts back together, mentally regaining her footing. It surprised him. Most women he knew—even the occasional honest one—would be hysterical, or begging him to exact revenge on their attacker. It was becoming obvious that this bargain she'd made with Melbourne meant a great deal to her. Much more than he'd realized.

As she sat in the hack, he handed the driver a shilling. "You've just come straight from Vauxhall," he stated, "and saw no one with the lady either there or here." He flipped a gold sovereign into the man's surprised reach as he gave the Griffin House address. "Yes?"

The driver doffed his hat. "Aye, my lord. I ain't seen no one between here and Vauxhall."

"Good." He reached over to close the coach door.

Eleanor put a hand out to stop him. "Thank you, Valentine," she whispered. "Thank you so much."

Valentine sketched a jaunty bow. "My pleasure, my lady."

He stepped back as the hack rattled down the street and turned the next corner. She would be safe from there. Melbourne would no doubt have some harsh words for her, but compared to what she'd been through, an argument wouldn't be difficult.

Of course he hadn't exactly made things easier for himself; if he'd turned her in to her brother, his obligation

would be over. It was amusing, in a way. Him, the least
honorable man he knew, touched by a chit's honest need.
And because of that one moment of weakness on his part,
he now had to carry her secret and continue to keep an eye
on her—unless the escapade at Belmont's had cured her
of her desire for freedom.

And there was one other thing he'd obligated himself
to, as well. At the moment, though, he doubted Stephen
Cobb-Harding would care to remember tonight, either. He
climbed back into his own coach.

"Home, my lord?" Dawson asked from the driver's
perch.

"God, yes. I need to get some sleep."

Chapter 6

When Eleanor awoke, the aching head she'd pretended the night before had become all too real. She groaned as Helen pushed open the curtains of her bedchamber. "What time is it?"

"Seven o'clock, my lady."

"Close the curtains at once. I am *not* ready to rise yet."

"His Grace has requested that all family members join him at the breakfast table, my lady."

Her heart, along with her sour stomach, lurched. Had he found out something? She thought she'd been convincing when he'd flung open the front door at her arrival last night, and he'd certainly been angry enough, but if Deverill—Valentine—had miscalculated, all of London could be talking by now about how she'd voluntarily accompanied Stephen Cobb-Harding to Belmont's, about how she'd had too much to drink, allowed him to paw at her naked chest—and then left with another man of far worse reputation than her original escort.

"I don't feel well enough to eat breakfast," she mumbled, and curled away from the window.

"My lady, His Grace said you must attend, or I am to be sacked for failing to pass on his instructions."

"What?" Eleanor struggled upright amid the mound of blankets. "He can't do that!"

Helen gave a nervous curtsy. "If you could possibly manage it, my lady, I would prefer not to test his resolve."

Neither would Eleanor, actually. "I will go down to breakfast," she stated, "just to tell him to stop threatening the household staff."

The maid's shoulders sagged in obvious relief. "Thank you, my lady."

Her head continued to ache dully as she dressed and headed downstairs. She wasn't certain whether it was because of the laudanum or because of the amount of spirits she'd consumed, but either way the pain served to remind her *never* to be caught unawares again.

Melbourne and Penelope were the only Griffins at the breakfast table when she entered the room. "Good morning," she said, in consideration of Peep stifling the protest she'd been about to deliver. Sebastian was diabolical, sometimes.

"Good morning," he said pleasantly, holding a slice of toast in one hand and an official-looking paper in the other. He had Parliament today, she remembered.

"You're walking funny," Peep noted, as Eleanor bypassed the platters of ham and the soft-boiled eggs in favor of dry toast.

"My head aches," she replied. Melbourne had already commented, several times, about how strongly she'd smelled of liquor last night, so lying would have been useless. In all likelihood she had more significant things she would have to tell untruths about, anyway.

And it was thanks to the Marquis of Deverill that she even had the option of lying. If Melbourne knew what had actually happened, he would have sent her back to Devon after last night.

She sighed heavily as she took the chair beside Peep. She owed Deverill both for saving her virtue and for giving her another chance at husband hunting or romance or adventure or . . . whatever it was she meant to do. Being more cautious was certainly at the top of the list. After Stephen Cobb-Harding's trap, her enthusiasm for finding a husband without first enlisting someone else's opinion of his character had waned—or rather had turned. And in the adventure yesterday, poorly as it had turned out, she'd noticed something else.

By daylight she could admit that the soiree had held a definite decadent attraction. But whoever she ended up marrying, whether she chose him or not, it would signal the end of that initial feeling of barely muted excitement and anticipation. Exploring more of that sensation—of freedom and everything that went with it—had literally overnight become her focus. And she knew precisely whom to thank for that.

She owed Valentine for saving her, and she owed him for turning what would have been nightmares last night as she slept into something more nebulous and heated.

"What's amiss, Melbourne?" Zachary said from the doorway. Stifling a yawn he headed for the sideboard and began loading up a plate.

"Not a thing," the duke replied. "Why do you ask?"

"Because it's bloo . . . blasted seven o'clock in the

morning," he grumbled, flicking Peep on the ear as he passed and making her giggle.

"I hope this isn't some sort of lesson for Nell," the drier voice of Shay took up as he entered the room, "because I would have preferred a later setting. I only went to bed three hours ago."

Their greetings were so typical of the two of them; Zachary, despite being half asleep, was still as much amused as he was annoyed—he'd never been truly upset or angry more than once or twice in her memory. Charlemagne was more reserved and less chatty, and with a much shorter fuse to his temper. He'd nearly been sent down from university once when a classmate had wrongly accused him of cheating and he'd broken the boy's nose rather than argue the point verbally.

Her own temper was beginning to fray at the moment. "Maybe it's a lesson for *you*," Eleanor countered with a frown, "because *I* was forced to attend school last night."

Melbourne set aside the document he'd been reading. "This is a new family tradition," he said. "Since everyone seems determined to go their own way without informing other members of the family, we will make an occasion where we will all sit down together. Three times a week. And for as long as we live under the same roof."

"At seven o'clock in the morning?" Zachary asked, gesturing for a second cup of coffee.

"On the mornings I have to go to Parliament, yes."

"He has to go this morning," Penelope added. "He always informs me of his whereabouts. *I* will be going to feed ducks in the park with Mrs. Bevins."

"Will you?" Shay asked as he filled his own plate.

"That sounds far more amusing than what I had planned. And the company more fair, as well."

"You were going to Gentleman Jackson's with me," Zachary protested.

"Exactly."

Peep laughed again. "You may come, then, but you have to bring your own bread crumbs."

As Charlemagne crossed to his seat, he leaned over to kiss Penelope on the cheek. "I'll bring extra bread crumbs."

Eleanor looked at her niece. Peep had no idea that in a few years all of this indulgence would vanish, and every move she made would be scrutinized and criticized and every liberty curtailed, both because she was a female and because she was a Griffin.

"So we've met for breakfast," she said, keeping her gaze on the slice of toast in front of her. "You've ordered everyone to rise, and we've obeyed you. I don't quite see what it's gotten you, but I suppose all that matters is that you've had your way."

"After last night I think a little enforced time with your family might do you some good," Melbourne returned, his tone still soft and mild, "since we are the ones who will be hurt if anything should happen to you."

Eleanor lifted her head, meeting his direct gray gaze. "I apologized last night, Sebastian. But I've kept to my part of the agreement. I haven't been involved in any scandal." That fact was thanks to Deverill, but they certainly didn't need to know that.

"It's only been three days, Nell!" Zachary protested. "You can't just vanish. Vauxhall is dangerous. If you want to go somewhere like that, one of us will take you."

"I don't want you to take me places, and I don't want to have to get your permission to go," she returned, reminding herself that facing their anger was a small price to pay. It could have been so much worse.

"Your declaration says nothing about endangering your safety." Sebastian finished his cup of tea. "You will inform one of us, at the least, of your schedule. And that is not negotiable."

As she considered it, Eleanor's hesitation was more for effect than because she meant to argue his decision. "Very well." She really didn't intend any more surprises like that anyway. And having them know where she was would at least help to keep incidents like the one last night from happening ever again.

For a moment the duke stayed silent, but she wouldn't venture to say aloud that her answer had surprised him. That never happened. "Good," he said finally. "Now if you'll excuse me?" Melbourne pushed back from the table and stood.

So that was that—another proclamation from the head of the family, and one that applied only to her. "Does this rule apply to everyone?" she blurted. If not for her throbbing head she probably would have kept her mouth shut, but in all fairness she frequently had no idea of Shay or Zachary's location, and while Sebastian might tell Peep where he intended to be, having to quiz a six-year-old for the information didn't seem to fit the spirit of the new Griffin law.

"It applies to whomever said they were going to be home in bed last evening and then slipped off to Vauxhall to see jugglers."

"Acrobats," she corrected stiffly. Perhaps she'd best concede the point. Deverill hadn't given her any further details about Vauxhall, and if Melbourne knew the truth, they wouldn't be talking about rules. They would be packing her things for an immediate return to Melbourne Park.

"I like acrobats," Penelope stated. "Why didn't you take me with you?"

Any answer she made to that would only prove Melbourne's point about the danger of her supposed actions. "My apologies, Peep," she settled for. "Next time, perhaps."

"We'll see about that." Melbourne kissed his daughter on the cheek. "Be good, Peep," he said, smiling fondly at her, then left the room.

Determined as she was to be angry with Melbourne, Eleanor hated when he was like that, when he showed obvious affection for his daughter and genuine worry over her. It was easier not to think of him as human, but he insisted on confusing the issue. He always had, she supposed, but absolute tyranny during her rebellion would have been easier to deal with.

In accordance with the new rule she informed both Shay and Zachary that she would be spending most of the day shopping with Lady Barbara Howsen. She left them debating whether to go back to bed, and went herself to ask the cook for cucumber slices to put over her eyes until a decent hour to meet up with her friend.

As she was putting on a new blue hat topped with an ostrich feather, the butler scratched at her door. She'd been hesitant to speak with Stanton, since he'd seen quite clearly in whose carriage she'd departed last night. But putting off conversing with him any longer would give her an apoplexy.

She gestured Helen back to the dressing table and pulled open the door herself. "Yes, Stanton?"

"You have a caller downstairs, my lady." He held out the salver, an embossed calling card resting in its center.

Eleanor picked it up, hoping with all her might that it wouldn't be one of the guests from Belmont's last night, someone who had recognized her despite the red gown and the black swan mask. As she read the elegant gold script, her heart skipped a beat and then began hammering again. It *was* someone from the soiree.

"Please inform Lord Deverill that I'll be down in just a moment," she said, her voice not quite steady.

"As you wish, my lady."

Now, Eleanor, she yelled at herself. "Stanton?"

The butler paused, facing her again. "Yes, my lady?"

"About last night. I . . . I would appreciate your discretion."

A slight smile touched the elderly gentleman's solemn face. "I am always discreet, Lady Eleanor. Last evening I believe your brothers assumed you left the house without my knowledge. Since you have safely returned, I see no reason to dissuade them of that perception. Will that suffice?"

"Absolutely. Thank you, Stanton."

"I shall inform Lord Deverill that you will join him shortly."

She closed the door again, shutting her eyes in relief. Apparently she had at least one ally in the household, anyway.

"My lady," Helen said, as she put away the remaining hat pins, "I will be discreet, as well."

"Thank you, Hel—"

"So long as you don't put yourself in any danger again, my lady. I was scared for you last night, going off like that and then returning hours later all alone. And even if you sack me, I won't—"

"I'll be more careful, from now on. I promise." She smiled. For heaven's sake, her actions seemed constantly to threaten Helen's employment, yet her maid was willing to risk that very thing to make certain she remained safe. "And thank you, Helen."

The maid curtsied. "You're welcome, Lady Eleanor."

Downstairs Stanton directed her to the morning room. Helen on her heels, she pushed open the door and entered. She wasn't going anywhere without a chaperone for a while. At least not until she could close her eyes without seeing a black fox half mask.

Valentine stood at the far window, a glass of whiskey in his hand as he gazed toward the street. From his brown coat, buckskin breeches, and Hessian boots, he'd ridden to Griffin House. She couldn't help noticing that for a hardened rake, he had an elegant, conservative taste in wardrobe.

"Good morning," she said, dipping a curtsy as he faced her. He could still cost her everything, she reminded herself. Just because he'd been kind last night didn't mean he wouldn't tell Melbourne what had happened. Lord Deverill seemed almost to live his life on a whim.

"It's still morning, is it?" he replied, sketching a shallow-enough bow that it wouldn't endanger his drink. "I seem to be beginning an alarming trend of rising early." His deceptively lazy eyes took in her wardrobe and Helen lurking behind her. "You're going out."

"Yes. Shopping. I thought you'd be in Parliament this morning."

"Do you know what bloody time they've taken to be-

ginning morning session? Eight o'clock! That's just un-
godly. I'll sit for the afternoon session."

She chuckled, a little more at ease since he hadn't
greeted her with a statement about Stephen Cobb-Harding
going to the newspaper with the tale about last evening.
His presence did bring up a question, however, and it was
one she couldn't afford to avoid. "Is there something I
may do for you, my lord?"

He sent another glance at Helen. "I came to inquire
about how you were feeling, since you weren't well
enough to attend the Hampton Ball last night."

Eleanor drew a slow breath. More gallantry, and from a
man she hadn't been sure was possessed of that quality at
all. She'd never been taken in by his seductive charm,
though in truth he'd never tried to seduce her. Not for the
first time, she wished he would.

Of course after last night, that wasn't likely to happen.
He'd seen another man pawing at her naked bosom, and
then had watched her vomit, practically inside his coach.
Even so, he'd known just what to say to reassure her, to
keep her from hysterics and make her feel safe. And he'd
rescued her reputation, the least likely man she could ever
imagine doing so.

"I'm feeling much better," she answered, meaning it. At
the thought of just what he'd done for her, a delicious
shiver ran down her spine. "A good night's sleep does
wonders, I've found."

"I'll take your word for that." He grinned. "I'm pleased
you're feeling improved."

Gesturing Helen to remain where she was, Eleanor approached Deverill at the window. "May I ask you a question?"

He nodded, taking a sip of whiskey. "Indulge yourself."

"How did you know that was me last night, in that room?"

Deverill looked down at her. "I didn't, at first," he said quietly, green eyes meeting hers and then trailing the length of her form and back again. "I saw a black swan in a crimson gown. You drew my attention."

Oh, my. "Did I?"

"Yes, you did." His fingers brushed against her skirt as they stood together at the window. "I don't know if you're aware, but red is a fine color on you, Eleanor."

Her pulse quickened. She could feel it, the rush of heat through her. Deverill was flirting with her—and not as he usually did, with broad comments and self-deprecating observations about his poor character. "It's unfortunate, then, that I tore that gown into several pieces last night."

"I don't blame you." His fingers curled, sending her skirt rustling against her legs. "Might I suggest you commission another?"

"I'll take your suggestion into consideration," she returned, though she wasn't sure she could do it. As she'd removed that gown last night, the memory of the rough, uncaring touch of Stephen Cobb-Harding's hands on her bare skin had left her feeling ill again.

Had that been freedom? Was that what it meant to be free? She studied Deverill's eyes as he gazed down at her. He would know, if anyone could.

"Last night," she said in a low voice, remembering Helen's promise of discretion only as long as her safety wasn't involved, "I wanted to feel free."

"Just for last night?" he murmured back at her, long black lashes half-curtaining his eyes.

Eleanor's bodice began to feel too tight. "I wanted an adventure, a little romance with a handsome stranger."

His gaze lowered to her mouth. "Does it have to be with a stranger? You might have mentioned your desires to someone with whom you're a little better acquainted."

"Do you have someone in mind?" she breathed, finding that speaking in a normal tone had become impossible.

"This is your fantasy, Eleanor. Perhaps you should tell me who you have in mind." Slowly he leaned a little closer.

For a dozen heartbeats she held absolutely still, hoping he would finish his advance and kiss her. Oh, she wanted to experience a kiss from the Marquis of Deverill. But he didn't move, and she knew why—and that was the reason she'd sought out a stranger. Decadent, hedonistic as he was, Valentine was still a member of the Griffin circle. "I have in mind someone who doesn't know the rules the Griffins have set up regarding how and when I am to be approached."

The half-raised whiskey glass paused at his mouth. She could almost see him pulling himself back, changing the track of his thoughts, though physically he didn't move.

"So you said," he returned, finishing off the whiskey. "I should be going. I can't tolerate the House of Lords on an empty stomach."

He turned away, but Eleanor grabbed his arm before he could leave. "Last night, was that it?" she whispered. "Was that freedom? Or romance?"

Deverill stilled, his gaze meeting hers again with startling clarity. "Neither. That was sin. I'm told there's a difference. All three, however, should be experienced at least once."

"Sin?" she repeated.

"Yes. Though it should have been done consensually,

and more pleasurably than what you nearly experienced."
Shrugging out of her grip, he strode for the door.

"I'll see you soon, yes?" she called after him.

He gave her a half grin and a jaunty bow. "I'll be about."

Eleanor listened as his boots padded down the hallway, followed by the opening and closing of the front door. He knew the answers. Even if he wasn't very forthcoming, he knew the differences between sin and freedom—and how to find both of them. And she suspected that he knew something about romance as well, though he might never have put it into practice. She imagined he would know, anyway. No one could have so deliciously wicked a glint in his eyes and not know something. In addition, she'd learned one thing about the Marquis of Deverill that she hadn't known before—she could trust him.

Obviously avoiding scandal was going to be more difficult than she'd realized. She couldn't believe that she'd been so naive where Stephen was concerned, but she wouldn't make that mistake again. These moments she'd wrested from her brothers were too important for that. What she needed was a guide around those barricades, and someone to lead her to a place she wasn't quite sure yet where or how to find. She needed Valentine Corbett.

"Valentine, I need you."

Valentine leaned back against the side of the coach parked along Bond Street and listened to the plaintive, disembodied voice inside. Or half listened, rather, since the majority of his attention was on the pair of young ladies strolling up the far side of the street toward a milliner's.

"Are you even listening to me?"

"I'm listening, Lydia," he said, pulling a cigar from his pocket. "Continue."

"Do you know what it's like for me, to have that wrinkled old man in my bed, inside me?"

"If it's so offensive to you, my dear, you probably shouldn't have married him." He nodded as Miss Malthorpe and Miss Elizabeth Malthorpe and at least three of their younger sisters strolled by. They giggled, and he heard the words "eyes" and "reputation" pass between them.

"You're not saying I should have passed up on all that money, are you? That's not at all like you, Valentine."

"Isn't it? How odd."

"I agree. And I do need you."

He lit the cigar. " 'Need' is a very strong word, Lydia. I don't think you *need* anything. If you *want* someone aside from your husband in your bed, I imagine you would have a wide range of choices."

Silence radiated from the coach. Even with the curtains pulled shut, he could practically see her sitting there on the crushed velvet cushions, eyes narrowed as she ruminated over what he'd said, examining it from every angle, looking for any opening or opportunity. "You've found someone new," she finally said.

He snorted. "That's the conclusion you've come to? Do you think that my finding another interest would have anything to do with you and me?"

"That depends. What, have you reached your quota of lovers so you have to let one of us go before you can bed another one?"

Valentine sighed, his gaze still on the shop door. "This is becoming tiresome. Make up any reason you like. Find someone else, Lydia. Having fun together is one thing, but I don't want to be needed, or nagged at. And certainly not by a married woman."

Her next comment was a slew of curses aimed at him and more directly, his cock. Thankfully, Eleanor and Lady Barbara left the milliner's to continue down the street, and he pushed away from the coach to follow them, leaving Lydia swearing in solitude behind him.

Technically he didn't have to be there. Shopping was one of the items on Eleanor's schedule, one of the events Melbourne had considered innocent enough that she didn't require watching. Valentine was fairly certain her brother was correct.

That didn't explain why he'd waited around the corner from Griffin House until she'd left to meet Lady Barbara, or why he'd followed them to Bond Street rather than joining his peers at the House of Lords.

He had no logical reason at all for being there, actually. Nothing other than a desire—a *need*, damn it all—to figure Eleanor Griffin out. For Christ's sake, he'd come within a breath of kissing her in her own morning room. In Melbourne's morning room.

It didn't make any damned sense. He'd hunted dangerous game before, game already owned by another man—though she never seemed to be held too dearly by her captor. Friends, however, were another matter. He didn't have many, and he didn't betray them. Ever.

Melbourne had asked him to keep an eye on Eleanor, to keep her out of trouble and theoretically to report on anything that might be construed as improper. Within one day of that he'd seen her half naked and accompanied her home without a chaperone—either of which might have forced him into a marriage with the girl if anyone reported it—and then he'd promised not to tell anyone what had happened.

What Cobb-Harding had attempted hadn't been her fault; of that he was certain. But she had gone to Belmont's of her own free will, so he should have felt perfectly comfortable with relaying that fact to her brother. His sense of fair play forbade that, or so he could tell himself, but after this morning he had a sneaking suspicion that his decision to keep this little surveillance going had nothing to do with fair, and everything to do with play.

Taking a long draw of his cigar, Valentine hung back far enough in the afternoon crowd of shoppers that all he could see of Eleanor was the curling ostrich plume atop her hat. Since he'd declared himself elsewhere, it wouldn't do for her to discover him trailing thirty feet behind her.

And he wasn't sure what the exercise was accomplishing, except to increase his level of frustration. Damn it all, if Melbourne hadn't gone to him and he'd learned about Eleanor's little rebellion on his own, he would have been first in line for the opportunity to educate her about freedom and sin and passion. Thanks to the duke, however, he'd effectively been gelded. Of course his head knew that, but the rest of him wasn't paying much attention to logic and loyalty. The rest of him wanted to bed Eleanor Griffin.

"Deverill? What are you doing here?"

Valentine stopped as Zachary Griffin emerged from a men's clothiers. "What do you think I'm doing here?" he returned, putting an unfelt edge of annoyance into his voice. "I'm paying off my bloody debt to Melbourne."

Zachary immediately dodged into the shadow of the

building. With almost comic urgency he sent a piercing gaze about the crowd. "She's here?"

Shaking his head, Valentine moved forward again. It wouldn't do to lose her now. "You have all the subtlety of a cannonball," he commented. "She's half a block ahead of us, shopping with Lady Barbara Howsen."

"She said she would be," Zachary admitted, falling into step beside him, "but she seems to be rather more devious than I'd realized. Did Melbourne tell you about her escape to Vauxhall?"

Damn. "She told me this morning," he improvised, "when I called to ask after her health."

"It's *my* health I'm beginning to worry about," Zachary countered. "There are rules of behavior, after all."

"Ah. So I hear. Personally, though, I have to applaud her for catching the lot of you by surprise. Did you just assume she would never grow up and wish to experience what the world has to offer?"

"I don't know," her brother grumbled. "I did think she'd be more reasonable about it."

"Women are rarely reasonable, my boy."

Zachary walked beside him in silence for a moment. "I suppose we might have been a bit overprotective, but that's not our fault. When she disappeared in Devon that time . . . I've never seen Sebastian so frantic."

Valentine hid a frown. "She disappeared? You mean she's done this before?" She'd seemed so genuinely lost last night. "Melbourne never said—"

"He knows about your dislike for family drama," Zachary cut in. "But it's not like that. Nell was twelve, and Melbourne was what, twenty-three? Shay and I were somewhere in between. Nell used to do everything we did—swim in the lake, fish, fence"— he chucked, obviously at some memory—"and even ride astride. Anyway, one afternoon she took out Seb's gelding, a big brute named Atlas. Forty minutes or so later Atlas came back without her."

The ladies entered a sweets shop, and Valentine stopped in the alleyway. "What happened?"

"The grooms and I rode out, but didn't see her along the riding trail she usually took. So Melbourne turned out the entire estate staff, and forty of us went looking for her. She'd been thrown before, and we'd taught her how to fall, so at first we weren't all that worried. I wasn't, anyway. But then the sun set, and we still hadn't found her."

Valentine realized his breathing and heart rate had accelerated, and he mentally shook himself. It wasn't like him to become so involved in a story, to the point where he actually worried over the main participant. Especially not when the events had taken place nine years earlier and he knew the outcome. Eleanor was in a candy shop twenty feet away from him, for God's sake. But he wanted to know what had happened. "And?" he prompted Zachary.

"We brought out torches and lanterns and kept looking. By then Melbourne was hoarse from calling for her, and I think he was half-convinced that someone had kidnapped her and meant to ransom her for the family fortune. He would have given it to them."

"That's uncharacteristic."

With a short grin, Zachary nodded. "You have no idea. We looked for six or seven hours. It was after midnight before Shay fired off his pistol and the rest of us came running. He'd found her four miles away in a pile of leaves, asleep, waiting for daylight to head for home. Her damned arm was broken, but otherwise she was fine." He chuckled again. "She wanted to know what had taken us so long, and why no one had thought to bring her something to eat."

Valentine smiled. "Sounds as though she was the only one of you with any sense."

"Perhaps so, but we were more careful with her after that. She was missing for nine hours, Deverill. And I count those among the worst in my life."

So he'd definitely done the right thing in not telling them about Belmont's. He couldn't imagine it himself, being so frantic to find someone that giving up the rest of one's life and livelihood for their safety seemed a fair exchange. "Another reason not to have family," he commented.

Zachary nodded. "For those nine hours I would have agreed with you. The five minutes after we found her safe, though, I wouldn't trade those for all the gold in the East India Company's coffers."

Valentine snorted. "And I would be even more wealthy than I am now."

"You say that, but wait until you have a family. Everything will change."

"I doubt it."

"I'll wager you anything that you're wrong."

"Ah, Zachary. I may be cynical, but I'm not a fool."

And given how angry he'd been at Stephen Cobb-Harding last evening, he wasn't willing to take that wager, anyway.

Chapter 7

"Why in the world do you want to attend a musical recital, Shay?" Eleanor asked, hands on her hips. If Melbourne was trying to alter the conditions of their agreement again by sending along the Griffin private army, he was in for a fight no matter whom he'd designated as his ambassador.

"I've decided I need to increase my exposure to culture. Shall we go?"

"Am I actually supposed to believe that?"

Charlemagne gave her an assessing look. "I suppose not. But you'll have to forgive me if I want to make certain you reach your destination safely."

"You will not—"

"After we arrive," he said, running a hand through his straight brown hair and refusing to lower his gaze from hers, "I will sit at the back of the room and flirt with any unmarried females in the vicinity."

At least her broad-shouldered middle brother was honest. "And when I do the same thing with every single gentleman in attendance?"

A muscle in his lean jaw twitched. "I am providing transportation. The remainder of the outing is yours."

Eleanor closed the distance between them, only two steps in the narrow foyer. "I will hold you to that, Charlemagne."

Though she'd never admit it to anyone except perhaps Deverill, the idea of having someone she trusted seated close by had become absurdly comforting since the Belmont House disaster. She would test Shay's word and forbearance tonight, because she intended on flirting, if for no other reason than to crowd Stephen Cobb-Harding from her memory. But now she would proceed with caution—or at least with her eyes wide open.

They took the coach to Lord and Lady Llewellyn's. Once they were through the door and into the ballroom where the recital was to be held, Shay did as he'd promised. Without a backward glance he crossed the room to converse with the host and hostess, leaving her to procure her own glass of punch. Eleanor took a deep, leveling breath. So what if her brother would see with whom she chatted? Other than telling Melbourne, there wasn't much he could do about it.

"My lady, allow me." Jeffrey, Earl Basingstoke, materialized in front of her, no easy feat for a man who weighed some twelve stone, and handed her a glass of punch.

"Thank you, my lord. You've read my mind."

A smile folded into the wrinkles of the earl's rotund face. "I always assume when a lady arrives somewhere that she will be in need of refreshment."

The statement didn't hold much logic, but at least it sounded harmless enough. "Do you often come to recitals?"

"I've found them a fair way to judge the talent of young ladies. Don't want to waste my courting on someone who can't entertain, don't you know."

"You're looking for a spouse then, my lord?"

He nodded, jowls wagging in agreement. "My mother, the Countess Basingstoke, has requested that I marry. And she likes to listen to the pianoforte in the evening, so I would like to find a chit who plays well."

"To please your mother," she repeated, wondering how Basingstoke had escaped Melbourne's notice. He was titled and had a nice income, and he certainly seemed to fit into the *dull as dirt* category of potential spouses. Goodness, she was surprised that they weren't already engaged.

The pleasant part of her agreement was that she could now spend time and converse with whomever she wished—not just the gentlemen who *would* be considered acceptable. "What would please *you*?" she asked. She generally didn't have the opportunity to ask men more than what they thought of the weather. Humorously as she regarded Basingstoke, it was still a real conversation.

"Finding a female to bear my mother company and play—"

"—play the pianoforte," she finished for him. So much for male insight.

"You understand. Do you play, Lady Eleanor?"

Good heavens. "Not well enough to claim any skill at it," she returned, shuddering.

She escaped the earl, but obviously by chatting with him she'd opened the floodgates. By the time the butler called for the guests to take their seats, and apparently seeing Shay's lack of attention to her, seven other gentlemen— the sum total of unmarried males in attendance other than

her brother—had approached to offer her punch or chocolate or their views on why she was by far the most attractive or most pleasant or most regal lady in the room.

Though she'd never been accosted in such a manner or
in such volume before, she wasn't so naive that she believed them. There was a reason Sebastian kept some of
them away from her. They wanted her money, or their
names joined with the Griffin standard. But for goodness'
sake, she didn't need her brothers to decide whether they
should be allowed to speak to her or not. True, Stephen
had fooled her, but no one else would. And a few of these
gentlemen, even the unacceptable ones, were at least
amusing.

On the other hand, so much for her seeking out men with
whom to flirt. It had taken all her energy to fend *off* their attentions, most of it so ham-fisted that she had to work not to
laugh. Conversationalists, yes, but no potential husbands
here tonight.

The first debutante took the low stage to a round of mild
applause, and Eleanor settled back to listen. Miss Sanford
looked terrified as she sat at the pianoforte, and Eleanor
glanced at the girl's preening mother. Little did Lady Sanford know that all her daughter needed was to make a
good showing and she could very well end up as Lady
Basingstoke.

"She can't compare to you, Lady Eleanor," another
would-be beau, Lord Henry Anderton, said from beside
her.

"Thank you," she returned, pointedly keeping her attention on the performer.

"And your—"

"I'm quite thirsty," she interrupted. "Would you please
fetch me a punch?"

Anderton happily scampered away, and Eleanor breathed a sigh of relief. Now she could simply listen.

"From sin to staid in one turn of the sun," Deverill's low voice murmured as he took the empty seat beside her. "How unexpected."

Her heart hammered at his arrival, but she kept her gaze on the stage. And he thought *her* attendance was unexpected. "Lady Barbara's older sister Mary is playing later. She invited me herself. But who invited you, my lord?"

"I'm not certain I *was* invited. I was driving by and saw coaches turning up the drive." He shrugged. "No one warned me away."

"They wouldn't, not when this many young women are here looking for husbands," she whispered back. "Even you might do for some poor chit."

"Ah, so I've landed in a trap of some sort."

She chuckled. "A very obvious trap, baited with punch and chocolate treats. And I thought you jaded."

"Minx," he drawled. "Any potential spouses here for you?"

Eleanor wrinkled her nose. "I'm only here for the chocolates, myself."

Henry reappeared, a glass of punch in either hand. The polite thing would have been for Deverill to make his excuses and give way. Instead, Valentine merely sent the younger man a single glance. Paling, Anderton stammered something that sounded like a request for forgiveness and vanished.

"Valentine," she chastised.

"What? I was merely saying that if I was seeking freedom and sin and romance, I'm not sure I would be spending my evening here. And as for husbands, you might—"

"Shh," she returned, though Miss Sanford's playing was enthusiastic enough that she didn't think anyone could overhear them. "I'm not trying to completely ruin my life; I'm trying to improve it. I have no intention of forgoing my more quiet evenings, or requests to socialize with my friends. You do things for your friends, don't you?"

"From time to time."

Well, she'd made an opening. Now was the time to see whether she had the courage to leap through it. "Valentine, would you . . . do something for *me*?"

He stayed silent for so long that she began to worry he would refuse her. She looked sideways at him. His own gaze was on her face, his expression unreadable but his green eyes glittering. Eleanor swallowed. If he ever realized how much time she'd spent thinking about him lately, she was doomed.

"What did you have in mind?" he murmured back.

A kiss. Your hands on me. "I need a guide."

"Are you going to Africa?"

"Don't tease. Not that kind of guide. Not precisely."

"I'm listening."

"I don't know how long Melbourne will honor our agreement," she said slowly, hoping that she hadn't misread him last night and this morning, and that she could indeed trust him. "But I do know that I won't have another opportunity when he declares this one finished. I want to find a husband, but that's not all I want to do. I want to have a moment where I feel . . . free. And I don't know how to go about it. I think you could guide me, help me figure out what I need to do."

Somewhere far below their feet, Lucifer was laughing at him. Valentine knew it, even though the banging of the pianoforte overwhelmed the sound of anything more subterranean.

"You don't want me for a guide, Eleanor. I'm not very nice."

"My experience says otherwise. Who else would I trust for such a thing? Mr. Cobb-Harding?"

This time he was sure he could hear devilish laughter. "Sin and trust aren't compatible. One betrays the other."

The slow smile touched her mouth again. "Then why are you protesting, my lord?" she asked.

Coming here had been a bad idea. It had been another of Melbourne's "safe" events, but he hadn't been able to resist. And now she was asking him to teach her how to sin. "You're my closest friend's sister," he grunted. "I doubt he would appreciate if I assisted you."

"You're correct. He would prefer that I sit in the morning room and embroider until he can find me some dull, proper husband. Then I'll be expected to pop out a few children, don a matron's cap, and host tea parties."

"Isn't that what all women want?"

She looked as though she wanted to punch him. "I can't speak for all women, but it's certainly not what I want. It's not *all* I want."

"Shh," came from behind them.

Ordinarily he wouldn't have cared whom he might be disturbing, but tonight he was grateful for the interruption. A female had never set him back on his heels before—and certainly not a chit ten years his junior. "Find a husband first," he put out, in a last effort to avoid becoming entangled, "and let him teach you what you need to know."

"What he needs me to know, you mean," she countered.

"I will be the one to decide what and how much I want to experience."

Where in the world had this come from? Sweet little Eleanor Griffin had definitely grown up, and in ways he'd never expected. "Perhaps we should continue this conversation later," he suggested, trying to give himself a little more time to think. His cock had already decided it wanted to help, but for once he intended not to listen.

"Yes," she agreed.

"Good. Now who is that playing—"

"Why don't you take me driving in Hyde Park tomorrow morning?"

"What? Me?"

She grinned again. "You've already admitted to rising before noon." Her gloved fingers discreetly brushed his sleeve. "Please, Deverill? Valentine? I don't know what else to do. And I don't want to make another mistake like last night."

He sighed to cover the shudder of his muscles. "At eleven. And have a damned chaperone."

"I will. Thank you, thank you, thank you."

"I'd hold on to most of those for later. I don't doubt you'll regret using them."

"I won't."

Perhaps not, but he would. Hell, he already did.

He'd noticed Shay Griffin seated several rows behind them. From the glazed expression in his eyes the middle Griffin brother had apparently lost the coin toss and been forced to escort Eleanor. After he heard from Zachary about the horse incident, the brethren's protectiveness toward their sister made more sense. Considering what he'd seen firsthand last night, he was glad she hadn't protested Shay's presence.

What surprised him more was Eleanor's seeming determination to break from her family's wishes and carve her own path. If she'd been a male, she would have been expected to make her own way. But she was definitely not a male. And in his experience chits didn't defy those who controlled their money and their future; they connived and manipulated beneath the surface while outwardly behaving as complacently and compliantly as milk cows.

The first set of performances ended, and Eleanor excused herself to go congratulate Lady Mary Howsen. Valentine considered it an adequate performance at best and that, coupled with his distaste for conversing with blushing, stammering virgins, was enough to convince him to remain seated.

"The strongest drink they're serving tonight is punch," Shay said, sinking into Eleanor's vacated chair. "It's a blistering combination, bad music and sobriety."

Wordlessly Valentine reached into his coat pocket and produced a flask of whiskey. He handed it over, keeping an eye on the host and hostess as Charlemagne took a long swallow.

"You've saved my life," the middle Griffin brother muttered feelingly, returning the flask.

Valentine took a swallow himself before screwing the lid back on and dumping the thing back into his pocket. "It does dull the pain a little."

"So I know why *I'm* here," Shay commented, sending a glance in his youngest sibling's direction, "but what the devil are *you* doing here? Melbourne sent me because he assumed nothing short of God himself could drag you here tonight."

"I just wandered by," Valentine returned, repeating the

lie he'd told Eleanor. The fewer versions of the tales he had to remember, the easier time he'd have of it. But it hadn't been God who'd convinced him to enter. It had been that horned fellow who obviously had no regard for, or loyalty toward, the already fallen.

"You and Nell seemed quite chatty."

Now would be the difficult part. "She thinks I'm the epitome of freedom and adventure, and she wanted some direction in finding her own way there."

Shay blinked. "And so she asked *you*?"

"Why not? I am irresistibly charming, and not one of her brothers."

"You know," Lord Griffin said slowly, "this could be to our advantage. You're supposed to be keeping an eye on her anyway, and if she's chatting with you she can't be encouraging ne'er-do-wells like Cobb-Harding or Anderton. God, the last thing we need to hear is that she's eloped with some professional gambler just because she thinks Melbourne handed her too many rules."

" 'Elope'?" Valentine repeated, lifting an eyebrow. "She said she's looking for a husband, but you think she's that desperate?"

"I think she's looking to escape. And now that Melbourne's opened the door, I doubt she'll voluntarily fly back into the cage."

"Did you tell him your opinion of this?"

Shay blew out his breath. "Several times. I've been ordered to abide by the agreement for as long as she does."

"Well, I'm supposed to take her driving tomorrow so she can attempt to convince me to assist her," Valentine commented, making an effort to sound reluctant and put-upon. He *was* reluctant, though not for any reason Shay could possibly realize. "I don't suppose you have a list of acceptable spouses for my reference? It would be easier if I knew who I was supposed to sponsor."

"I'm certain Melbourne has a list, but I'm not privy to it. Don't you think that'd be a bit suspicious, anyway, if you were to suddenly begin pointing out potential husbands? Especially since they're likely to be gentlemen you'd ordinarily never speak a word to."

"That dull, are they?"

"Compared with you, Admiral Nelson is dull."

He shrugged, unable to argue with that. "I'm just trying to repay my debt to Melbourne and free myself for decadence and debauchery again."

"Hm. Really, then, her request should make that even easier for you."

"I don't see—"

"I mean, if she thinks she's learning something nefarious from you, she can't be parading about and causing a stir now, can she? And then hopefully Melbourne will come to his senses and put a stop to this before she can actually do anything questionable."

It was too late for that already. And she'd been exploring on her own, without anything but her own nose to guide her into trouble. With his assistance, and even without his active participation, there was no telling what might befall.

Valentine reflected that he should have stayed in this evening. All he needed was for someone else to encourage him to spend time with Eleanor, when what he should do was stay as far away from her as possible. "You can't possibly want her to spend time with me," he stated. "Not in public or for any reason. I'm the wolf that mamas warn their daughters about."

Shay grinned, clapping him on the shoulder. "Yes, but you're *our* wolf at the moment, now aren't you? And you know the rules where Nell is concerned."

With his last breath of sanity, Valentine uttered another protest. "This is *not* what Melbourne asked me to do."

"It will be, as soon as I return home and tell him about it."

Scowling, Valentine pushed to his feet. "I'm warning you, Shay. This is a bad idea."

"No, it's perfect, because you know what's going on. Eleanor's already asked you to help her out, *and* you're one of our cronies so we know her reputation is safe with you." He chuckled again. "She may be the only female whose reputation *is* safe with you."

"Ha ha," Valentine grumbled, and headed for the door.

He'd landed precisely where he didn't want to be—in the middle of a family quarrel, and with an obligation to both sides. And a definite lust on one.

The safest, most logical route would seem to be for him to play the poor example that he was to the utmost, and convince Eleanor that she was better off safely back in the Griffin fold. Then it would be her own decision to forgo using his services, and at the same time the end of her rebellion would free him from his obligation to Melbourne.

He paused in the doorway to look back at Eleanor, chatting with the Howsen sisters. His abdomen tightened in pure lust. And the devil laughed again.

"He's late," Eleanor said, pacing the foyer.

"Yes, my lady," Stanton returned, turning his head to watch her stride back and forth.

She felt restless and agitated, and sitting demurely in

the morning room to wait for Deverill's arrival would have driven her mad. Even pacing only moved her feet at a quarter of the speed her mind raced.

It made so much sense, recruiting the marquis for her plans. If she wanted to learn how to be carefree, who better to teach her than the most carefree man in London? It also made sense that any man he knew and liked would also be possessed of those same qualities—so perhaps he could be the one to point her to her future husband. She certainly wasn't going to marry one of the dull, dim crowd just because Melbourne allowed them to speak to her. Yes, she felt attracted to Lord Deverill, but that had nothing to do with her decision to include him. Nothing at all.

Her only hesitation was that as titillating as she found his presence, he was a friend of her brothers. He was relatively safe, and he was familiar. And he, like any of her brothers' male friends, knew the rules.

"Rules," she grumbled, cocking her hat a little more jauntily on her head as she paced. That was why she needed to use Valentine to meet someone new. The rules. The rules about not touching Nell, not taking her seriously as a female or as anything but a . . . a . . . a puppy dog. Yes, that was it, pat her on the head and send her on her way with an admonition to be a good girl.

Well, damn it all, she was tired of being a good girl. Admittedly her first foray had gone horribly wrong, but she wouldn't be so unwise in her choice of companion—or activity—again.

A sporty curricle turned up the drive. Eleanor walked out onto the portico to draw a breath as the Marquis of Deverill pulled his matching pair of gray horses to a halt. He wore a complementary gray coat with a black waist-

SIN AND SENSIBILITY   107

coat and trousers, the image of a proper nobleman—
except for the devilish twinkle in his green eyes.

"Good morning," he said, doffing his gray beaver hat as
his liveried tiger jumped from the back of the curricle to
hold the team.

"You're late," she complained, mostly to give herself a
moment to take in the sight of him and to remind herself
that she'd requested his presence.

"I thought this had something to do with freedom," he
drawled, hopping to the ground. "I freely decided to remain in bed this morning." He flashed a grin. "I tossed and
turned all night."

Whatever he baited her with, she would rise to the occasion; how else was she to learn, except by example?
"And what caused your restless night?" she asked.

"A very nice y—"

"Valentine," Sebastian interrupted, moving past her
down the step to offer his hand.

"Melbourne. Lady Eleanor and I are going for a drive."

"So I see." The duke slid his gaze to her. "Am I permitted to request that you return early enough to join Peep
and me for tea at Aunt Tremaine's?"

Aunt Tremaine. For goodness' sake, their one close
blood relation, the nearest thing she had to a mother, and
she'd completely forgotten they were to have tea. "I'll return by two," she said, and her brother nodded.

Deverill stepped in to offer his hand to her, but when
Sebastian took her elbow to help her into the curricle's
high seat, the marquis gave a short grin and went back
around to climb up the other side. Despite the quickness
and the ease of it, something had happened just then. Had
Melbourne warned Deverill off? For goodness' sake, she

hadn't asked Valentine there to seduce her—just to learn how it was done, and to take advantage of his knowledge of like-minded men who had better reputations and who wouldn't resort to drugging her. And besides, there was still the entire "rules" complication. Still, she wondered what Sebastian thought of her going driving with his friend. His rakehell of a friend.

"To the park, then?" Deverill asked, as Melbourne helped Helen onto the small back platform and the marquis's tiger joined her there.

"Unless you can think of somewhere with more opportunities," she returned, still determined not to be cowed by him and his much greater knowledge of sin.

"Opportunities?"

"For me to observe and learn from your example."

His soft grin deepened. "The park will suffice." They rumbled down the drive and turned toward Park Avenue. "I thought you were determined to become free and unfettered," he commented after a moment.

"I am."

"Then why did you let Melbourne dictate how long your outing would last?"

"Because I want to see my aunt. He only reminded me of my promise to visit her."

The marquis sent her a glance as he navigated through the heavy traffic. "There are no rules regarding a true state of freedom, I suppose," he said, "but I do know that I don't make promises."

"Because you worry you won't be able to keep your word?"

"No, because I don't like to feel obligated. That's the thing, Lady Eleanor. I do as I please, when I please."

Eleanor furrowed her brow. "I think you're wrong," she

said slowly. "Being free is not about disobliging everyone else."

"True. It's about not caring about anyone else."

"That's horrid!"

"It's the truth. You are here to learn, you said."

She wondered whether he was baiting her, playing devil's advocate so she could convince herself that her little adventure was wrong. Still, Deverill did have a definite streak of jaded cynicism running through him, so thick sometimes that she could barely see him for it. "So you don't care about anyone else? Then why did you rescue me the other night?"

Deverill indicated Helen seated behind her. "Firstly, are we free to speak?"

"I trust Helen," she stated, hoping that her trust wouldn't be misplaced, as she couldn't think of any other way to hold a conversation with Deverill without being ruined. "But by asking me about my maid you've once again demonstrated that you care about someone besides yourself—and specifically about my reputation."

"Yes, I did, didn't I? Odd, that." He turned his attention to the street for a moment. "I like you. So I suppose that seeing you ruined would make me unhappy."

For a moment her mind seized onto the words "I like you" and refused to look beyond them. Oh, she was such a goose. Valentine chewed up and spit out females much more worldly than she, and on a regular basis. "You don't consider helping me to be an obligation, then?"

"Not when I agreed to it because I wanted to."

"So it's just a happy coincidence when what you want to do happens to be the right thing to do?"

"Exactly."

Eleanor drew a breath, frustration pulling at her. She

wanted answers, a guideline, some sort of rule book to follow that would enable her to change her life permanently without alienating her family. She wanted something that would allow her to obtain what she wanted, to marry whom she wanted, without everyone else dictating to her and making their priorities hers. "I'm beginning to sense that you're not going to give me a straightforward answer."

"Ask me a straightforward question, and we'll see."

"I think I may have to kick you," she said.

Laughter burst from his chest. She'd never heard him laugh like that before, easy and carefree and genuinely amused. The sound alone made her heart race. *Good heavens.*

"I was serious," he finally said, still chuckling. "I would prefer having a better idea of what it is you want to accomplish."

"All right." She sat beside him for a moment, thinking and trying not to notice the way his thigh brushed hers as he turned the pair into Hyde Park. "When your father . . . when you became the Marquis of Deverill, were you ready? For the responsibility, I mean."

For a second, gone almost too quickly for her to notice, his expression changed, hardened, then eased again. "My father spent his last few years as a stark raving lunatic. I ran the properties for three years before I took his title. So yes, I was ready for the responsibility."

For a moment she didn't know what to say. She'd known when Valentine had inherited, but Sebastian had never mentioned how it had come about. To do so, she supposed, would have been highly uncharacteristic of her overprotective brother.

She'd been schooled in etiquette since she could talk,

and of course she knew how to reply appropriately to someone's news of a tragic loss. This, however, was a great deal more complicated than that. Valentine didn't sound so much hurt or bitter as he did relieved.

"How old were you?" she asked quietly.

"When he died? Eighteen. My uncle, Lord Waddell, was furious that the old man lasted until I reached my majority. He used to practically drool, he was so anxious to get his hands on the Deverill guardianship." Valentine snorted. "I haven't seen him since then."

"That must have been a great deal of responsibility for you to shoulder at age fifteen."

He shrugged. "I did what I had to do. Now I do as I please."

"So your flaunting of the rules now is your way of rebelling, like Sebastian says I'm—"

"It's not a rebellion," he stated flatly, drawing the team sharply to a halt.

"Deverill, what—"

He gestured his tiger around to the horses and hopped to the ground. "Walk with me."

"But—"

Valentine circled to her side of the curricle while she tried to figure out what he might be up to. He did know the rules, but the Marquis of Deverill disregarded them on a regular basis. And if she'd made him angry . . .

He held a hand up to her. "I'm taking a stroll. You may wait here if you wish."

She had no doubt that he would leave her sitting there while he strolled off to meet some female or other. Eleanor stood and lowered her arms to him. For a swift, breathless moment he placed his hands around her waist and lifted her to the ground.

Behind them Helen started to scramble less gracefully to the grass, but Deverill jabbed a finger at her. "You wait here."

Helen sank back onto her perch.

This was all falling madly out of control. Eleanor put her hands on her hips. "Do not tell my maid what to do."

He leaned closer, folding his own arms across his chest. "Is your worry over propriety, or scandal?"

"Scandal," she returned promptly.

"Then don't worry," he said dismissively. Deverill offered her his arm. "And we'll be back in a moment. We're just taking a short stroll though a very crowded park."

They headed for the nearby pond, turning to follow the path that paralleled its reed-choked bank. For a moment Eleanor walked quietly beside him, trying to read his expression. If he was trying to remind her of how . . . helpless she'd felt in Stephen's company, he was having moderate success. He wasn't holding her against her will, or drugging her, or taking her somewhere she couldn't find her way back home, but she was still basically alone with a man who'd taken pains to earn his very poor reputation. And one who already held a secret of hers.

"I'm not afraid of you, you know," she blurted.

He glanced sideways at her. "I'm not trying to frighten you."

"What I meant was, if you're trying to intimidate me by not telling me where we're going or what you're planning, it's not working."

Deverill's mouth curved in a brief smile. "I could change your opinion in a heartbeat," he murmured.

Oh, dear. Wonderful, provoke the rakehell into doing something she would undoubtedly regret. "I—"

"You and I need to have a chat, Eleanor. Without loyal servants or anyone else to overhear."

She swallowed. "I'm listening."

"What do you want? Really? And tell me the truth, if you please."

So he'd guessed. He'd realized that all she'd known the night she wrote her declaration was that something had to change. What that was or how to accomplish it, she had no idea. "Promise me you won't laugh."

He shook his head. "I don't make promises."

"Fine." She pulled her hand free from his arm and strode ahead on the path. "I don't know."

"I didn't think so."

"But that's why I've requested your help, Deverill. You have infinitely more experience in . . . everything, than I do."

He caught up to her, but didn't offer his arm again. "You can't want to pattern your life after mine, so I can't figure what it is you want from me."

"I *do* want to pattern my life after yours. Part of it, anyway."

Deverill snorted. "Which part? The section where I have affairs with married women because they have the degree of experience and impermanence that I enjoy? Or the bit where I miss appointments with friends when something more amusing comes along? Or the wagering? Or the drinking?"

She stared at him for a moment, surprised into silence. "That is not what you're like."

"Yes, it is."

Eleanor stomped to a halt, flicking her hand over a stand of reeds and wishing she knew enough of the real

Valentine Corbett that she could sound more confident. "Well, perhaps it is, but that's not *all* there is to you."

His eyes narrowed as he stopped a few feet from her. "Really? Please tell me my character, then, if I've been misleading myself."

"Don't forget, you saved me the other night. And you were angry at Stephen's behavior. My recollections may be a bit fuzzy, but I remember that. And you saw me home safely, and didn't try to take advantage of me."

"My dear, one good deed in a lifetime does not a hero make. But this isn't about my poor habits; it's about the poor habits you want to cultivate in yourself."

"I don't want any poor habits."

"Then what, pray tell, am I doing here?" he repeated at higher volume.

How could she explain that the man he described was not necessarily the one she saw? Yes, he had some abysmal tendencies—he'd been the first one to acknowledge them. But he also had some fine qualities, aside from his obvious intelligence and wit. And honesty. She'd never heard him tell a lie, even to protect his own best interests—except to protect her.

"I like you," she answered.

Deverill blinked. "Beg pardon?"

"You said you liked me, and I like you. I like the way you don't try to elevate yourself above everyone because you have a title, or an old, respected name. You are who you are. You don't change your appearance for anyone else's pleasure or comfort, but you can still be charming and kind when you choose to be."

"At the risk of sounding sentimental, you seem to be describing yourself. If that's what you're looking for, you've already found it."

"No," she returned, trying not to be distracted by the unexpected compliment, "those things are why I like you. What I want is the *way* you live."

"The—"

"Not the way you described it, but that . . . freedom. You don't have to chat about the weather, or dance with someone because he's rich and titled and doesn't *need* you, or not dance—or even talk—with someone because he's not titled and *does* need you. You don't have to measure every word you say even to your friends for fear that you might cause a bump in eight hundred years of Griffin superiority and arrogance." She drew a breath, frustration pitching her voice higher. "It's all of that, and everything in between."

"Then be that person," he returned after a moment of silence.

"I'm trying to be. But I can't . . . I can't figure out how to do it without causing my family pain and damage. There are other people whose lives and reputations I have to consider. I love my family. They will always matter."

He shook his head. "If your first thought is that you might do something wrong, that's not freedom, Eleanor. That's fear."

"But I do have more than being free to consider. I'm not a man, and—"

"I noticed that."

"—and I don't want to be forced into my brother's idea of a good marriage. I want to make my own. In order to do that, there are rules I have to follow. Ignoring that would just be stupid."

"Then follow them." At her reluctant expression, he moved closer. "I think you *do* know what you want, and I know that I'm not the one you should emulate if your concern is making everyone happy. And for damned sure you're not going to find the kind of husband you would want to marry if you insist on *my* company and guidance. I assume that you want a good man. And I have it on good authority that there are good men in London—who I'm certain would be happy to have you."

"But I—"

"The best way to do that is to continue being who you are. From what you're telling me and what I've seen, you want to be good—a good sister, a good Griffin. You have no intention of giving up your obligations, and you don't wish to become a sinner. My best advice to you, Eleanor, is to go home and tell Melbourne 'no' until he brings home the spouse you want."

Damnation. She hated that he was absolutely correct—again. A tear ran down one cheek before she could swipe it away. "I have ideas about what I want, but in the Griffin fortress I'll never see them. Maybe I don't know precisely what I want or who I want," she retorted, her voice shaking, "but I'm not giving up until I find out. I won't go back to being dull and dreamless without at least one grand adventure. I won't. I can't, Valentine."

To her surprise, he cocked his head at her. "An adventure," he repeated. "What sort of adventure?"

She took a deep breath, closing her eyes to imagine what she might do, if she could do anything, anything she wanted, just once. "Something wild and free, and completely mad. Something wicked." Eleanor opened her eyes again. "And then I think I could find a husband who would suit me and at least not anger Melbourne."

Deverill's mouth twitched. "Very orderly. You're determined, then."

"Yes, I am. So, what do you think, Valentine?"

"What I think would fill volumes," he said. "I'll look
into finding a suitably wicked adventure for you. I'm not a
matchmaker, so you're on your own with the husband bit."

Well, she had an offer of assistance from him. She
could talk him into more, later. What mattered at the moment was that she had an ally. Impulsively, Eleanor
stepped up and threw her arms around him. "Thank you."

Valentine took her chin in his fingers, tilting her head
up. Slowly he leaned down and touched his lips to hers,
soft, beckoning, tantalizing. She stopped breathing. Elec-
tricity shivered down her spine. Though they didn't move,
she could swear her feet had left the grass. No wonder
women practically swooned at his feet. As he straightened, she found that she was leaning along his chest.

"I told you not to thank me yet," he murmured, setting
her back onto her own feet and then turning to continue
their walk.

But she already was thanking him. The memory of
Stephen Cobb-Harding's hard, selfish, fumbling mouth
attaching to hers abruptly fled. She had something much
nicer, and much more troubling, to think about now.

Chapter 8

Claiming a nonexistent appointment with his tailor, Valentine returned Eleanor well before her two o'clock deadline. As soon as he left the Griffin House drive he stopped the team again.

"Wiley, drive them home," he said, handing over the ribbons and jumping to the ground.

"My lord?" the tiger queried, climbing forward into the driver's seat.

"I'm going to walk."

"Yes, my lord." With a cluck, the servant sent the curricle rolling down the street.

Nothing had gone as he'd intended. For one thing, he'd meant to convince Eleanor to abandon her plan of rebellion, or at least to abandon him as her instructor. But now he appeared to be firmly entrenched in the middle of the Griffin clan battlefield. He'd actually *volunteered* to help her find something that would satisfy her craving for adventure. Him. Volunteering. And then it had gotten worse.

True, her query about his father had hit him like a fist in the gut; he'd thought he held no more than a vague memory of the old scarecrow, but obviously he'd been wrong. The entire first eighteen years of his life held nothing worth remembering, but once the thoughts stole in . . . At least today he had something to keep the memory of those mad, blind green eyes at bay.

And that something was even more disturbing. *He had kissed Eleanor Griffin.* "For God's sake you're an idiot, Valentine," he grumbled to himself, ignoring the questioning looks from passersby. "And a madman. And a fool."

Soft, virginal lips, the soft sigh of her breath—that would haunt him even more than thoughts of his mad, raging father. Her brothers trusted him. *She* trusted him. And she had a good heart, and a good nature, which under normal circumstances would have sent him fleeing. Nothing made sense.

And to hear her define the whys and wherefores of her plan to find freedom and a husband who would understand that had been nearly as unsettling. Women were supposed to be prizes and games. Before he'd gone mad, his father had at least taught him that, and had demonstrated it at every opportunity and with commendable regularity. All of the women he'd known during and since that time had only served to prove the old marquis's point. This female, though, seemed to have goals of her own—goals that didn't involve climbing into the beds of wealth and power. How very strange. And how strangely arousing.

He'd said he had nothing to teach her. That hadn't been strictly true, though the sensation of a man's hands on her bare skin, the feeling of a hard cock moving inside her—

those probably hadn't been among the items on her list. Jesus Christ, he needed a drink.

A horse snorted directly behind him, so close he could feel the animal's hot breath on the back of his neck. Instinctively he dodged sideways. A carriage wheel rolled past nearly on top of him. It scraped his elbow, shoving him between it and the stone line of fence wall.

He slammed back around, ready to flog whichever idiot cart driver thought it clever to send his vehicle up onto the sidewalk and attempt to run down pedestrians. The carriage, though, didn't slow down.

Phaeton, he corrected, though there was no crest on the back and the driver was hunched so low between hat and greatcoat that he couldn't make out much more than an inch of blond hair. That, though, and the pair of bays pulling the vehicle, was enough for him to be fairly certain who'd just nearly killed him.

"Stephen Cobb-Harding," he breathed, fingering the ripped sleeve of his coat. The heavy material was likely the only thing that had kept him from a broken arm. If he'd been a chit wearing a gown, he might very well have been caught up in the wheel spokes and dragged.

Other pedestrians closed on him with mutters of "Are you injured?" and "By God, that's Deverill."

"I'm fine," he muttered to the crowd in general, otherwise ignoring them.

Well, this was an interesting development. Act of a coward or not, it didn't make Cobb-Harding any less dangerous. Just the opposite. And not only to him.

His first thought was to return to Griffin House and warn both Eleanor and Melbourne that they should be ready for further trouble from the bastard, but he'd made a promise. And this was precisely why he hated giving his word. It led to all sorts of nasty predicaments. He couldn't warn Melbourne without betraying Eleanor's trust. And Eleanor's previous interest in Cobb-Harding had been both surprising and public enough that if he took it on himself to roust his attacker, her name would come up as well. "Damnation."

And to top everything off, his lie to Eleanor about needing to see his tailor had just become the truth. After that, he would be calling on a few friends to see what they might know about a man who drugged females and then attempted to rape them, and who now apparently had a new hobby of trying to run down noblemen who objected to his methods of seduction.

"Aunt Tremaine!" Peep squealed, dashing around the butler to slam her slim body into the legs of the sturdy matron standing outside her morning room.

"Decorum, Peep," her father cautioned, entering the foyer behind Eleanor.

"Nonsense, Sebastian," Lady Gladys Tremaine scoffed, embracing her grand-niece's head—the only part of Penelope she could bend enough to reach. "Decorum is for acquaintances. Hugs are for families."

"I stand corrected," the duke said, stepping forward to offer his aunt a kiss on one round cheek.

"And you, Nell?" the Countess Tremaine continued, "which are you going to offer? A hug or a kiss?"

"Both." Eleanor swept in, hugging her aunt over Peep's head and making the young girl giggle hysterically.

"You're squishing me!" She made a show of wriggling out of the sandwiched embrace and then scampered into the morning room. "Biscuits with globs of chocolate!" she reported.

"Oh, good God," Melbourne rumbled, following her.

Eleanor chuckled, her grip still tight around her aunt's shoulders. In her brothers' company she felt safe and protected, but only Aunt Tremaine could make her feel so . . . cozy.

"My goodness, Nell," Gladys muttered, hugging her back just as firmly. "You'll worry an old woman, holding on so tightly. What's wrong?"

"I've just had an interesting few days," Eleanor replied, releasing her aunt reluctantly and stepping back, "and I felt in need of a good embrace."

"Aunt Nell declared her independence," Peep announced stickily from the doorway, her mouth already smeared with chocolate.

"Did you, then?"

"She did," Penelope supplied, tugging on Eleanor's hand to drag her toward the morning room, "and at first I thought she was going to move to the Colonies, but she's not."

"I may yet," Eleanor muttered, catching the superior look Melbourne sent her as she entered.

"You must tell me all about it," Aunt Tremaine said, sending a footman for more chocolate biscuits. "It sounds very exciting."

Eleanor did want to tell her aunt all about it, but certainly not with Peep and Sebastian sitting three feet away. "It wasn't that dramatic," she returned. "I only wanted to have a bit more freedom, and the opportunity to find my own husband before Melbourne picked one out of the barrel for me."

Peep looked at her father. "You don't keep husbands in a barrel, do you, Papa?"

"No. They're in a box. A very large one, with holes knocked into it for air."

Aunt Tremaine laughed. "Your father is bamming you, Penelope. If potential husbands were in a box, someone would have to feed all of them. And I can't think of anyone who would want to have to pay for that."

"Not if they eat as much as Uncle Zachary."

"Out of the mouths of babes," Melbourne drawled.

They chatted for the next hour about what Peep was learning from her governess, Mrs. Bevins, which seemed to concern monkeys and Madagascar, and about fashion and who was engaged to whom and who had held the best and worst soirees so far this Season.

"I've heard there's already been at least one fight over a girl this Season," Aunt Tremaine commented. "Lady Easton told me."

"And we know how seriously to take anything *she* says," Sebastian commented. "Really, Aunt."

"Whether her tales are true or not, at least they're interesting. But Lady Easton said that she heard the story from an acquaintance who heard it from someone else, because she would never attend one of Belmont's naughty soirees herself, so I'm not certain how seriously to take it. It does make for good gossip, though."

"Who got into a fight?" Peep wanted to know.

Eleanor wanted to sink through the Persian rug and into the floor. If Melbourne *ever* found out what had happened and that it had occurred at Belmont's, everything would be over. And she would deserve whatever fate he assigned her.

"No one knows, dear. It was a masked party, so all Lady Easton could say was that a panther reportedly punched a fox in the nose, and then carried a crimson and black swan out and bundled her into a carriage."

"I think that's romantic," Penelope stated.

Closing her eyes for a brief moment, Eleanor sent up a silent thanks that no one had seen her in that dress. Deverill had been right to tell her to destroy it—though after Stephen Cobb-Harding had mauled her in it, she would never have worn it again anyway.

"Whose carriage was it?" Melbourne asked, waggling a finger at Peep when she tried to sneak another biscuit.

"That, I'm afraid, is where the details get absurdly fuzzy. Since Marigold heard it thirdhand, she wasn't certain whether it was Prinny's coach, Lord Westfield, or your friend Lord Deverill's." She chuckled. "I would tend to believe Westfield, myself, since he's been known to punch people before."

Melbourne snorted. "I'd wager it wasn't Deverill. I've never known him to get into fisticuffs over a woman."

"Valentine?" Peep commented. "He's very strong. He picked me up in the air with one hand once. Of course I was little, then."

Aunt Tremaine chuckled at the six-year-old, but Sebastian's attention was on Eleanor. For a moment she nearly panicked. Until the accusation was made, though, she wasn't going to confess to anything.

"And *that* is why you have to show some decorum, even in this little adventure of yours," he said. "If that had been you in that swan mask, you would no longer be residing in London."

"It's hardly fair to make threats based on other people's actions," Gladys commented. "And I'm sure Nell knows precisely what's expected of a young lady of her family and station."

Yes, she did know, but that didn't make *doing* what was expected any easier. "I thought you didn't even believe the tale, Sebastian."

"I heard a similar one myself, this morning," he returned. "Which doesn't make it true, but does make it more likely."

"I want to know when I can go to a masked ball." Peep sat on her father's lap and looked up at him. "I would be a princess. Or a peacock."

"You would make a lovely peacock, my love," he returned, kissing her upturned nose. "But at the moment, I think we need to take our leave before you eat every chocolate biscuit in London."

"I didn't eat every one."

"You tried." He set her back on her feet and stood. "Kiss your Aunt Tremaine, and let's be off." The girl complied, and they walked together out to the foyer. "Eleanor?"

"I'll be there in just a moment," she said, grasping her aunt's hand.

Melbourne and Peep headed out to the coach, but Eleanor pulled Aunt Tremaine back toward the morning room. "May I call on you tomorrow?" she asked.

"Of course, my sweet. Something *is* wrong. I sensed it."

"It's not that it's wrong, but that it could be," she returned. "Please don't tell Melbourne."

"We young ladies must form a united front. You may tell me anything, Nell. You know that."

"Thank you, Aunt." Delivering another kiss to Gladys's round cheek, Eleanor joined her brother and her niece in the coach.

"What was that about?"

"It was private. But don't worry, we weren't discussing you."

"That doesn't make me feel any better." He straightened one of the curls on his daughter's head. "Are you attending the Feryon soiree this evening?"

"I think so."

"And who will be escorting you?"

"Sebastian, this is not part of our agree—"

"I'm not preventing you from doing anything," he countered. "I'm merely asking a question."

True enough. And it was still close enough to her near-rape by Stephen that she was grateful for the question. "I thought I might join you, if you haven't made other plans."

"I never make plans that exclude my family."

Eleanor frowned a little. "That's because you're perfectly happy with your life as it is. You can make grand statements about your benevolence because you have everything you want, just where you want it."

Gray eyes looked calmly back at her for a long time, giving her a glimpse into their depths of what for a moment looked like pain. "That is a very short-sighted statement, Eleanor. And not at all like you."

Penelope reached across the seat and took her hand. "Aunt Nell is fighting for her independence," she said wisely. "I think it's difficult for her."

Eleanor sighed. "Thank you, Peep." Gazing back at her oldest brother, she gave a small smile. He didn't have everything, though at one time he had. If Peep hadn't been there three years ago when Charlotte had died and he'd become a widower, she wasn't entirely certain what Sebastian would have done. What he *had* done was round his bachelor brothers back up and give them free rent in the old ancestral manor just to keep all of his family close by him and safe. No, Melbourne had a great deal, but he didn't have everything. Not any longer. "I apologize, Sebastian," she said quietly. "But you could make this a little easier for me."

"I know I could. But I have no intention of doing so."

Rather than arguing back and forth about who was making life difficult for whom, Eleanor elected to retreat to her bedchamber with a book. Once she was inside her room, though, she stopped by the window. She couldn't exactly imagine Valentine retreating to his private rooms with a book when the late afternoon crowds of Bond Street and Hyde Park beckoned.

She supposed she could have a groom drive her to either location, or to the London Zoo or the British Museum— though those didn't sound particularly exotic today, either. What did one do when one wanted to be wild and wicked?

One could always kiss the Marquis of Deverill again. Eleanor ran a finger along her lips. She'd dreamed about being kissed by him for six years, since she'd been fifteen. Then she'd been a child, and as she'd grown older there of course had been the rules. Friends of her brothers were allowed to chat with her and dance with her when the occasion called for it, but they were never to look at her as a woman, and they were never, ever, to kiss her.

Deverill obviously knew the rules, and yet he'd kissed her anyway. And oh, my goodness, what a kiss. She'd been kissed before, in those rare moments when some rake or beau or other had managed to maneuver her away from her brothers for a second or two, but no one had ever made her toes curl before. Of course, she'd never been as . . . infatuated with anyone as she was with Valentine Corbett.

Eleanor shook herself. Her agreement wasn't about Deverill; it was about her. Her choices, her wishes—and yet a great deal of her time seemed to be spent thinking either about the marquis or what he would do in a given situation.

"Oh, stop it," she muttered, and plunked herself down at her small writing desk. What she needed to do was make a list of what she wished to accomplish and a list of potential husbands. That would do it. Then she could focus on her goals, and dismiss those things—and those people—standing between her and her adventure. Perhaps she could even match the adventure with the man, and in choosing her most-desired activity, find her best matrimonial prospect.

She pulled out a piece of paper and dipped her pen into the ink. "Number one," she stated, writing the number neatly at one edge of the page. "Acquire a more daring wardrobe which better reflects how I feel," she wrote.

That was a splendid start, she decided. She could even check that one off, since she now had nearly a dozen gowns from Madame Costanza, even without the infamous red one.

"Number two," she continued. "Speak with any man or woman I choose, and not just those preapproved by my family."

Well, she'd begun that, though her first real attempt had drugged and attacked her. She couldn't let that stop her, however. Melbourne's elitism was well and good for him, but he'd already experienced the world. She couldn't allow his standards to control her life.

"Number three." Pausing over this one for a moment, she dipped her pen several times and then cleaned off the excess ink again. "Drive a phaeton as well as any man."

Eleanor frowned, and nearly scratched the line out again. Not everything, though, had to be earth-shattering. And just because it had been Stephen who'd offered to teach her, it didn't mean she had to stifle the desire to learn. She simply needed a different, a better, instructor. Deverill would probably do, if she could manage to convince him.

"Number four," she continued. "Have an adventure."

Hm. That was rather vague. Deverill had said he would look into something for her, but as she thought about it, she realized that she needed to find one for herself—and not simply because whatever he came up with would probably be scandalous enough to ruin her and anyone standing within fifty feet. Once she found her own adventure, everything else would fall into place.

Still, she'd only made her declaration four days earlier. Choosing an adventure merely to get it out of the way would be both ridiculous and counterproductive—and quite possibly dangerous to the rest of her plans. After all, the adventure was to come before the finding of a husband. At the same time, she couldn't put off making a decision about either point indefinitely; her independence wouldn't last forever, and if Melbourne put a halt to her rebellion before she'd done that one thing, she would never be satisfied or content.

Eleanor left a space to fill in the subject of her adventure later, and went to the other side of the page to begin on her list of husbands. She decided to label them by letter rather than number. After all, she wasn't ranking them yet; it was merely a list of potential mates.

" 'A,' " she began, carefully writing the letter, and adding swirls and flourishes for artistic accent. Hm. Leaving space again, she labeled spaces "B" through "G" giving each of them the same attention she had the "A" so that she couldn't assume a preference by design intricacy.

That done, she returned to the top of the page. " 'A,' " she repeated.

Nothing.

After twenty minutes she realized what the problem was. She hadn't finished with goal number two of meeting a wide variety of people, so she hadn't met enough single gentlemen—other than the Griffin preapproved—to compose a useful list. For heaven's sake, the only name she was tempted to write down was Valentine's, and not even she would go that far to make her point.

Aside from the fact that the Marquis of Deverill would make a terrible husband, aside from the fact that the choice would absolutely kill Sebastian, aside from a thousand other reasons, Deverill would never agree to it. She knew his taste—married women with few morals, and no hearts involved. Since she wanted to love her husband, and to have him love her in return, Valentine would never do.

And so her goals list remained unfinished. And her husband list nameless.

Nothing had altered by the time Helen arrived to help her dress for the ball. This evening's gown, a midday blue at the neckline that deepened to midnight in the bottom folds of the skirt, she'd been saving for a special occasion. Tonight for some reason felt like one.

She debated wearing a cloak again, but by now her brothers knew the style of gown she favored, and she certainly didn't want them thinking she'd worn something terribly scandalous. This gown was more beautiful than daring, anyway. As far as she was concerned, Madame

Costanza had outdone herself. From the dressmaker's conversation she'd been looking for a noblewoman client for years. She was obviously enjoying the challenge.

Zachary gave a low whistle as she descended the stairs. It had to be a sign that her wardrobe had improved, or at least become less conservative. Certainly none of her brothers had ever whistled at her before.

Charlemagne's face folded into disapproving frown, but Melbourne's reaction was more difficult to read. He looked at her for a long moment, then with a nod signaled Stanton to pull open the front door. "Shall we?"

As Zachary helped her up the steps into the coach, he squeezed her fingers. "You're going to have every chit imitating you next Season," he murmured. "We'll see nothing but a whirl of Madame Costanza gowns. And I, for one, would like to thank you for that."

She gave him a quick kiss on the cheek. "Are you becoming a sympathizer to the cause?" she whispered back.

"Don't tell anyone, or I'll be strung up as a traitor, but obviously you haven't been happy lately. If this is what it takes to make you smile again, then you have my support."

With that unexpected bit of good news, Eleanor rode to the ball feeling more optimistic than she had for the past few days. The situation remained far from perfect, but she did seem to be acquiring a few allies along the way.

The Feryon butler introduced the family, and she strolled into a swirl of light and noise and music. Her brothers made themselves scarce, though she could still feel Melbourne's gaze on her even from across the room. So far, though, he'd kept his word, and hadn't interfered.

Every male in London society seemed to have discovered that her chaperones were off duty, and her dance card filled in what felt like less than a minute. She did manage to keep one waltz free, though she had no idea whether Deverill would attend this evening or not. The Feryons were a bit staid for his taste.

She supposed she should give the dance away to further her quest to find at least one gentleman to put on her list, but she wanted an update from Valentine about both her adventure and whether he'd heard anything from Cobb-Harding. If someone had punched her like that she would have kept her mouth shut, but she wouldn't have been in that situation in the first place. And rumors were circulating. Had Valentine heard them?

After two quadrilles and a country dance, the guests and the orchestra took a much-needed rest. Eleanor spied Barbara Howsen as she made her way to the refreshment table, and she changed direction to join her friend when a large male form blocked her path. Her heart skittered. He'd decided to come.

As she looked up, though, anticipation dropped into dismay. Stephen Cobb-Harding stood squarely in front of her, his blue eyes taking in the neckline of her gown. Eleanor flinched, fighting the instinct to cover her bosom and flee.

Slowly his gaze lifted to her face. "Good evening, Eleanor. Might I request a dance?"

The question was so absurd that for a moment she didn't know how to answer. "My card is full," she finally said, backing away to give herself some breathing room and so she could go around him.

He stepped forward, matching her retreat. "Surely you have one spot left for your future husband."

"You are the last man in London—in all the world—that I would ever marry," she retorted. "And you should feel lucky that I haven't contacted Bow Street to have you arrested."

"Yes, and why haven't you? Oh, that would be because you would have to admit to joining me at the Belmont party. And then I would have to confess that you had too much to drink, and that you and I went to a private room."

She blanched. "You wouldn't dare."

"Wouldn't I? I could even describe the small freckle you have right . . . there." He pointed just outside her left breast.

Eleanor couldn't breathe. Nothing, no one had ever been so dastardly. But she was still a Griffin, and Griffins didn't back down from anything. "You think that will convince me to marry you?" she asked, both wishing that he'd chosen a more private setting for this discussion and relieved that he hadn't.

He smiled. "No. But I don't need to convince you, do I?" Cobb-Harding looked past her shoulder.

Melbourne. Oh, he would be so angry, and so disappointed in her. She couldn't allow this. "If you tell anyone what happened, I will make certain everyone knows what an animal you are, and how much your behavior disgusts me."

"My dear, I asked if you wanted to join me at Belmont's, and you agreed. I didn't drag you there. And you're the one who dressed like an actress and then tried to seduce me—no doubt to defy your brother. If I chose to take advantage of your misbehavior, that was my prerogative." He stepped closer. "And I did and I do choose to take advantage."

"And what if I choose to put a ball between your eyes?" Deverill's low voice came. He stepped up beside her, close enough that his fingers brushed against hers. "That would be my prerogative."

Cobb-Harding shook his head, backing away a step. "I

didn't come here to fight with you. I'm merely here to discuss some things with the Duke of Melbourne."

"Then you shouldn't have threatened Lady Eleanor, and you shouldn't have tried to run me down this afternoon."

Eleanor ripped her gaze from Cobb-Harding to look at Deverill. "He what?"

"Tore the sleeve of my damned coat. So the more pressing question for you, Stephen, shouldn't be whether you wish to speak to Melbourne, but whether you wish to meet me at sunrise somewhere private."

The arrogant, confident expression on Cobb-Harding's face slipped a little. "You have no proof about anything."

"I don't need proof. I was there, both times. And I have good eyesight, and a very long memory. Now turn around and leave this house, or choose a location for our meeting tomorrow. I've already selected pistols."

"This is—"

The marquis edged closer. "If you don't leave immediately, I won't settle for embarrassing you or causing a scandal. I'll kill you, Cobb-Harding. But I leave the choice up to you."

Stephen pressed his lips together, sent a glare at Eleanor, and then with a stiff nod to Deverill turned on his heel and strode for the ballroom door. Eleanor looked after him, letting out the breath that had been locked into her chest for what felt like an age. "My goodness."

"Apologies," Deverill said, turning to take her hand and bring it to his lips. "I didn't mean to barge in, but Cobb-Harding seems to bring out the worst in me." He cocked an eyebrow. "Or is it the best in me?"

"No need to apologize," she returned, taking her fingers back, but not before she knew he felt them shaking. "Thank you."

"It wasn't for you, Lady Eleanor. He ruined my coat. And I liked that coat more than I like most people." The marquis offered his arm, tilting his head down as he did so. "You bit your lip. Lick it before anyone sees blood."

She hadn't even been aware that she'd done so. Eleanor licked her lip, tasting warm salt. "I didn't expect to see him here."

"I didn't, either. The man's a coward in the worst possible sense of the word."

"And you threatened to kill him."

"I knew he wouldn't stay. He tried to hide his face this afternoon when he attempted to run me down, and he didn't approach you in front of your brothers. He's still sorting out the best way to get what he wants. Hopefully I gave him a third possible outcome to consider."

"So you did." She drew another breath, squaring her shoulders. "How much did you hear?"

"I heard him threatening you. That was enough."

Eleanor had the oddest desire to smile, despite the upset of the evening. "He said that he wanted to marry me, and that he would go to Melbourne and reveal my indiscretions if I didn't agree to it."

He nodded as they reached the refreshment table. "I'm not surprised. Punch?"

She accepted the glass gratefully. "I wish this was stronger . . . No, I don't. What am I saying?"

"There's a difference between rum and rum topped with laudanum; though Lady Feryon would faint if she saw someone imbibing in her house." With a faint smile he pulled a flask from his pocket and took a swallow.

Eleanor couldn't help looking around for their rabidly teetotaling hostess. "Valentine!" she exclaimed, "put that away!"

"Only if you promise to smile."

"That sounds very civilized of you. And very thoughtful."

"Really?" he returned, his gaze touching hers. "You seem to bring out some very odd sentiments in me."

Oh, she enjoyed looking at him, trying to decipher what he might be thinking. He surprised her at every turn. "Perhaps we're good for one another," she suggested.

His voice lowered. "If you had any idea how very bad I wish to be for you, Eleanor, you would run away screaming."

Good heavens. Heat swept just under her skin. "Tell me how bad," she said unsteadily.

He took her fingers again, raising them slowly to his lips. "Very bad."

"Do you think you could seduce me?" As she spoke, it occurred to her that he'd half done so already.

His fingers curled around hers, eyes lowering behind those dark lashes. "Yes," he murmured, "I do. But I won't." Abruptly he released her hand, even taking a step back. "I suppose sometimes there is a good reason for rules."

She felt as though she'd been dumped into a snowbank. "That is not fair."

"So I should push you down on this table and lift your skirts? It would definitely be an adventure, but I don't think it would do you much good."

"It sounds to me like you're the one who's running now," she pursued, hurt that he could have been . . . toying with her. "So that's it?"

"That's it."

"Then should I tell Sebastian about Cobb-Harding? He'll kill me. And he'll send me home to Melbourne Park, and then he'll send some . . . walking tree stump to marry me. But I will have followed your stupid rules."

"They aren't my rules. They are merely *the* rules." Valentine replaced his flask, using the moment to check on the location of her brothers. All three of them had certainly noticed her conversation with Cobb-Harding, but he didn't think they had any idea how unfriendly it had been. No agreement would have kept Melbourne from storming to the rescue of a family member if he'd sensed that anything was amiss.

To himself he could admit that his first thought when he'd seen Cobb-Harding hadn't been for his torn wardrobe. It had been for Eleanor, facing a man who'd drugged and assaulted her, a man who'd chosen to confront her when she stood without allies.

She'd obviously been dismayed, but at the same time she'd faced him squarely, her chin up and her eyes defiantly meeting his. Whatever freedom or adventure she craved, Eleanor was through and through a Griffin.

"Be angry with me if you wish," he said in the mildest tone he could manage, "but don't expect me to apologize for anything. I spent a great deal of time and energy becoming who I am. And I'm not changing for anyone." And he had no intention of admitting that recently the idea of who he was had begun to take up some of his valuable drinking and gaming—and sleeping—time.

"Fine," she said after a moment. "Just don't you quote the rules anymore."

She was still speaking to him. Hell, she hadn't even stalked away. Eleanor Griffin was a remarkable woman.

"No promises." With a sideways glance at her, he faced the refreshment table. "And tell Melbourne whatever you choose," he said, handing her a biscuit, "but don't do it because of Cobb-Harding. I warned him once what would happen if he confronted you again. Obviously he didn't believe me."

Eleanor curled her fingers into his sleeve, tugging him around so she could look up into his eyes. "You're not going to kill him," she exclaimed, thankfully just as a footman dropped a tray of glasses.

"I haven't ruled it out," he returned more quietly, wondering at the way his pulse sped when she touched him. "But it would only be a last resort. I told you that you wouldn't have to worry about him, Eleanor, and I meant it."

She looked down, tears welling in her eyes. Valentine handed her his handkerchief, and she made a show of pretending a sneeze so she could dab at her eyes. When she lifted her head again, he couldn't read her expression at all.

"You, my lord," she said, "are a conundrum."

He lifted an eyebrow, trying to hide the realization that her comment pleased him. "I've been called worse."

She grimaced. "And you're very kind, but I hate being the damsel in distress even more than I hate you, of all people, throwing rules at me."

"You made a mistake in trusting him, Eleanor. The rest of it is no fault of yours." He smiled. "And believe me, I know far more about being underhanded than you—or Cobb-Harding—could ever hope to learn." Valentine turned her back toward the dance floor and her waiting quadrille partner. "Now, is there anything else I can do for you?"

"Hm, let's see. Vanquish my enemy, distract me from his threats, help me find freedom, conceal my poor behavior from my brothers . . . No, I can't think of anything at the moment."

He chuckled. God, she was a wit. He'd known before that she had a sense of humor, but had only paid enough attention to note that she could be mildly amusing. Obviously, though, she had a mind and a backbone to go with it. "Then I'll see you later."

As he started away, she clutched his sleeve again, bringing him to a halt as effectively as if she'd thrown a wall down in front of him. "I forgot," she said. "There is one thing."

"Yes?"

"I've one place left on my dance card. Would you—"

Valentine looked down from her face, taking the card from her free hand and penciling his name into the empty spot. "Are you certain you want me to take your waltz? You have an adventure to find."

Color crept up her cheeks. "Yes, I'm certain."

Chapter 9

With an hour to wait until his waltz with Eleanor, Valentine made for the gaming rooms. In keeping with the lack of liquor the games were excessively dull, but even whist and ombre were better than standing beside a wall, gawking at nothing.

He might dance with other women, he supposed, but Lydia Franch was there. Once his feet touched the thrice-waxed dance floor, she would manage to wrangle her way into his arms. Previously he wouldn't have minded, but tonight he had little patience for the romantic complaints of women who married for money.

How did he end up with unhappy fortune hunters, time after time? He knew the answer, though, even as he asked the question. They were familiar. He'd grown up with them. "Aunties," his father had expected him to call them, as if an eight-year-old couldn't recognize that the parade of women falling onto their backs in Corbett House weren't his relations. They wanted to be—the more hopeful, ambitious ones had even called him son. That hadn't fooled him for a moment, and his father for even less time than that.

Every one of them had looked at the old Marquis of Deverill and thought to become the new marchioness. After all, it wasn't as if he'd married the love of his life and would never recover, and he'd been a widower since Valentine was five. Alastair Corbett let them all think whatever they wanted, took them to bed, used them up, and then discarded them when they became too clinging or too dull or another, prettier, younger one caught his attention.

Valentine had asked him once if he ever meant to remarry, and his father had laughed at him. "I already have an heir," he had said. "Why should I fund what they give for free?" None of the ladies knew that, of course. Not at first, anyway.

In the end, they had gotten their revenge. The fifty-two-year-old marquis who finally succumbed to madness and disease little resembled the tall, handsome wastrel they'd so wanted to marry. By then, they'd turned their greedy attention to his eighteen-year-old son. And so he took his own revenge, scorning the single, eligible ladies in favor of those who offered and wanted nothing but a little passion.

None of that, though, explained his attraction to Eleanor Griffin. It would pass, he was certain, but at the moment every time he was in her company, he had the oddest desire to sweep her into his arms and kiss her. And more than that—he wanted to rip those revealing new gowns from her slender body and run his hands over her warm, smooth skin, and bury himself deep inside her.

"Deverill."

He looked up from the whist table. "Melbourne."

"I need a word with you."

Of course he did. The duke wanted a report on Eleanor's behavior—and Valentine had promised not to deliver one. "Give me a moment to take all of Everton's money. I'll meet you on the landing."

With a nod the duke left the gaming room. His concentration broken, Valentine lost the next hand and departed twenty quid lighter. He'd spent some time trying to decide how much he wanted to tell Sebastian, and how much he *could* tell without breaking his word to Eleanor. Nothing had seemed satisfactory, and now he'd run out of time.

Sebastian had actually gone out to the adjoining balcony beyond the gaming room and was puffing on a cigar when Valentine joined him. "I hope you have another one of those," he said, breathing in the heady scent of tobacco. American cigars. Melbourne had expensive tastes, but then so did he.

The duke pulled one from his inner coat pocket and handed it over. After Valentine lit it on one of the balcony lanterns, the two men crossed to the railing that overlooked the garden. They smoked in silence for several minutes, while Valentine made another effort to figure out what to say, and Sebastian tried to give the impression that he already knew everything that was going on and merely wanted confirmation. Valentine had known of that tactic for sixteen years, however, and it had never worked on him before.

"All right, what's going on?" the duke finally said.

"Nothing much. A few dances with a few gentlemen, and a ride in Hyde Park with Cobb-Harding."

"Has she shown favor to any other particular man? She did claim to be husband hunting, after all."

"Not that I've seen." Valentine paused. He needed to give Melbourne something, or the duke would begin to suspect duplicity. "You did just grant her complete freedom. I doubt she's in a hurry to settle into any damned marriage shackles."

Melbourne glanced down at the garden. "Since we're discussing Nell, I'll refrain from pointing out that your word choice implies a certain . . . cynicism."

"If you want my help, you also get my refreshing point of view."

"I suppose so. Now what were you discussing with Nell tonight? And don't attempt to look innocent, because that is something you've never been."

"You wound me. Shay told you that she asked me for advice on debauchery, didn't he?"

The duke nodded. "And just what advice did you give her, pray tell?"

"I haven't given her any, yet. Do you think I have a clue what to say? I have no desire to be chased out of London and hunted down by the Griffin brethren. So instead I asked her to waltz with me."

"And Cobb-Harding? I'm not going to have to call that fortune hunter brother-in-law, am I?"

"No. From my observations, on closer acquaintance she finds him less than appealing."

"Good." Melbourne tamped out his cigar. "I'd hate to have to make her a widow if she were to elope or make some other foolish mistake."

"I don't think you give her enough credit, Seb. She might be angry with you, but she's still a Griffin."

"I thought that was part of what she disliked about her life."

Valentine started to reply, then realized that he

shouldn't know the answer. As far as Sebastian knew, he was the same disinterested Deverill, only involved because of a rare matter of honor. He didn't care why Eleanor did anything—only that she didn't do anything scandalous. Which would include kissing him, but he wasn't about to discuss that. Whether Melbourne suspected something or whether it was an honest query, he didn't know, but he wasn't falling for it. "You would know that better than I. I'm only to keep her out of trouble, not decipher her motivations."

"I just thought she might have let something of her plans slip. You do have a way of getting people to chat."

"I'm naturally charming." Valentine took one last puff and ground out his own cigar. "And just how long am I to be your lackey, anyway?"

With a short grin, Melbourne walked back through the balcony doors. "Until I decide your debt to me is repaid, or until Eleanor ends this nonsense—whichever comes first."

"That's encouraging." Considering that he could have ended the nonsense a week ago with one word to Melbourne, Valentine decided that he had only himself to blame. And surprisingly, the task of providing guardianship to Eleanor had become more appealing than he would ever have expected. With one rescue, and one kiss, his life had turned upside down. And at the moment, he rather liked it that way.

After their last break of the evening for refreshment, the orchestra would play the waltz. Once Stephen Cobb-Harding had vanished, nothing else at the soiree mattered as much to Eleanor as that one waltz; not the heat of the room, not Francis Henning stepping on her foot four times during the country dance, not the silly, overabundant compliments from her sudden glut of suitors or the lack of appealing single gentlemen. She had to admit, in some instances her brothers had done her a favor. The fortune hunters were crawling out of the woodwork.

"Nell, I've barely seen you this evening," Barbara said, detaching herself from Mr. Robert Melpin to give her a hug and a kiss on the cheek.

"Yes, I seem to be quite popular," she returned, hiding her grin as a previous partner walked by, favoring her with a deep, reverent bow.

"I thought you and Mr. Cobb-Harding would be causing a stir this evening. I saw him chatting with you earlier, but you haven't danced with him once, have you? Your brothers didn't drag him out behind the stable and shoot him, I hope."

Eleanor forced a laugh. "I'm afraid Mr. Cobb-Harding and I weren't entirely compatible. He has the silliest ideas about females and marriage."

"What a shame. He's so handsome. But I suppose your brothers would have made life miserable for both of you if you'd decided you wanted to marry him."

"No doubt." She cleared her throat, desperate to change the subject. Thankfully Robert Melpin still lurked in the background, favoring Barbara with a lost-puppy gaze. "I believe you and Mr. Melpin have danced twice this evening," she commented, relieved as Barbara blushed. The Cobb-Harding conversation had just been forgotten.

"He's very determined," her friend admitted. "And Papa seems to like him."

"But what about you, Barbara? Do you like him?"

"I think so, but I would hate to commit to him and then realize that there's some other man out there that I like even more."

"Then don't agree to anything, for heaven's sake."

Barbara smiled. "I won't yet, but I don't have your limitless resources or your family's patience on my side. I'm expected to agree to a suit by the end of the Season. You know that."

Eleanor *had* known that, and in the confusion and chaos of her own ill-managed life, she'd forgotten. "I wouldn't so much call my family patient as I would skeptical and overbearing, but who else is on *your* list?"

"There are several. But I don't think this is the place to dis—"

"Of course not. I have a luncheon with my Aunt Tremaine tomorrow, and I have boat races in the morning, but I happen to be free all day on Sunday."

From Barbara's relieved expression, Eleanor had not been fulfilling her duties to her friend. "Might we go riding in the park in the morning, then?" Lady Barbara asked.

"That would be wonderful. I haven't ridden in ages. Shall I come by for you at ten o'clock?"

Barbara kissed her on the cheek again. "I've been wanting to chat with you, but you've been so busy."

"I'm never too busy for you, for heaven's sake."

"Are you too busy for me?" Valentine's low voice came.

She was going to have to ask him how he snuck up on people so effectively. At the sound of his voice, low shivers ran down her arms. He might have been teasing her earlier about how much he wanted to seduce her, but part of her wondered whether that had been a tease, at all. "Not if you're here for the waltz," she said breezily.

The orchestra began to play. With a lifted eyebrow Deverill glanced over his shoulder at the musicians. "That was timely, wasn't it? And yes, as it happens, that is why I'm here. If you'll excuse us, Lady Barbara?"

Barbara sketched a curtsy. "Of course, my lord."

He offered his hand, and Eleanor slipped her fingers into his. She wished she wasn't wearing gloves, and in the same moment decided that was foolish. With Cobb-Harding's threats she certainly had enough to concern her without adding a doomed flirtation with a hardened rake into the mix.

Valentine led her to the dance floor, where he slid a hand around her waist and stepped with her into the waltz. She'd seen him dance before, though rarely, and knew he was quite skilled. Being in his arms, though, was another experience altogether. This was a man who knew what he was doing, and what he wanted. And he was dancing with her.

Across the room, Melbourne conversed with the Duke of Monmouth and remained apparently oblivious to what she was doing and whom she was with. Eleanor furrowed her brow. "Has my brother asked you anything about why we went driving yesterday?"

"Which brother?"

"Melbourne, of course."

She thought he hesitated, but at the sight of his crooked smile and what it did to her pulse, she couldn't be certain. "He wanted to know if you were up to anything."

"And you said what?"

"I said I wasn't aware of anything in particular, but that I would teach you how to cheat at vingt-et-un if you asked me to."

Eleanor chuckled. "Perhaps next week. Thank you. I know from experience that Sebastian isn't easy to lie to."

"Ah, but I'm an expert in matters of deception. Half the time I don't even trust myself."

"That's not completely reassuring."

He smiled down at her, those deceptively sleepy eyes saying things she had no idea how to interpret. "It's not meant to be. Are we following the rules, or not?"

Oh, his way of behavior was so tempting—and it would be so bad for her. "I don't know yet," she whispered. As she looked up at him, a thought occurred to her. "If I were some simpering miss who happened to be Melbourne's sister, would you still be assisting me?"

"No," he answered promptly. I'm helping you because I like you. Not because of your bloodline."

"That's the truth, isn't it? And it sets you a step above most of the other men I've danced with tonight."

"You're wrong about that. My reasons for being here don't make me a hero, and they don't mean I'll do right by you. Best keep that in mind, Lady Eleanor."

They waltzed in silence for a moment. Melbourne might be pretending ignorance, but she couldn't help noticing Shay eyeing the pair of them from the game room doorway. And he wasn't the only one. Proper girls didn't dance with Deverill; if he hadn't been her brother's closest friend, waltzing with him might have been enough to void her declaration.

"Why do you keep warning me?"

"For the same reason I kissed you, I suppose."

She swallowed, hoping her cheeks didn't look as warm as they felt. "And why was that?" she whispered.

His lips curved into a smile. "Because I wanted to."

Oh, my. "You've never wanted to before."

"Warn you, or kiss you?"

"Kiss me. You've warned me before, though mostly

about the dangers of excessive drink and the eating of tomatoes."

He drew a breath, his gaze lowering to her mouth. "You've lately caught my attention. Which is why you should keep in mind the only thing I've said which is in your best interest: Find another tutor."

"No, thank you. I'm quite satisfied with the one I've selected."

What would he say, she wondered, if she confessed that he'd always had her attention? More than likely she would find herself in another private room with her skirt pushed above her waist. And with no one to come to her rescue, this time.

Except that she wasn't certain she would wish to be rescued. That sort of freedom would definitely go to her head, and it would just as instantly ruin her. She'd heard enough rumors about women he'd bedded and forgotten to know that one night of sin would be all she would have from him.

"What are you thinking about?" he asked in an intimate murmur.

"Freedom," she answered.

She'd surprised him; she could see it in his eyes. Even so, all he did was deepen his smile. "That's not quite the response I'd anticipated. You are determined, aren't you?"

"I am extremely determined. But at the moment, you hold the future of my quest in your hands." The waltz ended, but she held on to his hand when he would have released her. "I need another moment."

With a glance about them, he indicated the door leading into the hallway. "Go to the library and look for an atlas."

"An atlas? What am I trying to find?"

"I don't give a damn. Some river in the Americas I wagered you over." Valentine turned around, strolling toward the refreshment table.

Her heart pounding, Eleanor made her way through the crowd of guests. With single men accosting her at nearly every step of the way, it took her several minutes to make it to the hallway. Valentine was notoriously impatient, and she was half certain she would be stuck looking through an atlas when she finally reached the library.

As she stepped through the door, it swung closed behind her. "We've only got a minute before your brothers pretend they're not coming to look for you," Valentine said in a low voice, leaning against the bookcases, "so what did you want to tell me?"

She stood there for a moment. Insisting that he tell her what he thought they could do to deter Cobb-Harding would probably only make him annoyed enough that he would decline to do anything. Aside from that, it abruptly occurred to her that this was the most private she'd ever been with Valentine Corbett—she couldn't count when she'd been in his coach, since she'd been half drugged and frightened out of her mind. "Will you kiss me again?" she asked instead.

"Bold, aren't you?"

"I—"

Valentine pushed upright, taking her arm and drawing her up against him. In the same motion he leaned down, covering her mouth with his.

Time stopped. The rest of her body felt as if it were floating on air, not numb, but not precisely part of her, either. Rather, every part of her being focused on the soft, expert ply of his mouth against hers; the warmth of his breath; the deep, needful yearning spearing straight through her heart.

She moaned helplessly, dragging her fingers through his hair. In response his kiss deepened—and then abruptly broke off. Dazed, Eleanor opened her eyes. "What . . ."

"You asked for a kiss," he murmured, drawing her hands from around his neck. "Is there anything else I can do for you?"

Oh, yes. A country dance began dimly in the background, and she started. Good Lord. He'd warned her that they only had a moment; they could absolutely be caught at any second. *Think, Eleanor.* "My adventure."

His brow furrowed. " 'Your adventure,' " he repeated, releasing her captured fingers. "Of course. As for that, can you hand me any clues which might point me in the right direction?"

"I haven't decided yet." She hadn't decided much of anything, and with Cobb-Harding still sniffing about for something, time seemed to be flying around her.

"You'd best give it some thought, since despite your momentary weakness you don't seem to want to make sin a way of life. And that does narrow your scope of possibilities."

"I know." She drew a hard breath. "For the moment, I've decided to join Lord Michael Fitzroy and his friends at the boat races tomorrow."

He opened his mouth and then closed it again. "Hm. As a participant or a spectator?"

She grinned. Only he would think her participation might be possible. "I've never rowed a scull in my life." Eleanor chuckled, imagining the sight she would make. "I suppose, though, that I could always just say I'm going, and let Melbourne come to his own conclusions."

"A dangerous tactic, but an adventurous one. Have fun."

He stepped back, offered his careless, elegant bow, and pulled open the door. Eleanor stood there for a moment, wondering what she could possibly do that would make her feel as wicked as that kiss. Shaking herself, she pulled a mirror from her reticule to check her face and hair, then returned to the ballroom. She'd barely entered when Zachary appeared before her.

"Are you mad?" he muttered, taking her elbow and guiding her toward one side of the room.

"About what? Dancing with Deverill?" she returned, hoping wildly that no one had seen them vanish into the library. "Heavens, Zachary, I've known him for . . . forever. And what about our agree—"

"Not that," he said dismissively, "Fitzroy. You can't go racing on the Thames. And certainly not with his usual boatload of drunken idiots."

And she hadn't had to say anything at all for the rumors to begin. "He asked me to accompany him, and I thought it sounded fun," she returned, actually grateful for the accusation. At least it distracted her from Deverill. "I've witnessed the races before. You've even taken me there more than once."

"Spectating and participating are two different things, Nell. And I don't—"

"Yes, they are two different things, aren't they? Thank you for pointing that out. Now either dance with me or go away."

"Why, so you can arrange to sail to India and learn how to charm cobras? There has to be a point where you realize a little adventure isn't worth your safety—or the complete loss of the freedom you've made all this fuss about."

"Zachary, *I* am the one who will judge what a 'little' adventure might be, and *I* am the one who will decide whether said adventure is worth risking my safety and my reputation or not. And it's not a fuss. It's a declaration, and it's important to me."

"Nell, I'm on your side, but you're being a fool."

"Deverill doesn't think so."

"Deverill? You're judging your sanity by Deverill's? For God's sake, Nell, he's mad as a hatter. You've heard the rumors of some of the things he's done. And most of them are true!" Her brother scowled, looking as though he wanted to shake her very hard. "Aside from that, you're a female. Like it or not, there are things a man may do freely that would ruin a woman. Rowing sculls is one of them."

And kissing was another. "If I find myself ruined, then you and Melbourne win. So don't distress yourself."

She would have walked away, but he grabbed her arm again, turning her to face him. "This isn't about winning or losing. This is about my sister. Be a little cautious, Nell. I don't want to see you married to some witless buffoon because Seb thinks he'll be a steadying influence or something."

Eleanor froze. "He's selected someone, hasn't he?"

Her brother flushed, abruptly releasing her. "No. I'm just saying—"

"Who is it, Zachary?"

"It won't signify if you stop chasing about like some high-flyer and choose your own spouse."

"I haven't even begun chasing about," she lied, sending a glare in Melbourne's direction. "And just all of you remember the agreement. No one's said a word about any ill behavior on my part. Therefore, I still have the reins of my own destiny."

"Not if you get killed on the Thames tomorrow."

"That would be better than marrying whichever old goat the lot of you have plucked out of the pasture for me." She turned on her heel. "Good evening."

Even as she stalked over to rejoin Barbara and a few of her other friends, she reflected that it was only by the grace of Deverill that her impending marriage hadn't already been announced in the *London Times*. If he couldn't do something to stop Stephen Cobb-Harding from wagging his tongue, she might as well throw herself into the Thames tomorrow.

How odd, though, that she had asked one rake to defend her from the blackmail of another. She would say a prayer this evening, that the unlikeliest of heroes would prove worthy of her trust.

Chapter 10

For the fifth day in a row, Valentine found himself out his front door before noon. Well before noon, in fact. It wasn't the only change in his sleeping habits, either, but the devil knew he'd had enough sex in his life that he could do without for a week or two. Anyone other than Eleanor wouldn't have satisfied this odd new craving of his, anyway.

He wolfed down his breakfast and then headed out the front door. The tide wouldn't be going out until just after eleven in the morning, but he had several things to accomplish before he made his way to the Thames for the boat races.

His household staff, used to his late hours, looked nearly as disheveled as he felt at this change of schedule. When one was hunting songbirds, however, one needed to rise with them. And the same theory applied to jackal hunting.

Jezebel's hadn't opened its doors yet for the day, most likely because the club had only closed two or three hours

155

earlier. Nevertheless, Dicken, the club's owner, let him through the doors with only a quick nod of recognition.

"What brings you here at this hour, my lord?" he asked, his carefully cultured words still betraying their Cockney origins to anyone who knew how to listen.

"I have a question for you, Dicken," Valentine answered. "Several, actually. And they may very well be to your monetary advantage."

The former boxer's thick face split into a grin. "I'm always glad to assist a loyal patron of my establishment."

Valentine sat at one of the gaming tables, taking in the worn cloth coverings and the stains on the deep red carpet with cynical interest. With the windows thrown open and daylight pouring in, Jezebel's had a shabby set to it that he'd never noticed by chandelier light. "You keep papers on several of your patrons, don't you?"

Dicken spat into a nearby cleaning bucket. "Aye. I've a few who ain't as diligent about keeping out of debt as you are, my lord."

"Drinking debt, or gambling debt?"

"Mostly both." The heavyset face grinned again. "Seems one follows the other."

"That would make sense." Valentine leaned closer, noting and ignoring the faint sour smell of vomit and urine that Dicken's hostesses usually managed to cover by night with their cheap French perfumes. "Would you happen to have any paper on Mr. Stephen Cobb-Harding?"

"That's confidential, my lord."

Valentine pulled his billfold from his pocket. "It's just that Stephen is a friend of mine, and to save his family embarrassment, I might be willing to buy his debts from you. For a fair price, of course."

Dicken stood. "Wait here a minute."

Jezebel's owner vanished into a small room off the main parlor and emerged a moment later with a ledger book and a wooden box tucked under his arm. He took the seat opposite Valentine again and opened the book, flipping through several pages before he found the entry he was looking for.

"Mr. Cobb-Harding ain't sat at our tables for over a month, but I would wager that's because the house beat him at faro by a margin of seven hundred eighty-six quid. And that don't include another thirty-seven quid for liquor. Mr. Cobb-Harding likes his brandy."

"Don't we all." Valentine would never let Dicken know, but the figure surprised him. As far as wagering clubs went, Jezebel's catered mostly to the less well-heeled gentlemen who enjoyed a bit of gambling together with a bit of muslin wriggling on their laps. Eight hundred twenty-three quid was a huge amount for the club to keep papers on without sending an enforcer to recoup.

"I can see what yer thinkin', my lord, that I've been patient with the gentleman. I would've been more persuasive, but he did tuck his head in here a week or so ago to tell me he had a plump heiress on his hook, and that he'd settle his accounts with interest by the end of the month."

That was damned optimistic of Cobb-Harding, considering. "I have it on good authority that his heiress has her sights set elsewhere," he returned, working to keep his voice easy and his jaw from clenching.

"Well, damn me. If anybody knows, it'd be you."

"That it would. And so what do you say I give you a reasonable return on your kind investment, and we'll leave settling Cobb-Harding's debt to me?"

Dicken narrowed one eye. "How reasonable?"

"Say five hundred pounds?"

"Eight hundred would let me sleep peacefully."

"Six hundred quid in hand would let you sleep better than eight hundred you'll probably never see."

For a long moment Dicken chewed on his lip. "Done," he said finally. "Six hundred in cash. No more notes."

"Done," Valentine repeated, counting the bills out. If the morning continued as he expected, he was going to have to visit his banker for more ready funds. "And the papers?"

The former boxer signed over the promissory notes and slapped his wooden accounts box closed again. "I'd consider it a favor if you informed Mr. Cobb-Harding that he ain't welcome in Jezebel's again without ready blunt."

"It would be my pleasure. Thank you, Dicken."

"Nice to do business with an understanding gentleman such as yourself, my lord."

As Valentine left the club, he stuffed Cobb-Harding's promissory notes into his pocket. Eight hundred pounds worth of blackmail down, and who knew how much more to go. With a whistle he hailed a hack. "Boodle's Club, if you please," he requested, tossing the driver a shilling.

After Boodle's, White's, the Society, the Navy, and a dozen so-called clubs that were little better than thieves' rookeries and houses of ill-repute, Valentine had paid out more than thirteen thousand pounds and bought precisely twenty-three thousand, two hundred and eighty-six quid in promissory notes signed by Stephen Cobb-Harding.

Most of the bookkeepers, club owners, and tavern masters he approached were more than happy to sell him the papers; none of them seemed to have much hope of being repaid. But several of them had recently received visits from Cobb-Harding and assurances that he would soon have the means to repay his debt, which served to increase the amount Valentine had to pay out to them. It also increased the level of his anger, but he and Cobb-Harding would settle that later.

The overall amount of debt appalled him. He wagered, and heavily, from time to time, but never more than he could afford to lose—not that he lost very often. Cobb-Harding didn't appear to be nearly as skilled. No wonder the baronet's son had decided it was time to marry into money. But what he had done in an attempt to net himself a bride—what he had planned, and nearly accomplished— that was what his more conservative friends would call beyond the pale. As for Valentine, he was simply . . . furious. Ruining some innocent's life to rectify his own stupidity was cowardly. The fact that it had been Eleanor Griffin's life made it criminal, as far as he was concerned.

His accountant hadn't been overly pleased at the amount of money he'd stopped in to request. Since he and his father had invested the family fortune wisely, however, he'd barely notice the absence. It would have been worth a pinch, anyway.

Once he had the stack of promissory notes in his possession, he'd been tempted to walk up to Mr. Cobb-Harding's front door and break it down. Though pummeling the bastard and ordering him to pay his debt or flee to America would have been infinitely satisfying, he crushed the idea. He had a plan, and he would stay with it. He'd bought those papers for a reason—to protect Eleanor Griffin's reputation.

Eleanor. With a curse he pulled the watch from his pocket. Half past eleven. The sculls would already be lining up on the Thames. He had few concerns about her safety; Fitzroy was an idiot, and Eleanor knew that. Unless she'd gone completely mad overnight, she wouldn't set foot in one of the narrow boats.

She would be there by herself, however, looking for an adventure and surrounded by gentlemen hunting her fortune. And any one of them might prove to be as desperate as Cobb-Harding.

He could tell her that, but she would have figured it out already. Eleanor was extremely bright. She also had a troubling habit of thinking for herself. It made her unpredictable, a trait he generally frowned upon in females. In this particular chit, however, he found it interesting.

As he paid off the hack and sprinted to the edge of the pier, she was standing there amid a crowd of onlookers and waving a handkerchief at the first flotilla of departing sculls.

"Where are your brothers?" he asked, skidding to a halt and approaching the last few feet through the crowd at a more civilized stroll. His heart still raced, but not from the pace. The sun brightened the brunette of Eleanor's hair into a rich, honeyed bronze, and through the thin green and yellow muslin of her gown his discerning gaze could make out the crisp white of her muslin shift beneath.

She glanced over her shoulder at him. "I would imagine they're on the far bank yelling at Fitzroy. They seemed to be under the impression that I would be rowing in the race."

"And how did that happen?"

Eleanor shrugged, her eyes dancing. "I never said anything."

"They're only worried for your safety, you know."

"I know. But they made it clear that I would be wiser to abstain from racing. That done, it was supposed to be my decision. They couldn't stop there, though. They had to—"

"No. I would have stopped you, too."

Lowering the kerchief, she faced him. "You? But—"

"This isn't about freedom. It's about drowning." He grinned at her. "I do, however, have an idea for an adventure that wouldn't require inhaling the Thames."

"And what might that be?"

Now he had to come up with something. Since he had little experience with propriety, thinking of an acceptable activity took more effort and energy than simple sin. "Joining me for luncheon," he stated, hoping it sounded more adventurous aloud than it did in his head.

"Luncheon," she repeated.

"It's all—"

"Very well."

Valentine closed his mouth again. "Yes? Oh. Good. Come along, then."

"As long as we don't inform the prison guards where we're off to."

Jesus, she was still taking stupid risks. "We could inform them and still go," he suggested.

"Since when are you the proper one?"

That was a very good question. "Since you asked me for assistance, and since I don't want to be pummeled by the Griffin brethren for damaging you. Or rather, I wouldn't want to have to pummel them when they threatened me."

"So your concern is merely out of self-preservation?"

He smiled. "You already called me a conundrum, I believe."

She sighed. "So I did. Might we settle for leaving them a note?"

Valentine was surprised—and extremely relieved—that she'd agreed. "Splendid idea. Less chance for anyone to get hurt."

Luckily he'd ended up with a spare scrap of paper during the purchase of Cobb-Harding's promissory notes. She produced a pencil from her reticule and informed her brothers that she was not boat racing, and would be dining at luncheon with the Marquis of Deverill.

That done, Valentine hired a hack and sent the note to Griffin House. He nearly hired one for himself and Eleanor, but in broad daylight the chances were too great that someone would see them entering a closed vehicle without a chaperone. This whole propriety thing was a damned nuisance all the way around, but it remained at the base of both Eleanor's quest and his obligation to Melbourne.

"Where to?" Eleanor asked, apparently having come to the same conclusion, since she wrapped her fingers around his sleeve.

Perhaps propriety had its place, after all. He looked over at her, her gray eyes alight with both amusement and a touch of anxiety. Cobb-Harding had made an impression with her—and though it was probably a good lesson considering how close to the edge she'd chosen to walk, it was still one he wished she hadn't had to learn.

"Prospero's is close by," he returned, naming the least offensive sidewalk dining establishment in the area.

She nodded, and they headed north away from the river. For a few moments they walked in silence, while Valentine congratulated himself on averting both a catastrophe and a direct intervention from her brothers. Well, she'd averted the catastrophe on her own, but if Melbourne had confronted her, she might very well have leaped into a boat just to be contrary.

"Do I seem like I'm being a complete fool?" she asked, leaning a little closer against him.

His damned heart beat harder. "Not that I've noticed. Are you referring to anything in particular?"

"I feel as though I'm meandering about making grand claims with no idea how to accomplish anything. And nice as your . . . kisses are, they seem to confuse the issue."

Nice? He could sympathize with the confusion bit, though. "You don't know what you want. You're hardly unique in that, Eleanor. At least you've recognized that you want *something.*"

"I have no idea why you're being so . . . understanding, Deverill. You've made fun of Zachary for the way his cravat is tied. And I . . . happen to have overheard some rather unflattering remarks you've made in the past about members of my sex."

"About your sex, yes. But not about you."

Her fine cheeks colored. "And why is that?"

Hm. She wanted her lesson in freedom; she needed to realize that kisses were only the beginning where scoundrels such as himself were concerned. On the other hand, he didn't want to frighten her, especially after Cobb-Harding's boorishness. The proper thing would seem to be to leave the choice up to her. "How straightforward would you like me to be?" he asked quietly.

Eleanor stopped, facing him. "Actually, I would like you to kiss me again," she stated.

That was straightforward. "I would like to kiss *you* again." Valentine took a breath, praying that his cock could control itself until he got out of this mess. "But I won't."

"What if that's the adventure I want, Valentine?" she asked softly.

He went hard. Good God. "Then I would suggest that you choose another. Two kisses for an innocent is my limit. After that, she doesn't get to remain innocent."

"You can't—"

"You said you didn't want to be ruined, Eleanor. Believe me, the next time I wouldn't stop at a kiss, and you *would* be ruined."

She pulled her hand free. "Then why are you here? You claim to be a selfish, mysogynistic heathen, and yet you arrived this morning just in time to make certain I didn't get smashed into Westminster Bridge and drown. And you promised to assist me with Stephen. Why?"

If he answered that question truthfully, he would never have to worry again about the temptation of kissing her soft, warm skin. He wouldn't get the chance if he whispered a word about his agreement with Melbourne to her. "I'm trying to be a friend, Eleanor. It's not something I'm accustomed to, and certainly not with a female. It's a new experience for me, and when I kissed you, it was a mistake."

"And the second time?"

"An even bigger mistake."

"A mistake," she repeated, putting her hands on her hips. "That is not very flattering."

Despite his frustration and the growing discomfort of his groin, Valentine grinned. "You're upset that I don't intend to seduce you, after all?"

She scowled. "I—"

"Be grateful. Remember, if there's a scandal, you marry—how did you describe your nebulous potential husband?—a tree stump. You're flirting with scandal just walking in public with me. So you need to choose. Are you looking for one adventure and a return to your safe, secure life, or are you looking to upend everything you know and pay the consequences?" He moved closer to her, breathing in the lavender scent of her hair. "Because if you bait me again I'll act on it, and then you will pay, and I won't."

"I know the consequences."

"Knowing in theory and knowing in fact are two different things. So I know you're lying."

She flushed. "Isn't that my prerogative?"

When she turned her gaze away, hurt, he drew a breath. Christ, she'd surprised him. Even suggesting she might want him to be her adventure proved well enough just how naive she truly was. In any case, being rude and threatening obviously couldn't dissuade her from liking him—she'd put him into some sort of daisies and roses fairy tale. And to himself he could admit that it would have been easier to be cold and brutal if he'd wanted to be excluded. "So tell me who you're considering for marriage," he suggested.

"Why, so you can make fun of them?"

"You asked for help. I'm offering it."

"Just so long as you can remain on the periphery, yes? Two kisses, but no more than that because you might feel something?"

And he'd thought *he* was the one who would have to be direct. "That's *my* prerogative," Valentine said stiffly. He took another breath. "Come on now, Eleanor. Back to you and your experiment. At the least I may know whether any of the prospects have some unsavory habits unknown to their peers."

"I'll consider informing you. I thought you were going to come up with an adventure for me, though."

Valentine forced a smile. "I'm still working on that particular task."

They reached the spread of outdoor tables at Propero's, and he handed her into a chair. As he expected, several acquaintances were there ahead of them, undoubtedly having been more enamored of the idea of watching scull races than actually doing so. And he heard the murmurs, the speculation as to why Deverill would be accompanying Lady Eleanor anywhere, and especially without a chaperone.

"Are you certain it's not considered a scandal to be seen in my company?" he asked in a low voice, seating himself at her right elbow.

"Melbourne trusts you. *I* trust you," she returned, though her gaze as she took in their fellow diners wasn't quite as carefree as she pretended.

"Very well." He signaled a footman. "Two glasses of Madeira," he ordered when the man scampered over, "and whatever your best meal is."

The footman bowed. "Immediately, my lord."

"Take your time. We're in no hurry."

Eleanor watched as he placed the order. Her brothers were the same way; even if the person to whom they were speaking had no idea who they were, the "my lords" and bowing began immediately. It was as if they simply had an aura of nobility about them that everyone else recognized.

Without any other effort on his part, Deverill took over the café. The head waiter approached to pour the Madeira himself, and spent nearly five minutes discussing the rapturous quality of their roast pheasant, known throughout England and the Continent.

It was foolish for her to be angry with him. He'd been honest, which she'd requested and which was one of the central things she admired about him. She was the one with the questions, and for heaven's sake, he'd agreed to answer some of them. And if he'd refused further intimacy, of course it was for her own good, whether it felt that way or not.

"Yes, that'll do," Valentine finally said, when the man seemed ready to weep as he discussed the complicated marination technique. "Leave us alone now, until it's ready."

The waiter bowed. "Yes, my lord."

Eleanor chuckled. "For a debauched rakehell, you certainly seem able to command attention."

He snorted, apparently as willing to forget their argument as she was. "My billfold commands attention. I could be a corpse, for all they care."

"I disagree, but what do I know? He barely glanced at me."

Valentine slid his chair a few inches closer to her. "The waiter didn't, but the rest of the café knows precisely who you are and who you're here with. And they all want to know why."

He made the question sound so . . . wicked. "Why? Because you offered to take me to luncheon."

"So I did." Valentine tapped his glass of Madeira against hers and took a swallow. "Gads. It's like pretty-colored water."

"No one forced you to request Madeira. Ask for whiskey. Isn't that your liquor of choice?"

"It does the most damage in the least amount of time," he agreed. "I'm attempting to remain sober this afternoon. Relatively so, anyway."

Sober. For her? *Stop it, Eleanor*, she chastised herself. More likely it was too early in the day to imbibe, even for the Marquis of Deverill. He'd agreed to help her with Cobb-Harding, but that didn't mean she suddenly had to view him as some sort of hero. It was better not to. Best to keep to safe topics, especially after she'd been such an idiot and actually suggested that he kiss her again—and *he'd* rebuffed *her*. "Any news regarding Cobb-Harding?" she asked, taking a rather large swallow of her own drink.

"I've taken care of it. Or I will have, rather, as soon as I return home."

"Might I inquire as to how you've stopped him from blackmailing me?"

The delicious smile curved his mouth again. "A gentleman would never tell."

"Yes, but—"

"Yes, I know. I'm not a gentleman. Very well, I'm blackmailing *him*."

She froze for a moment. "With what?" she returned carefully. Good heavens, what had Deverill done to Cobb-Harding? Knowing the marquis, there were so many possibilities, she couldn't begin to guess.

"Unfortunately, I've had to resort to the dullest of methods. Money."

"Money."

His eyes dancing, Valentine took another sip of Madeira. "You look so dubious. Shall I explain?"

"Please do."

"Cobb-Harding is a gambler. And not a very proficient one. I've merely bought up all of his promissory notes. As soon as I return to Corbett House I'll send him a letter informing him of that fact, and demanding that he either pay me for them or leave the country—in either case keeping his damned mouth shut regarding a certain dastardly attempt he made to steal a woman's virtue."

" 'Dastardly?' " she repeated, hearing the anger in his voice. "That doesn't sound like your usual vocabulary."

"I was being considerate. That's not the exact phrasing I intend to use in my letter."

"What if he simply repays you for the promissory notes?"

Valentine laughed, the sound devoid of humor. "He won't be able to. Not unless he finds an . . . He won't be able to."

Eleanor studied the marquis's expression for a long moment. "You were going to say that he would only be able to repay the debt if he finds another heiress to marry, weren't you?" He would have answered, but she shook her head at him. "I'm not hurt by his motives; I expect them, to a certain degree, and from every man who approaches me. For God's sake, I knew it wasn't love." She frowned.

"Then I apologize for not being more direct, but you're wrong."

"You must always be direct with me, Valentine. But just what am I wrong about, pray tell?"

"About every man's motive for approaching you being money." He gave a short smile. "I mean, far be it from me to protest your cynicism, but you're a very attractive young lady, Eleanor. Sometimes a man's sensibilities aren't able to run much beyond the thought of sex."

She felt her cheeks warm. "I did ask you to be direct, didn't I?"

"Yes, you did. I'll stop, if it bothers you."

"It doesn't." It felt more like a privilege. Still, the vain part of her, the part that was insanely attracted to him, couldn't leave it at that. "Do you always speak so frankly with your female friends?"

His brow furrowed. "I don't have any female friends."

"You certainly know enough women."

His jaded smile appeared again. "Yes, but I don't talk with them."

Oh, my. Now she was embarrassed again, and they were dreadfully off-topic. "I see," she returned vaguely, "but I was about to make another request of you when you distracted me."

To her surprise, his smile deepened, lighting his eyes in a way that made her breath catch. "I distracted you?"

And now he was doing it again. Concentrate, Eleanor. He was right; he could seduce her in a second, and until it ruined her, she'd be thankful for it. "Only momentarily. What I intended to say was that I won't have Stephen forced into kidnapping some other poor girl and forcing her into marriage in order to satisfy his debt to you."

Valentine sighed. "I suspected you might have some objection to the choices I offered him. Very well. I'll put in a stipulation that he has one month to settle his affairs, and that if he attempts to marry in that time I'll make sure that whoever's in charge of the girl knows about the level of his debt—and his tendency toward being underhanded."

"That doesn't sound very . . . upstanding," she muttered, realizing that her real objection was to his assumption that some male would be making all of the girl's decisions on her behalf.

"Blackmail never is, my dear."

"But how much is this costing you?" She also wanted to know what he might expect in return, but if she asked that question, he would respond. She wasn't certain she was ready for that.

"No more than I'm willing to spend," he answered. "In fact, I would be willing to spend quite a bit more to cut into Cobb-Harding's hide."

Their pheasant arrived, carried to the table by two waiters and led by the head man. It looked like a parade. Valentine shooed them away when they would have stayed to watch their customers savor their first mouthfuls, and she chuckled at him. "You've whipped them into a frenzy. The least you could do is let them know we appreciate their efforts."

"I'll let them know when I pay the bill—if the pheasant's any good."

He took a bite, chewing and swallowing with such serious concentration that she laughed again. Heavens, she'd known he was witty, but she hadn't suspected until now that he was also quite funny. "And?" she prompted.

"The poor bird gave up its life for a good cause," he stated, motioning her to eat. "I'll reward them for well-executed sycophancy and a very nice wine sauce."

Eleanor took a bite herself, closing her eyes at the tender, succulent flavor. "Oh, my."

"I'm glad you like it."

Her eyes met his. The things she imagined in that deep green gaze made her breath come faster, her pulse speed. He didn't say any of them aloud, though, and in fact he was the one who looked away first.

"So, Eleanor," he said conversationally, when they'd both returned to eating, "you were going to tell me which prospective husbands appear on your list."

"No, I wasn't."

"Yes, you were. You might as well tell me anyway, or I'll simply wheedle it out of you."

He probably would. "I haven't thought that much about it," she lied. Confessing that she'd spent two unsuccessful hours plus endless nights trying to come up with anyone she even wanted on her list would make her sound unbearably snobbish—and that was precisely what she didn't want to be.

"Was Cobb-Harding on the list?"

The question, and the honest curiosity in his tone, surprised her. "Yes. I mean, if on better acquaintance I had liked him, I would have considered him."

"Odd, isn't it, that if he'd behaved himself, he might have gotten what he'd planned to take by force," he mused quietly.

She'd never thought about it that way, but it dismayed her to realize that Deverill was probably right. "I would like to think that I would have realized his true character sooner rather than later," she said slowly, suppressing a shudder.

"Well, I think we can safely say he's been crossed off the list now." He leaned toward her. "So tell me, you must have at least another name or two in mind."

"Lord Dennis Cranston seems pleasant enough," she blurted, just so he wouldn't think she hadn't found anyone else who intrigued her at all—no one but him.

"Nerriton's son? Come now, Eleanor. You can do better than that mush-for-brains."

"He's handsome," she protested. "And you said you wouldn't make fun."

"I distinctly recall *not* promising any such thing. Who else?"

"Hm. I believe, my lord, that you're familiar with the saying, 'Once gullible, twice a fool'?"

Deverill laughed. It was the same merry sound she'd heard before, and it had the same effect on her insides. By rights no one should be that attractive and at the same time that black-hearted—though she had the growing feeling that much of his cynicism was a defense, a reaction to the self-involved, fawning people of his past. As for the womanizing, she could surmise, but she knew very little about the old marquis, his father. From what Sebastian had said,

Valentine had nearly been sent down from Oxford twice for having a female in his room. A married female, as she recalled.

"Very well, no potential spouses. What about your adventure, then?" he asked, still chuckling. "Have you given it any more thought? Any direction in particular I should focus my efforts?"

"What would you do, Valentine? If you could do anything, just once, what would it be?"

He cast his gaze to the far side of the street, his jaw working. "I'm not you," he finally said, looking back at her. "I can't make that decision."

"But—"

"I can make suggestions, of course. Riding in a balloon, singing on an opera stage, sailing across the Pacific Ocean, meeting an Indian, journeying to India or to China, riding bare-breasted through Grosvenor Square, flinging a cake into Prinny's carriage, shooting a weapon in Parliam—"

"Oh, stop it!" Torn between horror and laughter, Eleanor downed the rest of her Madeira. "Nothing like that—though the balloon ride might be interesting."

"Out of all those suggestions?"

"Most of which would cause me to be arrested, in addition to ruining me," she pointed out.

"There is that, I suppose." Reaching across the corner of the table, he took her fingers in his. "Consider what you want, my dear. I'll find a way to see it happen for you."

It should have been easy to choose something wild and wicked and free. It probably would have been, except for one troubling fact: She'd told him the truth before—he *was* the adventure she wanted.

Chapter 11

V alentine sent Eleanor home in a hack again. When she arrived at the front door, the greeting committee looked much like the one who'd been in attendance after the fiasco at Belmont's—with one exception.

"Aunt Tremaine!" she exclaimed, shaking her mind free of visions of seductive green eyes. Quickly she stepped down from the carriage with Stanton's assistance and hurried up to her aunt. "We were to have luncheon! I'm so sorry!"

"No worries, my dear. I was only concerned about you, since you didn't send over a note."

"Oh, I have abysmal manners, and a worse memory." Eleanor took in Sebastian's still, grim countenance, and gripped her aunt's arm. "Have you eaten? Should I have Stanton bring some sandwiches? Or would you prefer tea?" she rambled, guiding her round aunt into the house and toward the morning room.

"Eleanor."

Her spine stiffened at the dark tone of her eldest brother's voice. "Yes?" she asked, turning around to face him. The expression in his eyes made her shiver.

"My office. Now."

Aunt Tremaine extracted her arm from Eleanor's. "I'll be in the morning room, my dear," she said. "Stanton will bring me my tea."

"Of course, my lady," the butler put in, gesturing a maid toward the kitchen.

So Aunt Tremaine thought she needed to be yelled at, as well. Considering how easily she'd forgotten a luncheon engagement when Valentine had smiled at her, she probably did deserve it. Keeping her expression calm and her gaze steady, Eleanor followed Sebastian into his office. She couldn't help flinching when he closed the door, but she hoped his back had been turned and he hadn't noticed.

"I received your note," he said, moving to stand at the window.

"I wanted to let you know where I would be, just as you instructed." Continuing her show of uncaring serenity, she took a seat in one of the comfortable chairs facing the desk.

"We looked for you at the boat races for an hour. Someone finally said they'd seen you stroll off in the company of Deverill." He sat heavily in the deep sill. "I was actually grateful you had decided against rowing a scull."

"Oh, Sebastian, I would never do such a foolish thing. You know that."

"No, I don't. I thought I did, but you've lately been challenging most of my notions about you. How did you come to meet up with Deverill?"

"He came looking for me, I think, to make certain I didn't join Fitzroy in his boat."

The duke nodded. "And where did you dine?"

"I don't have to tell you that."

"No, I don't suppose you do." For a long moment he sat silently, his gaze on the small garden outside. "I'm surprised that with the risks you're taking, not only have you arrived home safely after each escapade, but you've managed to avoid a scandal at the same time. I think it's only fair to warn you, though, that even the most proficient gambler loses on occasion."

"I know that. I'm willing to take the risk."

"I'm not finished. One of the reasons we—I—allowed you so much freedom when you were a child is that I didn't know any better. I hadn't even started at Oxford when I inherited the title, Shay, Zachary, and you. But ignorance, I suppose, is no excuse. And perhaps that makes your rebellion my fault."

Eleanor stood. "If your solution would have been to allow me less freedom, you would have been doubly wrong."

"Most female children of noble families don't go fishing or jumping naked into lakes or riding off on their brother's horses to break their arms, Nell. And when they grow up, they don't venture into Vauxhall on their own, and they don't wander off to have luncheon with hardened rakes without informing anyone first, or even after that."

"I thought Deverill was your dearest friend."

"He is. But *you* are my sister." He blew out his breath. "I suppose what I'm trying to say is that if you want to find your own husband, do so. If you want to visit Vauxhall or view the boat races, one of us will accompany you, and without complaint. But don't . . . for God's sake, don't put yourself into danger. Please."

Eleanor closed her eyes for a moment, trying to gather

her thoughts so she could finally explain this. "Sebastian, I love you. No, don't give me that look. I do. But the blood that makes you a leader, that makes you hate limitations and demands that you think for yourself—that blood runs in my veins too."

"I know that."

"Then you should also know that until I was fifteen I could . . . do the same things that you did. And then I couldn't."

"Elean—"

"But now, for this moment anyway, if I'm willing to take the risk, I can do those things again. This time, though, it's my responsibility, my decision. If I break my arm or get lost, it's my fault. Not yours."

"That may be how you and I see it, but it won't be how the rest of London views it. They'll see—"

"I don't care what they see. I know that eventually I'll have to go back to small dreams and small ambitions, and that because of the dictates of Society and the Griffin bloodline I'll be forced to marry some fool of your choosing, but in the meantime, I *will* have some fun. Short-lived or not, at least I will have done it."

"My concern is that when you look back on this moment of yours, you'll see it as the greatest mistake you ever made."

"Then at least it will be a mistake that *I* made for myself."

He let her have the last word. That felt significant, but considering the doubt and worry she still read in his eyes, he remained unconvinced. She'd given the explanation her best effort, and still no one was on her side. No one except perhaps Valentine—and that hardly counted.

Tears starting down her face, she half stumbled into the morning room, surprising her aunt by collapsing on her shoulder in sobs she hadn't even realized she was holding in. "I'm sorry," she wailed, her voice muffled against Aunt Tremaine's shoulder.

"Oh, dear, and me without a parasol," her aunt returned, patting her on the back. "You go on and cry, Nell. It seems as though you need to."

"I don't want to cry. I want to punch someone."

"Not me, I hope. I would guess Melbourne, which I wouldn't recommend, either. He's quite muscular."

"No, not him." Eleanor wiped her eyes, straightening. "I don't know who I could actually punch, anyway. All of this frustration is my fault. But I won't just give up and do what everyone else thinks I should. It's not fair."

Gladys took her hand, leading her to the couch and seating her, before going to pour them each a cup of the tea Stanton had provided. "I think I should refrain from comment until I know what in heaven's name you're talking about."

With a hiccup, Eleanor sipped at her tea. "Oh, yes, I suppose so. I apologize, Aunt Tremaine. It's just been in my head so much that I—"

"—that you can't believe no one else could know about it. I understand. But you must tell me."

"Yes. All right." Eleanor took a breath and sipped at her tea again. She wanted to tell her aunt. Other than Deverill, she couldn't think of anyone else she could include. Barbara knew a little, but only Deverill knew everything. Kind blue eyes looked at her as she sipped again. Gladys Tremaine was a perfect lady. She'd loved her husband, despite his lower rank, and before, during, and after her marriage had never even looked at another man, as far as

Eleanor knew. She'd certainly never been tempted to kiss a rake—but Eleanor hoped she would understand the reasoning behind those unhelpful cravings.

"I made a declaration of independence," she said.

"So Peep said. What sort of independence?"

"From the Griffins. I announced that I meant to find my own husband without their aid or interference, and that I would act as I chose and associate with whomever I pleased. And I would dress as I liked."

Her aunt sat on the couch and sipped her own tea. "And Melbourne didn't agree to this?"

"No, he did."

"He did? Ah. Then might the problem be that you aren't enjoying your new freedom?"

"No, that's not it, either."

"My dear, I'm afraid I'll need a bit more information before I can offer any advice or assistance."

"I wish I could explain it to you, Aunt." Eleanor flung her hands up in the air and back into her lap. "I have this opportunity to be free to do what I want, and I don't know how to do it—or even what it is that I want."

"You went to luncheon with the Marquis of Deverill, unchaperoned. That seems like freedom to me, Nell."

"It isn't. Not with Deverill. I mean, he does say things in my presence that most men wouldn't, but he's Sebastian's best friend. He knows the rules."

"The rules," Aunt Tremaine repeated in a dubious voice.

"The rules about behavior toward me as established by Sebastian, Shay, and Zachary."

"You mean you feel too . . . safe in Deverill's presence?" Gladys chuckled. "I didn't think I would ever use those two words in the same sentence. 'Safe' and 'Deverill.' How odd."

It had perhaps begun that way, but it wasn't precisely true any longer. Not since Valentine had kissed her. But despite his occasional verbal flirtations he'd already said nothing else would happen, and she wanted it to, blast it all.

Eleanor shook herself. There he was again, just the thought of him, of his warm mouth, distracting her from not merely her conversation, but her larger goals. "I feel as though I'm wasting this time," she said. "I know that eventually, probably sooner rather than later, I'll go one step farther than Sebastian is willing to tolerate, and he'll put a stop to this. In the meantime, I have no idea what to do. To make the most of this moment, I mean. And all the while, everything I *am* doing seems to hurt or disappoint my brothers—Sebastian especially. I don't want to do that, either."

"It's a difficult dilemma. Freedom, I believe, always has a price."

"That's precisely what Deverill said."

"He has a great deal of sense, then." Aunt Tremaine raised an eyebrow. "Surprising, that."

Yes, it was. In fact, Valentine's compassion and understanding had been a constant source of amazement to her. Eleanor swirled the tea in her cup. If she told anyone else, though, she had the feeling that all of it would disappear. That once she said it aloud he would instantly return to being the same jaded, cynical rake to her that he was to everyone else. And she didn't want that to happen.

What it all came down to, though, was that whatever happened was required to have meaning only to her. And the doing of it, and the consequences, were for her alone. "What I really need right now," she said with a deep breath, her thoughts barely running ahead of her words, "is to know that you, at least, understand what I'm trying to do."

Her aunt looked at her. "You don't even understand it, my dear."

"But—"

"I do understand. Your mother was my sister. An earl's daughter, suddenly married and a duchess. And not just any duchess, mind you, but the Duchess of Melbourne. An eight-hundred-year-old title, belonging to a family and a name dating back to the Romans."

"Grifanus," Eleanor supplied. She'd grown up knowing that, knowing that her family had practically founded the British nobility.

"It wasn't easy for Elizabeth, either," Aunt Tremaine continued. "But she decided it was worth it. She was very proud of who she was, and of the legacy of which her children became a part."

"So I should just stop this and beg Melbourne to find me a husband of his choosing? Someone worthy of me?"

"No. You should do what you think is necessary to be happy. Only keep in mind that your name doesn't stand by itself, Eleanor. Others share it."

"I know that." She kissed her aunt on the cheek. "And I won't forget it, either. Thank you."

"I don't think I did anything, but you're most welcome. And any time you need a friendly ear, I have a pair of them." Aunt Tremaine set aside her tea and stood. "I won't even tell you to be careful, because I know that you will."

"I will try," Eleanor amended, walking her to the front door. And she'd best try harder, considering what had almost happened with Stephen Cobb-Harding. What would have happened, if it hadn't been for Valentine, who had twice now come to her rescue. Counting on him to do it again would be foolhardy, however infatuated with him she might be.

But she would have to trust him at least one more time. Everyone's talk about adventures, and about what she'd used to be able to do as a child, had sparked an idea. Eleanor smiled as she headed back into the morning room and the small writing desk there. She had her adventure. Now all she needed was the courage to ask Valentine for help in achieving it, and most of all, the courage to go through with it.

Valentine had one of his grooms deliver the letter to Cobb-Harding, but waited down the street himself to watch and see what might happen next. As he had expected, within ten minutes Stephen Cobb-Harding had stormed out to his tiny stable, grabbed a mount, and thundered off toward Pall Mall. Following at a discreet distance, Valentine allowed himself a grim smile as the fool went from one club to another, obviously trying to verify whether they'd sold off his papers or not. The answer had to be devastating. And as far as the marquis was concerned, every ounce of agony and dismay was well deserved.

Now Cobb-Harding could scream and curse and rage at the sky, but there was little or nothing he could do to rectify the situation. Though Valentine hadn't said anything about it to Eleanor, his concern hadn't been for every naive debutante in London; it had been to prevent any harm from befalling her or her reputation.

And so his letter to Cobb-Harding had been very specific. He was to pay, or to leave the country. And if within the month he had remaining in England the fool came near her again, spoke one word to her or to her family under any circumstances, the day would end with him being locked into debtors' prison—or on board a convict barge, if Valentine could arrange it. A twenty-three-thousand-pound debt with no hope of repayment was a serious offense.

When Stephen didn't emerge from White's, Valentine approached more closely. Cobb-Harding sat in the bay window, drinking his way through a bottle of bourbon. Undoubtedly he'd paid cash for it.

Valentine smiled darkly. He didn't ruin other men's lives as a rule; he didn't care enough about most of them to bother with it. This particular man, though, had stepped directly into the middle of a friendship. And more than that, though Valentine couldn't even put a name to it. All that mattered was that Stephen Cobb-Harding go away. Permanently.

He had no intention of standing there watching a man drink himself into oblivion, so he returned to Iago and swung into the saddle. His options for other activities at this time of afternoon were fairly limited. No heavy games would have begun at any of the clubs, Parliament had no afternoon session today, and any ladies whose company he might desire would be out visiting with friends.

With a frown he turned Iago for home. He hadn't desired any female's company for over a week. No, that wasn't quite true, because he practically went hard every time he conjured a thought of Eleanor Griffin—which seemed to be with alarming frequency. No good rake spent this much time and effort on one woman, and especially on one whose favors he could never hope to win— would never sanely attempt to win. It was ridiculous.

If not for his idiotic debt to Melbourne he could be off arranging a rendezvous with Lydia or Lady Danning, or any of two dozen other chits he'd ensnared over the course of the last Season or two. But at the moment he couldn't imagine it. He couldn't imagine being satisfied by one of them while Eleanor still roamed London looking for the perfect adventure, and getting herself into God knew what mischief.

That was it, he decided. It wasn't so much that he couldn't stop thinking about her as that he was anxious to settle his debt and move on. The only way he could remove his obligation to Melbourne was to stop Eleanor's mischief. And the only way he could do that would be to help her find her adventure—and her husband.

"Bloody, bloody hell," he muttered, turning for home.

It bothered him more than he cared to admit that until Belmont's, Eleanor would have considered Stephen Cobb-Harding a potential husband. They'd danced together, chatted about nonsense for an afternoon, and she considered him a possible mate. That scenario hadn't exactly gone well—and he wasn't precisely sorry about it.

She wouldn't name any other potentials for him to review, and he wondered why. Yes, he would probably make fun of them, but how could she expect him not to? Most young, single gentlemen were good for nothing so much as a joke. They certainly weren't good enough for her.

"What?" he asked aloud, frowning. Where had that come from? A man not good enough for a woman? Such a female didn't exist. Except that she apparently did.

"Hobbes," he said as the butler opened the front door of Corbett House for him, "do we know of any young, handsome gentlemen of the unmarried persuasion who might appeal to a young lady seeking an adventure?"

"You, my lord," Hobbes answered immediately, accepting his coat, hat, and gloves while he toed the door closed with one foot.

Valentine snorted. "I said 'young.' I'm two-and-thirty. And I may have neglected to add 'upstanding' to the list."

"Oh. In that case, Lord Zachary or Lord Charlemagne? The Earl of Everton? Roger Noleville? Stephen Cobb-Harding? Thomas Chesterfield? Thomas Atherton? Lord Warefield? John Fitz—"

"Enough already," Valentine interrupted. "You might have replied to my query with something along the lines of 'a great many, my lord,' or 'nearly a dozen, my lord.' I didn't ask for a litany."

"Apologies, my lord. There are a *great many* young gentlemen who might suffice, my lord."

"Bugger off."

Hobbes bowed and started down the side hallway toward the servants' quarters. "At once, my lord."

"Wait a moment."

The butler turned smoothly around, his unflappable expression unchanged. "Yes, my lord?"

"Any news?"

"You have received a *great many* letters and calling cards, my lord."

"Are you and Matthews in league to kill me with an apoplexy?"

"I wasn't aware that your valet was trying to do you in, my lord. I shall speak to him about it."

Ah, so they were working separately—until this moment, anyway. "Letters and calling cards from whom, Hobbes?"

"Lady Franch, Lady DuMont, Lady Caster, Miss Anne Young, Lady Eleanor, Lady Bethenridge, Lady Field—"

"Thank you, Hobbes." Valentine stopped his retreat up the stairs. "Did you say Lady Eleanor?"

"Yes, my lord."

His heart skipped a beat, then began pounding harder to compensate. "Calling card or letter?"

"Letter."

"I'll take that one."

The butler returned to his station, retrieving a letter from the pile littered across the side table and salver. Climbing the stairs to reach Valentine, he handed it over. "Will there by anything else, my lord?"

"No. Go away now."

"Yes, my lord."

"And I'm not home to anyone but a Griffin. Unless it's Melbourne. If he calls, I've fled to Paris."

"Yes, my lord."

Valentine retreated to the small office adjoining his private chambers and seated himself behind the desk there. He placed the letter in front of him, adjusting it so that it sat exactly parallel to the front of the mahogany desk. And then he looked at it.

The anticipation coursing through him was new. He wasn't accustomed to feeling so . . . expectant about a measly note, about some chit's correspondence, but his hands shook as he lifted the letter to his face.

A faint scent of lavender practically had him pointing the way to Griffin House and Eleanor. "Jesus. It's a letter, Deverill," he swore at himself, running a finger under the wax seal to open the thing.

" 'Deverill,' " he read, " 'I've thought of an adventure. When may I tell you about it? Eleanor.' "

With a frown Valentine turned the paper over. Nothing. "That's it?" he said aloud.

That was disappointing. No protestations of yearning from the woman who, after all, had said she wanted him to be her adventure. No pleas for assistance, nothing more than a six—no, seven, he corrected, counting—word inquiry as to when she might inform him of her decision. No "dear," no "Valentine," no "Yours." Nothing clandestine at all. Hell, she could have shown Melbourne the note without fear of censure or reprisal.

Perhaps that was it, he thought, cheering up. Melbourne was reading her correspondence, so of course she couldn't have included anything more personal—like his Christian name. She'd called him by it before, after all.

He would be just as cool in his response, then. With a deep breath Valentine pulled a paper from a drawer and dipped his pen. "Eleanor," he wrote, saying it aloud as he went, "I will be at the Caster Grand Ball this evening. If you plan to attend, we can speak then."

"Hm. No," he decided. It sounded too clandestine. Crumpling the paper, he started over again with the same greeting and information. "I will be happy to listen to your plan there."

That was better, but it needed something to assure Melbourne that he was merely being polite. He began a third note, ending it with "Save a quadrille or something for me. Deverill."

"That will do." Blowing on the ink, he folded and sealed the note and summoned a footman to deliver it for him.

He had approximately five hours until he planned to arrive at the Caster Grand Ball. A dozen pleas from ladies awaited him downstairs; any one of them would be pleased and gratified if he should summon them or choose to call. At the moment, though, he didn't want to be satisfied. He wanted to feel this odd anticipation running just under his skin, the sensation of looking forward to something with genuine excitement—and, of course, arousal.

And so instead of answering or even looking through his ample correspondence, he went downstairs to do something completely uncharacteristic for him. He went to his library to read.

Eleanor read her note. " 'A quadrille or something'?" she repeated, scowling. "Heavens. If it's not too much trouble, of course."

Zachary looked up from his own correspondence. "What was that, Nell?"

"Nothing. Just a comment."

She'd tried to respect Deverill's wish to avoid any personal entanglements, though privately she didn't see how they could become more involved than they were now, short of becoming naked. That thought, of course, made her blush, and sent heat skittering along her skin.

"You're attending the Caster event tonight, aren't you?" Zachary pursued, scratching through a line of his writing. "Caster says it'll be the crush of the Season."

"That's because Lady Caster always says that. I'll withhold judgment for the moment."

"But are you going?"

Since she had to save a quadrille or something for Deverill, she supposed she had to. "Yes, I'm planning on it."

"With us?"

"I'll share the carriage ride, if you don't mind."

For a moment he was silent, then blew out his breath with an audible sigh. "How long are you going to do this?"

"I thought you were on my side."

"I would be, if I thought it was gaining you something that would make you happy. But to be honest, Nell, I don't see what this is getting you except for more arguments with Melbourne and tears when you see Aunt Tremaine."

"Who told you that I cried?"

Zachary pushed to his feet, the expression on his lean face frustrated. "I'm not blind, you know. Your eyes were all red and puffy. And—"

"You aren't supposed to say that to a lady, Zachary."

"You aren't a lady; you're my sister. And between you and me, I would never let Melbourne force you into a marriage with someone you disliked."

Marriage. She'd actually forgotten that had been her main reason for rebellion, as far as her brothers were concerned. "Thank you for the thought, but you would never stand against Melbourne if he forced the issue. Both you and Shay bow to his every order, as if he's something more fantastical than simply older by five years."

"Eight years, in my case," he pointed out. "And eleven, in yours. That's eleven more years of experience and wisdom than you have. Not just age."

"I still know what I want, and who I like. Eleven more years won't change that. I won't be dictated to, Zachary."

Her brother raised his hands. "All right, all right. I surrender. I don't want to argue with you. It just strikes me as odd that you're taking advice from Deverill, when you won't take any from me."

"I'm listening to advice," she amended. "I'm doing as I please."

"And listening to Deverill advise you about matters of the heart is ridiculous. He doesn't even have a heart. And that makes him probably the least qualified man in England to help you find a husband."

Eleanor tucked Valentine's missive into her pelisse pocket and stood. "I'm not going to discuss this any further. Just consider who you might ask for advice when you want to make a change in your life."

"But I like my life," he said to her back as she left the room, but she pretended not to hear him.

She did appreciate that Zachary was happy, but it only made her long harder for the same thing. She wasn't happy; everything seemed like a fight and a challenge, and still the chances of her getting something she wanted out of life remained abysmal.

Even her rebellion didn't seem to be turning things entirely in her direction. The man in whose arms she wanted to be wrote her extremely bland letters and promised nothing, only suggesting they meet for a quadrille or something so that she could tell him her dreams. And how he might respond to what she had to say, Eleanor had no idea—and a great deal of nervousness.

"Men," she muttered, going upstairs to examine the new arrivals from Madame Costanza and decide what she wanted to wear for the evening.

Chapter 12

❦

❝Just how many new gowns do you have?❞ Charlemagne asked as they entered the Caster ballroom.

Eleanor twirled in the emerald creation so that it swished around her ankles. "They're still arriving. I've ordered at least fifteen. Why do you ask?"

"No reason, except each one you wear shortens my life span by at least a decade."

Grinning, Eleanor headed off to greet some friends. "Then I'll expect to attend your funeral by next Wednesday."

When they'd arrived she hadn't been able to help looking around the room for both Cobb-Harding and Deverill, dreading seeing the first and anxious to see the second, if only to inform him that his letter-writing skills left something to be desired. Neither man, though, appeared to be in attendance. She supposed this might be one of those myriad events Valentine neglected because something more interesting had come along, but artfully or not, he had said he would be there.

191

Once she began thinking along those lines, however, she couldn't help wondering what—or rather, who—the more interesting something might be. She knew of at least three lovers he'd had already this Season, but lately he seemed to appear whenever she needed assistance. Maintaining a schedule that flexible and still keeping a lover would not have been easy, even for someone of his skill and imagination.

She greeted her friends, chatting and laughing about the Season and about who had already received proposals from whom, but half her attention remained on the doorway. It continued to flood with guests, but not one of them was the Marquis of Deverill.

"Did you hear that Phillipa Roberts eloped?" Rachel Edderly whispered, just loudly enough for the dozen giggling and laughing ladies in their circle to hear. "With Lord Ulbright."

"No!" Barbara gasped, covering her mouth. "Her father threatened to disown her if she saw the baron again."

"Yes, but with Ulbright's fortune, what does she care?"

"But he's twenty years older than she is," Eleanor put in, glancing again at the doorway. *Blast him, where was he?* She'd managed to save a stupid quadrille, since that was the dance he'd suggested, but she hadn't been able to help reserving a waltz as well. If he didn't appear she'd either have to sit out the most popular dance of the evening or attempt to ascertain whether one of her brothers would partner her. Considering Sebastian's mindset about her rebellion, she didn't hold out much hope for that.

"Can you imagine Ulbright climbing a ladder in the middle of the night to whisk her away? It's pure luck that no one's neck was broken."

"She'll hate living through the scandal when she returns," Barbara commented. "She's so shy."

"Not that shy, if she inspired an elopement," Rachel countered, chuckling again. "It must have been romantic, even with Ulbright involved."

"I hope so, for Phillipa's sake," Eleanor muttered.

Rachel looked in her direction. "Speaking of scandal," she said slyly, "what about you and the Marquis of Deverill?"

Eleanor frowned, feigning puzzlement even while her heart pounded. They hadn't done anything, for heaven's sake. Just one secret ride in a carriage and one luncheon. And two kisses. And quite a few heated thoughts on her part. "There's nothing between myself and Deverill. He's Melbourne's dearest friend."

"I know, but my mama saw you at Prospero's with him, having luncheon. Unescorted," she added, for the edification of the rest of the group.

This was where the scandal could start. Deverill had warned her that his company was dangerous, even with her brother's blessing. "For heaven's sake, Rachel," she exclaimed, waving her fan in the air for emphasis, "I think I have the right to dine with a family friend if I choose to do so. At an outdoor café, with thirty other diners."

"Well, yes, I suppose so," Miss Edderly conceded grudgingly. "Though I'm not certain I would have the courage to go anywhere with Deverill, escorted or . . ." She trailed off.

Without turning around, Eleanor knew that Valentine was standing behind her. She waited a moment, enjoying the stir of her pulse, the anticipation skittering through her muscles, before she turned around to look at him. "Good evening, my lord," she said, curtsying.

"Lady Eleanor."

The look in his eyes made her mouth go dry. Considering the nature of the adventure she'd decided on, perhaps she shouldn't include him in her plans for it, after all. The problem, though, was that she didn't know of anyone else she could trust. As if that were the only reason she wanted him to know. Now did not seem the moment, though, to strip away her delusions.

Practically in a line behind the marquis stood the usual gaggle of single gentlemen, all undoubtedly waiting to take the two remaining places on her dance card. Briefly she wondered what he would do if she gave away the quadrille. Unpredictable as he was, though, she wasn't willing to take the risk of not being able to speak with him.

"I'm blocking the way to paradise, it seems," he noted, obviously hearing the herd milling behind him. "Shall I see you later?"

"Only if you take a spot on my card," she returned with feigned nonchalance, handing it to him.

His mouth twitched. "As long as you don't think it'll begin a riot." Not waiting for a reply, he scratched in his name and handed it back. When he'd returned it to her, he aimed his gaze at Rachel Edderly. "If you ever drum up the courage, let me know," he murmured. He glanced at Eleanor, his eyes dancing, then strolled away toward her brothers.

Rachel clapped both hands over her mouth. "He heard me," she whispered in a muffled voice. "Oh, no."

"He only offered," Eleanor said, torn between amusement at her friend's apparent terror and jealousy that Valentine would flirt in front of her, even in such a blatantly teasing way. "You don't have to accept."

"The only reason you can be so stoic," Rachel retorted, "is because Deverill wouldn't dare try to seduce you with your brothers about. I don't have any such protection."

Eleanor could have informed her friend that Deverill only pursued where the attraction was mutual, but that would have been admitting to her familiarity and friendship with him. Besides, she wasn't all that happy about what Rachel had said regarding Deverill's restraint, especially because despite a few deliciously weak moments it was the truth.

She looked down at her dance card as the rest of the male horde swarmed around her. And swallowed. Valentine hadn't come for the quadrille. He'd written his name beside the waltz—the first one of the evening.

Barbara leaned over her shoulder while in front of her the first gentleman took the quadrille and the rest of them handed her card around—or snatched it from one another, rather like a pack of hungry dogs. "Friends, hm?" she whispered. "Are you certain *he* knows that?"

"Of course he does. We both do. He has some information I've been finding useful, is all. And as luncheon companions go, at least he doesn't spend the entire encounter bemoaning the weather or the color of the sky in London this Season."

"Just be careful, Nell," her friend continued in the same low tone. "Rachel's an amateur compared to some of the wags in attendance tonight. They would love nothing better than to imagine some sort of sordid episode between you and the marquis."

"I know." Eleanor sighed. "At least Melbourne knows not to pay attention to any such nonsense. Otherwise my declaration would have been void a week ago."

"Do you have any prospects in mind?" Barbara contin-

196   SUZANNE ENOCH

ued, nodding as the card returned. Roger Noleville had penciled in his name beside the one remaining dance, the quadrille.

"A few," Eleanor lied. "I'm not quite ready to name the contenders, yet."

"Well, if you're lucky, some of them will kill one another, and you'll have only the fittest to choose from."

With a laugh, Eleanor put the completed dance card back into her reticule. "I'll only have to step over the fallen challengers to find my mate," she chortled.

"Are you ready, Lady Eleanor?" Thomas Chesterfield made his way through the crush of guests to offer his arm. "I believe the country dance is mine."

"Of course, Mr. Chesterfield," Eleanor returned, trying to stifle her chuckles. In an out-and-out brawl, she would have to give the advantage to Lord Deverill, because she couldn't imagine that he would bother to follow the rules of fair play. Except that he wouldn't be involved in the fight, because he was a friend rather than a suitor, and because he didn't like to be involved in any stickiness.

With the start of the music she and her partner bowed to each other and then began the winding parade around the other dancers. She actually liked country dances; they provided the best opportunity for seeing who else was in attendance, and she could actually smile at persons with whom she might otherwise not be permitted to socialize. That restriction didn't hold true any longer, of course, and she could smile at or chat with whomever she chose, but the thought of that only made her enjoy the dance more. Over the course of the last few soirees she'd ended the evening with her face hurting, she'd done so much smiling.

"You look lovelier than Venus," her partner said as they met and parted again.

She hoped he didn't mean Botticelli's naked *Venus Rising from the Clam Shell*. True, she'd worn another low-cut gown, but after Stephen Cobb-Harding, she had become a little sensitive to compliments about her bosom—especially when her dance partner hadn't even discussed the weather or the number of guests in attendance.

"And lovelier than Aphrodite," Thomas Chesterfield added as they passed each other again.

So that was it. He was merely comparing her to goddesses in general, and not to naked ones in particular. Though technically Venus and Aphrodite were one and the same, depending on whether one followed Roman or Greek mythology.

Eleanor shook herself. She was supposed to be flattered, for heaven's sake. A handsome young gentleman happened to be complimenting her, and all she could think of was whether he'd confused his mythology or not. Apparently some of Deverill's jaded view of life was rubbing off on her.

The rows of dancers crossed again, and she found herself taking Charlemagne's hand. "Who's your partner?" she asked as they turned.

"Lady Charlotte Evans," he returned. "Who's yours?"

"Chesterfield."

"Blockhead," he replied, and was gone again.

Well, that was nice. She'd only agreed to dance with Thomas, not marry him. And Chesterfield had a reputation as being an upstanding young man with a future in the House of Commons, if he so chose. It wasn't his fault if he was a little . . . bland. Hm. Everyone was bland when compared with the Marquis of Deverill.

She was still ruminating on why Thomas Chesterfield wasn't more enticing to her when the dance ended and he led her to the refreshment table. "Thank you, Mr. Chesterfield."

"It was splendid, dancing with you," he said, his words stumbling over one another a little. "I was wondering whether . . . if, that is . . . you would care to join me on a picnic." He flushed. "I have a great many prospects, you know."

"Yes, I've heard," she answered. "I—"

"I believe everyone has prospects of some sort or other," Deverill's low drawl came from behind them. "Perhaps you should have claimed aspirations."

The fair skin of Thomas's face reddened. "But I do have pros—"

"Keep them to yourself," the marquis interrupted. "I have a waltz."

With that he took Eleanor's hand and wrapped her fingers around his arm. Behind them Chesterfield stammered for a moment, then wandered toward the gaming room with its well-stocked supply of liquor.

"Was that really necessary?" she asked. "He only asked to take me on a picnic."

Valentine slowed. "Was he one of your potential husbands?" he asked, lifting an eyebrow. "My apologies. Go back and finish your conversation. You must be desperate to know what his prospects are."

"You've made him so nervous now that I'll never have a decent conversation with him."

His lips curved. "I doubt you could have before."

The waltz began, and he faced her, slowly sliding his hand around her waist and tugging her a little closer than propriety dictated. Her heart hammered, both with excitement and anxiety—she needed to tell him her plan tonight, if she wished to accomplish it. At the same time, she wondered what it was that made him so much more appealing to her than other men, even more decent, proper gentlemen.

"Deverill, give me a compliment," she said, gazing into his lazy green eyes.

"A compliment?"

"Something you would say to impress a young lady."

His smile deepened. "Most of what I would say wouldn't be appropriate in public."

"Give it a try, will you?"

He sighed. "Very well." They waltzed in silence for a moment. "A compliment. Hm."

"Oh, stop it," she protested, blushing. "Surely you can think of something."

She waited for the inevitable comment about her eyes, or her hair, or her resemblance to one or other of the goddesses of love. Instead, Deverill's gaze became surprisingly serious.

"You are the most interesting female I've ever encountered," he said.

And that was probably the best compliment she'd ever received. "Considering the number of females with whom you are acquainted," she said, smiling so he wouldn't notice her stammering and see that he'd nearly left her speechless, "I'll merely say thank you."

"You might also tell me which adventure you've decided on," he said in a lower voice, tugging her a breath closer.

Goodness. If Melbourne and Deverill hadn't been friends, the marquis would be in a great deal of trouble with the Griffin brethren right now. And so would she be. She blinked. Being in his presence had become rather . . . distracting. Again.

"Yes. I've been trying to think about what I would most like to do, and I realized that it's something I used to do, but can't any longer."

His gaze studied her face. "Enlighten me, then."

She drew a breath. This was the embarrassing part. "I want to . . . I want to go swimming."

"Swimming."

"Yes."

"That's easy enough. I have to admit, though, I'm a bit disapp—"

"It's what I want to do," she cut him off. *Disappointed.* She'd disappointed him. And that bothered her to a surprising degree. "I'm sorry if it's not something . . . spectacular, but it's important to me."

"Why?" he asked.

Eleanor tightened her lips. At least he wasn't making fun yet. "I . . . when we were children, we used to go swimming in the lake at Melbourne Park nearly every day during the summer. Half the time we were completely naked. No one cared—we were children, and it was fun. I want to feel that way again, Valentine."

" 'Naked'," he repeated.

He *would* seize on that word. "That's not the point. I hardly think I would do that again. But I would like to go swimming. In a pond." She drew a breath. "At midnight. In Hyde Park."

Slowly he closed his mouth, and she thought he might even have paled a little. In the same moment, as they twirled about the room, the distance between them abruptly became proper again, though she hadn't been aware of him pulling away.

"Is something wrong?" she asked in a whisper, feeling heat flood her cheeks. She wasn't being ridiculous. If that was how he saw it, she wouldn't be able to hold another conversation with him without embarrassment.

"It's more spectacular than you might think, Eleanor," he finally murmured. "That's a very public place."

"It will be completely dark."

"You're determined, then?"

"I am. I would like you to . . . assist me as my lookout, but if you don't want to be involved, I'll find another way. It's not—"

"When?" he interrupted.

"You'll help me?"

"I'll help you."

Abruptly she was more nervous than before she'd told him anything. Now it was real. Now she had to go through with it, or both she and Valentine would know she was a coward, and that this rebellion of hers was nothing but a sham, a plea for attention or some other pitiful thing.

"I looked at the almanac," she said, her voice beginning to shake despite her best efforts to remain as calm and cool as he seemed to be. "Tomorrow night is supposed to be both good, mild weather, and a new moon."

He grinned, humor touching his eyes. "You've done your research. That's quite admirable."

"I know how much trouble this could be for me."

"It won't be. I won't allow it to be."

The waltz ended, but he wrapped her fingers around his dark sleeve. "Can you get out of Griffin House without anyone knowing?"

"I'll manage it."

With a glance in Melbourne's direction, he nodded. "My coach will be waiting for you around the corner from Griffin House at midnight. If you change your mind, send me a note."

"I won't change my mind," she whispered, forcing a smile as Barbara joined them again.

Deverill released her to her friends, and moved away to observe from a distance. *Jesus*. He'd expected something wild, something closer to the adventures he'd suggested previously. But a swim—he would never have suspected that. On the surface, it sounded simple and naive and childlike, and that was probably why it bothered him so much. Of all the things Eleanor Griffin might have chosen, she wanted a simple, private gesture just for herself.

She meant this rebellion. It wasn't a boast, something with which to antagonize her brothers or to make her the center of Society's attention. Hell, she had that regardless of what she might be wearing or with whom she might be dancing.

No, this was something she meant, very seriously. And if he had any sense of self-preservation, he would march straight over to Melbourne and tell him everything that had transpired, starting with Belmont's and ending with their conversation this evening. But he knew that he wouldn't do any such thing.

Across the room Lydia, Lady Franch, sent him a glare. She was clinging to the arm of Earl Pansden, so apparently she hadn't spent more than a night or two with only her husband for company. What had made her decide to seek out a lover after her marriage? Had the decision been a difficult one? She was jaded and cynical and held a grudge, but that was now. She'd been married for six years, and they'd been lovers on and off for nearly two. He was fairly certain he hadn't been her first, but the whys and wherefores had never occurred to him before.

Until the past week or two, the mathematical equation had been simple: He wanted something, or someone, and he either achieved his goal or he didn't. Now, though, he'd become acquainted with Eleanor Griffin—not the girl he'd always thought of her as, but the young woman she'd become. And the equation didn't seem quite so straightforward any longer.

Eleanor wanted things that weren't tangible, that couldn't be counted among conquests or wealth or property. Everything he'd seen, everything he'd learned from his father and from observing the parade of females in and out of the old marquis's bedchamber—and his own—had taught him that women were scheming manipulators, and that they thought of nothing but their own security, freeing him to think of nothing but his own pleasure.

"You feeling well, Deverill?" Shay asked, relinquishing his dance partner and freeing a glass of port from a footman. "You look as though you've inhaled a bug."

"I'm fine," Valentine said absently, watching as Eleanor's next partner joined her circle of friends by the refreshment table. "Just contemplating."

"Gads. I suppose Nell's to blame for that. Any idea what she's plotting now?"

Forcing a chuckle, Valentine claimed his own glass of port. "Do you think she would trust me with anything? I'm the incarnation of sin, if you'll recall. I give advice; I don't listen to confessions."

"Yes, well, I shudder to think what advice you'd give her. She's not talking to us at all, except for those pronouncements that we can't tell her what to do."

Looking down at the ruby liquid in his glass, Valentine felt the pricking of his conscience, or rather of his strong sense of self-preservation. Sternly he locked it back up again. "How often do you tell her that, anyway?" he asked.

"Tell her what?"

"What to do, or what not to do."

Charlemagne frowned. "What kind of question is that? We're her brothers. We all tell each other what to do or what not to do."

"So why is *she* rebelling, and not Zachary, for example?"

"I'm not sure I like this line of questioning, Deverill. Melbourne asked you to keep her out of trouble. The rest of it really isn't any of your affair."

Male aggression was something Valentine very much understood, but even though inside he was preparing for battle, he offered Shay a loose shrug and a grin. "I just thought if I knew what she was rebelling against, I might have a clue about her intentions here. Which means I might not have to keep chasing her all over the damned town."

His shoulders visibly lowering, Shay took another sip of port. "If I had the least idea what she thought she was doing, I could probably head this off myself. But I don't. I mean, what good brother wouldn't be concerned over who his sister spoke with or danced with? We don't want some bloody fortune hunter marrying her and then bleeding the lot of us dry, now do we?"

"So that's your concern? Her association with unacceptable men who might inconvenience you?"

"I wouldn't word it that way," Shay grumbled, "but I suppose so."

Valentine wondered whether Melbourne thought the same thing, and whether the brothers had any idea at all that this had very little to do with men and with whom she was allowed to dance. No wonder they'd been so baffled by her rebellion. And no wonder the duke had had to call in reinforcements, even in the sorry person of himself. If Eleanor didn't find what she was looking for soon, the

Griffins were going to be in a great deal of trouble. And he'd be right at the forefront.

"Uh-oh," Shay muttered. "Nell's looking this way. I'd best go elsewhere; don't want her to think we're conspiring or something."

"No, we wouldn't want that."

As Charlemagne strolled away, Valentine turned his full attention once again to Eleanor, now dancing a quadrille with Thomas Atherton. She smiled as she turned, obviously enjoying herself. Atherton was quite the charmer, but Valentine doubted she'd be going on any solitary drives with him. Not after Stephen Cobb-Harding.

He wasn't doing any more dancing tonight himself, so with a sigh that he refused to acknowledge might be regret, he left the dance floor and headed downstairs to summon his coach. It looked as though he had twenty-four hours to find a pond in Hyde Park where a young lady might go swimming without being discovered.

Chapter 13

Eleanor slid between the covers of her soft, warm bed and closed her eyes while Helen pinched out the candle on her bedside table and left the room, shutting the door quietly behind her. Then Eleanor counted to one hundred to make certain the maid would be well downstairs and nowhere close to the bedchamber door.

"One hundred," she whispered, and flung off the sheets.

Hurrying to her wardrobe, she selected a simple, plain gown and pulled it on over her night shift, then padded in her bare feet to the dressing table to comb her hair into a long, wavy tail that she coiled up and pinned to the top of her head.

"Shoes," she muttered, heading into the dressing closet. She couldn't very well run down to the corner in her bare feet. Heavens. No one was that brazen.

Squinting, she could just make out the hands of the clock over her fireplace. Two minutes after twelve. She'd tried for half an hour to get her brothers to take her home from dinner with the Gurnseys, but Zachary had been determined to win at least one game of charades. *Damned charades*. And now she was late.

She knew the Marquis of Deverill had a very finite amount of patience, and while he'd likely waited around the corner for young ladies to join him in his coach before, she doubted it had been with so little reward for himself in the offing. She had no idea how long he would wait before he decided to drive off and find amusement elsewhere, so with barely a thought as to whether they matched, she pulled out a pair of soft slippers, yanked them on, and hurried to the door.

At the last moment she decided to wear a bonnet; if someone saw her climbing into or out of his coach, at least her face would be partially concealed. After all, this was about freedom, not being ruined beyond repair.

The bonnet on, she then remembered it had been quite cool when they'd returned from the Gurnseys', so she freed a shawl from her wardrobe and pulled that across her shoulders. "Stop stalling," she hissed at herself, and resolutely stalked to her door.

Her fingers on the handle, she paused again, taking a deep breath. This was it; this was where she had to decide whether she was actually going to go through with it or not. On the surface, of course, going for a late-night swim with a trusted friend to keep watch seemed insignificant. When she took into account, though, that she was one-and-twenty, and that she hadn't been permitted to swim for eight years, and that the trusted friend was an infamous rakehell with whom she seemed to be quite infatuated, the idea didn't seem nearly as brilliant, if no less appealing.

Open the door, Nell, she ordered herself, and with a last breath she turned the handle and stepped into the hallway.

A few of the hall candles were still burning, which at best meant at least one servant was still on duty. At worst, one of her brothers still roamed the house. Eleanor prayed for a servant even as she moved quietly to the stairs and started down, avoiding the fourth stair with its infamous squeak.

Her heart pounded. If this was what an adventure felt like, she wasn't certain she would be able to survive anything more strenuous. In fact, the actual escaping of the house—and Melbourne's watchful gaze—concerned her more than what would come after. That, however, would change as soon as she reached Valentine's coach. If she reached Valentine's coach.

She paused in the foyer, listening for footsteps or voices or anything that might indicate she wasn't the only soul awake in Griffin House. Complete silence met her ears. According to the rules, she should have been able to inform her brothers of what she was doing, and then be perfectly free to go swimming. Since the Vauxhall lie, she was *supposed* to inform them of her whereabouts. In the face of reality, though, she was far from being that naive. Sebastian would never allow this, no matter what he might have agreed to in principle.

The clock on the landing kept ticking, reminding her that she was already several minutes late. Testing Valentine's patience was an uncertain prospect at best, and she didn't think she would have the nerve to do this again, rebellion or not. "On the count of five," she whispered soundlessly, then had to go through the count twice before she could make her legs move to the front door.

Gripping the handle, she slowly turned it until it clicked free. Even more gently now she pulled, and the door smoothly, silently, swung open. Before she could change her mind, Eleanor stepped onto the front portico and closed the door behind her. The click as the latch engaged seemed deafening, but she couldn't afford to wait and see if anyone had heard and would come to investigate.

Gathering her skirt in one hand, she hurried for the corner, running with every few steps as she neared her destination. "Please be there," she muttered, rounding onto Brook's Mew.

Silently beneath one of the gas lamps, a black coach waited. There in the dark it abruptly occurred to her that someone could possibly have overheard their plans, that it could be Stephen Cobb-Harding waiting in the black night for her to wander by. She slowed, but made herself keep walking. She was not going to stop just because of her wild imaginings.

As she drew nearer, the yellow crest of Deverill became visible on the door panel, and she let out the breath she hadn't realized she'd been holding. He'd come, and he'd waited. The driver ignored her, and in fact seemed to make a point of looking in the opposite direction. Undoubtedly he was used to the marquis and his odd hours and secretive rendezvous.

Eleanor rapped on the coach's door, and it swung open. "Good evening, my dear," Deverill's deep voice came, and he extended a hand to help her up the steps into the vehicle.

"I didn't think you would be here," she panted, taking the seat opposite him and grateful for the lamp lit beside his head. In the dark, wearing a black, austere coat and trousers with a gray waistcoat, he seemed even more . . . arousing—especially now, when all her senses felt awake and attuned to the world around her. Whether that was from excitement or anxiety she wasn't certain, but her heart had never pounded so hard in her life.

"I said I would be," he returned, pulling the door closed

and rapping on the ceiling with his walking cane. It wasn't for walking; she'd seen him with it before, mostly in the late evenings when he stopped in to see Melbourne after a night at some club or other. It held a razor-sharp rapier, for "unwelcome encounters," he'd said.

"I know, but I'm late."

"I expected you to be." He pulled a flask from his pocket, lifting an eyebrow as he offered it to her. "Whiskey?"

She was tempted. Tonight was not about liquid courage, however, and after a moment she shook her head. "No, thank you. But keep it close by; I may require it later."

He pocketed it again without drinking. "I may, as well."

That was the first time she'd heard anything that might be reluctance from him. "I didn't mean to drag you into anything," she said quietly, abruptly disappointed—not in him, but in herself. This adventure scheme of hers must be terribly boring for someone of his experience and reputation. "I can hire a hack if you don't—"

"That would be a sight," he interrupted, eyes shadowed in the dim carriage. "You arriving home, sopping wet, in a hired hack."

"Then what did you mean?"

"I rarely know what I mean, Eleanor. Don't let it trouble you. I never let it bother me."

She smiled despite her nerves. For someone so dangerous, he had an uncanny knack for putting her at ease. And always at times she never would have expected it. "Very well. Are we going to Hyde Park?"

"That's what you requested. I wouldn't let a duck bathe in some of that water, much less a pretty young lady, but I found a nice, secluded pond in the northwest corner. And it has the additional attraction of being at the farthest possible point from Griffin House."

"Oh." Secluded and far from home and safety. For a moment the realization left her distinctly uneasy.

Valentine seemed to sense the swaying of her courage, because even as he sank back in his seat, he offered her a calm smile. "I told you how I pursue chits," he said. "It must be mutual, or I'm not interested. And any time you wish to turn around, tell me, or tell Dawson, and it will be done. He has instructions to take your orders over mine."

The gesture surprised her, and though she would never admit it, it calmed her immensely. "So what if I should tell Dawson to leave you behind and return me home?"

"Then I will be walking. And not very happily."

"I shall try to refrain from doing so, then."

"Thank you." His gaze, which had been steady on her face, wandered down the length of her body and back again. "Interesting choice of wardrobe."

Eleanor fought to keep the blush from her face, though she couldn't help the warmth spreading beneath her skin everywhere his eyes had wandered. "I thought something simple would be appropriate."

"Since you won't be wearing it long, you mean. Unless you plan to swim fully clothed?"

Hm. "I do trust you, Deverill, but it seems to me the less you know about my precise plans, the better."

"As you wish. I'm merely curious, anyway. I can't re-call a single chit of my acquaintance who has made a point of swimming through a London pond. Not on purpose, anyway."

"Then I shall feel sorry for all of them when I've done it."

"I feel sorry for them now, just for being well-enough acquainted with me that I should know of their bathing habits."

"You're not so bad, Valentine," she said, keeping her

voice as distantly friendly as she could manage, considering that she was torn between fleeing home and throwing herself on him. "I don't mind being acquainted with you." Not at all. What would he do, she wondered, if she altered what she wanted for her adventure?

His teeth shown in the dimness. "You've only seen my good side. Think of me as a triangle. What you've witnessed is the narrow point. To the rest of London I show my broad backside."

She grinned. "But you've forgotten two other complete sides. If you're isosceles, which I assume you are."

The expression in his eyes softened for a brief moment. "Thank you for noting that I might have them."

"I've seen them, Valentine. What you've done for me wouldn't fit on the point of a triangle."

The marquis shifted. "Yes, well, the thing with triangles is that you can never see all three sides at the same time." The coach bumped, turning sharply. "We've reached the park. Do you care to enlighten me about the general plan? Am I to lead you to water and then turn my back and stand guard? Or should I wait in the coach and let you splash about in peace?"

She wanted him to be there, even though it seemed like the worst idea in history. "I would feel . . . better if you would remain somewhere in earshot, but once you point out the direction of the pond I shall proceed on my own."

He nodded. "And a blanket? Something to cover your wet body?" Valentine moved again. "Not that I'm trying to discover details, but this coach does have rather expensive leather seats."

Eleanor flushed. "I forgot a blanket."

He produced one from the cabinet beneath his seat. "I didn't."

Their fingers brushed as he handed it over. It might have been an accident, but since their last kiss, she couldn't be as certain any longer. Nor did she truly wish to be. Wondering whether the Marquis of Deverill lusted after her made life seem much more exciting. "Thank you."

"No detail forgotten. That's my motto."

She couldn't help smiling. "I thought your motto was *carpe diem*."

"Actually, it's *carpe femme*, but I'm expanding my repertoire."

Glancing toward the curtain-covered window, Eleanor couldn't help a nervous fidget. "What time do you think we'll be back? Stanton rises before five o'clock, I believe."

"We can be back in twenty minutes or less, so I suppose it depends on how long you plan to go swimming."

"And that would depend on how cold the water is."

He grinned. "I found a location; I make no guarantees about temperature."

"Fair enough." For a moment she debated whether to ask the next question, but with the dark and the coach and her companion, she couldn't help thinking about a similar situation last week. "Have you heard anything new from Mr. Cobb-Harding? I have to say, I expected to see him present at the Caster soiree."

"I haven't heard anything. And I don't expect to."

"So you sent him your letter. What, precisely, did you say in it, Valentine?"

He liked when she used his Christian name. Females used it often in his company; they seemed to find it romantical. For as long as he'd known Eleanor, though, she'd only begun using it over the last few days, only since they'd started this odd partnership, and that made it seem somehow more . . . significant.

"Nothing to worry about," he returned. "Unless he's shot himself, of course. One can always hope for the best, I suppose."

"Valentine! I may find him disgusting, but I certainly don't wish him to kill himself."

"Then you may hope he doesn't, and I will hope he does, and we'll all have done our duty."

"But what did you say?" she insisted.

Eleanor had a tendency to be very hard to distract. Valentine blew out his breath. "That I had discovered his level of indebtedness and made him responsible to me for it. And that unless he wished me to force repayment and the consequences thereof, he needed to make plans to leave the country."

Her soft lips pursed. "Thank you. I have to confess, though, that the further I get from the actual incident, the stronger my desire to confront him myself and deliver a punch to his nose."

There she went again, expressing that odd independent streak, that desire to do for herself. Considering how much experience he had with females, the level of confusion she caused in him was astounding. And as few morals as he had, he was still aware that the level of arousal he felt around her was completely unacceptable and best throttled and killed. A damned difficult prospect for someone far more used to indulging his passions than stifling them.

While she sat silently opposite him, Valentine concentrated on thoughts of ugly old chits and losing at faro. It didn't help much, but the more he had to think about, the less opportunity he had to dwell on any one thing.

The one thing stirred in her seat. "How much did you have to pay?" she asked.

"For what?"

She made a frustrated sound. "For Stephen's papers. To take over his debt. How much did it cost you?"

How could he tell her that the amount of Cobb-Harding's debt appalled him? And not merely the amount, but the carelessness of it? The bastard's idea of a solution to his monetary troubles had infuriated him, but he didn't want to let her know that, either. The Marquis of Deverill didn't get angry or upset over other people and their dilemmas—not unless they directly affected him. "Why the interest?" he said instead. "Unless you wish to find a way to repay me and take them over yourself. I wouldn't recomm—"

"It's a simple question," she interrupted, folding her arms across her lovely bosom.

"Yes, I suppose it is. And I'm 'simply' not going to answer it."

"I think I have a right to know."

Valentine shook his head. "I said I would take care of a problem, and I did. The details are my affair. Suffice it to say that Stephen Cobb-Harding is a reckless man who wouldn't have deserved you under the best of circumstances."

That seemed to stop her for a moment, but just as he began to relax a little, she leaned forward and touched his knee. "You are a very nice man," she whispered, her voice shaking a little.

The emotion in her voice bothered him. "Good God, don't go about saying that. I'm taking more pleasure from torturing Cobb-Harding than from helping you. That's not nice."

"Tell yourself anything you like, but you're wasting your breath if you're trying to convince me. You're forcing a man to leave the country because he attacked me."

He lifted an eyebrow. "Your faith in me is somewhat dismaying. I'll have to do something nefarious to convince you of my poor character."

She laughed, a sound he'd recently become surprisingly attuned to, and absurdly pleased to hear. "Just not tonight, if you please."

"Very well. Another time, then."

Eleanor settled into silence, and for the moment he let her be. A declaration of a wish to go swimming might sound innocent enough, but he knew her well enough to realize that she had to be supremely nervous about it. Ladies might take the waters in Bath, but that was considered medicinal. The shore at Brighton also attracted bathers of the female persuasion, but in addition to the god-awful attire they wore, that setting obviously lacked the solitude and the propriety-flaunting dimension that interested Eleanor Griffin.

As for himself, he could only admire the great restraint he'd been showing in her presence. Mentally he'd been undressing her and making love to her for days, but that didn't count. He was being good. "Nice," as she'd called him. Probably the oddest label he'd ever had applied to him, but on occasion he almost enjoyed it.

The coach turned onto a bumpier stretch of road, and he leaned over to brush aside the window's curtain. "We're nearly there," he noted, surprised at the low tremor of excitement that ran through him. For Lucifer's sake, *she* was the one going swimming; he wasn't even going to watch.

"Good. I'll try not to be long."

"Take as much time as you like, Eleanor. This is your moment of freedom."

He heard her quiet sigh. "Yes, I'm being so terribly bold, aren't I?"

Valentine sat forward. "You are. I'm beginning to understand that this isn't about making a statement to the world, but to yourself." He conjured a smile. "And besides, if this doesn't satisfy your cravings, I can still arrange a balloon ride or a voyage to the Congo for you."

With a chuckle Eleanor glanced out her own window. "I shall keep that in mind." The line of her mouth straightened. "It's very dark out there, isn't it?"

"I'll set a torch at the edge of the pond. And I'll be close by, standing guard. But if you don't want to do this, I—"

The coach bumped to a halt, and she stood. "I want to do this," she returned, turning the handle and pushing the door open herself.

The driver flipped down the steps, and Eleanor emerged before Valentine. He would have preferred it otherwise, just in case someone might be in the area, but he hadn't chosen this pond by accident. It was neighbored by an old church, and was used for the occasional baptismal on Sundays and otherwise abandoned.

"This way," he said, removing the lantern from one of the coach posterns and offering her his free hand. She took it, her bare fingers warm in his and shaking just a little.

They walked across the narrow stretch of meadow between the pond and the road, then entered the small, dark stand of oak trees that circled the water. Eleanor stopped at the sloping edge of the pond to gaze about at the lantern-lit darkness. "This is what I imagined," she said, her voice quiet.

That pleased him to an absurd degree. "It's used as a baptismal, so the bottom should be fairly firm." He set the lantern down on a rock, then straightened again. "I'll be just outside the trees. Call me when you're ready to return."

"Thank you, Valentine."

He shrugged, watching as she set down the blanket and then went to work pulling pins from her hair. Brunette waves cascaded over her shoulders, caressing her smooth cheeks and stirring in the slight breeze. With a swallow he turned his back. "Have fun."

Jesus. After he'd seen a hundred women letting down their hair, this one doing so innocently shouldn't have the ability to make him hard, but it did. She did. And with an obligation both to her and to her brother, he needed to put some distance between them immediately.

After striding away so quickly that he nearly brained himself on a low-hanging branch, he stopped at a convenient tree stump and sat down. "Stop it, Deverill," he mumbled at himself, rubbing his hands over his face. So he'd told her to have fun; it was far from the wittiest thing he'd ever said, but at least it had gotten him away from her before she could see his groin straining at his trousers.

Behind him he could make out the dim, broken light from the lantern, but he refused to look more closely than that. And he wasn't certain whether he could hear the swish of her gown as it softly fell from her shoulders or whether that was just the sound of the breeze, but he definitely knew which sound he wanted it to be.

He did hear the splash of water as she entered the pond. Keeping his gaze resolutely on the new moon, he refused to imagine her thin shift rendered transparent and clinging to the soft, wet curves of her body. This was about her freedom, damn it, not about how attractive he happened to find her. He'd already stepped too far by kissing her, and he wouldn't make that mistake again. Not even if it killed him.

Chapter 14

Eleanor held her breath as cold water rose up to her thighs. A warm afternoon would have been more ideal for this excursion, but that would played into the ruination clause Melbourne had put into their agreement. She took another step forward, gasping a little as the water rose to her hips. Her shift clung to her legs, making her feel clumsy and weighted, and the slap of the cold, wet material against her still-dry parts made her gasp again. With a glance over her shoulder in the direction Valentine had vanished, she yanked it over her head and tossed it onto the shore.

She shivered. "Oh, stop it," she muttered, and deliberately sank to her knees, letting the water flow up past her bosom to her neck.

The shock of the cold froze her there for a moment. As her body grew more accustomed to the temperature, she acknowledged that it wasn't that bad. She drew in her breath and submerged completely, stroking toward the center of the pond. The fingers of cold water sank in through her thick mane of hair, pricking and electric as they touched her scalp.

Swimming through darkness was an eerie sensation, as was the realization that her body felt different moving through the water than it had when she'd been a young girl. As she surfaced she smiled and flung hair from her face.

Tomorrow when she went down to breakfast she would know that she'd gone swimming naked in the middle of London, and that she'd done it simply because she'd wanted to do so. Her brothers had said they would serve as her escorts anywhere she wanted to go, but she seriously doubted they would have agreed to this. Certainly if Melbourne knew what she was doing, and who was standing guard, he'd drop dead on the spot.

Out here in the dark she could admit to herself that at least half of her excitement was from knowing that the Marquis of Deverill stood close by. Valentine Corbett, the notorious rake—and her surprisingly loyal friend. While she appreciated the friendship part, she'd be a fool to deny that she spent more time thinking of his kisses and wondering what would happen if she dared to bait him again.

She swam until her arms and legs began to tire. Even then she was reluctant to leave the pond, but she couldn't very well stay until daylight. Still, she would never do this again, and it was difficult to name the last moment of her freedom. Finally, though, she waded back to the point where she'd first gone into the water. And froze.

A pair of beady eyes, red in the reflected lamplight, gazed at her from beneath the skirt of her gown. It was probably a squirrel, she told herself, taking another step toward shore and waving her arm. A squirrel, or a hedgehog. "Shoo."

A low growl answered her. Eleanor yelped, backing into the water again. Hedgehogs didn't growl, as far as she knew. And naked, she didn't feel nearly as brave as she might have otherwise.

Something crashed through the shrubbery toward her. "Eleanor?"

With another shriek she sank down in the water just as Valentine emerged from the trees. He skidded, nearly sliding down the muddy bank into the water before he came to a halt.

"What's wrong?" he asked, his unabashedly curious gaze fixed just below the waterline in the direction of her chest.

"There's a . . . a thing under my dress."

His lips twisted. "I've actually had a chit tell me that very thing before."

"I'm serious, Valentine! It growled at me."

He gave her pile of clothes a dubious look. "Are you certain?"

"I've never had muslin growl at me before. Get rid of it so I can come out of the water."

Valentine looked around for a moment, then set aside his nice walking cane and instead bent down and picked up a hefty stick. Rather than shooing away the growling hedgehog, he hooked a strap of her shift and lifted the damp material into the air. "You're naked," he announced.

Warmth crept down her spine. "And feeling extremely vulnerable. Make it go away, Deverill."

With a sigh he lowered the shift and turned his attention to the larger pile of material. "Shoo," he said experimentally, poking at her gown.

A long dark form shot out from beneath the skirt and swarmed at him, growling. With a curse Valentine shifted backward, brandishing the stick like a sword. The weasel grabbed the end of the wood with its teeth and shook it. The marquis flung the weasel and the stick into the bushes, skidding to keep his footing on the damp ground. A rock went out from under his boot, and with a curse he fell into the water.

He lurched to his feet, splashing water into the air and over Eleanor. He was soaked to the chest, water dripping from his fine coat tails and his sleeves. After a stunned moment Eleanor burst into laughter.

"Well, thank you very much," he muttered, turning around to glare at her.

"I'm sorry," she gasped, trying to control her laughter. "The notorious Marquis of Deverill falling into a baptismal pool. It's a wonder the waters don't boil!"

Deverill started to respond, but the weasel trotted back out of the shrubbery. It stopped a few feet from the shore, and marquis and weasel glared at each other. Then with a sniff, the animal headed back into the trees, low tail twitching.

"I showed him," Valentine stated, slapping at the pond with the flat surface of his hand.

"You know, you might have told me you wanted to go swimming. I would have invited you."

"You sing prettily enough now, my bird, but I heard you squawking a moment ago."

Eleanor chortled. "There was a weasel under my skirt!"

"Yes, and who can blame him?" Swinging around, the marquis shed his coat and flung it beside her shift.

Abruptly she remembered that she was stark naked, only the dark and a few inches of water concealing her body from the world as she crouched in the shallows. "What are you doing?"

He stopped, tilting his head as he looked at her. "Going swimming. You did say you would have asked me to join you."

Her heart skipped a beat. "But I . . . I don't have any clothes on."

Deverill pulled his shirt from his trousers and yanked it over his head, sending it over to join his coat. "I'm attempting to catch up."

She meant to reply that it wasn't necessary for him to join her, but her gaze and her mind couldn't seem to move beyond the sight of his bare, well-muscled chest and abdomen. *Oh, my.* "But I was . . . getting out," she stammered, forcing her gaze up to his face again.

"Then do so. Do you require assistance?"

"Valentine, I—"

He faced her. "Do you want me to leave?" he asked quietly.

Her breath stilled. "No."

Deverill submerged completely in the water. A moment later a Hessian boot came soaring out of the pond and onto the shore. The second one followed it and Valentine surfaced, snorting. "Damnation. Wet boots. I nearly drowned."

"Then you should have gone back on shore to remove them," she pointed out, surreptitiously backing into deeper water so she could straighten from her crouch. She was insane to allow this to continue—but at the same time the naughty voice in the back of her mind told her she'd be insane to let the moment pass.

"Yes, I suppose so," he replied, and the wad of his wet trousers slapped onto a rock beside his shirt, "but then I would have gotten my backside muddy."

With a breath he submerged again, only the kick of a bare foot giving a clue about the direction he might have gone. The abrupt chatter of crickets and the quiet slap of water against her skin seemed absurdly loud in his absence. Her breathing was fast and deep, her heart pounding. When he surfaced a few feet away, slinging water from his black hair, she spent a long moment studying his face, his easy, amused grin and his eyes that could speak so much more than he allowed himself to say.

"Valentine?"

"I think a turtle bit my toe," he observed. "Yes, my dear?"

"Will you kiss me again?" she asked, her voice shaking.

"I warned you about a third kiss, about baiting me," he returned softly.

"I know that."

"I'll consider it," he said, and dove again.

Eleanor felt poised on the edge of something, waiting, listening, wanting—and potentially furious if he meant only to tease. Tonight was hers, her one night. And she'd done it; she'd told him what she really wanted. Him.

Warm lips touched her shoulder, and a hand brushed her wet hair forward across her breast. For goodness' sake, she hadn't even heard him rise. She stood frozen as his mouth moved up along the nape of her neck, warm breath caressing her cheek. "Valentine," she breathed.

"I considered it," he murmured from behind her, sliding his hands slowly down the length of her arms to twine his fingers with hers. "But I'll give you one more chance. Are you certain this is the adventure you want?"

She didn't have to think about her answer. "Yes, this is the adventure I want. For tonight only." Deverill needed to understand; she had no intention of embarking on an affair with him. That would kill her brother, and ruin her future.

And obviously she couldn't tell him that her stipulation

was more for her peace of mind than for his, that she'd said it so that when she saw him tomorrow in the company of some other woman, she could tell herself that it had been part of their agreement.

"For tonight only," he repeated, humor touching his voice. "That is actually something a gentleman longs to hear."

Hands still joined with hers, he tugged backward. Eleanor lost her balance, leaning back against his chest with her face upturned. Valentine leaned down, kissing her upside down. Oh, God, she'd dreamed of his mouth on hers, the tug, the heat, the insistent, knowing pressure. She moaned, freeing one hand to sweep up into his hair as she twisted to face him.

"This is your night, Eleanor," he murmured, lifting his mouth away from hers. "What do you want to do? What do you want me to do?"

"I don't want there to be a plan," she returned, twining her fingers into his dripping hair and pulling his face to hers again.

Hands swept around her waist, lifting her half out of the water. The marquis bent his legs, lowering them both below the surface. The sensation was extraordinary; his hot mouth, hot skin, touching hers, and cool water everywhere else around her. She pressed her body along his, kneeling as he had. Their bodies interlocked, she could feel his hard staff pressing against her abdomen, aroused and ready—for her.

Abruptly the air left her and she sputtered to the surface. He rose in front of her. "Christ, I didn't mean to drown you."

"You weren't. Deverill—Valentine—I . . . I want to see you."

"Ah. Lucky, then, that we have a blanket."

He didn't seem surprised by the request, but then he'd probably done this before with some other female, probably in this same pond. Eleanor frowned, then gasped as he swept her up into his arms and captured her mouth with his once more. How could he be so jaded, so accustomed to bedding women, and still feel so . . . electric? So full of passion?

"I hope the damned weasel's gone," he muttered, wading to shore. He freed one hand to grab the blanket off the rock where she'd flung it and dumped it onto the bare ground.

Heavens. She'd forgotten all about the creature, though considering the havoc it had caused, she was beginning to feel somewhat more kindly toward it. "Perhaps we should stay in the water," she suggested, casting a glance at the dark tangle of shrubbery around them.

He chuckled, the sound resonating into her. "The problem with that, my dear," he returned, laying her on the blanket and sinking down on one elbow next to her, "is that I want to see you, as well."

"But you've seen naked women before." Her already warm cheeks heated. "You've seen me half naked before."

"Yes, I have. Every woman, however, is different. And though I suppose the gentlemanly thing to say would be that I didn't look that night, I did. You've been occupying a fair share of my thoughts since then, Eleanor. And I will attempt to do your night justice." Grinning, he ran the fingers of his free hand along her cheek, then leaned over to kiss her again. A moment later his fingers brushed across her breasts. Light and languid, the anticipation of each pass constricting her breath, they circled, breathlessly closer and closer, until fingertips rubbed across her nipples.

She gasped, arching her back. Her nipples hardened at his light caress. As they did, his touch became more insistent, roving from one breast to the other, rolling her nipples between thumb and forefinger.

"Valentine!" she rasped, her head falling back.

He shifted over her with another plundering kiss, then sank slowly down, lips and tongue marking a heated, shivering trail down her throat, along her shoulders, and then, following the trail of his fingers, onto her breasts. Eleanor writhed beneath him, every new touch and new sensation sending her soaring.

Her muscles turned to water. Logical thought was impossible; every bit of her brain became focused on memorizing sensation and scent. A white haze wrapped around her, but she fought against it. Tonight was hers, and nothing was allowed to pass without her taking note of it.

"Wait," she rasped, tangling fingers into his damp hair and pushing his face away from her.

Half to her surprise, he straightened a little. "What?"

"Will you bring the lantern closer?" she whispered.

Closing his lips, he nodded. Something had changed, if Valentine Corbett couldn't manage a quip. But he stood, making his way barefoot through the scattering of sticks and dirt to the rock where he'd set the lantern. Abruptly conscious of how she must look disheveled and breathless on the rumpled blanket, Eleanor sat up to watch him return.

His damp skin glowed golden in the lantern light, his arousal large and impressive at the dark apex of his thighs. He wanted her. And the unabashed way he showed it as he put the lantern down and sank onto his knees beside her drew her toward him, tight and breathless. Her gaze lifting to his face, Eleanor reached out one hand to wrap her fingers around his cock.

His eyes closed, his head lifting. He felt warm and hard, and tentatively she stroked the length of him. His eyes flew open. "Jesus. Are you certain you've never done this before?"

"That feels good?"

A slow smile curved his lips. Leaning over her, he trailed a hand down her belly. His own gaze lifting to hers, at the same moment he dipped a finger between her thighs. "Does that feel good?"

Eleanor couldn't even speak. Instead she gave a nodding gasp, releasing him to fall back onto the blanket while he parted her thighs further and his finger roved inside her. His mouth returned to her breasts, then slowly meandered down the length of her torso. He shifted to kneel between her thighs and leaned in, his mouth joining his fingers. She bucked as his tongue flicked inside her.

"Valentine," she rasped, fingers grasping at his shoulders while he continued his sweet torment. He didn't relent at her plea; rather, his hands and his mouth continued downward, sliding along her legs, inside her thighs, and slowly back up along her abdomen again. He paused once more at her breasts, this time using his palms to knead and caress while he took her mouth again in a blistering, tongue-tangling kiss.

She was going to die. No one could stand this heat, this focus of passion and attention, and not simply expire from it. But she couldn't stop wanting it, wanting even more from him—and there was more. She knew it. The certain knowledge, the sharp arousal and desire, swirled around and around her in a confusing haze of heat and wonder and passion.

Valentine stretched out along her body, resting his knees between her thighs and leaning down for another deep, soul-stealing kiss. Skin pressed against skin, damp and hot and heavy. Eleanor stopped breathing as he angled his hips forward.

He pushed against her, slowly but steadily. She felt pressure, and then a slight, sharp pain, followed by an indescribable slide as he buried himself completely inside her.

"I thought it would . . . hurt more," she managed, overwhelmed by the sensation of him filling her.

"So did I." The sound reverberated through him and into her. His sensuous mouth quirked again. "You used to ride horses astride, you said once."

"Yes. But . . . You mean that makes a difference?"

"Apparently, though I'd really prefer to discuss it later." Valentine lowered his face to hers again, holding the rest of his body still while they kissed. "You amaze me," he whispered, his gaze locking onto hers as he began pumping his hips slowly and then more strongly, moving with a tight, hot, slick slide inside her.

Eleanor wound her hands around his shoulders and concentrated on breathing, but she couldn't move her mind beyond the sensation of Valentine Corbett inside her. She'd wanted this for so long, before she'd even known precisely what it was. His attention, his passion, his body, for this moment they all belonged to her.

He moaned, deepening his thrusts and pinning her to the blanket with his lean, hard weight. Eleanor panted, unable to help the mewling sound coming from her throat any more than she could fight the exquisite tension spreading through her. If this was dying, she could welcome it. Valentine shifted, increasing his pace and taking her ear gently between his teeth. It was too much. Eleanor lowered her hands to his pumping buttocks, digging in her fingers as she drew still tighter and then shattered.

She cried out Valentine's name, clinging hard to him as her mind shut down completely. All she could feel was him joined with her as they floated skyward. His thrusts quickened, and with a grunt he found his own release.

He gently settled his weight onto her, lips caressing her neck. Pressed to each other, she could feel the hammering of his heart, beating as hard and swiftly as her own. Slowly the veil around her mind began to lift, the sounds of crickets and frogs and the rustling of leaves returning her to the world again.

But the world was different now. She had held—still held—a man in her arms, inside her, and even if this one night was all they would have, it had changed everything. Every other man she met from this night on wouldn't be Valentine, and yet they would have to live up to him. To the way he made her feel, inside and outside and everywhere in between. And he still held her, even after he'd given her pleasure and taken his own. That meant something, but she wasn't about to ruin it by trying to explain it or even give it a name.

Valentine lifted his head to kiss Eleanor again. Her lips felt warm and soft and swollen. It was a new sensation, even for him. He rarely kissed after he'd gotten what he wanted, or given what he needed to satisfy himself. Christ, tonight had been nothing like that. No games, no seductions, no promises. She'd wanted him, and he'd wanted her. The honesty, aside from being refreshing, had been startlingly arousing.

He couldn't count the number of women he'd been with, but he would remember this one. His skin against hers felt warm, but as the rest of him dried in the slight breeze, the chill of the evening became more difficult to ignore. Reluctantly he lifted his head again. "How is your adventure progressing?"

She smiled, running a finger along the line of his jaw and somehow managing to make the gesture seem intimate and friendly rather than clinging. God, he hated clinging. "Quite well," she returned. "Does once count as one time, or one night?"

Valentine chuckled, using the gesture to cover his reluctance as he pulled away from her and sat up. "Considering the time of morning and the damage to my wardrobe, I—"

"I know, I know. If I don't return soon, half the staff will be awake to greet me at the front door."

"And we wouldn't want that." Of course not. That would mean he would be forced into a marriage with her—if Melbourne didn't just shoot him in the head and dump him in the garden to fertilize the turnips.

"I should say not." She sat up beside him, her gaze lowering to his now-diminished member. "No wonder you enjoy doing that so much, Valentine."

He found himself hoping that she wouldn't ask for a ranking of tonight among all of the others in his life. Not because it wouldn't hold up, but because it would. This made no damned sense at all. He'd been with women renowned for their sexual prowess, spent hours rutting in their heavily perfumed boudoirs, and in his earlier days he'd taken a virgin or two—though their tears and histrionics had caused him to swear off that particular breed. All of this, and yet with Eleanor Griffin he hadn't been able to pass by a single opportunity to peel her out of her gown— even if she'd actually taken care of that part herself.

She kept glancing at him as she pulled on her clothes,

which at least were mostly dry. He'd be lucky if he didn't come down with pneumonia. *Say something,* he ordered himself, seeking some suave and witty phrase to put her at ease and extricate himself without sounding like a moon-struck fool.

"Marrying you to some drooling old halfwit would be a waste in every possible way I can imagine," he drawled, handing her a shoe as he dug in a bush for his boot.

"At least now I can say that I've done something I wanted to first," she replied. "Thank you."

He scowled. "For God's sake, don't thank me, Eleanor. It was my pleasure. Believe me."

Eleanor cleared her throat. "But you . . . do that all the time."

With an irritated sigh Valentine stood, taking her shoulder to spin her around so she faced him. Moving in, he kissed her hard and deep, tilting her chin up and tasting her sweet mouth again. "I don't do that all the time," he muttered, releasing her to yank on his wet coat. "Now let's get you home before you regret this."

"I won't." She smiled, an expression that made his mouth dry. "Don't worry about that."

Chapter 15

E leanor awoke late and took her time with dressing. Her body ached in some unexpected places, but that wasn't the reason for her gliding about as if she were sunk into a waking daydream. Everything felt different; she felt different, and it was a sensation she was rather enjoying. And to think she'd only meant for her great adventure last night to be a swim.

It was past eleven when she made her way downstairs. She hummed as she slipped into the breakfast room.

"Good morning," Zachary said, looking up from the newspaper.

The paper appeared a little wrinkled, but then he would have been the third one to read it, after Melbourne and Shay. By the time it reached her, none of it would be pristine. She stifled a grin. Rather like her, now, thanks to Valentine Corbett.

"Good morning," she returned, shaking the image of

those sleepy green eyes from her mind. "Are there any peaches left?"

He nodded, indicating the sideboard. "Stanton had the bowl refilled when your maid announced that you'd risen."

She glanced at the butler. "Thank you, Stanton."

"My lady. And—"

"Oh, and there are three men waiting in the morning room to take you driving or some such thing," Zachary interrupted.

"What?" Eleanor glanced toward the hallway and the morning room beyond. "I didn't agree to join anyone for any outings this morning."

"Apparently they just appeared, hoping you would be available. And as ordered we didn't chase them off, so you're on your own."

"Who are they?" she asked, browsing through the sideboard offerings, and at the moment not disposed to rush her breakfast. None of them had been invited, and none of them would be the Marquis of Deverill. Aside from the fact that he wouldn't wait in a herd of hopefuls, he wouldn't call on her anyway. Last night had been their— her—moment of freedom and passion. He'd helped her find it, and she had been the one to say there wouldn't be anything more.

And of course that had been precisely the wisest thing to do—even before she'd discovered just how enjoyable last night would be. It made a great deal of sense to put an end to anything before it could begin, especially since it might also save her from wondering where he might be— not that it seemed to be working at the moment. Valentine didn't precisely have a reputation for faithfulness or lengthy romances. In fact, she would hardly call them romances at all. More like liaisons. And she'd been just another in a long line of those. Eleanor frowned. That was what she'd wanted. Wasn't it?

"Ask Stanton who's here," Zachary returned. "I'm busy."

Sighing, she raised an eyebrow at the butler. "Stanton?"

"Mr. Roger Noleville, Lord Ian Woods, and Lord Chambrey, my lady."

"Oh."

Zachary glanced over the edge of the paper at her, then went back to reading when she looked in his direction.

"What?" she asked.

"Nothing. Just noting your good mood and not asking you about it, because I don't want to ruin it or break the rules or anything."

And how was she supposed to reply to that? "Good," she attempted. "Thank you."

"You're welcome. And the hopeful herd in the morning room?"

"I thought you were too busy to concern yourself with them."

"I am. I'm merely reminding you of their presence."

"Fine." None of the callers stirred her in the least, though she supposed Noleville was an upstanding young man, if rather dull. Still, it showed some spirit, if he'd bothered to come calling without an invitation to do so.

On the other hand, she wasn't particularly interested in spending the day with any of them. Eleanor picked up a peach, then set it back in the bowl. "I suppose it's rude to keep them waiting."

"So you're going driving with all three of them?" Zachary asked.

She stuck her tongue out at him just as Peep pranced into the breakfast room. "My governess said she would wash my tongue with soap if I stuck it out at her again," she commented, snatching up the peach Eleanor had rejected and biting into it. "But I won't tell her about you."

"Thank you, Peep."

"You're welcome. And who are these new men coming to call on you?" the little girl continued. "I've never seen them before, so they can't be friends of Papa or the uncles."

"No, they're not," Zachary agreed.

"They're here to call on me," Eleanor explained. "They want to take me driving."

"All of them?"

"Yes," she returned, trying not to sound reluctant. This was supposed to be what she wanted, and Zachary would report any hesitation on her part to Melbourne. Her social calendar used to be much more organized, but she wouldn't exactly call this new chaos any more fun than the old, staid life she'd had before.

"Well, I don't think you can go with all of them."

Obviously not. An idea struck her, and she turned to the butler again. "Stanton, which of them arrived first?"

"That would be Lord Chambrey, my lady."

Of course—the one with the neck like a goose. Eleanor pursed her lips. Chambrey would be the fair choice, but even as she opened her mouth to have Stanton dispose of the other two, a thought struck her. She didn't need to be fair. She could choose to spend the day with the one who appealed to her the most, and she didn't need to make an excuse for it. Valentine had taught her that—it wasn't about being cruel, but it *was* about being fair to herself.

"Stanton, please inform Mr. Noleville that I'll be ready shortly. And let the other two know that I appreciate their interest and hope to see them soon."

The butler nodded, in one fluid movement turning on

his heel, exiting the room, and closing the door behind him. Eleanor took a breath and chose another peach.

"Hm," Zachary muttered, turning a page of the newspaper.

She ignored him, instead seating herself next to Peep. "What are your plans for today, my darling?"

"Well," the little girl answered, "I'm supposed to take a lesson on the pianoforte and then do my studies, but I was thinking of going to the museum instead."

"Oh, you were?"

"Yes. Papa won't like it, but he's at Parliament."

"I'll make you a bargain, then," Eleanor suggested. "You do your pianoforte lesson, and when I return from my drive, I'll take you to the museum."

A peach-juice-covered hand gripped her wrist. "You would? That would be grand. Because Uncle Zachary only likes to look at the naked statues, and I like the mummies."

Zachary cleared his throat. "That is not true."

Eleanor ignored him. "Then we have a—"

"It's only that I admire the workmanship," her brother interrupted.

"I like some of the statues, as well," Eleanor said, meeting his surprised gaze. She didn't know what possessed her this morning, except that her adventure with the Marquis of Deverill had fulfilled her in a way she'd never thought possible, and that she simply didn't . . . care as much what other people—including the members of her own family—might think of her.

"You—you're not supposed to say that," Zachary stumbled. "Good God, Nell. That's infamous."

"If you're free to admire marble breasts, I may admire what I choose, as well."

Peep put both hands over her mouth, which didn't even come close to stifling her giggles. "You said 'breasts,'" she tittered, her voice muffled.

"Oh, now see what you've done?" Zachary snapped, the color of his tanned cheeks deepening. He pushed to his feet. "I'd wager you won't talk that way in front of Noleville."

"Hm. I hadn't considered that," Eleanor mused, allowing her own grin to show. "It would certainly make for an interesting morning."

Pressing his fingers to his temple, Zachary shot her a last glare and stomped out of the room. She and Peep giggled for a moment, then went back to their peaches. Eleanor felt hungry this morning, but she did have a caller waiting for her in the morning room, and she wanted to be out-of-doors. The morning—what was left of it—looked glorious, and sunshine seemed a very good idea. Wanting to go driving in Hyde Park had nothing to do with looking for anyone in particular, of course.

"Aren't you going to stay and breakfast with me?" Penelope asked, as her aunt stood.

"I can't, Peep. I have to go driving."

"But you'll be back to go to the museum with me?"

"In two hours," Eleanor returned. "I promise."

"Very well. I should go take my lesson. Mrs. Bevins has been waiting for me, I think."

Penelope obviously had everyone in the household wrapped around her little finger, and Eleanor could only hope she would enjoy the indulgence while she could. It certainly wouldn't last.

Or would it? Since last night, she had to admit that her pessimism over her dull, planned-out future had faded a little. Or rather, it had been replaced by a sense of hopefulness and self-confidence that she hadn't been aware she lacked. At least she had a basis for comparison in the bedchamber now—though comparing *after* she was married would be too late.

"Good morning, Mr. Noleville," she said, strolling into the morning room.

The earl's son jumped to his feet. "Lady Eleanor. I'm so pleased you decided to go driving with me this morning."

She took in his crisp cravat, his carefully pressed jacket, and the hope in his pleasant, open countenance. He would make for a cheery companion, though she couldn't even fool herself that her mind wasn't elsewhere. She almost felt sorry for poor Roger, except that he'd called on her without first making an appointment and she would have been perfectly within propriety to refuse to join any or all of the three men this morning.

"Shall we?" she asked, gesturing him toward the door.

He'd driven a curricle, his older brother's if she recalled correctly. Evidently the Nolevilles had selected her as the perfect spouse for Roger. Well, she had nothing of the sort in mind.

Eleanor frowned as he handed her into the seat. That wasn't right. She'd decided already that once she'd had her adventure, she would find the man she wanted and marry him before Melbourne could step in with some walking mummy for her. Roger Noleville was far less offensive than some of the other suitors who'd been hounding her heels lately, so obviously she should be keeping an open mind about going driving with him.

"My lady, your maid?" he asked, hesitating as he stood on the ground beside the carriage.

"We're driving in an open curricle through Hyde Park," she said dismissively. "We'd hardly be able to commit an impropriety even if we wished to."

He flushed. "I would never," he stammered.

"No. No, of course you wouldn't," she replied, nearly as nonplussed as he was. Her life had changed last night—or rather, her perception of it had changed—but that didn't mean she could suddenly disregard everything she'd ever learned about propriety and proper behavior. Apparently Valentine had done more than take her virginity, though he would probably laugh if she told him just how earth-shattering she'd found the experience. He'd gain a swelled head in addition to that other swelled body part.

Oh, goodness. Blushing and hoping Roger would attribute it to her poor manners, she sent Stanton back inside the house. A moment later the butler emerged with Helen, already dressed for the outing, behind him. At least her maid knew her duties, even if Eleanor couldn't seem to keep hers in mind today.

As they entered Hyde Park she blinked. Roger had been chatting about something for ten minutes, and she hadn't a clue what it might be. From the smile on his face she decided that a small chuckle would be appropriate, and she forced one from her chest.

"Yes, I thought you'd appreciate that," he said, his smile deepening. "Though I can't imagine why Lady Pugh would wear satin to Vauxhall in the first place."

She had no idea how to reply to that, and settled for shrugging. Usually she hated gossip about her fellows, and made a point not to encourage it, but he might have been talking about a poor batch of satin fabric and the tragic consequences of it, for all she knew.

"You know, last year I asked His Grace your brother for permission to call on you," he went on, glancing at her. His pretty brown eyes didn't seem to carry an ounce of duplicity or insincerity in them. "He didn't precisely refuse me, but neither did he introduce us to one another. I don't suppose he mentioned my interest to you?"

"No, he didn't." And she was hardly surprised by that fact. "Why have you decided to make another attempt now, after a year?"

"Ah. Well, I have . . . noticed that your actions have been a bit more independent of late. I thought I might broach the topic with you. If we deal well, I will approach the duke again."

So he already had the progression of their relationship planned out. She could hardly blame him, she supposed, but she did intend to have some say in the course her life took. Especially now. "Then we shall have to see how well we deal," she returned, smiling back at him.

That statement seemed to please him excessively, and he launched into a discussion of the finest soirees of the Season so far. He certainly knew the nuances of Society, where to be seen and where not to be seen. No doubt Roger Noleville would never make a false step.

"So what did Melbourne actually say when you spoke with him last year?" she asked.

Roger gave a short laugh. "I remember it quite well. It took me three weeks to gather the nerve to approach him. I had a friend introduce me, and then asked if I might have his permission to call on you. His Grace looked at me as though I were an insect, and then he said, 'I shall let you know.' He never did, of course."

"Of course not." What Roger didn't realize was that a

nondenial from Melbourne was tantamount to a ringing endorsement. Sebastian had probably expected Mr. Noleville to proceed, or at least to ask permission a second time.

So there was at least one man her brothers considered adequate for her. And she'd voluntarily gone driving with him. *Drat*. She meant to marry, but not to someone who'd received the Griffin stamp of approval more than a year ago. Neither, though, did she intend to ruin a chance at happiness just to spite her brothers. Damnation, this was complicated.

She opened her mouth to make a comment about the unique decorations at the Granden soiree, but abruptly swallowed the words. *He was here*.

He sat on his bay stallion, Iago, to one side of an intersecting driving path. His blue beaver hat was tilted at its usual jaunty angle on his head, his black, wavy hair touching his collar and swept across one green eye. Her insides clenched in pure lust. *Heavens*. Had it been only twelve hours since they'd held each other, naked, beside the baptismal pond?

Valentine turned his head as though he sensed that she was there. He met her gaze and smiled with easy familiarity, touching his hand to the brim of his hat. And then he turned away.

For the first time she realized that he wasn't alone. A barouche had stopped beside him, a pair of young ladies on the rear seat. The Mandelay sisters, she noted, hiding a sudden frown. A worse set of flirts she'd never met. He needed to be care—

Eleanor shook herself. He knew what he was doing. Precisely what he was doing. For goodness' sake, he probably knew the sisters better than she did. Eleanor swallowed. He and she had had their evening. As she'd already considered, the Marquis of Deverill would hardly look upon it as life-changing. He probably did that sort of thing nightly, anyway.

"Lady Eleanor?"

She started. "I beg your pardon, Mr. Noleville. What were you saying?"

"No begging is necessary. Lord Deverill is a good friend of your family, I believe."

"Yes, he is." And she desperately wanted to talk with him, to find out if he'd given last night—or her—another thought once he'd returned her to Griffin House. But the question would probably prove both painful and pointless, considering where he was and with whom he was chatting.

"Did you need to speak with him?" Roger continued. "I can drive us over there."

"Oh. No, no. I just didn't expect to see him this morning." Eleanor cleared her throat. "He seems somewhat occupied, anyway."

"Yes, he does. Hardly a surprise, given his rather . . . robust reputation."

"They're only talking," she returned, though she wasn't quite certain why she felt the need to defend him. "Just like we are."

"Not just like we are," he said, his brow furrowing. "I called on you at your home, announcing my presence and my interest, and giving any of your brothers ample opportunity to turn me away. And I certainly didn't accost you in the park while you were out taking the air."

"I'm sure he didn't accost anyone," she retorted, at the

same time telling herself to keep her blasted mouth shut. She didn't feel any particular need to be pleasant to Mr. Noleville, but she was *not* going to speak up for Deverill. Not after seeing him happily flirting with Lilith and Judith Mandelay.

"Perhaps not. I would wager the young ladies' parents, though, would be happier seeing them elsewhere."

Well, she couldn't argue with that. "No doubt," she muttered, determinedly turning her attention elsewhere.

The sun shone through a pretty patchwork of clouds, and the light southeast breeze sent the smoke from a thousand chimneys away from Mayfair and in the direction of the Channel. Eleanor took a deep breath. Today was different. Her entire life was different, changed because a man she trusted had helped her find . . . herself. So what if he'd turned his attention elsewhere? So had she.

"Mr. Noleville, you have several older brothers, do you not?" she asked after a long moment of silence.

He looked sideways at her. "I do. Why do you ask?"

"I have several older brothers myself."

"Yes, I'm aware of that."

"My point being, do your brothers ever attempt to . . . govern your life?"

Roger laughed. "No, that would be my father's sworn duty. The rest of the brood barely gets a word in edgewise." Abruptly his amused chuckling broke off. "Well, that was unspeakably rude of me. I beg your forgiveness, Lady Eleanor. I'd forgotten that you lost your par—"

"Please don't worry yourself, Mr. Noleville. I was six when their yacht capsized. While I do miss them, I certainly don't begrudge you your own parents. That would make me a very pitiful creature."

"Which you are not."

Eleanor forced a smile. "Thank you." She shook herself, remembering that her questions did have a point.
"Do you acquiesce to your father's rules and orders?"

"What an odd question. Of course I do; he is the patriarch of the family."

"And he holds your purse strings."

The line of his lips thinning, Noleville drew the curricle
to a halt. "I do not discuss monetary matters with young
ladies. It's not gentlemanly. And if I may be so bold, my
lady, it isn't seemly for you to carry on such conversations, either."

For a moment Eleanor wasn't certain whether to be angry or mortified. It couldn't be a good sign when prospective beaux began criticizing her behavior—she'd never
met a group of men so willing to forgive anything. And
the fact that this beau was correct didn't leave her feeling
any better. "Perhaps you should take me home, if my conversation offends you."

He nodded. "I think that's best. I shall do so at once. I
daresay you are merely out-of-sorts, my lady. A cup of
peppermint tea and a nap will no doubt do you a world of
good."

Eleanor refrained from rolling her eyes, but just barely.
Yes of course there must be something wrong with her. No
female in her right mind would ever question the value of
patriarchal influence or wonder whether even men had
free choice.

Neither of them spoke again until the curricle stopped
at her front door. As soon as Stanton helped her and then
Helen down to the ground, Noleville doffed his hat, said,
"Good day to you," and sent his team back down the drive.

She didn't bother to reply as she stomped inside and up
the stairs, her maid at her heels. "Stupid," she grumbled,

not certain whether she referred to Roger Noleville or herself.

"That was quick," Zachary said, sticking his head out of the billiards room door.

"Yes, I suppose it was. I made the mistake of asking an honest question."

Her brother took a step farther into the hallway. "How honest?"

"Oh, don't worry, it wasn't scandalous or anything. Just something about authority and freedom."

"Good God, Nell, you're supposed to talk about the weather and who's courting whom. Not treatises on free will."

She grimaced at him. "It was hardly that. And his reply was less than enlightening. He told me I needed peppermint tea and a nap."

Zachary laughed. "If I told you that, you'd try to blacken my eye."

"Both of your eyes. Now leave me alone."

"Yes, my lady."

Before he could vanish again, though, Eleanor remembered her promise about escorts. "Zach?"

Dark hair and gray eyes peered around the doorway again. "Yes?"

"Will you escort me to the Goldsborough dinner tonight?"

"Oh. Ah, certainly."

Eleanor put her hands on her hips. "What now?"

"Nothing. I was going to go to the Society and play faro, but I can do that tomorrow night."

Another head appeared, much like the first, except for the green tint to the light gray eyes. "I'll take you."

She nodded. "Thank you, Shay."

"He only volunteered because of the Goldsboroughs' cook," Zachary put in.

"What?" Lifting both eyebrows, Eleanor looked at the middle Griffin brother. "A cook?"

"Gads, Nell, Mrs. Neal is at least ninety. It's her chocolate desserts I'm after. Now if you'll excuse me, I have to kill Zachary."

"Could you wait an hour or two? I'd like him to take Peep and me to the museum. He can visit the statues."

"Ha ha."

Shay brushed past her, calling for his jacket. "In that case, I'm coming, too."

Valentine sat at his desk, four invitations spread out on the mahogany surface before him. A dinner, a recital, and two small soirees. All for tonight, and all at approximately the same time.

He tapped his finger against the recital. It was in all likelihood the one Eleanor Griffin would be least likely to attend, and it was the least appealing to him of the four. Therefore, that was where he should go for the evening. Of course he also had a myriad of clubs where he could spend several hours. Clubs also had the additional bonus of liquor and cards—and no young ladies of good standing.

Grimacing, he pushed the recital invitation off the desk. A club definitely had more appeal than two hours of squeaky viola or strident pianoforte. With a nod he swept the other three invitations into a stack and dumped them into his top drawer. Halfway to his feet, though, he stopped and sat again.

Maybe he could fool anyone else, but he'd long ago moved past attempting that with himself. Besides being counterproductive, it never worked. And so he had to admit that he wasn't looking to avoid seeing Eleanor, or trying to steer clear of any postcoital clinging or hysterics—the sort of thing he usually avoided with a passion. He had even more cause to do so now, since seeing her in the park today with Roger Noleville had been like having a ramrod driven through his chest. Considering the nastiness of that particular sensation, he wasn't at all sure why he wanted to see her again. But he did, and he wasn't going to any damned club tonight.

"You are mad, Valentine," he muttered, yanking the drawer open and freeing the other three invitations again. All three were possibilities, since the Griffins knew all three households and would have been invited to all three events.

With a grumble he grabbed one of them and stuffed the other two into his pocket. One in three; he generally liked those odds. As for the reason *why* he was so determined to see her, that would require self-reflection, and he avoided that whenever possible.

Chapter 16

As he entered the ballroom of his second soiree of the evening, Valentine began to consider that he should have engaged in at least a little self-reflection before he went scampering about Mayfair looking for a woman he supposedly didn't want to see. Especially considering that he couldn't seem to find her.

He detested so-called intimate soirees; all it meant was that the hostess invited strictly those people with whom she wished to be linked, or more commonly, those with whom she wished her son or daughter to be linked. And Mrs. Stewart had two daughters. Even though he was seldom the target, circumstances had been known to cause all sorts of odd behavior among the marriage-challenged.

"Deverill," the Duke of Melbourne said, clapping him on the shoulder with far too much enthusiasm.

Valentine started, then realized he actually had reason to be relieved to see Eleanor's brother. "Don't be so happy to see me," he murmured, dodging behind a potted plant as Iris Stewart began a turn in their direction. "I'm not here to frighten off the chits who want to approach you. In fact, I have no intention of being pulled into this Hades at all. I'm only here looking for Nell."

"Bastard," the duke grunted, talking behind clenched teeth and a faux smile, his gaze on the young Miss Stewart as she approached.

"Sorry, there's only room for one of us back here. Now where's Nell?"

"She and Charlemagne went to the Goldsborough dinner. Leave while you can; I'll distract the natives this once, but that will put you in my debt again."

Valentine scowled. "No, it won't. I'm escaping in order to fulfill my previous debt. You can't tack on another one, especially since your damned calendar listed four potential destinations for your sister tonight."

The duke sighed. "Fine." He took a step forward, out of Valentine's line of sight. "Miss Stewart. You are looking especially lovely this evening."

At the sound of a grating giggle, Valentine grinned. As soon as Melbourne had maneuvered the older Stewart sister away from his hiding place, he dodged out the side entrance and returned to his coach. "Goldsborough House," he instructed.

He thought Dawson sighed just before the coachman clucked to the team, but considering that Goldsborough House would be their third destination in an hour, he decided to overlook the insubordination. At least the earl's home was close by. He would be arriving almost halfway through the meal, but as the Marquis of Deverill, he was expected to do such things.

His tardiness would also mean that he would be relegated a place at the foot of the table; Lady Goldsborough would have reshuffled the seating to cover a vacant space farther up the table as soon as the butler confirmed that he wasn't present. But that was a good thing, since Lady Eleanor would be nowhere near the end of the table. He could look at her, but he wouldn't have to speak with her.

The Goldsborough butler announced him, and he followed the servant into the large dining room. Since he was titled, everyone stood to acknowledge his presence, but he deliberately refrained from looking about for Eleanor. "My apologies, George, my lady," he said instead, stepping forward to greet the host and hostess. "I had some business I needed to attend to."

"Ah, and what was her name?" the earl muttered with a grin, shaking his hand.

"George," his wife chastised, curtsying. "We're pleased you could join us, Lord Deverill."

"Thank you, Lady Goldsborough."

"Deeds, please show Lord Deverill to his chair," the countess instructed, seating herself again.

As he strolled the length of the table behind the butler, he finally looked at the gaggle of fellow diners. The most prestigious guests would of course be seated closest to the head of the table, and Eleanor and Charlemagne were on either side of the earl and the countess, respectively. "Shay, Lady Eleanor," he greeted, nodding.

"Valentine. Makes sense you'd arrive in time for Lady Goldsborough's famous chocolate dessert," Shay returned, chuckling.

"It'd take Bonaparte attacking London to make me miss that," he said, though he'd never heard the dessert mentioned before.

Eleanor didn't say anything, though she inclined her head politely enough. His abdomen tightened as he scented her lavender perfume. Sweet Lucifer, he should have gone to a club.

As he'd predicted, he ended up at the foot of the table, with Amelia Hartwood at one elbow and Roger Noleville at the other. "Miss Amelia, Mr. Noleville," he said, accepting the wine one of the footmen offered.

"M-my lord," Amelia stammered, her cheeks darkening to an alarming shade of red.

Valentine stifled a sigh. Of course he would end up seated next to the daughter of a minister. Lucifer was laughing at him again, but after last night he supposed he deserved it. Bedding the virginal sister of his best friend when he was supposed to be protecting her. It had to be among the lowest things he'd ever done.

"Deverill. Saw you at the park this morning," Noleville said, his own tone rather gruff.

Noleville was rather stiff as well, Valentine recalled. Wonderful. All this because he wanted a glimpse of Eleanor, when he might simply have called on one of her brothers at their house and avoided having to spend at least the next hour between the holier-than-thou duo.

Now that he was trapped, however, he might as well have a little fun with the circumstances. "Yes, I saw you as well," he replied to Roger. "Driving with Lady Eleanor, if I'm not mistaken."

"Yes, I was."

"Courting her, are you?"

Roger blinked. "That's a bit personal, don't you think?"

It probably was, and it certainly wasn't his usual roundabout way of finding out information. As he asked the question, though, he'd felt that wrench inside his gut similar to what he'd experienced when he'd first seen Eleanor sitting in another man's curricle. "I'm a family friend."

"So she said. In fact, she even defended your behavior toward the Mandelay sisters."

"What behavior?" Valentine countered, stiffening a little. "We were chatting, I believe."

"I don't wish to argue with you, my lord. But neither can I condone a single gentleman accosting young, unescorted females in public."

"You—"

"Deverill," Shay called from the head of the table, "who was it that sold you Iago?"

Valentine took a breath. *Be calm,* he told himself. He hadn't come to begin a fight with anyone. And besides, given Noleville's lack of imagination, he doubted Eleanor could seriously look at the young man as a suitor. "I didn't purchase him," he said in a more carrying voice. "I won him in a hand of ecarte. From Wellington."

From the murmur that ran along both sides of the table, several of the guests were surprised that the Duke of Wellington played ecarte—much less that he ever lost. Given his skill at strategy, however, the duke was a surprisingly poor gambler. And Valentine had badly wanted the half-mad Iago.

Before Noleville or someone else could then accuse him of cheating the duke or some other nonsense, footmen brought out the next course, the apparently famous aforementioned dessert. It looked like raspberries in melted chocolate with some sort of cream topping. Tentatively he raised a spoonful to his mouth and looked up to see whether anyone else had already tasted the concoction.

Pale gray eyes met his from down the length of the table. Valentine stopped, the spoon halfway to his mouth, and tried to interpret the look she gave him. He expected anger or remorse, or more pleasantly lust, but unless he was mistaken, she was disappointed.

In him? Why, in God's name? His performance last night had been exceptional, if he did say so himself, and she knew him well enough to be unsurprised by both his tardiness and his halfhearted flirtation with the Mandelay twins in the park. If they weren't so chatty and simpering he might have pursued the conversation more seriously, but even before he'd sighted Eleanor, his heart simply hadn't been in it.

Holding her gaze, he took a bite of dessert. Not bad, but hardly worthy of the fame Shay accorded it. But now he had something more significant to contemplate, anyway. He needed a word with Eleanor. Yes, he was supposed to be guarding her, and he was doing a damned poor job of that, but she couldn't possibly be contemplating settling into matrimony just because he'd provided her with a swimming and a lovemaking session. And she certainly couldn't be serious about marrying someone as stuffy and dull as Roger Noleville. And she had the nerve to be disappointed in *him*.

Directly following dessert, the ladies abandoned the table, going to gossip or embroider or whatever it was they did when no men were present. The butler brought around a box of fine cigars and some port, while Valentine rose to seat himself beside Shay.

"What the devil are you doing here?" Eleanor's brother whispered, lifting his glass to cover his words. "I'm only in attendance because Nell requested an escort."

"I have a duty, if you'll recall," Valentine pointed out, grateful for once that Melbourne had wrangled him into this fiasco. Otherwise he would have to be admitting some rather troubling things to himself, such as the fact that he hadn't liked seeing Eleanor in another man's company today, and that whatever look she'd given him earlier bothered him.

"I would think this would be considered a 'safe' outing. I'm here, at any rate."

"Well, I didn't know that, now did I?" Valentine lied. "How many times do I have to tell your brother to send me a note?"

Charlemagne chuckled. "At least the dessert was worth the trip."

Valentine took a breath. It was the best opening he was likely to receive. "Speaking of dessert, Nell didn't eat much of it. Is she feeling well?"

"She's swamped with suitors," her brother replied, humor still in his voice. "I don't think she had any idea that calling off her guards would open the floodgates like this. Three this morning, and four more after luncheon, all just coming by in the hope that she'll grant them a few moments so they can charm her into matrimony."

"Seven in one day?"

Her brother nodded. "Truth be told, if they weren't so obviously the dregs, I'd be concerned. But I know she'd never settle for one of them."

"Is she looking seriously toward anyone at all?"

"Not as far as I can tell. She doesn't talk to me much, though. I've become one of the enemy."

"Men?"

"Her brother."

"I think she'll come around, Shay," Valentine supplied. "She just wants a chance to experience new things before she settles down."

"Aren't you enlightened tonight? What brought that

on?" Charlemagne reached over and felt of Valentine's forehead. "Are you well?"

Valentine knocked his hand away. "I have moments of clarity which surprise even me. This is simply one of them."

That had been close. Yes, he and Eleanor were friends, but he absolutely didn't want to give any of her brothers the tiniest clue that he'd been doing more than keeping an eye on her.

Lord Hennessy began some bawdy tale about a milk-maid and a baron. He claimed it was all true, but considering that if turned inside out the chit's gown would have been nearly impossible to fasten, Valentine didn't believe a word of it. Stating his disbelief aloud, however, would have meant sitting through the explanation and everyone else's opinions on the manner, and he wanted to be else-where. Only when the men were finished with their idiotic gossiping would they join the ladies in the drawing room.

Of course he really didn't need to talk in depth with Eleanor; he merely wanted to know what that look had been about, and to be certain that she had no interest in Noleville. After all, until Melbourne called off the hunt, he still had an obligation to look after her.

"Shall we join the ladies, then?" Lord Goldsborough finally said around a belch. "Don't want them forgetting us."

"Thank God," Valentine muttered, pushing to his feet.

Shay chuckled. "You need more practice at spending time in civilized settings."

"No, I don't. I need to spend less time there. Then it won't bother me."

"You're hopeless."

"So I've been told."

When they entered the drawing room the ladies were all

laughing about something. As long as it wasn't he, he didn't much care, but Eleanor was smiling as well. He slowed, gazing at her. It was so odd. Until a few weeks ago he'd never thought of her as more than the sibling of a friend, a child he'd known for years and one he would classify more as a pet than a female, not that he had much respect for either.

But then they'd engaged in an actual conversation—several of them, in fact, and he hadn't known what to make of things. He did know he'd enjoyed the time he spent with her, but that certainly hadn't led to anything good. Enjoyable, yes, but not good.

Lady Goldsborough lurched to her feet as he entered the room. "Lord Deverill, there's a seat next to Lady Wendermere," the countess exclaimed, gesturing at the old bat.

"So there is," he agreed, taking the chair beside Eleanor.

"You should have sat with Lady Wendermere," Eleanor murmured. "She's hard of hearing and could use some charming company."

"Then someone else can be charming. I'm not the only damned man present, and I prefer my conversations to have two sides."

He wanted to ask how she was, whether she had any regrets about last night. Asking, though, would mean staying to hear the answers—and he was quite certain he didn't want to do that.

"I was surprised to see you wander in here this evening," she continued in a low voice, while the other guests cajoled Lady Goldsborough into sitting at the pianoforte for a tune or two.

Valentine shrugged. "Seemed as good a place as any to get a meal."

"So it had nothing to do with me?"

For a moment he just looked at her. Eleanor preferred being direct; he knew that about her. He generally preferred it himself, but not tonight. "Should it have?" he asked.

"No, I suppose not."

"I mean, I flipped a coin," he lied, "about whether to venture here or to the Stewart soiree. The Stewarts actually won, but then I recalled that their only offspring are two unmarried daughters with large feet. Hence my presence here."

"I see." She looked away, toward the group of guests gathered around the pianoforte. "Might I ask you a question?" she said slowly.

Valentine hid a grimace. "Yes."

"Did last night mean anything to you?"

Damnation. "Last night? Of course it meant something. It was quite pleasant, you are exceptionally lovely, and I hadn't been swimming in a very long time." He almost added that he wouldn't mind repeating the experience, but restrained himself at the last moment.

"Swimming is the thing you hadn't done in a while," she repeated. "The other is more frequent."

"I've never made a secret of that, Eleanor," he returned, a creeping unease shivering along his spine. God, she couldn't be jealous. He didn't want her to be jealous—but neither did he want to discuss last night any further. "How was your drive with Roger Noleville this morning?"

"How was your chat with the Mandelay sisters?" she retorted.

"Dull as dirt," he said smoothly, "but it passed the time."

She gazed at him. "So there was nothing you would rather have been doing?"

He didn't know whether she was looking to comment on

his lack of usefulness or whether she wanted a simple compliment. Either one meant admitting to something he wasn't quite ready to confess to, but neither was he prepared to tolerate that disappointed look of hers. "The thing I would rather have been doing wasn't possible, since you were unavailable."

Eleanor blinked. "Oh. So you—"

"Yes, I would. You, however, made a stipulation, and I will honor it."

"Then it's just on to the next chit for you?"

As if he could get Eleanor out of his thoughts long enough to call on anyone. This conversation was becoming a little too personal—and a little too close to encouraging him toward self-reflection. "Eleanor, I'm not the one who wanted to change any part of my life. That was you. And if there's more you wish to do, I'll be happy to oblige. But don't expect that I will alter an inch. I'm quite happy with my life as it is."

"You mean to say that you're happy with complete frivolity and never making any more than a brief physical connection with anyone," she said, her tone still quiet.

"That's none of your damned affair. And besides, you're the one who said 'one night only.'" He stood, still careful to keep his voice lowered. "Don't expect me to become a bloody monk or something, just because—"

"Excuse me," she said, rising as well. "But if you don't mind, *I* need to face some responsibilities and make some serious decisions about my future. Your determination to be frivolous is giving me an aching head."

"You're giving me an aching head," he shot back. "Insult me if it makes you feel better, my dear, but spend a little time looking at yourself in the mirror. I think you might just find that you envy me more than you disapprove of me."

"Maybe I do, in some ways," she admitted, surprising him to his bones. "Your freedom to do and say what you want, and keep company with whom you please. But I do not envy your lack of . . . feeling for anyone but yourself."

That was enough of that. "Thank you for your insightful conversation," he snapped, turning on his heel.

He was outside and back inside his coach before he realized he still held a snifter of brandy in one hand. With a scowl he downed the remainder of the liquor and tossed the crystal onto the opposite seat. If he'd been thinking clearly he would have reminded the damned chit that just last night she'd declared him to be some sort of hero. Of course he had feelings for and about other people; just because he chose not to share them with anyone, including himself, didn't mean they didn't exist.

Valentine growled. Thinking was bad. He'd learned that a long time ago. Leaning out the window, he slammed the flat of his hand against the door panel. "Dawson, take me to Boodle's."

"Yes, my lord."

Eleanor sat again, trying to ignore the empty place beside her when everyone else was practically seated on top of one another in the small drawing room. The high titter of women giggling, Shay's suave drawl, Lady Goldsborough's sure fingers coaxing the pianoforte into a jig. Well, she should have expected that Valentine wouldn't sit about and listen to her insult him.

Today was supposed to have been easier. Everything after last night was supposed to simply fall into place, leaving her content with the path she was now supposed to see clearly before her. She'd had her adventure, she'd indulged her most deep-seated, naughty daydreams—and every time she set eyes on Valentine, she wanted to indulge again. Damnation, she was supposed to be able to set all of yesterday behind her and look forward to settling the rest of her life.

Perhaps that was the problem. Deverill had done precisely that, and she still couldn't move beyond how freeing it felt to be with him.

"Nell," Shay said, making her jump as he dropped onto the cushions beside her, "I've seen hanged thieves who looked happier than you. What's wrong?"

"Nothing. I'm just thinking."

"You've been thinking since you came back from your drive with Noleville this morning." Her brother glanced in Roger's direction. "Did he say something to you? Because agreement to stay out of your affairs or not, I'll happily break him in two for you."

Eleanor wondered whether he would still make so generous an offer if he knew Deverill, rather than Noleville, was to blame for her pensiveness. Breaking Valentine in half would certainly be a more challenging—and dangerous—prospect. "That's not necessary," she answered. "I am tired, though. Would you mind seeing me home?"

"Not a bit." Standing, Charlemagne pulled her to her feet. They made their excuses to Lord and Lady Goldsborough, and her brother led the way outside. As soon as their driver brought the coach around, he helped her inside and climbed in behind her.

"My apologies for dragging you away," she said, still trying to pull her thoughts together. She just needed to not think about Deverill, and not think about last night. Eleanor stifled a scowl. *How difficult could it be, to not think about the most important moments of her life?*

"I was actually looking for an excuse to leave," Shay

drawled. "I only came because of you and the dessert, remember?"

She forced a smile. "How could I forget?"

"So what's wrong? Really?"

"I told you, I'm just t—"

"Tired. Yes, I heard you. That looked like an interesting conversation you and Valentine were having. Until he left, that is. Did *he* say something to you? One of his usual nasty little tidbits?"

That *had* been what he'd said, she realized. Some of his usual cynical, jaded observations on life. She was used to hearing them—and she'd always found them amusing. But not now. Not when he was trying to say that nothing touched him, or meant anything to him. Not when he implied that *she* meant nothing to him. "Oh, I suppose so. But one has to expect to hear nonsense when one listens to Deverill."

"I suppose so," he repeated.

They sat in silence for several minutes, Eleanor feigning sleepiness and pretending she hadn't managed to worry Charlemagne. Of course he'd probably been worried for the past few weeks, since she'd begun her rebellion. She sighed. "So who do you consider the best prospect to join the family as my husband?"

He started. "What? You're asking me? I thought this entire exercise was about you not listening to our advice."

"I didn't say I'd heed it," she teased. "I'm only asking your opinion."

"Well, not Noleville, the dull sock," he muttered.

"Isn't he on Melbourne's list?"

"I think there are several dead people on Melbourne's list."

"Aha!"

Shay scowled. " 'Aha' what?"

"I *knew* Sebastian had made a list of potential husbands for me. Now you tell me ev—"

He scooted back as far as he could from her in the confined carriage. "No, you don't. You ask Melbourne if you want to know anything about Melbourne."

"Coward."

"Damned right. And I won't be responsible for you refusing every eligible man on that list just to spite His Grace."

"Then I'll have to refuse every eligible man in London just to be sure one of his favorites doesn't sneak through."

Shay cursed. "Don't act like a child, Nell. We've done everything you wanted. You can't keep acting like an Amazon forever."

An Amazon. She actually liked the comparison. "It's not about being a child, Charlemagne; it's about *not* being a child. Give me a good reason why no one ever bothered to share this list with me. For heaven's sake, they're supposed to be men you have in mind to spend their lives with me. And yet I'm not allowed to know their names? Who decided that?"

"And what's wrong with someone you choose also being someone who happens to appear on Melbourne's list?"

Eleanor wanted to scream. The more she found herself changing, the more her brothers' intractable manner left her frustrated and angry. "Obviously I'm taking this up with the wrong brother."

"And that is what I've been trying to tell y—"

"I had thought you might have some standing in Melbourne's eyes. I wonder whether he'll tell me which females appear on the marriage list for you?"

Shay's expression darkened. "There is no list for me," he enunciated. "And you won't trick me into revealing anything. Talk to Sebastian. Or better yet, make your own damned list and show it to him. Then you'll have somewhere to start your negotiations."

She almost retorted that she had no intention of negotiating, but she knew her oldest brother well enough to realize that of course she would at least be expected to make some sort of concession. Perhaps Charlemagne was correct. For a moment her mind snapped to the image of the man who'd most been on her mind over the past weeks. But she couldn't put Valentine on a list. Besides its being a useless exercise in penmanship given the marquis's infatuation with bachelorhood, Sebastian would never seriously consider him. And neither could she. But after last night, and even after their annoying conversation earlier, he wouldn't leave her thoughts—or her dreams.

"Nell?"

With a start she straightened. "Hm?"

Her brother leaned forward and swiped a finger across her cheek. "You're crying," he announced.

"No, I'm not."

He lifted an eyebrow. "Do tell."

"Really," she attempted. "I'm terribly happy. I'm accomplishing everything I dreamed of. Everything's proceeding precisely as I imagined."

"So I see." Charlemagne looked at her for a long moment, while she tried to fade into the shadows and not sniff. She knew Valentine's character, and even liked most of what and who he was. But was she still simply the sister of his dearest friend? Once she brought anger and emotion to whatever it was they had, did that signal him to move on?

"So it's not Noleville," Shay said slowly. "I don't think he has enough imagination or personality to make you cry."

"Leave be, Shay."

"It's Valentine, isn't it?"

"Val—no! Who cares about Valentine? I certainly don't."

He looked as though he wanted to respond to that, but luckily the coach rolled up their front drive. She climbed down to the ground as soon as Stanton pulled open the carriage door.

"My lord?" the butler queried, glancing into the coach when Charlemagne remained seated.

"It's still early," her brother replied, rapping on the ceiling to signal the driver. "I have someone I need to see."

Chapter 17

～⌒◯◯⌒～

"Will there be anything else tonight, my lord?"

Valentine glanced over his shoulder. Hobbes leaned into the doorway, his feet already turned in the direction of the servants' quarters. "No. Go to bed. And send Matthews off as well. I'm not in the mood to check for traps."

"Thank you, my lord."

Nodding, Valentine took another deep swallow of brandy. Boodle's hadn't provided what he'd wanted tonight, either. Eleanor's damned questions about his life had cursed his luck at faro, vingt-et-un, and loo, and as drunk as he wanted to get, he'd realized he'd be safer at home.

Down the hall someone rapped at the front door. Wonderful. It was either some chit he didn't want to see, or some chit's husband, whom he definitely didn't want to see. Hobbes would still be close enough to take care of it. Settling deeper in his chair before the library fireplace, Valentine finished off the snifter of brandy and refilled it to the brim. Amber liquid sloshed over the rim of the crystal onto his antique mahogany end table. Hm. He *was* drunk, if he was spilling perfectly good liquor.

The knock repeated. A moment later, he heard Hobbes pull open the door and engage in a low-voiced conversation with someone. The butler's voice grew louder, and another male voice joined in. Valentine frowned.

"Charlemagne?" he muttered, twisting his head to face the library door as it shoved open.

"So you're not in," Eleanor's brother grumbled, slamming the door closed behind him again.

Valentine's first thought was that Eleanor had told her family about their tryst last night. If that had been the case, however, it would be Melbourne and a pistol charging into the room—not the middle brother. "Not socially," he returned. "But you usually don't require me to be social, so what can I do for you?"

"What did you say to Nell?"

"Beg pardon?"

Shay dropped into the seat opposite him. "At dinner. You had a conversation with her, and then you left. What did you say?"

"I don't remember. But whatever it was, it's not any of your damned affair. I was blackmailed into keeping an eye on her, not into reporting *my* conversation."

"You made her cry, Deverill."

Valentine lifted an eyebrow to cover his abrupt dismay. Thank God he could blame the emotion on being three sheets to the leeward. "Are you certain it was me?" he drawled. "It seems that her family's been providing her with a fair share of aggravation."

"It was you. And you damned well remember. Melbourne didn't recruit you to make things worse."

"Is that was he's calling it? Recruitment?"

"Don't change the subject."

"I don't remember what we talked about," Valentine lied. "Chits are all watering pots, anyway. How do you know the wind merely didn't start blowing in the wrong direction? I hope you don't go out on a rampage every time a chit cries, Shay. You'd never get a moment's rest."

"I only go on a rampage when this one cries, Deverill. She doesn't do it often."

Valentine took another swallow of brandy. Damnation. They'd only been chatting, and she'd made him angry. She'd started it, anyway. "I wouldn't put much store in anything a female says, Charlemagne. No doubt she wants something from you. A new gown, perhaps. One of those low-cut ones, hopefully. Delicious, those."

"That's enough of that. And how the devil do you manage to make women like you, when you view them with such disgust?"

"It's not disgust. They have their place, just like a . . . pig, or a donkey. But I wouldn't make the mistake of treating a pig like anything but what it is, or using it for anything but bacon."

"Tell me you don't seriously believe that." Charlemagne stood again, no doubt preparing to storm out in a burst of indignity.

Valentine climbed to his feet as well, with considerably more difficulty than usual. He hated missing a good show. "Of course I do. And so do you. You're just too squeamish to admit it."

"It's not squeamishness, Valentine," Shay said, no trace of humor in his voice. "I don't have the luxury or the inclination to be that kind of bastard—I had a mother, and I have a sister, and a niece. I don't view any of them as bloody farm animals. Whatever you said to Eleanor, you owe her an apology."

"Nonsense." Valentine snorted, taking another generous swallow of brandy. As it traveled down his throat, it didn't burn with the fire it used to; good God, if he'd come to the point that not even brandy could engage him any longer, he might as well put a ball in his head. After tonight he didn't believe he could sink much lower in life, anyway.

"You will ap—"

"I had a mother as well, my boy," he drawled. "When I try and conjure her countenance, however, the faces of all the whores my father bedded after her demise twist and mingle about until I can't remember which one is dear Mama, and which one is the lightskirt." He shrugged. "Then again they're all the same, I imagine."

Charlemagne hit him. If Valentine hadn't been drunk he would have seen it coming, but as the fist met his left eye he stumbled backward and landed hard in the chair behind him.

"I don't know what the devil Sebastian was thinking when he sent you to look after Eleanor, but consider yourself relieved of your duties, you swine." The Duke of Melbourne's middle brother wiped his fingers on a kerchief, dropping the thing onto the floor as if he no longer wanted to be associated with it. "To make it perfectly clear, Deverill, stay away from my sister. Very far away."

Even after the library door slammed shut, Valentine remained in his chair. Gazing at the remains of the brandy in his glass, he ignored the further yells and the additional door slam from the direction of his foyer. If he'd been sober, he would have retaliated—either by calling Charlemagne out, or more likely by simply beating the living hell out of him.

But for what? For calling him a swine? The devil knew he'd been called far worse than that, and for far less reason. No, even drunk, his first thought after being knocked off his pins had been that no one—*no one*—was going to prevent him from seeing Eleanor Griffin again.

"Fuck," he muttered, and downed the rest of the brandy.

"I want to see the list," Eleanor stated, marching into her eldest brother's office.

Sebastian looked up from an accounts book, but not to gaze at her. His eyes flicked instead in the direction of Mr. Rivers, the Griffin family finance man. "Rivers, give me a moment, will you?"

"Of course, Your Grace." With a bow in Eleanor's direction, the accountant slipped out of the room and closed the door behind him.

"Now, what was it you wanted, Nell?" her brother asked.

"Firstly, I didn't realize you were engaged with Mr. Rivers," she muttered, walking to the window and back. Damn it all, she'd meant to appear all suave confidence and reasonableness. "I apologize for interrupting you."

Gray eyes assessed her. "No matter. You said something about a list?"

Eleanor cleared her throat, resolutely seating herself in the chair that Rivers had vacated. "Yes. The list you've made of men you feel would make me a suitable husband."

"I don't have any such thing."

"Yes, you do. Charlemagne said—"

He leaned forward. "Do you actually think I would sit down and put pen to paper to name men you might marry?"

It didn't sound like him when he described it that way. "But—"

"I have several persons in my mind, as I imagine you do yourself. But I wouldn't write them down. That would be fairly piggish and arrogant of me, wouldn't you say?"

That had been precisely what she'd meant to say once he refused to give her access to the list. Now, foundering to sort out a new road to take, Eleanor frowned. "Then will you please tell me some of the names you have in mind?"

"Why?"

"You're the one who knows everything," she snapped, too quickly to draw herself back.

"Evidently not where you're concerned. So are you interested in my opinion, or do you mean to avoid everyone I name just out of spite?"

"I'm . . . interested. In truth this rebellion has done little but cause a stampede of silly males to camp themselves on my doorstep. That is not what I wanted from it." Her rebellion had also taken her several steps beyond where she'd meant to travel, and the ease with which she'd erred stunned her. As did the way she couldn't stop imagining repeating her mistake—and with the same man, despite the fact that at this moment she was furious with him.

"So you want to call this war off?" he queried, lifting an eyebrow.

"No! I'm only asking who you might envision as my perfect mate."

Sebastian looked down for a moment, closing the accounts book. "Perhaps we might discuss this later," he said slowly.

"Why is that? Are you afr—"

"At the moment you have five gentlemen waiting in the morning room for your appearance."

Drat. "But—"

"This is *your* rebellion. If you want to end it, then end it. But I'm not going to offer my opinion of a gentleman when you've specifically asked me not to. Just remember that some of these men would love nothing more than to put you in a compromising position to force a marriage. Tread carefully, Eleanor. Freedom does have a price, as I believe I've already pointed out."

She had to stifle the urge to growl. "So I shouldn't bother attempting to make amends to you. It's either fight or surrender for me."

"If you wish to negotiate a ceasefire, I suggest you come with concessions. I have all the time in the world, and will outlast you in a siege. And don't expect me to step in when a natural consequence of one of your demands becomes inconvenient for you. By now you could have as many as a dozen callers awaiting your presence."

Frustrated beyond anything she could tolerate, Eleanor pulled herself to her feet. "I won't surrender. If you'd shown me the least bit of compassion just now, I might have. But you've only demonstrated again what an unforgiving tyrant you are. Good morning."

"If I were a tyrant, Eleanor, you'd already be married. So good morning," he returned. "And let Stanton or one of us know where you'll be off to, and with whom."

She slammed the door behind her, but Sebastian could still practically feel her glare through the heavy oak. Drawing a breath, he reached for the bell to summon Stanton and have Rivers returned to the office. But before he could do so, the office door swung open again. This time Zachary strode into the room, towing Charlemagne behind him. That sight was unusual enough in itself, since it was usually Zachary being dragged in to see him over something.

"Did you hear what this idiot did?" Zachary asked, dropping into the chair Rivers and then Nell had vacated.

"I believe I'm about to," the duke said dryly. "Enlighten me."

"It was necessary," Shay said in a clipped, angry voice. "And you should never have allowed it in the first place, Melbourne."

If there was one thing Sebastian didn't like, it was other people deciding he'd done something wrong and then taking steps to correct it—especially without seeing him first, and especially when they didn't have all the facts. "What did you do, Charlemagne?"

The middle Griffin brother folded his arms across his chest in a typical show of stubbornness.

"He hit Deverill," Zachary supplied. "And warned him to stay away from Nell."

Sebastian clenched his jaw. "You hit Deverill? And he didn't kill you?"

"He was drunk."

"And why, precisely, did you feel it necessary to hit my friend and to relieve him of his obligation to me?"

"He . . . he said something to Nell last night that made her cry."

Well, that was unexpected. "What did he say?"

Shay grimaced. "I don't know."

"You don't—"

"She wouldn't tell me. And neither would he. But she'd been out of sorts all afternoon, and then—what do we need him for, anyway? She's been asking us to escort her, and isn't that what you had in mind? Someone you trust keeping an eye on her? We're better suited for that than Deverill. I wouldn't trust him near anything female, anyway. You should have heard what he said."

Melbourne straightened. "Did he say something disrespectful about Nell?"

"Not specifically. It was about females in general. About his own mother, particularly. While I don't think Nell has the slightest clue about what she's doing, no one who thinks that of her sex should be allowed within a hundred miles of her."

Slowly Sebastian pushed to his feet. "So you confronted a drunken man, coaxed him into saying something regrettable, and then hit him for it. In public, no doubt."

Shay shifted. "No. In his library."

"A private drunk. Did you stop to think what might have prompted Valentine to do something uncharacteristic like drink in private?"

"Like perhaps he felt badly that he'd said something to hurt Nell's feelings?" Zachary supplied, nudging Charlemagne in the back with one elbow.

"As if Deverill feels anything."

"When did this happen, pray tell?" Sebastian asked, anger and frustration curling down his spine. Damn it. The only person Nell seemed inclined to confide in, and not only had she and Valentine argued, but Charlemagne had assaulted him. And *he'd* just lost his best weapon in keeping Eleanor safe.

"Last night," Shay muttered. "Late."

"Since he hasn't called you out, I'll assume Valentine's in a forgiving mood. You will apologize to him."

His color darkening, Shay shook his head. "I will not."

"You will, or I will on your behalf."

"You're too forgiving, Melbourne."

Sebastian snorted. "Tell that to Nell. You might give him today to engage himself elsewhere, but do it by tomorrow, Charlemagne. I thought you were the sensible brother."

"I say," Zachary contributed indignantly, but the other two ignored him.

With a curse the middle Griffin brother stomped out of the room. Zachary reached for a cigar and lit it on the table light.

"This is a fine tangle, isn't it?" he commented. "And thank you for the insult."

"You haven't exactly been helpful, Zach. I'm in the middle of doing accounts. Leave. And send Rivers back in."

Zachary stood. "Just watch that you don't run out of allies, Melbourne. You're beginning to make Nell look reasonable."

The duke took a breath. None of this was reasonable, and the sooner everyone came to their senses, the better.

That reminded him of something, though. With a glance toward the half-open door he pulled a piece of paper from a desk drawer, took a quick look at it to make certain he had the correct parchment, and held it up to the light at his elbow. Once it was engulfed in flames, he tossed it into the fireplace brazier. No sense leaving that about for Eleanor to find.

Hot air leaking from the open front door fogged when it hit the cold night as Valentine let one of the Halfax footmen take his coat, hat, and gloves. He'd nearly bypassed attending the soiree, but after Charlemagne's assault, he wasn't going to give the hothead the satisfaction of thinking he'd been intimidated. And besides, he hadn't seen Eleanor in an entire day, and he wanted to apologize.

Why he'd been in the wrong he didn't know, but it made sense. She was intelligent and compassionate, and she'd been the one crying. Ergo, he'd gone too far in expressing his damned opinion. He hadn't meant for her to cry.

He hadn't meant for a great many things to happen where she was concerned. And he knew himself well enough to realize that the best thing he could do for Eleanor Griffin was keep his distance. He'd been relieved of his duties in spying on her, anyway, and thank God for that. So of course at his first opportunity he'd gone looking for her.

As he entered the ballroom to the sound of the self-important butler announcing his presence, he saw her. She'd worn a new Madame Costanza creation, yellow and maroon silk that looked as though it would blow off her shoulders in a stiff breeze. His mouth went dry.

She turned around as the butler finished his announcement. Her eyes met his and then slipped away again when Lord John Tracey approached her. *Wonderful*. John Tracey. He hadn't even known that bastard was back in London. Tracey was probably making the rounds, telling all the chits stories of his heroic deeds in the Peninsula.

For a moment he stood watching them, watching rose tint her cheeks and her soft, amused smile. When someone approached to block his view, he couldn't hide a scowl.

"Deverill," Charlemagne Griffin muttered, offering his hand.

"What the hell do you want?" Valentine returned, declining to complete the handshake.

"I want to apologize. For last night," Shay said, clenching his fingers and lowering his arm again.

"Why, for the devil's sake?"

Charlemagne eyed him for a moment. "Honestly?"

"If you please."

"Because Melbourne ordered me to."

"Let's clarify one thing then, shall we? If I hadn't been drunk, you wouldn't have gotten a blow in. But having done so, I would hope that your reasons for it are valid enough that they don't require an apology."

"You are a strange man, Deverill."

"I think it makes sense. Don't do something unless you mean it." Automatically his thoughts turned to a late-night swim in a baptismal pond, and the lovemaking afterward. If he followed his own philosophy, he had some more thinking to do. He'd been doing a bloody lot of that lately.

"I don't want you for an enemy, Deverill."

"Then never do that again." Glancing over Shay's shoulder, he saw Melbourne approaching. "And one more bit of friendly advice. For tonight, the Griffin clan had best leave me be." With a nod, he turned for the refreshment table, leaving the two brothers standing in the middle of the room behind him.

Considering he'd ruined their sister he probably should have attempted being more charitable, but his mind had been such a swirling mess over the past few days that he could barely manage to keep his balance. Eleanor had joined Tracey on the dance floor for a waltz, and she seemed to be making a point of not looking at Valentine again. Perhaps, then, she'd found someone else with whom she'd rather repeat her adventure.

His fists clenched. No, this was worse than that. This had never been about an evening's pleasure. She'd sought a moment of freedom, found it, and now fully intended to march back into Society's fold. And where the Griffin clan was concerned, that meant marrying.

John Tracey would be a splendid prospect for that. Hell, he'd even been granted a field promotion to major, if what the wags said was true. Young, dedicated, handsome, the brother of Earl Heflin also had a guaranteed income from properties his brother had given over for him to manage. "Bastard," Valentine murmured.

"Are you still finished with me?" a soft feminine voice cooed from behind him.

He turned around. "Lydia. Heavens, no. Is gouty old Franch here?"

"Yes, he's holding court by the fireside."

Valentine held his hand out to her. "Then he won't mind if his wife dances with a charming gentleman?"

"He'd be grateful for it." With a smile she curled her fingers around his and allowed him to lead her to the dance floor. "I knew you would be back, dear heart."

Actually, she was the one who had come looking for him, but now didn't seem to be the time to point that out. Not when he could take the dance floor with her and let Eleanor Griffin know just how little her attentions and her approval and her body meant to him.

Determined not even to glance in the direction of Eleanor and Tracey, Valentine concentrated on complimenting Lydia about her fine choice of gown, her china blue eyes, the sweep of her low-cut neckline. And he ignored the fact that he hadn't the slightest desire to touch her, to kiss her, to take her, and that despite his lack of eye contact, every ounce of him was attuned to the woman happily dancing a few feet away.

"You're being very charming tonight," Lydia observed, smiling again. "One might almost think that you missed me."

"I'm fairly certain I did," he returned absently, trying to hear whatever nonsense it was that Tracey was telling Eleanor. The damned orchestra was playing too loudly for him to be certain, but it sounded like a bloody war story, just as he'd predicted.

"You know, Franch's physician recommended that he take the waters at Bath again," Lydia continued. "And I've already suggested that I stay behind in London to keep the house open."

"That makes sense."

"I thought so. Which means that I'll be there all by myself for at least a fortnight. And you know how I hate sleeping alone."

"That's not what you tell your husband."

Her brow furrowed. "Of course not. Do you expect me to encourage his attentions? I'd much rather have yours."

"Who wouldn't?" Hiding a scowl, he turned Lydia in a sharper circle to keep the other couple in earshot.

"Valentine, don't think you can make me jealous. As a matter of fact, Lord Fowler offered to hire Lawrence to paint my portrait, if only I'd give him one of my gloves as a token of affection."

He looked down at her upturned face. "Good God. Fowler's older than your husband."

"And not nearly as well heeled. I turned him down, obviously. But you see, you are not my only admirer."

"I don't admire you, Lydia. I use you. You're convenient and uncomplicated."

She blinked. "So did you used to be."

"No. I'm quite complicated. It's just that I usually try to ignore that fact. Lately, though, it's been giving me a bit of trouble."

"Valentine, are you going to sleep with me tonight or not?" she whispered, anger and frustration touching her pretty eyes.

"No, I'm not." Her lack of concern for him matched his for her. A few weeks ago it wouldn't have mattered—or rather, it would have pleased him. Now, though, a virginal chit had told him some confidences and had trusted him enough to allow him to be her first, and his damned world had tilted on its axis.

"I could be very angry with you."

"You've already cursed me, Lydia. I haven't forgotten that, even if you have. I told you, I use you. And tonight I choose not to do so. Be grateful."

She started to pull back from him, but he tightened his grip on her hand and around her waist. "Let go," she hissed.

"Let's not make a scene, shall we?" he returned. "The dance is nearly over. You may stomp away after that."

"I wish that one day you would get precisely what you deserve."

Finally he glanced over at Eleanor, to see her chuckling at something Tracey had said. Her eyes danced, the flash of her smile warmer than sunlight. Damn it, this was killing him, and he didn't even know why. "I think your wish may already be coming true," he told Lydia. "And you may not believe me, but I'm probably doing you a favor by not having you around me when it does."

"It hardly seems like you to be selfless."

"Odd, isn't it?"

* * *

"Well, isn't this interesting?" Stephen Cobb-Harding leaned against the wall beside the Halfax conservatory.

"What's interesting, besides Deverill looking like he's turning away a fair bit of tail for no good reason?" Andrew Perline stopped his careful, long-distance examination of Miss Deborah Grayling's bosom long enough to cast another glance at the dance floor.

"Keep your damned voice down, Perline, and pay attention. Deverill's practically been attached to Lady Eleanor's shadow for weeks, and now she won't even look at him. And he's turned away both Charlemagne Griffin and Melbourne. Something's afoot."

"Maybe they've all tired of one another," Perline suggested.

"Precisely."

"So what good does that do you? Deverill's still got your papers. And you've got a fortnight remaining before you have to start calling Paris home."

"Thank you so much for reminding me, and keep your bloody voice down. That's not what I'm talking about. Not precisely, at any rate."

"Then what—"

"If there's a wedge between Deverill and Melbourne, I have been handed an opportunity to tell my side of the story to His Grace." He gazed at pretty Eleanor for a long moment. "And I'd wager that he hasn't heard any other side, so my task should be simple."

"You don't think he'll let you marry his sister."

"By the time I'm finished with my tale, he'll be begging me to take her. And the Griffins certainly have enough money for me to pay off my damned papers. Hell, if they're feuding with Deverill, I might not even have to ask twice."

"Well, whatever you're planning, if it's got something to do with taking Deverill down a peg or two, I'm all for it. After he practically wagered me into oblivion he actually made me ask him for the blunt to pay for the port I'd already drunk. In front of Prinny, yet."

"Aye," their third companion agreed. Mr. Peter Burnsey sipped a glass of whiskey. "He may have your papers, but you two aren't the only one whose prospects he's ruined. If he'd left me any blunt I'd pay to hand him and the mighty Griffins a bit of a bruising."

"If tomorrow goes as I plan, we'll all have the chance." Stephen sent a last look in Deverill's direction, then turned his attention to Melbourne. The marquis might have delayed his marriage plans by his interference at Belmont's, but he hadn't destroyed them. Not when Stephen had a verifiable and substantiated story to tell the duke. And not when he had a good description of what Lady Eleanor's bare bosom looked like, and a proposal to keep anyone else from hearing about her indiscretions.

No, tonight it looked as though his luck was finally turning.

Chapter 18

"I'm pleased you've returned to London as well, Lord John," Eleanor said, smiling as they strolled toward the refreshment table. "You've certainly brightened up the evening."

"I believe you are tonight's brightest constellation," John Tracey returned with a warm grin of his own. "I'm merely an admiring astronomer."

With a chuckle, Eleanor accepted the glass of punch he procured for her. Thank goodness for John Tracey. When she'd set eyes on Deverill earlier, her heart had stopped. It was dreadful, not knowing whether she wanted to throttle him or kiss him—and being determined not to do the latter.

And then he'd made it worse when he'd decided to dance with that awful Lady Franch. Everyone knew they'd been lovers, and apparently that hadn't changed. He'd made no promises to her, but it still . . . hurt her that her defining moment had been nothing to him except a way to pass an evening—though with the sensation that ripped into her chest, "hurt" seemed completely inadequate to describe it.

"Tracey."

At the sound of Deverill's voice she turned, her breath catching. Valentine stood there, his attention on Earl Heflin's brother. As she watched, he held out his hand.

"Deverill." Tracey shook it.

"I wanted to welcome you back to London," the marquis continued, releasing the grip first. "How's Wellington faring without you?"

John chuckled. "I shudder to think. I'm only on leave for a few weeks, though. I'm due to return to the Peninsula in August."

"Hopefully that won't be enough time for the French to realize you're not there." Deverill finally turned in Eleanor's direction. "I wondered if I might intrude for a moment. Lady Eleanor's planning a surprise for her brother, and I had a suggestion about it."

Tracey inclined his head. "Of course. I hadn't meant to monopolize you, my lady."

Eleanor sniffed. "I would have told you if I found your companionship unwelcome, Lord John." *Ha.* She'd learned a few things about speaking her mind, and about enjoying her freedom, anyway. "Might I trouble you to find me a glass of Madeira?"

The major saluted. "At your command. I'll be right back."

As soon as he was out of earshot, Eleanor looked back at Valentine. "Don't tell me that *you're* chasing men away from me now."

"He's very . . . shiny, isn't he?"

"Stop it. What do you want?"

"A word with you."

"Then speak."

A muscle in his jaw twitched. "Not here. On the balcony, perhaps?"

"No."

"In the hallway, then."

"No."

"Eleanor, I need to speak with you in private." He held her gaze for a moment, then heaved a deep breath. "Look at it this way: If you feel the need to pummel me, in private you can do it without fear of scandal."

"My, you do make it sound tempting," she said scathingly. "And that's a lovely bruise on your cheekbone. Who do I have to thank for that?"

"Eleanor, please."

She didn't think she'd ever heard him use the word before—not so directly, anyway. He was a master manipulator, of course, but she knew that. The problem was, she wanted to see him in private, to have him pay attention only to her. As long as she was aware of that weakness, she supposed, no harm could come of it.

"Very well. But only for a moment."

He inclined his head. "And the location?"

"I'll join you on the balcony in five minutes."

With a stiff bow he turned and walked away. Immediately she wished that she'd refused his request, but she didn't have time to fret about it. As soon as he walked out of her sight, a horde of young men mobbed her, looking for an open spot someone might have accidentally left on her dance card, or wanting to compliment her on her gown, or her hair, or the fine weather she was apparently responsible for providing.

She hadn't realized that Valentine's presence kept men

at bay as effectively as her brothers' did. It wasn't because he warned them away from her; she knew enough about him to realize that. No, it was because of who he was, she decided, and the way he had of commanding people's attention without appearing to make an effort to do any such thing. Charisma, Melbourne had called it once. Oh, yes, Valentine Corbett had that in spades.

Given a choice between being fawned over by men who didn't know anything about her but her family name and the amount of her fortune, or a private meeting with the man to whom she'd given her virginity, she actually preferred Valentine. She kept her eyes on the clock. As soon as five minutes had ticked by, she made her excuses, turned away all offers of escort, and strolled toward the balcony for a breath of fresh air.

Chilly as the evening was, no one else had left the ballroom to take advantage of the relative privacy. In fact, she appeared to be quite alone. Oh, that was splendid. He'd found something more entertaining with which to occupy himself. She turned back to the doorway.

"Going so soon?"

Valentine emerged from the shadows at the far end of the vine-tangled balcony. Eleanor made her breathing stay normal, though she couldn't control the fast patter of her heart. Well, he wasn't going to get close enough to detect that, anyway.

"I'm here," she stated. "What do you want?"

"I want to apologize."

"Apo—You don't even know why I'm angry with you."

His sensuous lips twitched. "No, I don't, but that hardly seems the point. I've made you angry, and I didn't mean to. And I certainly didn't mean to make you cry. I'm sorry."

Eleanor scowled. "How do you know I cried?"

Valentine touched the bruise on his cheekbone. "Charlemagne told me."

Her hands flew to her mouth. "Oh, dear." So *that* was where Shay had driven off to last night. "I didn't ask him to do that."

"I don't think you needed to. Do you accept?"

"Accept?"

"My apology."

"You're not supposed to ask that."

He took a half step forward. "I don't do this well, Eleanor. I just wanted to know if we're still friends."

She tilted her head, trying to figure out whether he was sincere, or whether he was playing another game. Or whether he even knew what he was doing. "Why do you care if we're friends? You've . . ." Eleanor looked about, lowering her voice just in case someone lurked near the balcony door. "You've bedded me, so move along. That's what you do, isn't it?"

"Are you jealous?" he returned, taking another step closer. "I thought that night was about your moment of freedom, your adven—"

"I don't want a *moment* of freedom any longer," she snapped before she could stop herself. Horrified, she turned her back, facing the railing and the garden below. Damnation. All she'd ever meant to tell him was that he would be happier if he could make himself care about someone or something besides his own well-being. She hadn't wanted to confess her continued yearnings to him, for heaven's sake.

"Oh."

"That doesn't mean I expect you to—"

Valentine grabbed her shoulder, spinning her back to

face him. Before she could utter a gasp, he lowered his mouth to hers. Sensation and yearning flooded through her. Eleanor swept her arms around his shoulders, pulling him hard against her, drinking in his heat, relishing the touch of his mouth on hers.

He kissed her until she couldn't breathe, then slowly lifted his head. "I'm sorry, what were you saying?" he murmured, his gaze on her mouth.

"The, um . . . I . . . I don't remember," she said truthfully.

"You want more than a moment of freedom. I remember that," he commented, running a thumb along her lower lip.

"Yes. Yes. What I was going to say is that I don't expect you to provide it. I imagine I've tested your charity far enough."

Valentine shook his head. "It's not charity, Eleanor. I don't offer charity. Ever."

God, she wanted him to kiss her again. "Even so, you—"

"You are a complicated woman," he muttered, kissing her again, hard and deep. "I want you. If that's the freedom you have in mind, we'll find a private place."

"Here?" she asked, less shocked than she would have expected to be.

Valentine swallowed. Jesus, she would, if he went along with it. And he wanted to, except that too many people would be keeping an eye out for her, and someone would discover them. Melbourne would shoot him, but he was more concerned that Eleanor would be ruined and forced to marry Noleville. Or worse for him, Tracey. He frowned. Someone was going to have to keep their wits about them, and apparently that was him.

"Not here. I'll find somewhere."

"You shouldn't give me time to consider," she returned, lifting a hand to brush hair from his forehead.

The gesture made him shiver. "Probably not. But I am."

She drew a breath, the motion drawing her bodice tight across her chest. "Or is it because you have a prior appointment with Lady Franch?"

He forced a laugh. "No. Actually, I've said my fare—" He stopped himself just before he could admit that he'd voluntarily parted company not only with Lydia, but with every lover he'd had this Season—except for Eleanor. "I've been ordered to stay away from you," he rephrased. "I don't want to have to pummel Shay on principle, and he's probably already seen us talking."

"Charlemagne and I are going to have a conversation of our own," she said stiffly. "My brothers are not to interfere with my social calendar. And out of every man I've conversed with, I would say you're an odd—and dangerous—choice to pick for a fight."

"Not if he knew the truth," Valentine pointed out.

She blushed. "But he doesn't."

Eleanor tucked her hands behind her back. Valentine noted the gesture with some disappointment. She'd finished with touching him for tonight, then. Pity, that. He felt as though he still had some ground to make up after seeing her chatting with Tracey after the waltz. The major obviously needed to be reminded to honor the rules of competition—whether Valentine had any intention of doing so himself, or not. No monopolizing a chit when other men were lined up to converse with her. He concealed a smile, enjoying every second of the monopolizing he was doing. "So why were you mad at me?"

Glancing past him toward the doorway, she shifted. "I'm just never sure who you are, Valentine. One moment you save my virtue, the next you take it, then you comfort me, and then you insult every member of my sex. Half the time I envy the freedom you have, and the other half I could scream at you for the waste you make of it."

So it hadn't been about jealousy. She *had* been disappointed in him, as he'd first suspected. "I've spent a long time becoming who I am, Eleanor. Judge me if you like, but I'm seeing some rather amazing similarities between us, lately."

"I am, as well," she agreed, not looking as if she felt insulted. "What I'm not certain about, though, is whether I've changed, or you have."

That shook him, mostly because he'd been wondering the same thing himself. Yes, he craved her, and yes, he enjoyed her companionship more than he ever had any other female that he could recall. That didn't mean he'd changed. It only meant he'd unexpectedly found a friend, and didn't want to lose her. Of course, even that degree of possessiveness was unlike him, but now wasn't the time to debate that.

He smiled. "Kiss me or kill me, but don't ask me any sticky questions."

"Hm. I'm not certain that's satisfactory." Slowly she leaned in and touched her lips to his, soft and brief and taking his breath. "Come and see me tomorrow."

"I—"

Before he could conjure any more of a reply than that, she swept past him and strolled back into the ballroom. Something had definitely changed.

" 'Come and see me tomorrow,' " he repeated, trying to sound cynical. That was the sort of thing *he* usually said, enticing a chit into coming to see him when he couldn't be bothered to make the effort of a seduction. Cynicism was difficult, though, when he knew he'd be calling at Griffin House sometime tomorrow—and probably before noon.

The Duke of Melbourne sat cross-legged on the morning room floor, listening to the tale of a rabbit and a very large carrot as read by his daughter. It was the seventeenth time he'd heard the story, but the opportunity to spend the morning with Peep was rare enough that he wouldn't mind hearing it another eighty or ninety times.

Penelope lowered the book. "How large do carrots actually grow, Papa?" she asked, her brow furrowed.

"Not terribly large," he returned, craning his neck to look at her seated above and behind him on the couch. "But keep in mind that the rabbit is rather small."

She nodded. "Yes, that's true."

A scratch came at the door. "Enter," Sebastian called.

Stanton pushed the door halfway open and leaned in. "I beg your pardon, Your Grace, but you have a caller." He offered a calling card.

The duke ignored it. "Who is it?"

"A Mr. Stephen Cobb-Harding, Your Grace."

Hm. He hadn't heard that name mentioned in a while. In fact, Cobb-Harding had seemed to drop rather abruptly off the face of Nell's map. "Show him to my office. I'll be there in a moment."

"Very good, Your Grace."

Peep clambered off the couch to her feet. "Remember, Papa, if he's one of Aunt Nell's suitors, you're not to speak to him."

"I'll keep that in mind," he returned, pulling himself upright as well. "I'll be back shortly. Hopefully we'll have time to finish the story before my meeting."

"Yes. I have some more questions about carrots, too."

Sebastian sent his daughter upstairs into the care of her governess, then made his way to his office. As he pushed the door open, Stephen Cobb-Harding bounced to his feet from the chair in which he'd been reclining.

"Good morning, Your Grace. Thank you for seeing me."

"Have a seat, Mr. Cobb-Harding," Sebastian returned, gesturing. He sank into the chair behind his desk. "What might I do for you?"

"I actually think that what I have to say will be to our mutual benefit."

The duke reflected that, apt as Peep's warning about Nell's suitors had been, if not for Cobb-Harding's association with his sister, the lout would never have been granted an audience at all. He nodded. "I'm listening."

"I couldn't help noticing a certain . . . distance in your family's dealings with Lord Deverill last night. Given that fact, and considering the delicate nature of the information I'm about to impart, I would be grateful for your understanding."

Cobb-Harding seemed to flap his lips a great deal, and as yet he'd managed to say absolutely nothing. Stifling his annoyance, Melbourne nodded again. "I do have a meeting this morning, if you'd care to proceed."

"Yes, of course." Cobb-Harding cleared his throat. "Lord Deverill has been attempting to blackmail me."

Well. Obviously he needed to acquire some better sources of information, Sebastian decided. "And what do you wish me to do about that?"

Cobb-Harding was silent for a moment, as though taken aback by Sebastian's lack of concern over his pronouncement. "I will be frank with you, Your Grace," he said finally. "A few weeks ago your sister accompanied me to a soiree. A soiree hosted by Lord Belmont."

Sebastian curled his fingers into the mahogany edge of his desk. "Yes?"

"Yes. I wanted to attend the Hampton Ball, but she insisted that Belmont's would be more to her taste. Once there, I'm ashamed to say that we engaged in a mutual indiscretion. I, of course, immediately offered to do the honorable thing and take Lady Eleanor's hand in marriage, but Lord Deverill interfered, attacking me and then threatening to bankrupt me if I revealed a word of your sister's behavior to anyone."

"I see." As he sat listening, Melbourne wondered whether Cobb-Harding had any idea just how much peril he was in. But the duke had long ago learned the virtues of patience, and so he remained in his chair. "Go on, if you please."

Apparently encouraged by the duke's seeming interest, Cobb-Harding sat forward. "Yes. With you and Deverill on the outs, I fear there is nothing to prevent someone from revealing your sister's scandalous behavior to the world at large. So I have come forward both to inform you first, and to once again offer to join my name to that of the Griffins and ensure that Lady Eleanor is not ruined."

"So your marriage to my sister will dissuade you from speaking of her alleged indiscretion."

"And it will protect her from Deverill if he should seek revenge on you by revealing the same."

Melbourne looked at him for a moment. Cobb-Harding obviously had no idea of the depth of the friendship between Deverill and himself—and thank God for that. Whatever happened, however, Valentine had some serious explaining to do. And so did Eleanor.

"Mr. Cobb-Harding, I presume there are no other witnesses save you and Deverill?"

"And a few guests who would only need a word to complete the puzzle. And Lady Eleanor, of course. Though I would call her a participant rather than a witness."

That was enough of that. "And what I would call you, I won't say in this house. Get up, and leave. You have one minute to be gone from my front drive."

Cobb-Harding blinked. "I beg your pardon? I came here with the idea of making a mutually beneficial match. I am saving your sister's—and your family's—reputation."

"You are attempting your own breed of blackmail. Unfortunately for you, however, you're an idiot."

"But I—"

"You what, Mr. Cobb-Harding? You'll ruin my sister if I refuse your kind offer? Whatever Deverill has been doing to ensure your silence doesn't even begin to describe what I will do to you if you ever speak one word of this nonsense to anyone. *Anyone.*"

He rose, and Cobb-Harding scrambled out of his own seat and around the back of the chair. "I will not be spoken to in this manner. I have proof, and I will use it if you force me to."

"What proof could you possibly have of such a lie?"

"I can describe your sister's breasts to perfec—"

Melbourne grabbed him by the throat, shoving him backward toward the door. "You forget yourself, sir," he said, using every ounce of hard-won self-control to keep his voice calm and quiet and steady. "I applaud your attempt to better your standing, but I will not tolerate your doing so at my family's expense." He bent his elbow, bringing his face to within inches of Cobb-Harding's. "Do I make myself clear?"

Cobb-Harding squeaked, his fingers grasping at the duke's. "Perfectly," he rasped.

With his free hand Sebastian opened the door. Still gripping Cobb-Harding's throat, he backed the shorter man toward the front door. Stanton, his face an immobile mask, pulled open the door and stood aside while Melbourne shoved. Staggering backward, Cobb-Harding stumbled down the shallow steps to the drive.

"Good day, Mr. Cobb-Harding," the duke said, nodding.

"Well done, Your Grace," Stanton commented, closing the door again with a thud.

"Get Charlemagne and Zachary," Sebastian rumbled, his temper beginning to flare past his hard control. "Now."

Not uttering a word, the butler turned and ran up the stairs. A moment later both of his brothers, one of them holding a newspaper and the other half dressed, emerged onto the balcony.

"What is it, Melbourne?" Shay asked.

"Down here," he returned. "I am not going to shout."

Obviously sensing that something was amiss, they hurried down to the foyer. "What happened?"

"Find me the Marquis of Deverill," Melbourne murmured. "I don't care where he is, or what or who he's doing. I want him here by the top of the hour."

They glanced at one another, then Shay handed the newspaper over to the panting butler and headed for the front door. Zachary turned back for the stairs. "I'll finish dressing and help him out."

"Is Eleanor still here?"

"Yes. She has a few hopefuls waiting in the sitting room. I think she was going on a pic—"

"Send them away. Keep her here."

"But what about your agreement with her, Mel—"

The duke jabbed his youngest brother in the shoulder. "Keep her here. And you are not to tell her anything."

"I don't know anything."

"You will. I just hope we're the only ones who do. Damnation." Still cursing, he strode back into his office and slammed the door. His little agreement with Eleanor had just ended.

"Who's in the gaggle this morning?" Eleanor asked, seeing Zachary lounging at the head of the stairs. She finished pulling on her lace gloves as she joined him.

"Come down and wait with me," he said, straightening.

"Wait with you? For what? I'm going on a picnic. Or perhaps shopping. I haven't decided yet. It depends on who I have to choose from." It was beginning to be fun, having this amount of power—especially after Valentine's kiss last night. For the first time she'd realized that she had some power over him, as well. The euphoria of that moment still kept her feet several inches above the floor.

Of course if she had only the likes of Francis Henning or Howard Fanner waiting to escort her, she was likely to land on the floor with a thud. But even that couldn't depress her overly much; Valentine would be calling sometime today. Of that she was certain.

Zachary looked as though he had more to say, but after a moment he only gestured her to proceed. Chatty as her brother usually was, she immediately began to wonder whether something was amiss. Obviously, though, her senses had been somewhat askew over the past few days. Or perhaps it was merely that Valentine was here already, though it would be frightfully early for him. A thrill of goose bumps ran down her arms. If he appeared this early, it would mean something.

The sitting room door stood open, and with a questioning glance at the nearby Stanton, she slipped inside. "Good morning, gentle—"

The room was empty. Surprised, Eleanor turned around and nearly bumped into Zachary as he pressed in behind her. He didn't look at all surprised, and when he closed the door and seated himself close by it, she knew for certain that something was afoot.

"What's going on?" she asked, abruptly worried.

"I don't know."

"You don't know, or you won't say?"

"I don't know, and I wouldn't say if I did. Just have a seat and drink your tea."

So whatever it was, she was supposed to stay out of it. How typical. And how very counter to their agreement—though Zachary wasn't the one with whom she would need to take that up. "Might we at least move to the morning room?" she asked, trying to pretend she wasn't that interested in whatever was going on. "The chairs are so much more comfortable in there."

"I don't think so."

"Oh, come now, Zachary. Did Melbourne say you had to keep an eye on me, or did he say I was to stay right here in this room?"

"No one said anything." He shifted, frowning at the stiff-backed chair. "But you're correct about the furniture. All right, we can move to the morning room."

"Thank you."

She would have led the way, but he actually took her hand to wrap around his arm. Eleanor suppressed a shudder. Whatever was going on, it wasn't good. Had someone seen her kissing Valentine? Or worse? Eleanor blanched, her imagination diving through logic and straight on to panic. Everything would be finished. *She* would be finished.

"Stop it," she muttered, shaking herself.

"Beg pardon?"

"Nothing." All she needed to do was fight her way back to logic. No one would have kept news of their tryst secret for this long and then tell. The gossip would have been too hard to resist.

As they crossed the hall, though, the front door opened, and logic leaped out the window again. Charlemagne entered, followed closely by Valentine himself. Neither man looked particularly happy, and Eleanor's already thundering heart skipped another beat. Valentine glanced at her, his expression unreadable, before he turned his attention back to Shay.

"You're beginning to perturb me," he said, shrugging out of his greatcoat and tossing it at Stanton. "What the devil is so pressing that you had drag me out of my own bloody house before I've had breakfast?"

"In the office," was all Shay said.

"Come on," Zachary told Eleanor, tugging her down the hallway.

She dug in her heels, pulling free of her brother's grip. "If this has something to do with me, I demand that you tell me what's going on, Zachary. I am not a child. And this subterfuge is ridic—"

Sebastian stepped out of his office. The dark, furious expression on his face stopped her cold. "Get into the morning room and stay there until I summon you," he growled. "This is not a game any longer."

Valentine watched the color leave Eleanor's face. Her wide gray eyes spoke her worst fear so clearly that he was surprised her brothers didn't drag him out and hang him from the front portico. He wanted to tell her to be calm, not to worry, that he had every intention of claiming responsibility for whatever it was the Griffin men were frothing about. And considering how uncharacteristic of him that sentiment was, he was almost as amused as he was annoyed when he followed Melbourne into his austere office.

"You're beginning to bear a frightening resemblance to the Spanish Inquisitors," he commented, noting that neither of the other brothers had been allowed into the room.

The duke moved with a measured stride to his desk. "I had a visitor this morning," he said, his voice the deceptively cool one that Valentine had heard on only a rare handful of occasions.

The hairs on the back of his neck pricked. "I assume you're going to tell me who came calling."

"Stephen Cobb-Harding."

It took everything Valentine had not to lurch to his feet. Melbourne was watching him, however, so he only crossed his ankles. "How exciting for you. I wish you'd waited until a decent hour to share the news with me."

"You're blackmailing him."

Thank God Melbourne had gone to him for information first. Confronting Eleanor with whatever accusations Cobb-Harding might have leveled would have been both unfair and unnecessarily cruel. He shrugged. "It's been a bit dull this Season. I had to do something for excitement."

The duke pounded his fist on the desk. "Dammit, Valentine! Do you know what he told me? How he offered to preserve my family's—my sister's—reputation through an offer of marriage?"

"Melbourne, you—"

"And I had to sit here and listen to it, because no one bloody told me about any of it! I recruited you to keep Eleanor out of trouble, not to let her do as she pleased and then conceal it from me!"

Valentine sat and listened to the duke rant. Since Melbourne didn't seem to expect an answer or even a response at the moment, it gave him time to think.

He could lie about it, of course, tell Sebastian that he had no idea what Cobb-Harding was talking about. That would suffice if he were the only party involved, but Eleanor complicated the issue immensely. In the first place she probably wouldn't sit for a lie, and in the second place she would consider the fabrication an injustice. This had been about her right to some freedom, and pretending now that she'd been sitting demurely on her hands that night at Vauxhall would counter everything her rebellion had been about.

"Deverill," Melbourne bellowed, jolting him out of his thoughts, "you owed me a simple favor. I hardly consider this appropriate repayment. Explain yourself."

For a fleeting moment he wondered how Melbourne would react to the information that the evening at the Belmont soiree was the very least of what Eleanor had done, and how integral his own participation had been. "I don't carry tales," he said shortly. "And keep your damned voice down. They could hear you in Paris."

Melbourne leaned over the desk, jamming his fists into the hard surface. "Don't change the subject. And this tale, you *will* carry."

"Sebastian, it's complicated. And it's not what you think." *It was worse, actually.*

"Then enlighten me, damn it all. I am out of patience."

"Cobb-Harding tricked her into attending the Belmont party. It was a masked gathering, so no one saw her face."

The duke made a strangling sound. "He offered to describe certain . . . aspects of Nell's anatomy to me."

Cobb-Harding was a dead man. "He drugged her. Laudanum. And then he dragged her into a room and attacked her. I arrived in time to prevent the worst of it. It wasn't her fault, Seb."

For a moment Melbourne remained where he was. Finally he sank back into his chair. "And why didn't you inform me about this? It would have ended Nell's little rebellion weeks ago."

"That's why I didn't tell you." That, and the fact that she'd begged him not to say anything. "It was her first attempt at freedom. She bungled it. I thought she deserved another chance."

"*You* thought. That's hardly your place, Deverill. You are not part of this family. Your involvement was to settle a debt of honor."

"There's a reason you recruited me to be her nanny, as I recall. None of you could manage it. I could. You said no scandal, and there hasn't been one. Even Cobb-Harding only came to you. No one else knows anything."

"True. All I have is that little scab lingering about and trying to worm money or power or influence out of me, now."

"Not even that. According to our . . . agreement, he has to leave England in the next fortnight."

"How fortunate for him. This is finished. As you said, she bungled it. Now it's my turn. She needs to be married and have a family and responsibility. I daresay she wouldn't feel the need to seek out scandal, then."

Valentine laughed. He didn't feel particularly amused, but he couldn't help it. "Yes. A married woman is immune to temptation and scandal. For God's sake, Sebastian, what do you think I do with my nights?"

The duke looked at him. "I am not going to overlook this. Someone will find out, and someone will talk. The gossip is too good to let pass by. If she's married, she'll be protected from the worst of the insinuations of her being some sort of lightskirt."

"She's not—" He drew a breath. "She'll resent you for the rest of her life if you take this away from her now. Don't do it."

"I thought you'd be relieved. You didn't want anything to do with this in the first place."

God, he hadn't, had he? "It's been more . . . interesting than I expected."

"I see. So what else has she done that you haven't bothered to tell me?"

Standing, Valentine walked to the window and back. He wanted to defend Eleanor, both her actions and the reasons behind them. If he did so, however, Melbourne would see just how involved he had become in this—not just with Eleanor's project, but with her. "Take a step back and look at this from her viewpoint," he suggested instead.

"What? *You're* telling me that a chit has a right to any viewpoint other than what we tell her?"

"She isn't just a female, the sister of my friend," Valentine spat, too angry to ignore the wise part of his brain which was telling him to keep his mouth shut. "She's a woman with wants and needs, and she will be miserable in any life you choose for her—especially now that she's experienced some freedom. Let her find her own happiness."

"What the dev—"

The door burst open, Eleanor storming into the room with both Zachary and Charlemagne on her heels.

"We tried to stop her," Zachary said, rubbing a red mark on his cheek where he'd obviously been hit.

"You were talking rather loudly," Shay added, his own tone tight and angry.

Valentine vaguely heard the duke order everyone out of the room, but he wasn't paying much attention. Rather, his gaze was on Eleanor as she stalked up to him and stood, hands on her hips, glaring at him. He couldn't put a word to the expression in her eyes, but it cut deep into his chest.

"You what?" she said tightly.

He frowned. "I don't—"

"*You were assigned to look after me?*" she continued, a tear running down her cheek. "Melbourne told you to keep me out of trouble, and you agreed to do this?"

Sweet Lucifer. "Eleanor, I—"

"You were a spy?" She drew a shuddering breath. "I thought we were . . . I thought we were friends."

"We are friends. Don't—"

She slapped him. More than anything else the blow startled him—not that he'd never been slapped before, but that Eleanor had hit him. Reflexively he grabbed her wrist, but she pulled free.

"How dare you," she whispered, her voice shaking.

"It's not just him, Nell," Melbourne put in, his voice surprisingly calm. "I asked him to help."

"So you did. You couldn't trust me for one second, could you? Nell couldn't possibly have been looking for something she felt was important just for herself. She must be trying to make some sort of trouble for the family, so let's assign her a keeper. That was shameful of you,

Melbourne." She glanced at her other brothers, her eyes cold. "And shame on you two for going along with it."

Before anyone could comment, she whipped back on Valentine again. "And shame on you for agreeing to this farce, and for choosing not to tell me about your little agreement." Tears choked her, but she took another breath and continued. "I thought I was free, Valentine. But this was all just part of another of my brothers' plans to control my life. And you were part of it. After everything you said, and your advice . . ."

He stepped forward, lifting a hand to wipe the tears from her cheek. "Eleanor, give me a chance to exp—"

"Did you hover about me because you truly wanted to help? Did you care for me at all? Or were you merely trying to distract me and control me—to keep me from doing something that might trouble everyone's busy schedule? And if my brothers trusted you, how could you behave in such an ungentlemanly manner toward me? I trusted you. I confided in you. How could you not tell me that you'd been 'assigned' to watch me?"

Valentine wanted to shake her. Before he could conjure a suitable retort, she stormed out of the office, slamming the door behind her hard enough to rattle the windows. He clenched his fists, but stayed unmoving. Perhaps it was just as well that she hadn't given him the opportunity to explain what he'd been doing. He had no idea how to do so, even to himself.

"And what, pray tell, was that conversation about?" Melbourne asked in a hard, cold voice.

"She didn't know you'd recruited me to be her bloody nanny," Valentine growled, not certain whether he was angrier at the duke for bellowing, or himself for not telling her. Or better yet, at himself for getting involved with this in the first place. He'd known from the beginning that entangling himself in Griffin business was a mistake.

"I was not referring to her ignorance about your assignment. She mentioned some—"

"What sort of 'ungentlemanly' behavior did you show Nell?" Charlemagne interrupted, grabbing Valentine's shoulder. "I warned you about distressing her, damn it all."

Valentine shrugged free, using all his self-control to keep from punching someone. "You interrupted a nice breakfast," he grunted, turning for the door. "If you don't mind, I'll return to it."

"I want some answers," Sebastian said in his controlled voice.

"Well, so do I," Valentine snapped, yanking the door open.

Shay made a move to block his exit, but Melbourne gestured him back. "Let him go. And don't come back, Deverill, until you can explain yourself."

"Go bugger yourself. The lot of you. Damned Griffins. This was *your* idea, Melbourne. Not mine."

Charlemagne had come to fetch him in one of the Griffin coaches, so it seemed only fair that he commandeer it to return home. With a scowl at the driver, he pulled open the door and climbed in. "Corbett House. Now."

"Aye, my lord."

The coach rolled forward, then jolted to a halt again. Cursing, Valentine stood and shoved the door open to lean out. "Damn it, I said—"

Eleanor stood in front of the team, her hands on her hips. "Wait here a moment, Frederick," she said to the driver, her voice unsteady. "I need a word with your passenger."

Chapter 19

❦❦ **I** am not in the mood for this, Eleanor," Valentine snapped. "Get out of the way."

She wasn't in the mood for it, either, but she absolutely was not going to let him escape without giving her an explanation. And whatever he said, it had best be something that allowed her to breathe again. At the moment her throat and chest were so tight, it felt like she was dying. "Don't you move this coach, Frederick," she ordered, moving from in front of the team and stalking up to the door. "Step aside and let me in, or I'll simply express my feelings right here."

His eyes narrowing, Valentine slammed the door open the rest of the way and then moved back into the shadows of the coach. He obviously wasn't going to help her in, so Eleanor gathered her skirts in one hand and clambered up herself.

Valentine sat as far from her as he could, arms crossed over his chest. Angry as she was, the expression in his eyes still made her hesitate; not many people crossed the Marquis of Deverill. Little as most things affected him, he had a rare and nasty temper. She'd certainly roused it, even if her brothers' participation had added considerable fuel. But she was furious as well, and with even more cause. She hadn't lied to him, after all. In fact, he was the one person she hadn't lied to. He couldn't make the same claim to her.

"You've made things somewhat more difficult for me than they needed to be," he stated.

She felt ready to explode. "Difficult for *you*? I trusted you, Deverill."

He snorted. "That would seem to be *your* error."

For a long moment she gazed into his eyes, trying to figure out once and for all who the real Valentine Corbett might be, as if anyone could ever hope to completely solve that conundrum. She had the distinct feeling that she'd been with him that night by the baptismal pond, and that today he'd made himself scarce. But she needed to speak to him, not to the flip, cynical rakehell who would never give her a straight answer.

"I'm not going to cry and tell you that you used me or ruined me. I entered into that experience with my eyes wide open."

"That's refreshing," he commented.

"Be quiet. I'm not finished." She drew a breath. "All I wanted was a little bit of freedom, one adventure."

"I gave you one."

"No, you didn't. The entire time you said you were my friend and that you sympathized with my feelings, you were following Melbourne's orders—though I'm certain he didn't know the specifics." If Sebastian had known, either she or Valentine would be dead or forced to flee the country. "The entire time you had in mind the limits of where I could go, and you had every intention of enforcing them. Sebastian made it your job to keep me from doing something truly wild, and you accepted your assignment."

"You're the one who decided to confide in me; that was your choice."

"And I won't make that mistake again. Damnation, Valentine. I'm not a child to be kept away from sweets; I'm an adult. And I thought I admired you. Ha. Be assured that the next adventure I choose won't have anything to do with you. And it won't be anything you can control." She drew a breath. "You should have told me."

"Would it have made a difference?" he asked almost grudgingly, as if curiosity was overtaking his better judgment.

Good. That was the Valentine she wanted to rail at. "I would have found someone else—someone not obligated to carry every tale and conversation to Melbourne."

"I didn't." He shifted. "That's why he was so damned angry this morning. Bloody Cobb-Harding stopped by and tried to describe your breasts."

She blanched. "Stephen Cobb-Harding was here?"

"He offered marriage as a way to protect your reputation. If I'd done as I should have and told Sebastian what occurred at Belmont's, he would have had some time to prepare for Cobb-Harding's approach."

Eleanor nodded. "Perhaps so. But you haven't done me any favors, regardless."

He gave a nasty grin. "That's not what you said the other night."

"The other night was my idea; not yours. You may have had your hand on the reins, but penned or not, this horse got something she wanted from you." She sat forward, jabbing a finger into his knee. "And have you considered that I'm not the only female who's used you for that? You are quite good at it."

"No one uses me."

"Are you so certain? Perhaps the chits you're so proud of having seduced and then cast aside were actually only playing with *you*. Maybe you provided something—one thing—they wanted, and so they used and discarded *you*." She stood, opening the door again. "Because frankly, Valentine, given your actions, I don't see much else that you're good for."

No one had ever spoken to him like that before. And no one ever would again, as far as he was concerned. Valentine remained seated, mostly because he was concentrating on not striking Eleanor. He watched as she stepped out of the coach, shutting the door when she reached the ground.

"All right, Frederick. Take him home. I'm finished with him."

That was bloody well enough of that. Before the coach could travel to the end of the drive, Valentine slammed open the door and jumped to the ground. "I'll walk," he snapped, glaring up at the surprised driver.

"Very good, my lord."

Now it was his turn to speak his mind. He turned around, but Eleanor's backside was vanishing into the house. As though sensing the danger she was in, Stanton gave him one look and closed the front door.

Fine. "You're wrong!" he yelled for good measure, ignoring the groomsman and driver giving him wary looks.

Walking home was probably a good idea. It would be better for everyone concerned if he calmed down a little before he reached the familiar depravity of his own house. He stalked down the street, glad he had nearly two miles to go. He would use every foot of it.

For a good half mile he simply cursed. So Eleanor detested him. What did he care? He'd just used her for a little fun and excitement and enjoyment, and now that the situation was becoming too complicated, it was time to end it. Good riddance.

But he wasn't a fraud. He hadn't lied about his participation, even if he had neglected to tell her why he'd made his first appearance as her shadow. At the moment he was loath to admit it, but he did enjoy her company. He enjoyed chatting with her, and trying to figure out the way her mind worked. Eleanor Griffin was one of the few females of his acquaintance who seemed to have a desire in life other than to settle herself as comfortably as possible.

And now he felt as though she'd kicked him in the teeth. Whatever she thought to do next, Melbourne would never make the same mistake twice. He'd said her rebellion was over, and he meant it. The duke was probably thanking his lucky stars that John Tracey had made an appearance in London. Surely not even Eleanor would object to a match with a war hero. Hell, he'd probably give her all the adventure she wanted every night in their cozy little marriage bed.

"Bloody hell," he growled.

"Deverill!" a familiar voice called.

He looked toward the road as a barouche stopped beside him. "Henning," he grumbled, giving a nod and continuing on.

"Some chit lock you out when her husband returned home?" the young, rotund man continued with a chuckle, urging his driver to keep pace. "Let me give you a ride."

"Thank you, no. I'm walking."

"But—"

"I'm not feeling social at the moment, Francis," Valentine interrupted, the last of his patience crumbling away. "Good day."

Henning nodded amiably. "I'll leave you be, then. I've seen many a gentleman with that look before. Driver?"

Valentine stopped. "What look?" he barked.

"The look that says some chit's got you all twisted around. I've even felt that way a time or two myself. No tell—"

"No chit twists me around," the marquis growled. Bloody damnation. Lucifer must be howling with laughter right now. Even dull-witted Henning had advice for him. "I twist them around."

"You don't have to tell me," Francis Henning returned, his good-humored expression faltering a little. "I've seen the results. Good thing you only break the hearts of married ladies."

"Why is that?"

"Too late for them to go into mourning and become old maids in your honor."

He doubted any of his conquests would even consider such a thing. They moved on to the next conquest—or conqueror—just as he did. Just as . . . "Right." Valentine made a show of pulling out his pocket watch. "I have an appointment. Excuse me."

With a nod Francis waved his driver on again, leaving Valentine standing in the street. Of all people to say something pointed, he would have thought Francis Henning the least likely. And yet the muddlehead's bent logic echoed almost exactly what Eleanor had yelled at him.

But it didn't make sense. She had to be wrong. Whatever she said, no chit had ever used him. The idea that she claimed to have done that with him—just used him so she could get the adventure out of her system—was ridiculous. And infuriating.

He was not some stud bull the cows sought out when no one better was available, only to be sent back to the pasture when they were finished with him. It was the other way around. They all knew that. *He* knew that.

Eleanor Griffin was a great deal of trouble. Other women had called him hardhearted or cruel, but they'd never called him worthless. And coming from her, the accusation was more . . . disturbing than he would ever have expected.

And simply because his initial reason for keeping her company might have been coerced, that was no reason for her to disregard the integrity of her adventure. She'd chosen it, and he'd delivered it. Even if he hadn't been obligated to Melbourne, he would have done the same.

Valentine frowned. That wasn't the truth. If he'd somehow been swept into her plot, hadn't known her brothers, hadn't been obligated to keep her relatively safe, he would have maneuvered her adventure to reflect what *he* wanted from her. And it would have involved considerably more sex, with much less attention paid to what she claimed to be seeking. What she had been seeking.

Had he somehow ruined that for her, simply by not telling her that someone else had asked him to stand by her? And why the devil did he even care? She'd insulted him, her brothers had insulted him, and he had a hundred other women he could use to purge her from his mind. Or they could use him, if what Eleanor said was true.

He swore again, ignoring the startled looks of the nearby pedestrians. She'd done something to him. She'd made him insane. That was why he couldn't stop thinking about what she'd said, couldn't stop thinking about her damned adventure, couldn't stop thinking about her. And that, of course, led to all sorts of speculation about when Melbourne would request Tracey's presence, and whether Eleanor would accept the match out of spite—or even worse, because she liked the damned war hero. She'd probably never call *him* useless.

"Damnation." He looked up, stopping as he realized he'd missed his corner and had ended up on South Audley Street in front of the modest Grosvenor Chapel. He'd probably passed by it a thousand times, but it being a church, he'd never paid much attention to it.

A church. He'd meant to enter one of God's buildings only two more times in his life: Once when he found the chit who could bear him an heir, and the second time when he was to be put under the ground, if the hallowed ceiling didn't crack in horror when they carried him in.

Glancing about self-consciously, Valentine pushed open the gates and entered the grounds. Lightning didn't strike him, but he remained cautious, nevertheless. A twining arbor of roses marked the entrance to the small cemetery, while more red blooms bordered the short walk to the four front steps of the stone and wood structure. With a deep breath he seated himself on the lowest of the granite steps.

"Good morning, my son," a quiet male voice came from the entry above and behind him.

Well, it wasn't God; that was for certain. Valentine lowered one shoulder and turned to look. "Father. Sorry to disturb you. I merely needed a moment to think."

The tall, thin man garbed in black nodded at him. "You're Lord Deverill, aren't you? Valentine Corbett?"

"I am."

"Ah. I believe I've delivered a sermon or two about you."

If there was one thing Valentine hadn't expected, it was humor from the clergy. "I'm honored."

"Yes, a little mention of sin always makes the flock pay more attention." The elderly priest lowered himself with a grunt to the stair above where Valentine sat. "I've always wanted to ask—are you named for the saint?"

The marquis shrugged. "I suppose so. I was born on St. Valentine's Day. My father always seemed to think it was some sort of joke. I didn't understand it until I grew a little older."

"Yes, I believe St. Valentine was a bit easier on the pure of heart than you are reputed to be. But is it only the need to think which brings you here?"

"Do you lurk on your doorstep waiting for pagans to convert?"

The priest chuckled. "If you must know, I was about to water the roses. All are welcome within these gates, though. Take your time, my son. Think all you want."

With another grunt the priest stood again, descending the remainder of the steps and walking stiffly to the small gardening shed. Valentine watched him emerge with a watering can and continue on to the small well in the middle of the garden.

"If this is a sign, it's a fairly weak one," he commented to no one in particular, rising to go help the priest draw water from the well. A few weeks ago he wouldn't have bothered, though a few weeks ago he doubted he would have set foot on church grounds.

"Tell me, Father," he said a moment later, hauling up

the full bucket to dump water into the watering can, "is it some sort of sin not to tell someone you're protecting them when that someone is under the impression that you are participating in their adventures without reserve?"

"A sin? Not one of the deadly ones. It is a lie, I would say."

"Yes, for her own good."

"That would depend."

"Oh, really? On what, pray tell?"

"Who decided that the lie was for her own good? And did it prevent this lady from accomplishing what she intended?"

"What if what she intended was sin?"

The priest looked at him. "You didn't ask me to debate morality—only actions."

Valentine lifted the full watering can and lugged it over to the nearest of the rose bushes. "Actions. Yes, I suppose then that my concealing my true reason for being there might have prevented her from realizing the true . . . spirit of her actions."

"Then you were wrong."

"Just like that?" he returned, lifting an eyebrow.

"I thought you might appreciate a direct answer. I could give you a parable, if you'd rather."

"Thank you, no." For a moment Valentine concentrated on doing enough watering to lighten the weight of the watering can. "Then I should take steps to make it right."

"I certainly can't advise you to act in a manner which would encourage sin." With a slight grin, the priest took the half-empty can to continue with watering. "But putting things right does seem a more worthy task than putting them wrong."

"A more difficult one, anyway. Thank you. This has certainly been an unexpected conversation, Father . . ."

"Michael. Father Michael. And I've found it rather interesting myself, Lord Deverill. Feel free to stop by for a chat on any Monday or Thursday."

"Why Monday or Thursday?"

"Those are the days I water the roses."

Valentine chuckled. Doffing his hat, he headed back for the front gate. Halfway through, though, another question occurred to him. It horrified him, but for Lucifer's—or rather God's, considering the location—sake, it was just a question. It didn't mean anything—and he certainly had no one else to ask. "Father Michael?"

"Yes, my son?"

"If I were to bring someone by, would you . . ." His mouth went dry, and he swallowed. *Just a question*, he reminded himself, not believing that for an instant. "Would you marry us?"

"Not without the banns being read, or a special license procured from Canterbury. If you're that desperate to keep from sinning, I might suggest Gretna Green." Father Michael frowned. "Though we don't encourage that sort of thing. Too scandalous."

Nodding, Valentine closed the gate behind him and turned back down the street toward Corbett House. It shook him that he'd even been able to say the word "marry," much less that he continued to contemplate it. One thing he knew for certain, though; he didn't want Eleanor marrying Lord John Tracey.

And even the priest had said he had an obligation to make things right. Eleanor wanted an adventure, something wild and uncontrolled and completely out of anyone's safety and protection. Well, he would just give her one—if he didn't give himself an apoplexy thinking about it first.

Eleanor stormed straight up the stairs from the front drive, all three brothers on her heels, and barricaded herself in her bedchamber. While Zachary pounded at the door, she even dragged her dressing table to block the entrance, and shoved one of her overstuffed sitting chairs against that.

"Go away!" she yelled, moving to the remaining chair beneath the window and dropping into it.

"This isn't finished with, Nell," Sebastian's voice came, though he seemed to be farther away—probably leaning against the wall while he let Zachary attempt the actual breaking and entering.

"I'm not listening. I may have some things to answer for, but so do you. And you will not bully me into doing anything. When I've considered everything, then I will come out and we'll have a calm, adult discussion. One to one. No overwhelming force of numbers allowed."

"But in the meantime you'll be up here hiding?" the deep voice returned, sarcasm finally seeping into his tone.

"I wouldn't have to hide if you'd stop pursuing me! Go away and let me think in peace." Recalling just what she'd overheard of Melbourne's bellowed conversation with Deverill, she lurched out of her chair and strode to the door again. "And you're a cheat, Melbourne. Don't think you've won!" she yelled.

"I don't think anyone's won," his quieter voice said. "We'll be downstairs, Nell. No one's leaving this house until we settle matters. And I do mean settle."

Eleanor grabbed a down pillow from her bed and held it up over her face so she could scream into the soft material. It helped relieve a little of the sharp fury, so she did it again.

As her striding-about, wanting-to-hit-something anger faded, though, the deep hurt beneath it began creeping heavily into her chest. Instead of yelling into the pillow, she clutched it to her. A sob wrenched her throat, followed by another and another, until she was shaking with tears.

It wasn't that Stephen Cobb-Harding had appeared and threatened her family. They would deal with that. However angry Melbourne might be, he wouldn't allow the Griffin reputation or standing to be damaged. For him, that meant everything.

No, she knew quite well why she was crying. And the fact that she was weeping and heartbroken because of *him* made it even worse. Why had she trusted him? Why had she just assumed that the uncaring Marquis of Deverill would suddenly take an interest in a friendship with her? Because she'd wanted to. That was why.

"Stupid," she muttered brokenly, blotting her wet face with the pillow. Valentine broke hearts with alarming regularity, and she'd just assumed that she was immune. But he'd only become her companion because Melbourne had forced him to. And his bits of advice and the example he'd set—those things she'd begun to admire about him— they'd all been given with his obligation to Melbourne in mind.

Her adventure, being with him—true, she'd asked for both, but . . . Oh, she didn't know what to think. And to her surprise, she wanted to talk to Valentine. Not to yell at him again, but to discover what he'd really been thinking, and more importantly, feeling, while they'd been involved in her so-called rebellion.

After what she'd said to him, however, it was entirely

likely that he would never speak to her again. He'd never kiss her, or touch her, or chat with her, and tomorrow he'd probably have some pretty, empty-headed chit on his arm so he could pretend he'd never had any interest in Eleanor at all. If he ever had.

She buried her face in her hands, rocking back and forth in her comfortable chair. Whatever conversation she and Melbourne had when she'd supposedly thought everything through logically, she already knew what the end result would be. Her brother would hand her a list of two or three names, give her the choice among them as though that meant she had freedom, and then he would arrange the marriage. If she was lucky, she'd get an actual proposal, though of course her presence would be the least significant part of the deal.

Eleanor didn't think she'd ever felt so alone, and in the back of her thoughts the person whom she most wanted to talk to, whom she considered a companion and a friend, continued to be Deverill. It was as if her heart refused to accept what her logical mind now knew perfectly well—that he'd cast her aside as too much trouble, and she needed to let him go and concentrate on making her future as tolerable as possible.

"Damnation."

The worst part of it was, she'd done it to herself. She'd wanted new experiences, a new way of looking at life, and evidently as Melbourne had told her, nothing was truly free. She only wished that fact had been demonstrated with less force and volume.

"Aunt Nell?" A quiet knock came at the door.

So they'd sent Peep to negotiate. Cowards. "What is it, my dear?"

"Are you going to come downstairs for dinner?"

Eleanor blinked, turning to look out the window. Blackness greeted her outside, lit by the occasional gas lamp along the quiet street. For heaven's sake, she'd been moping all day. But if she went downstairs, she would have to be ready for another fight, and she simply wasn't up to it. Not yet.

She rose, going to lean against her dressing table, which still rested in front of the door. "No. If you would please have Helen bring me some soup and bread, I would be very grateful."

"Eleanor, you can't stay locked in there forever."

She'd had a suspicion that Sebastian lurked nearby. "I know. Just until tomorrow."

He was silent for a long moment. "Very well. You're not a prisoner. I only want you in the house until we assess the damage from Cobb-Harding."

"I'm not going anywhere," she returned, putting the flat of her hand on the door. "Thank you for giving me a little time."

"We'll see you in the morning."

"Good night, Aunt Nell. Don't be sad. If you want me to help you yell at anyone tomorrow, let me know."

"Thank you, Peep. Good night."

Helen brought up her soup and bread, and helped her move her furniture back into place. "Shall I make down the bed, my lady?"

"No. I'll do it myself. In fact, you can go. I'll put the dishes outside the door."

"Very good, my lady. What time shall I wake you in the morning?"

Eleanor managed a smile. Some things never changed, no matter the chaos in her life. "Half past seven, if you please. Good night, Helen."

The maid curtsied. "Good night, my lady."

Sitting at her dressing table, Eleanor ate her soup. It was barley and chicken, usually her favorite, but after the first bite she barely tasted it. Her mind refused to let go of scenarios and conversations where she confronted Valentine and he went down on his knees to admit that he cared for her and to beg her forgiveness for his deceit. She sighed. It sounded nice, but she couldn't imagine anything more unlikely.

After she finished eating she put out her dishes and then spent an hour wandering around aimlessly, sitting down four times to try to read and another three to do some of her correspondence, and failing miserably at all of it. "Blast," she muttered. "Just go to bed, Eleanor. Things will look better in the morning."

She didn't believe it, but as long as she was attempting to fool herself, it might as well be with something pleasant. It was just unfortunate that both the most pleasant and the most unpleasant thing she could think of was Valentine Corbett.

Chapter 20

◦─◦◡◦─◦

Valentine managed to find John Tracey at the third club he searched that morning. The war hero looked calm and confident, and probably had no idea that today might very well be his chance to join one of England's most powerful families. At least it hadn't happened last night when Valentine had been formulating and discarding plans in the midst of drinking a bottle of whiskey. If it had happened already, Tracey would no doubt have been breaking his fast with his family-to-be.

Valentine took a seat at a table across the room, far enough away that he wouldn't be noticed, and close enough so he could see anything that might transpire. Tracey ordered a plate of ham and two boiled eggs, while Valentine settled for toast and coffee. It didn't make sense. Tracey should be the one with no appetite, worried over whether the Griffins—and Eleanor in particular— would find him worthy of joining the clan.

Aside from the drinking and plotting, he'd spent the

night doing a distressing amount of that damned self-reflection, focused mainly on why he'd abruptly become so determined that he wouldn't lose Eleanor to anyone else, why the idea of making things right for her had crept into his soul and refused to loose its grip.

For God's sake, if he'd decided to wed he could have any woman he wanted. Even a married one could probably be persuaded to leave her husband with the proper inducement. The problem was, he didn't want any other woman. And he couldn't have Eleanor. True, he could talk to priests and plot elopements, but he was the damned Marquis of Deverill. And Deverill didn't embarrass himself, compromise his principles, lose his mind, over a chit.

The worst moment had come just before dawn. He'd tried out words like "possession," "obsession," "spite," "jealousy," and "ownership" to describe why he felt as he did toward Eleanor—and then the right word, the perfect word, had struck him squarely between the eyes.

The word. It didn't make any sense. How could he be in love with Eleanor when he didn't even believe in the emotion?

Once his mind had found the word, though, every bit of him refused to relinquish it. So whether he'd ever be able to do anything about it or not, whether he'd be able to even say it aloud, he loved Eleanor Griffin. And now he was about to lose her.

Tracey finished breakfast and then headed out to Tattersall's horse auctions, with Valentine still trailing him. If he wanted to know firsthand what Melbourne might be plotting, he could probably apologize and be let back into the fold. Then he would have to sit and listen to it—listen to the brothers plan a life for Eleanor and know they had no real concept of what she wanted or needed or deserved.

Twenty minutes after Tracey settled in to view the auctions, a servant in Griffin livery approached him with a note. *Damnation.* They were doing it. Of course, Nell might end up liking Tracey, even being happy with him. Well, that wasn't acceptable. Not when he would have to watch from a distance and know he might have had her for himself if he'd only taken action.

So it was time, then, to take action, and damn the consequences. With a deep breath, Valentine approached the war hero. "Tracey, I see you've been favored with Melbourne's correspondence," he commented, gesturing at the note.

"Deverill. Yes, apparently I'm to appear there this afternoon for an audience."

"Any idea why?"

John looked at him. "I have an idea, yes. But if you don't, then I don't believe I should be discussing it with you."

"Of course I know why you've been summoned," Valentine returned, managing his usual uncaring drawl. "Are you interested in the match?"

"Who wouldn't be? Lady Eleanor's a beautiful woman."

"And the dowry won't be anything to laugh at, either."

Tracey frowned. "If I might ask, what, precisely, is your interest here?"

"I'm a family friend. I just want to be certain that Eleanor will be happy."

"Then ask her." The auctioneer called off another horse, and Tracey turned his head. "If you'll excuse me, I have a team to bid on."

Valentine inclined his head and moved away. He knew enough, now. Melbourne, and perhaps even Eleanor, had settled on a candidate, and the potential husband had no objection to the match, either.

Well, *he* had an objection. No one had asked him who he thought might be the best match for Eleanor, and no one would consider him for it. No, not the blackhearted Marquis of Deverill. Not even if he managed to convince them how . . . important Eleanor had become to his life, or how he couldn't imagine going through his days without having her to chat with, to kiss, just to look at.

According to the Church, in the person of Father Michael, he needed to make amends to Eleanor. It was simply the right thing to do. And with the amount of time he'd spent on the slopes of Hades, he'd best listen. Valentine chuckled grimly. He was about to do the one thing he'd sworn to avoid at all costs: Lead with his heart. He hoped the shriveled thing was up to the adventure.

Eleanor awoke abruptly. She felt thick and disoriented, as though she'd slept too hard and awakened too fast. The clock on the mantel sat cloaked in inky blackness, but from the silence in the house and on the street, it must have been sometime after two and before five o'clock in the morning.

Sighing, she turned onto her side and resolutely closed her eyes again. *Don't think about anything*, she ordered herself when her mind threatened images of the charming John Tracey and how happy he'd been to meet with her brother. *Count farm animals*.

A hand clamped over her mouth, and another pinned her crossed arms to the bed.

Her heart slammed against her rib cage. She yelped, the sound muffled beneath the hard grip. Kicking out beneath the heavy blankets, she tried to wrench her hands free.

"Surprise," a harsh male whisper came in her ear.

In her mind she was shrieking. She had three formidable brothers lying only yards away. A breaking vase, a cry, anything would wake them. And then the sound of his voice began to sink through her panic.

He yanked her upright, face-to-face with him. She could dimly make out a black panther's half mask—and a pair of glittering green eyes—set beneath a battered-looking black hat. "*Valentine?*"

"Shh."

"Get—get out of here!" she rasped.

"I can't do that." Before she could flinch away, he tied a kerchief around her face, covering and muffling her mouth. "Hold still," he whispered, pulling her hands forward and binding them in the same way.

Plunking her back flat on the bed, Valentine went to her wardrobe and pulled out a large portmanteau. He began opening drawers and flinging clothing into the bag, hesitating and changing his mind about articles several times.

Even knowing who it was rifling through her things, Eleanor couldn't quite believe it. And as hard as her heart was pounding, it only took a few seconds for her stark terror to twist into anger. Whatever he had in mind, and however mad at her he might be, she was through with being manhandled.

The hem of one of her gowns caught in the edge of the wardrobe, and with a curse he glanced down to free it. Seizing her chance, Eleanor lurched to her feet and ran barefoot to the door. With her hands bound together it took her a moment to rattle the latch open. She was a second too slow.

One strong arm curled her into his hard chest, while with his free hand he gently shut the door again. "Stop that," he murmured into her hair, half dragging her back to the bed again.

She kicked him. Valentine grunted, flinging her onto the rumpled bedsheets before he bent to rub his knee. If she'd had another second to aim or if she'd been wearing shoes, he would have been on the floor. One didn't grow up with brothers and not learn how to kick effectively.

Eleanor wriggled off the side of the bed and onto her feet again. Before she could aim another kick at his lowered head, he tackled her back onto the mattress, landing her on her back with him on top of her.

"And I thought you wanted an adventure," he muttered, grabbing her hands to keep her from punching him two-fisted in his masked face.

"What the devil are you doing?" she attempted around the gag.

"Sorry, haven't a clue what you're saying. So shut up."

He dumped a last item into the portmanteau, fastened it closed, and returned to the bed. Dragging her to her feet by one arm, he hauled her toward the door.

"I'm not going anywhere with you," she snarled, her heart still pounding at quadruple its normal pace.

Valentine looked at her for a moment in the dim moonlight. Her hair was wild, coursing down her shoulders and sticking out at odd angles beneath the tightly tied kerchief. The terror had fled her eyes, but they remained large and filled with suspicion. He hadn't wanted to frighten her, but obviously he'd underestimated how angry she would be. If she kicked him like that again she'd probably reduce his cock to pudding.

He couldn't understand a word of what she was muttering at him, but she didn't sound happy. He could guess the gist of her dialogue. "You're having an adventure. So stop fighting and come with me."

Eleanor shook her head, digging in her heels. The word she mangled sounded distinctly like an insult, but he ignored it. Instead, Valentine heaved her up over his shoulder, lifted the portmanteau in his other hand, and opened her bedchamber door. The house was as still as it had been when he'd broken in through the morning room window, but even so he kept all his attention on the closed doors lining the hallway as he made his way to the stairs. Running into another Griffin right now would lead to bloodshed.

She refused to remain still, and her struggling nearly sent them both headlong down the stairs. Leaning one shoulder against the wall for balance, he continued to descend. The fourth step down, though, let out a godawful squeak. Valentine froze, listening for a long moment. Nothing stirred above.

Hoping the sound was something the family was accustomed to, he tightened his grip across Eleanor's bottom and continued down. Waiting about would only ensure that they were caught. And since Eleanor was wriggling but not attempting to shout, she evidently didn't want him dead.

He'd already unlatched the front door from the inside, and it took only a moment to swing it open on well-oiled hinges and escape onto the portico. Closing it took a bit more effort, but if the damned stairs hadn't roused the brethren, the front door latching wouldn't, either.

His coach waited at the end of the drive, and his driver fastened the portmanteau at the back of the vehicle while Valentine waited, Eleanor still slung over his shoulder. Dawson held the door steady while he hauled Eleanor up and dumped her onto the soft leather opposite him. "Go, Dawson."

"Aye, my lord."

They rolled onto the street, and Valentine sat back to remove his borrowed hat and the black mask. "That wasn't so bad now, was it?" he said conversationally, running a hand through his ruffled hair.

Eleanor had pushed herself upright, and with both hands still tied together in front of her she managed after a moment to lower the kerchief from across her mouth. "This—you—" she sputtered, "what—what the devil do you think you're doing?"

"I'm providing you with an adventure to replace the one I ruined with my duplicity," he returned, offering her the flask from his pocket.

"Untie me."

"In a moment. I don't wish to be pummeled by a chit."

"A pummeling by me will be the very least of your worries, Deverill," she snapped. "Stop this coach and return me home at once!"

"No. And don't threaten me with your brothers—if you'd let out a shout we'd never have made it out of the house."

She drew a breath, obviously trying to assess his sanity. He wished her luck with the task; he'd given up on being reasonable hours ago, even before he'd come up with the word that explained his lack of common sense. "I do not need your help to plan another adventure," she finally said in a more reasonable tone. "I don't need you for anything. Let me go."

"At the moment you need me," he returned, "considering that you're wearing nothing but a cotton shift." He finally let himself look at more than her face, and felt warm desire curl down his spine, as it had when he'd watched her sleeping. "A very thin shift, by the way."

"This is ridiculous."

"No, this is something you can't control. Enjoy it, or not. I'm not turning around."

Eleanor studied his expression for a long moment. "Then where are we going?" she finally asked. "You can tell me that, at least, can't you?"

"Certainly." He drew a breath of his own. "We're going to Scotland."

"*Scotland?*"

"Gretna Green, to be specific."

She audibly swallowed. "Gret—So you . . . you think you're going to marry me? Melbourne's already spoken with John Tracey. You're too late. And I wouldn't have you in a million years anyway, Deverill. So you might as well turn this coach around now. If you do, no one needs to know that you kidnapped me."

"I'm not letting anyone else have you." Anger and worry clenched into his chest as he tried to imagine her in Tracey's arms. In any man's arms other than his.

"You've gone mad. What's driven you to this non-sense?"

"You have," he snarled. "You, with your pretty gray eyes and your smile and the way you speak your mind. The sound of your laugh, your tears when something makes you sad." He closed his eyes for a moment, trying to imagine anyone else who had ever made him feel the way he did when he was with her. Emptiness looked back at him. There wasn't anyone else. "You're the only woman I've ever . . . liked."

"'Liked'?" she repeated stiffly, her gray eyes deep pools of midnight.

He cleared his throat, uncomfortable. "That's quite the confession for me, my dear. And more than you've gotten from Tracey, I'll wager."

"It is, isn't it? But if you became acquainted with more females, I think you'd find I'm not that unique. And I'm all but engaged to someone else."

It jolted him, that she could so easily go along with Melbourne's plans for her. Was it his fault? Had he hurt her that much? "I'd venture to say that I'm acquainted with more women than you are, Nell," he countered, "and I—"

"I don't mean acquainted physically. That doesn't count."

"I don't know about that," he argued, amused.

She straightened. "I thought I was here because you wanted to marry me. I wouldn't recommend discussing—"

"I didn't want to talk with them," he interrupted. "There's a difference between spending time with someone until something more interesting comes along, and spending time with someone because you can't imagine not doing so."

"Oh," she whispered, her gaze half wary and half surprised. "But if you felt this way, why didn't you tell me before? All of this—"

"Because I didn't know before," he returned sharply, beginning to become annoyed. He was fairly certain that a chit wasn't supposed to question the whys and wherefores of a declaration like this.

"How do you know now, then?"

"Damnation, Eleanor. I didn't know until you started

yelling at me and calling me worthless, and then I realized that probably the next day Melbourne would go out and find a husband for you. And he did, didn't he? I . . ." He trailed off, studying the soft lines of her face. "That isn't acceptable. It shouldn't be for you either."

She hesitated. "I knew my rebellion wouldn't last forever."

"But you didn't have that adventure you wanted, did you? You said I ruined it. And therefore your rebellion isn't over."

"So *you* decided *you* would marry me? Without even asking me? How does that give me an adventure?"

"The adventure is the journey," he returned. "And I didn't have a chance to ask you. Instead I discussed it with someone else. He gave me some very good advice."

"And who might this someone be? A butler? A horse trader?"

"A priest. He said if I'd done something to wrong you, I should do something to set it right."

"And to you that meant marriage."

Unless he was mistaken, most of the anger had left her voice. That was a very good sign, especially considering that he was perfectly serious. He wasn't taking her back home. If she didn't want to marry him, he would convince her otherwise. She was not marrying John Tracey.

"Well, Father Michael did speak rather strongly against sin. And when I asked him about how quickly he could marry us, he said if I was that desperate, Gretna Green was an alternative I might consider."

" 'Consider'. That means 'think about,' not 'rush headlong into'."

He grinned. "Yes, but as I said, this way it has the added attraction of being an adventure."

"I didn't think you ever meant to marry, Valentine. What about all of your lovers and paramours who keep you from boredom? Isn't that all you want?"

"I haven't touched another woman since I kissed you, Eleanor. My butler's ready to call in a physician. He's convinced I'm ill." Valentine paused. "I think I am ill. And there's no cure." Swallowing, he sat up straighter. "I like this sickness, Eleanor."

"But I said that I'd used you," she said slowly, holding her bound hands out to him again.

He was going to have to release her sooner or later. With a frown he untied the bonds, careful not to scratch or bruise her soft skin. "I don't think you used me, Eleanor," he returned. "And the only thing I kept from you was that Melbourne asked me to keep an eye on you. After that first night, I would have done it, regardless."

Slowly she reached out to touch his cheek. "I just wish I could rely on this being the real Valentine Corbett. I like this man, but sometimes I can't find him at all."

"He's new to this," he replied, leaning forward to touch his lips to hers. His pulse sped as her mouth softened to his embrace. "But he's trying. And he does have three days to convince you. Will you give him a chance?"

Rising, he moved to sit beside her, drawing her arms up over his shoulders as he took her mouth again. God, he could kiss her forever. The thought of not being able to see her whenever he wished, of not being able to chat with her and hear her warmer view of the world, had driven him into a near panic. He'd only been half serious when he'd spoken to Father Michael, but hell, if a priest thought it was a good plan, who was he to argue? Besides, it seemed the very best idea he'd had in three decades and two years of life.

She moaned softly against his mouth, and he went hard. True, she hadn't agreed to marry him, but she hadn't said no, either. And he had nothing against doing some convincing—especially if it involved being inside her again.

"You're truly going to ruin me," she said quietly, a small tremor shaking her voice.

"I am. That way you'll have to marry me."

"I won't, if I don't want to. Melbourne could probably still convince Tracey."

"I'll convince you, first," he murmured, pulling her onto his lap so he could kiss her more deeply.

"Or I could enter a convent," Eleanor suggested, licking his ear.

"Not now," he said with a soft chuckle. "You'd never be able to stand going a lifetime without feeling a man's touch again." He slowly ran his hand up her leg, pulling her thin shift up as he went from her ankle to her thigh.

Immediately he realized that he'd said something wrong, because she lifted her head away from his throat to look at him. "What about you going a lifetime without feeling another woman's touch? *You*, Valentine. Because if you think I'll tolerate you having mistresses, you can—"

He ignored the "tolerate" part of her sentence, feeling a small tremor run through him at the jealousy in her voice. "All I have is my word, which probably isn't worth much. But I . . . don't want anyone else. I want you."

"This is all very nice, but it's also convenient."

" 'Convenient'? You think it was convenient for me to arrange all this? To break into your house and kidnap you?"

"Convenient that you only decided to do this after Melbourne told you to stay away from me, and after he summoned John Tracey."

That definitely had something to do with it; he was in a weak position, and he knew it. "Before that, I'd thought we—I—would have more time to figure out why you make me feel this way. Cobb-Harding's idiocy slammed that door." He gave a short grin. "So I broke in through the window."

"Is this for me or for you, then, Valentine?"

"Can't it be for both of us?"

"You—"

"I don't know how to be proper, Eleanor," he breathed, kissing her again, feeling her melt against him in response, "and I don't suppose I'm capable of doing something completely against my own self-interest. If I could, I still wouldn't let you marry Tracey."

She sighed. "I don't think you would," she agreed slowly, tangling her fingers through his hair. "But are you better for me than he would be?"

He smiled against her mouth. "Much better. Consider this: Since you don't want to be proper, perhaps we'll make a good match."

She took a ragged breath. "This is all well and good, for you to seduce me while I'm in a night shift and completely reliant on you for protection and for my reputation. But what about tomorrow?"

Part of what Valentine enjoyed so much about Eleanor was the way she looked at the world, and the way she spoke her mind. Tonight, though, he would have accepted her quiet acquiescence without complaint. With a last smoldering kiss that had him pointing the way to Gretna Green, he set her back on the opposite seat.

"What I know is that you have no feelings for John Tracey, or you would have leaped out of the coach by now, moving or not. But you're right. I can't convince you to trust me, and you don't have to believe that I would never do anything to hurt you. I could try to bribe you, tell you that I'll build you a private bathing pool if you'd like, and that I'll never try to stop you from riding astride or speaking to whomever you please. And I would do those things, if you wanted them."

"Val—"

"But I'm just going to tell you what you already know," he continued, "that you and I are good together. We have fun, and we understand one another. Hell, you understand me better than I do, and I think I can say the same about you." Valentine brushed a finger along her cheek because he needed to touch her. "But that's just words, and you need to think. So I'll be over here, napping, if you should make up your mind tonight."

He settled back into the corner, closing his eyes and trying to convince his nether regions that the delay was for a good cause. He wanted her, more than he'd ever wanted anything in his entire life. More than he would want anything ever again. But neither did he want to be a haphazard decision that she made in a last effort to thwart Melbourne.

Good God. *He was closing his eyes.* He never closed his eyes in the company of a female—but it wasn't the first time he'd done so with Eleanor. That gesture on his part spoke more to him than all of the rationalizations and protestations he could make. He trusted her. Not just with his physical well-being, but with his heart—which apparently meant that he had one.

As the silence lengthened, he opened one eye. She was sitting in the opposite corner, her arms crossed over her chest and her gaze steady on him. Valentine frowned.

"Are you cold?"

"A little."

"Why the devil didn't you say something?" he asked, shrugging out of his greatcoat and standing to wrap it around her shoulders.

"I'm not familiar with the rules for a kidnapping," she returned, tucking her chin into the heavy coat.

He let the comment go, considering that he'd half expected an all-out battle. "So had you decided to marry Tracey?"

She sighed. "I don't know. He's certainly the least offensive of the candidates Melbourne and I discussed."

"He discussed candidates with you? That's a surprise. I expected a sweeping pronouncement immediately followed by a special marriage license."

"So did I, at first. He did make it clear that I was to stop carousing about London and marry, both for my own safety and for the good of the family."

" 'Carousing'? Is that what he called it?"

"Yes. What would you call it?"

"Having a bit of fun," he returned. "Exploring. Deciding the course of your life."

Eleanor smiled a little. "You do understand."

"That's what I've been trying to tell you, my dear. And that brings up something else which bears mentioning. I'm good at sex."

"I assumed that, after—"

"But I've never been as good as when I'm with you." Valentine drew a breath, willing her to understand what he was trying to say. "And I don't think you'll find anyone else who makes you feel the way I can, Eleanor."

"Oh, my." Her color deepening, she sat forward. The

coat sagged from her shoulders. "Tomorrow will you still be this Valentine Corbett?"

He was only just discovering that there *was* another Valentine Corbett, and that aside from the insanity, he didn't seem to be a bad fellow. "You hate the other one— and for good reason."

She shook her head. "No, I don't. And I'm beginning to realize that they're both you. You've done some awful things, but in the past few weeks, I've discovered that you can be . . . frightfully insightful."

"You're making me blush."

"Valentine, I'm trying to be serious. You know, I remember meeting your father. I think Melbourne had dragged the family to Scotland, and we stopped by Deverill Park overnight."

He nodded. He wasn't particularly proud of anything in his past, but since he'd kidnapped Eleanor, he supposed he owed her a discussion of it—even if that meant more damned self-reflection on his part. In some ways, and to his surprise, he'd actually been able to figure some things out lately. "I remember. You were what, seven?" He glanced down at his hands. "My father was raving by then. You probably didn't know, or don't remember, but Melbourne had planned to stay for a fortnight. My father got it into his head that the lot of you were his illegitimate children, trying to take his fortune. He actually attacked Sebastian."

"What was wrong with him?"

"I'm sure you've heard all the gory details by now, Eleanor."

"Rumors galore, yes, but I'd prefer the truth."

So this was the talk about his bloodline. He supposed she deserved to know that, as well. "Syphilis."

"That must have been awful for you, Valentine."

"By then I just wanted him to hurry up and die, and leave me in peace." He cleared his throat. "Christ. I don't think I've ever said that before. My apologies."

"For being honest?" Eleanor shrugged the rest of the way out of his coat and leaned across the open space of the carriage to put her hands on his knees. "You know, I have to admit that the entire time I was chatting with John Tracey, I knew precisely what he would reply to everything I said. I could have held the conversation all by myself."

Valentine stopped breathing. "That does save time," he drawled, supremely conscious of her fingers creeping up his thighs.

"I suppose so, if one's dream is to never have any surprises, or even a good discussion about something." She leaned in closer, her lips feather-light running up his throat, along his jaw, and up to his mouth. At the same time, her hands went to work on the fastenings of his trousers.

"And who would want that?" he murmured, shifting to run his hands down her rib cage, drawing her closer into him.

"Exactly," she returned in a whisper, tugging his trousers down and freeing him. "What self-respecting chit would want anything unexpected to occur?"

Swallowing, his eyes closing at the exquisite sensation of her hand closing around him, Valentine slid her shift up past her thighs and around her hips. "It would seem to get in the way of an ordinary life," he agreed, lifting her up and then guiding her down to slowly impale her on his cock. God, he loved the feel of her, of every tight, hot inch engulfing him.

She threw back her head, gasping, as she sank down to

take him fully. "Oh, God, Valentine," she moaned, writhing against his hips.

He nearly came right then. "Eleanor, kiss me."

Hot and openmouthed, they kissed, tongues teasing. Putting both hands on her hips, Valentine rocked her forward. Immediately she took up the rhythm he'd begun. In and out, back and forth, the rolling of the carriage running through them with every movement. Their gazes locked as she moved on him, and he thrust up to her, a moan ripping from his chest.

He felt her come, heard her shuddering sigh. Speeding his own movements, he joined her, clasping her to his chest as she sank bonelessly against him.

Valentine lifted her chin in her fingers, kissing her lips softly. "Now you have to marry me," he whispered.

"No, I don't," she returned. "But I'll consider it."

"Didn't you steal anything demure?" Eleanor asked, twisting to look over her shoulder at Valentine as he fastened the back of her silk azure gown.

"Why would I do that?" he returned, the soft grin he'd worn for most of the morning deepening. "Besides, it was dark, and you were trying to castrate me."

Thankful she hadn't managed that, Eleanor leaned forward to dig into her portmanteau. They'd stopped the coach only once, and only long enough to move her luggage into the passenger compartment so she could dress. "There's not a thing here suited for less than a ball. I think you chose every Madame Costanza gown I own, and nothing else."

"You can hardly fault me for that, my dear."

"But what about breakfast? Do you expect me to wear this?"

"You don't have to wear anything, as far as I'm concerned."

"I'm certain all the innkeepers will appreciate that."

"I would, and that's what counts." He pushed open the curtain, glancing out at the passing countryside for a moment. "We won't be lingering anywhere too long, anyway."

"Are you afraid I'll change my mind?" She'd told him the truth before; she might be inescapably ruined now, but if the match wasn't to Melbourne's liking, he could still send her away from London, never to return, and never to marry at all. Valentine had narrowed her options considerably, but as she'd dozed against his shoulder through dawn, she couldn't be angry with him.

This was a fine mess, but he seemed to have jumped into it with her. And that in itself pushed her toward simply enjoying the adventure. At least one thing Valentine had told her was absolutely true; no one could make her feel as free, as hopeful, as he did. She loved him. And until reality came crashing down around her shoulders, she would let that be enough. For weeks she'd only imagined—and wished, and hoped—that Valentine was the type of man whom she could seriously consider for marriage; apparently she owed a great deal of thanks to this Father Michael, whoever he was.

"I'm afraid your brothers will hunt us down. It'd be poor taste for me to kill one of your close relations before our wedding."

Eleanor looked at him. He'd said the words in jest, but she had more than a suspicion that he was utterly serious. A thrill ran through her. Exhausted or not, she'd never felt so . . . alive as she did now. He excited and surprised and pleased her, but he was right about her brothers' objections. With Valentine's reputation for both impropriety and womanizing, Melbourne would never sit for a match between the two of them, and he would do everything in his power to stop it once he realized where and with whom she'd gone. "Let's not stop at all," she suggested.

Valentine pulled her around and kissed her. "I think we can afford a few moments to eat and change horses. Melbourne would only have risen an hour or so ago."

"And he still has to figure out where I've gone."

"Well, he might have an idea about that," Valentine muttered, looking sheepish.

Eleanor frowned. That look from him worried her. "What do you mean?"

"I left a note. On your bed."

She went cold. "Why would you do that?"

"Because I didn't want him to think you'd been dragged off by some stranger, and because short of asking his permission ahead of time, it seemed like the most gentlemanly thing to do."

"I see. And it wouldn't have anything to do with you *wanting* them to chase after us?"

He shrugged. "Well, the thought might have occurred to me. And this *is* an adventure for you. One that neither of us can completely control, now."

"You are a dangerous man."

"Thank you."

She scowled. "That wasn't a compliment."

Despite the fact that she would have been happy to flee to Scotland without stopping for anything, Eleanor had to admit that a chance to stretch her legs would be heavenly. And the hot, naughty part of her wanted to spend an entire night with Valentine Corbett, stretched out in a nice, soft bed. The thought that in two days she would have the freedom to do that every night for the rest of her life made her shiver with delight and indescribable anticipation.

"A penny for your thoughts," he murmured, handing her a bright coin.

She grasped it in her hand. "I still can't quite believe that yesterday morning I was resigned to . . . to being resigned," she said slowly, hoping the insightful marquis would realize that she could accept the adventure of all this, and even the breathless boldness of what he'd done, but that she hadn't *wanted* to be rescued. On the other hand, she had resigned herself to propriety as soon as Sebastian had ordered her to—so perhaps she had *needed* his rescue. "How could I give up? How could I just decide I'd had enough of being happy?" she muttered.

Valentine curled his fingers around hers. "Yesterday morning I was following John Tracey about, watching to see if and when Melbourne would send for him. I wanted to call him out, shoot him, run him through, anything to keep him from seeing you—and to keep you from liking him enough to marry him."

Tears gathered in her eyes. It seemed that sometimes dreams really could come true. Or she desperately hoped so—for both of their sakes. "I've always liked you, you know," she whispered.

"I know. Half the time I couldn't figure out why." He smiled again. "But odd as it sounds, you made me want to be that man. The one you liked."

It sounded wonderful. And only to herself, in the very back of her mind where she still retained some sanity, was she worried that this was nothing but an adventure for him, that he saw her as some sort of possession that he simply didn't want another man to have. For a while it might be enough that she had him, but if he didn't love her, if she was only an obsession, she was far more doomed than she would have been if she'd married John Tracey. At least if Tracey left her or took a lover, it would only disappoint her. Losing Valentine would kill her.

Chapter 21

‿‿‿◦◯◯◦‿‿‿

They stopped at the Greenbriar Inn for breakfast and to change horses. The inn was on the main mail route to London, so Valentine wasn't surprised to see it fairly crowded with stage passengers as they pulled into the yard. That meant potential witnesses for anyone who might follow, but Melbourne would know exactly where they were headed, anyway. Nervous though Eleanor had been on hearing that he'd left a note, he couldn't in good conscience have done otherwise.

Good conscience. No one was more surprised than he to learn that he had one. As the coach bumped to a halt he hopped out and lowered the step, offering a hand to Eleanor as she descended to the ground.

She was right about her wardrobe; he'd chosen five gowns to cram into the bulky portmanteau, and not one of them was suitable for daylight hours. Still, seeing her in low-cut azure beneath the bright sunlight made his heart flip-flop.

345

"People are looking," Eleanor said through her teeth as she curled her hand around his arm.

"Let them look. The stage is about to leave; they won't be here long." He glanced over at her. Something more than her brothers' pursuit troubled her, and he had a suspicion that it was he. "I'll rent us a private dining room," he decided.

It felt odd that the more time he spent with her, the more he wanted to be with her. Usually after a tryst with a woman he didn't even spend the entire night. With Eleanor, though, it wasn't just the sex, arousing as he found her. No, he enjoyed being in her presence. His father was probably spinning in his grave—but then, his father had slept with one woman too many and then died blind and mad. Not precisely an example he wished to follow. Not any longer.

The innkeeper showed them to a small private room set with a table and a sputtering fire. "I'll be with you in just a minute, my lord," he said through an impossibly curly beard. "The mail coach is leavin', and I have to get them passengers on board."

"Just send in some tea for a start," Valentine agreed, nodding. "And we'll be wanting breakfast."

"Aye, my lord."

"He looked at me rather oddly," Eleanor noted, stretching her back as soon as the door closed.

Valentine's veins heated as he watched her. No one else got to have her—not even for a moment, or in passing thought. He'd finally done the right thing—for both of them, he hoped. "Of course he did; you're wearing an evening gown."

She stuck her tongue out at him. "And I saw you sign us in. Lord and Lady Smith? You're not even trying to escape Melbourne."

"No, I'm counting on outdistancing him. My best scenario is that your maid decides you deserve to sleep in, and she doesn't go to wake you until eleven o'clock. She'll see the note and take it to the butler, who'll take it to Melbourne, who'll read it by half-past. Then he'll have to track down Shay and Zachary and formulate a plan, so they'll be on horseback and after us by half-past twelve." He pulled out his pocket watch and flipped it open. "Which is in another . . . four hours."

"Putting us ten hours ahead of them. Will that get us to Scotland in time?"

"If I have to drag the horses there on foot, it will," he returned. She might be used to her brothers and their self-assured view of the world, and so was he, but he well knew that the rest of England would fall before the Griffins' every demand. And he'd just crossed them in the most serious way possible.

"And what about your worst scenario?"

"They'll be here in ten minutes," he said, grinning. "But I'm going to be optimistic. It's my new philosophy."

Eleanor chuckled. "Good heavens. If this is a disaster, at least it'll be a spectacular one."

Valentine gazed at her sideways while she wandered to the window to look out at the departing mail coach passengers. The way she'd said "disaster" bothered him. She'd already made several leaps of faith in this adventure; whatever he'd said, if she'd truly wanted to stay in London, he would have turned around. But neither was she some carefree, naive young miss who believed everything without question. Her eyes were open; it was what she saw that troubled her. And she was looking at him.

A maid entered the room with their tea, curtsied as she set it on the table, and then hurried out again. Wordlessly

Eleanor went over to pour two cups, adding one sugar to hers and two to his.

"You remembered," he said, indicating the sugar.

Her soft lips twitched. "I used to have something of an infatuation with you."

Standing, Valentine walked over behind her. "Did you, now?" he asked softly, bending to kiss the nape of her neck.

"When I was fifteen, you seemed very dashing." Her soft intake of breath at his kiss made him hard again. Jesus, he couldn't get enough of her.

"Was that why you always used to give me the lemon biscuit with the most sugar powdered on it?" he murmured, brushing aside her long tail of hair to continue trailing his mouth along her neck to her soft throat. Her pulse beat wildly beneath his lips.

"You noticed that?"

Turning her to face him, he kissed her lips, gently but thoroughly. It wasn't enough, but there would be time for more once they started north again. "I'm very observant."

"So I see." She slid her arms around his neck, pulling herself up along his chest.

"Here you are, my lord," the innkeeper said, pushing open the door. "I took the liberty of bringing in some fresh, hot bread."

"Yes, thank you," Valentine said, torn between annoyance and amusement as Eleanor pulled away from him and retreated to the far side of the room. He ordered ham, eggs, and fresh peaches for the two of them and sent the innkeeper away again. "Are you going to stay over there?" he asked, facing Eleanor again.

She demurely seated herself beside the fireplace. "I

think so. You know, I have a few questions for you before I agree to become your wife."

"Oh, you do?" he drawled, to cover the sudden uneasy thud of his poor, misused heart. "I was counting on simply sweeping you off your feet, past all logic and reason."

Eleanor smiled. "And so you did. But they've caught up."

He was doomed. "Then ask away."

"Very well." She took a breath. "Children. Do you want to have them?"

Valentine stopped the flip answer he'd been about to make. She was serious, and if he didn't answer seriously, he could still lose her. "A month or two ago," he said, leaning back against the edge of the table, "I would have said I wanted one son, to inherit the title after me." The mail coach rattled out of the inn yard to the sound of shouts and squeaking springs, and Valentine relaxed a little. Melbourne could still run across the passengers, but those odds shrank with every mile they traveled. More likely, they'd just gone from a dozen available witnesses to two or three.

"Now," he continued, "the idea of domesticity has an . . . appeal I never expected, as does simply growing old. With you. I'd like to have children with you, Eleanor." He hesitated again, hoping he didn't sound like an idiot, and hoping she would keep in mind that he'd never expected to have this conversation, much less these feelings. "I don't know what kind of father I'll make, but I'd like a chance to do a better job of it than my own father did."

She nodded, looking away for a moment while she touched the corner of one eye. "And when I'm older and not so pretty, and my hair turns gray? What will—"

"I'll be older and not so pretty, and my hair will gray

before yours, Eleanor," he interrupted. "I may even get fat and become jolly. I haven't decided yet."

"The point being—"

"No," he interrupted again. "I don't want anyone else. I won't want anyone else. You've . . . you've made me see things differently. I can't explain adequately, because I don't think the words have been invented. But my heart has recently begun beating, and hurting you in any way would make it stop again. And that would kill me."

"Oh," she whispered.

Well, this new thing—this honesty—seemed to be working. And it wasn't as painful as he'd been led to believe. He pushed upright. "No one else—nothing else—can affect my happiness like you do. I wasn't willing to risk you turning me down."

Eleanor sighed. Should she tell him that what she really wanted to know, all she really wanted to be certain of, was that he would look at her that way forever, with a mixture of affection and exasperation in his expression? He would probably give his promise of adoration if she requested it, but that wasn't the same as *knowing* that he would do it. Valentine certainly said all the right things, but when it counted, would he still be the man she'd fallen in love with? Anything less than his entire heart would ensure her a miserable, hopeless rest of her life.

The door behind him opened again. This time Eleanor was grateful for the innkeeper's interruption. Oh, she needed to figure out what she could expect from Deverill, and whether that would be enough to satisfy her heart.

"Just leave it on the table," Valentine said, continuing to approach her.

Someone moved up fast behind him, and swung a heavy platter at the back of his head. It struck him with a thud. Rolling back his eyes, Valentine fell bonelessly to the floor.

Eleanor drew in a breath to scream, but the sound froze in her throat as Stephen Cobb-Harding tossed aside the tray and stepped over Valentine's limp body. "You've had quite an adventure, haven't you?" he said conversationally.

With a shriek Eleanor snatched up a piece of firewood and ran at him. "Go away! Go away!"

He caught the blow against his forearm, stumbling backward as she slammed the wood at him again. Her mind refused to go beyond the thought that he couldn't be there. They were finished with him. He'd tried to ruin her before, and he'd failed. Valentine had stopped him.

A sob ripped from her throat. "Help!" she screamed, swinging at him again.

Cobb-Harding grabbed her arm and yanked the firewood out of her hand. "Stop that!" he bellowed, pushing her onto the floor.

She fell beside Valentine, who lay prone half on his face. "No, no, no," she whispered raggedly, touching his cheek.

The door opened again. "Keep her quiet, damn it all," another voice said. "The innkeeper's already asking for more blunt." The man dressed like a gentleman, and he looked vaguely familiar—one of the male horde who had been swarming around her for weeks, but to whom she couldn't even remember speaking. Looking over his shoulder, he left the room again, leaning back in as he swung the door closed. "And hurry up. You know we don't have much time."

Cobb-Harding jerked her upright by one arm. "You heard him, Nell. Keep quiet. I don't want to hit you."

"Then what do you want?" she rasped, pulling away so hard that her sleeve ripped off.

He shifted his grip to her shoulder. "It's a simple business proposition," he grunted, "if you'd calm down and listen."

"Calm down? You attacked Valentine from behind, you coward!"

"Be glad I didn't kill him, Nell. That would remove a considerable amount of debt and embarrassment—and the need for relocation—on my part."

Oh, God, she'd forgotten about that. "I don't—"

"I tried to explain to Melbourne that I am in an untenable position. Unfortunately, *you* are obviously my only solution."

She kicked at him, and he flung her into the fireside chair. A third man pushed into the room, and Eleanor frowned as he dragged the limp Valentine out of the way. "I know you. Peter Burnsey. You play cards with Charlemagne."

"I *lose* at cards with Charlemagne," the grandson of the Marquis of Sneldon returned, lifting an eyebrow. "And Deverill. I also lose at other things. Until today, of course."

"You must be desperate, to throw in your lot with this idiot," she snapped, wishing her voice were steadier. She glanced over at Valentine, now crumpled in the corner. He hadn't moved, and her throat constricted. *Please let him be all right.*

"A little risk, for a lot of reward," Mr. Burnsey said. "His coach is ready. Are we taking it, or do you want to wait for the next mail coach north?"

Cobb-Harding gave a short grin. "Since Deverill was kind enough to bring it this far, we might as well avail ourselves of it." Rubbing at his forearm, he jerked Eleanor back to her feet. "You might have dressed a little less conspicuously, Nell."

She pulled against his grip. "I'm not going anywhere with you. Let me go at once!"

"You don't get to give orders here, my lady," Cobb-Harding returned. "Besides, we're only continuing the journey you began. Deverill was taking you to Gretna Green, was he not?"

Deep dread froze Eleanor's heart. "Stop this."

"No. I need twenty-five thousand pounds to pull me out of my debt to Deverill. Short of killing him, that is, which I really don't wish to do. That would serve to banish me from England, and that's what I'm trying to avoid. I gave your brother the opportunity to assist me and to keep your reputation safe. He refused."

"You attacked me!" she snapped. "You tried to—"

"I tried to secure our marriage. And now the match is even more necessary than before. So you and I will marry, with Burnsey and Perline as witnesses, and your brother will *have* to make good on my debts."

Burnsey came forward to eye her as well. "And perhaps *my* debts."

"In any case," Stephen continued, "I'll be free from Deverill, and I'll be part of the Griffin clan. Do you see a negative side to any of this? Because frankly I can't see one."

"I can."

Valentine hit him in the chest. His arms flailing, Stephen slammed backward into the hard wood table. Burnsey stumbled out of the way as bread and tea flew in the air. Cobb-Harding tried to roll sideways, but Valentine hit him again, this time with a fist into the jaw.

She jumped forward to help. Before she could reach Valentine, a foot caught Eleanor's skirt, dumping her onto the floor. Pain shot through her right knee, but she didn't care. Valentine needed her help, or at least her distraction.

She scrambled away, pulling herself back to her feet as Burnsey stormed past her to grab Valentine's shoulder. "No," she shrieked, slamming him across the head and shoulder with the remains of the teapot.

As Burnsey staggered backward, hot tea dripping from his hair, Andrew Perline charged into the room. "Deverill, behind you!" she yelled, throwing the bread platter at Burnsey.

Whipping around, Valentine took Perline's charge in the ribs instead of in the back. They crashed through a chair, splintering the heavy thing and sending pieces scattering. Eleanor snatched up part of the armrest and limped forward.

A hand grabbed her arm, wrenching the club free of her grip. "None of that," Cobb-Harding growled. "Come along, Nell."

"Let go!" She tried to bash him with her elbow, but he slapped her hard enough to stun.

Even with a bloody nose and a cut across his forehead, he managed to look smug. But then he had Valentine outnumbered three to one. "My friends will be along shortly. I'm sure they'll tell you Deverill's fate if you ask them nicely. Of course if you were to cooperate, this episode might end a bit more pleasantly—for him."

Valentine. "You may as well stop this and let me go," she snapped, digging her thin slippers into the floor and fighting his pull with every ounce of strength she had, "because I will never agree to marry you."

"Of course you will. If you don't, your reputation will be ruined beyond repair."

"Not over a forced kidnapping."

"I only secured you from Deverill. You were in the midst of an elopement, were you not? It's Deverill who's

ruined you; not me. I'm only stepping in to finish the job."
He gave a slow grin, made lopsided by his swollen lip.
"You should be thanking me, rather than fighting me."

"I don't care if I have to spend the remainder of my life
in a French convent," she returned, swinging her fist at his
face. "I will not marry you!"

"Eleanor!" Valentine bellowed, half buried beneath the
other two men.

"Shut him up. Permanently," Cobb-Harding snarled.
"I've been reasonable beyond all expectation."

Oh, God, they were going to kill him. She did have more
to risk than her reputation. And she couldn't, wouldn't,
give away Valentine's life. Not for anything. "Stephen, I'll
go with you," she said quickly.

He stopped, looking down at her with suspicion clear in
his sunny blue eyes. "Oh, really. And why is that?"

"I'll go if you'll leave Deverill alone. Tie him up or
lock him in a room, and I'll go with you."

"And you'll agree to marry me."

A tear running down her face, she nodded. "If you don't
hurt him anymore."

He yanked her up against him, reminding her horribly
of the night he'd attacked her. She could tolerate his company for a short while, she told herself, until she could
get free, or until her brothers caught up. Or until Valentine could figure out a way for them to get out of this.

"You heard her, Deverill!" Cobb-Harding yelled.
"She's going with me. You lose."

Blood dripping from his hairline, Valentine shoved to
his feet, Perline clinging to his back and half choking him.
"Eleanor," he rasped. "Don't."

"Stop it, Valentine," she ordered, another tear joining
the first. "Don't fight them. I'm going with Stephen."

He glared at her through his disheveled tangle of dark hair. "So you're just giving up?"

"No, she isn't. She's choosing me. Tie him up."

Valentine yanked an arm free of Burnsey's grip. "Don't bother. I thought you were a fighter, Eleanor. If this is how little your freedom means to you, then good riddance. This is all too damned sticky for me."

Eleanor blinked. A short time ago she would have believed his easy dismissal of her. Now she could only watch, wide-eyed and not having to pretend her look of horror, while she wondered whether Burnsey and Perline knew the old Deverill better than the new one.

"Do you expect me to believe you would just abandon her, Deverill?" Cobb-Harding asked.

Valentine shrugged his torn coat back onto his shoulders. "I was in this for a bit of fun, a romp at the expense of the almighty Griffins," he returned, and looked pointedly at Eleanor. "In truth, she's a bit too stiff, and this is no longer fun."

Play along, Nell, she told herself. "How . . . how could you, Valentine?"

"Don't look at me," he snorted, wiping blood from his face. "You made the agreement. Not me."

"But—"

Moving so quickly his arm seemed to blur, Valentine shot out his fist, catching Burnsey flush on the jaw. The man collapsed without a sound. Perline lunged at him again, but he'd lost the angle. Deverill's knee caught him in the face, and he went down with a *wumph*.

"There now," Valentine said, dusting his hands together. "That's better."

"But you agreed—"

"*She* agreed, Stephen," he countered, stepping over

Burnsey's legs as he advanced. "I didn't. And I'd guess she was probably lying to you."

Cobb-Harding tightened his grip on Eleanor's arm. "She's coming with me. Stay back, Deverill. I don't want to hurt her, but I will if you don't give me another choice."

"A choice," Valentine repeated, wiping the back of his hand across his mouth. His tone remained calm, but the look in his eyes was frightening. Eleanor was abruptly doubly glad that she wasn't Stephen Cobb-Harding at this moment. "I'll give you a choice, then," he continued. "Let her go, or I'll skin you alive and feed your carcass to the hogs."

"No," Cobb-Harding replied. "You don't get to win, Deverill. You've treated me poorly, when you would have done the exact same thing if our positions were reversed. You can have any woman. You don't need her. I do."

"You're wrong about that, Stephen." Staggering a little, Valentine gripped the back of the one upright chair in the room. "Eleanor . . . *duck!*"

She threw herself down. The chair whistled over her head, catching Cobb-Harding high in the shoulder and sending him sprawling over the table and to the floor. As soon as he went down Valentine was on him, twisting an arm behind Cobb-Harding's back until Stephen screeched.

"You're breaking my arm!"

"And your complaint is?" Valentine panted. "Lie down, facedown on the floor." He glanced over his shoulder at Eleanor. "Get ropes or blankets or draperies. Anything we can use to bind their hands."

She hurried for the door, shoving it open and nearly falling over the innkeeper and his wife. "You heard him," she barked. "What do you have?"

"They threatened us, you know," the innkeeper blustered, backing away.

"I don't care. Find me some rope, instantly."

Apparently he realized that the bribe he'd been promised was no longer forthcoming, because he produced a length of rope from a storage closet and handed it over. "Shall I fetch a constable?"

She nearly agreed to that, but first she wanted to check with Valentine. In her mind the optimistic ten hours lead they had kept ticking away. Calling in the constabulary would eat it away entirely. "I'll inform you in a moment," she hedged, running back into the private room.

Together they bound the three men. Valentine knotted Cobb-Harding's legs, pulling the rope so taut that Eleanor wouldn't be surprised if the earl's son ended up with gangrene.

"There," Valentine said, finally straightening. "They aren't going anywhere now."

"You're all right?" she asked.

Slowly he held out his hand to her. She placed her fingers in his, and he led her to the far side of the room. "You have blood on your cheek," he murmured, reaching out to touch her face.

"I don't think it's mine. You're the one with the cracked skull." She realized that his fingers were shaking, and she tightened her own grip. "You scared me a little."

"I know. I needed them to relax for just a moment. I would never . . ." He stopped, clearing his throat. "I would never let anyone hurt you, Eleanor. I should have realized Stephen wouldn't give up so easily. I put you in danger. This—"

"Shh," she whispered. "I'm not hurt."

"Yes, you are." He leaned down to kiss her. "I'm not the sort of man that women trust. I know you don't trust me."

"I trust you with my life, Valentine."

He smiled a little. "But not with your heart."

"That's not what I meant. You scared me because I thought for a second that he'd killed you."

For a long moment Valentine gazed at her. "Thank you for that." Then to her surprise, he took her other hand and clasped it as well, then sank down onto both knees before her. "I . . . I couldn't stand to lose you, Eleanor," he continued in a husky whisper. "You make me feel optimistic, and happy, and content. You've taught me so much."

With his face upturned, blood running down one cheek, and his deceptively sleepy eyes more earnest and sincere than she'd ever seen, Eleanor could believe him. She *wanted* to believe him. "You've taught me a great deal, as well. More than I thought I had to learn."

His smile deepened into his eyes. "You and I, we aren't so different, you know. You worry about too many things, and I worry about too few. Except for you, now. You've caused me a great deal of thought recently."

Oh, goodness. "Have I, now?"

"Yes, you have. I lo—"

The common room door slammed open again. Before she could even gasp, Valentine shot to his feet, pulling her behind him. She could feel the tension in his shoulders, every muscle taut and ready to defend her. To protect her.

But he didn't move. Taking a breath, Eleanor peeked around his shoulder. "Oh, no," she whispered.

His calculations had been off by approximately nine and a half hours, but Valentine had been correct. Her brothers had caught up with them.

Chapter 22

❧◦◦◦❧

Damnation, Valentine thought as he fought for control over both his temper and the dizziness slogging through his brain. For the Griffin brethren to have any worse timing, they would have had to have caught him and Eleanor naked.

"Sebastian," Eleanor gulped, gripping Valentine's hand tight enough to leave a mark.

The duke stood just inside the doorway, his brothers ranged on either side of them. After the first second, though, Melbourne's attention shifted to the broken furniture, strewn-about bread and tea, and the three men bound and stretched out on the floor.

"Shay, gather anyone who might have heard what happened in here," he said quietly, pulling his pocketbook from his coat and handing it over. "Make certain they don't know anything."

Charlemagne nodded, taking the billfold and vanishing back into the main part of the inn. Valentine opened his mouth to say something typically witty and dry, but all he could think of was ordering Melbourne to stay the hell away from Eleanor and himself. Considering his wrenched shoulder and throbbing skull, he wasn't up for another three-on-one battle at the moment, but he kept his fists clenched, waiting. No one was going to stop him from making Eleanor his.

"What the devil is going on?" Zachary demanded, moving farther into the room.

"A misunderstanding," Valentine supplied, shifting a little to keep both brothers in sight.

"That's a bit of an understatement, I'd say," Zachary shot back. "And it would be worse if you hadn't squeaked the damned stair. Jesus, Deverill, you stole our sister."

"Yes, you should really get that stair fixed," Valentine returned.

"I think everyone should calm down," Eleanor said, tightening her grip on Valentine's arm.

"And I think Deverill should move away from you, unless he wants more of whatever's been handed him already." Zachary's fists clenched.

"I hope you can back up your mouth, boy," Valentine bit back. "Stay away."

"You—"

"Zachary," the duke interrupted. "We're going to try to be civilized about this. Questions and answers. Not accusations."

"And what if we don't like the answers?" the youngest Griffin brother returned.

"Then we'll still have time for being uncivilized." Melbourne righted one of the intact chairs. "Why don't we all sit down?"

Valentine would have refused, but he could feel Eleanor

shaking beside him. Aside from that, as much as his head hurt, he was ready to fall to the floor. With a tight nod he handed Eleanor to the bench on the near side of the table and then carefully seated himself beside her, keeping close enough that he could hold her hand, and far enough that he still had room to move quickly if one of the brothers tried to jump him.

"I can explain," Eleanor said unexpectedly.

The duke lifted an eyebrow. "Please do, then. Keeping this in mind, of course." He pulled a folded note from his pocket. "I doubt you've read it, so I'll tell you. It says that you've been kidnapped by Deverill, and that he is taking you to Gretna Green with the idea of marrying you to keep you from my," he looked down, "my 'overstuffed, self-important ignorance' of your needs."

"I left voluntarily," she blurted, flushing.

"So the note is a lie, and this is an elopement?"

"I kidnapped her," Valentine put in. Whatever happened, Eleanor loved her brothers. He wouldn't allow her to drive a wedge between them, even for his sake. "I couldn't sit by and watch you force her into a—"

"—a life of misery?" Melbourne finished. "A little dramatic, I think. Especially for you. You're a pragmatist, Deverill. And a cynic."

"I was going to say a common, ordinary life," Valentine countered.

"But I asked him to help me in the first place," Eleanor interrupted again. "This is my fault. Don't be angry at Valentine. He saved me." She glanced over at Cobb-Harding, mumbling in a pained, muffled tone. "He saved me."

"Oh, stop it, Nell," the duke cut in. "Deverill doesn't look after anyone's skin but his own. Everyone knows that."

"Yes, they do," Valentine agreed, anger threatening to overthrow the calm he'd forced on himself. "So why would you choose someone as jaded and irresponsible as I am to watch over your sister in the first place?"

Charlemagne slipped back into the room and tossed the billfold back to Melbourne. "Taken care of," he grunted, striding over to stand beside the fireplace. "What did I miss?"

"Nothing yet. Melbourne was about to explain why he would select someone unacceptable to guard his sister," Valentine said, before Zachary or Sebastian could color the conversation with their version of events.

"I didn't," the duke said slowly.

Even Shay looked puzzled. "You didn't what?"

"Select someone unacceptable to guard my sister."

"I beg to differ," Zachary said with a snort. "Jesus, Melbourne, he kidnapped her out of our house in the middle of the night! And you consider him a friend. I say we call for the constable and have all four of them dragged before the bar and carted off to Australia."

Valentine ignored the insults, instead looking at the duke for a long moment. A hundred conversations, a dozen scenarios, played through his mind. He'd known Melbourne for a long time, and he'd never seen him make a false step, misjudge a business proposal or a partner. No, by God, the duke had known precisely what he was doing when he blackmailed Valentine into the middle of this mess.

"You were matchmaking," Eleanor gasped. Evidently she'd been coming to the same conclusions. "You were trying to put Valentine and me together."

"*What*?" Shay straightened. "Don't be ridiculous. Why would Melbourne think Deverill would ever commit to—"

"But he did," Melbourne interrupted.

Eleanor stood, her face white. "You can't possibly be saying that you arranged all of this." She looked down at Valentine, her hurt expression like a thousand knives in his chest. "You didn't—"

"I didn't know anything about it." And if Melbourne's smug assumption of the responsibility for everything that had happened continued, he was going to lose her. He gingerly stood beside her, forcing himself not to wince. "And I don't care. Whatever happened to this point to bring us here, I don't care."

"Valentine, I am tired of being manipulated. I am not going to tolerate another instant of this. How am I—"

Valentine kissed her. It had little finesse, but it stopped her argument. Slowly her mouth softened against his, and he deepened the kiss in response, sliding his hands around her waist. "Eleanor," he whispered, lifting his head a little, "I love you. I truly don't care about the circumstances which brought it about."

She blinked, lifting her gaze from his mouth to his eyes. "What did you say?"

"Oh, just ignore us," Zachary broke in. "You're the ones who ran off to—"

"Shut up, Zachary," Valentine interrupted, grasping Nell's hand. "Eleanor, walk with me."

"We're not letting you out of our sight." Charlemagne started across the room toward them.

"Then stop us," Valentine said, lifting his chin.

"Let them go," the duke broke in, before the fighting could begin again. "They know better than to leave without us."

Valentine wouldn't have wagered on that, but he didn't say anything more as he led Eleanor from the room, through the kitchen, and out into the small, simple side yard.

"Do you really think he masterminded all of this?" Eleanor asked, facing him. "That he arranged for us to end up together?"

He shook his head. "I think he figured I'd be a good influence on you, and you'd be a good one on me. As for the rest, he couldn't have had any idea."

"I'm a good influence on you?" Eleanor studied his face. Somehow he looked even more handsome now, with his hair disheveled and his face bruised and bloodied. It was as if with the polish gone, she could see the true value of the gem.

"Yes. Especially in the way you wanted your moment of freedom, but not in a way that would hurt anyone else." He hesitated. "Responsibility isn't something I've ever had much use for. I always thought it would feel like a shackle, or a noose around my neck. And then I realized that I felt responsible toward you, that I worried over what could happen, that I didn't want you to be sad or disappointed. And it didn't make my world feel smaller, Eleanor. Just the opposite. And I do love you."

Eleanor cupped his face in both hands, leaning up to kiss him. She couldn't help herself. He meant it. He'd said that he loved her, and he meant it. "I went swimming naked in a baptismal pond in the middle of Hyde Park," she said softly, chuckling against his mouth. "I went for drives without an escort, and I spoke about my interests to people without worrying what they might think." Slowly she kissed him again.

"And you can still do all of that, Eleanor. You don't have to live a small life."

"I don't think I could, with you."

"With me?" he repeated, brushing hair from her face. "This hasn't been too much of an adventure, even for you?"

"Never. I've known what I wanted for my adventure—for my life—since the night you saved me from Stephen at the Belmont soiree. I just didn't know whether it would be wise or not."

"And now?"

"And now I know that you may be rather unconventional, but you're also kind and caring and honorable." Her smile deepened. "I do want to be like you, Valentine."

"You are like me. In only the good ways, of course. Marry me, Eleanor."

She nodded, another tear running down her face. "I want to marry you. More than anything."

He kissed her again, slow and feather-light. "Good. Then let's be off."

Eleanor lifted both eyebrows. "To Gretna Green?"

"Melbourne thinks he knows everything. But I'll wager he won't expect us to continue with this particular adventure."

She covered her mouth with both hands. Now that her brothers were there, now that she knew what she wanted, she'd just expected that everything would settle back into easy convention. Where Valentine Corbett was concerned, though, she supposed she shouldn't expect anything but surprise. And that, for her, was perfection.

"Yes," she agreed, laughing aloud. "Let's go."

If you've enjoyed her historicals, then you're going to love *USA Today* bestselling author Suzanne Enoch's dazzling romantic suspense debut! Be the first to read this thrilling tale.

Raised to appreciate the finer things in life, Samantha Jellicoe has no trouble divesting the wealthy of their treasures. But an attempt to steal a valuable item from a Palm Beach estate goes horribly wrong—a bomb goes off, a guard is killed, Sam ends up saving millionaire Richard Addison, then making a desperate escape before she's implicated for murder.... When the dust settles, Rick knows the only person with answers to his questions is the mystery woman. He has to find her... even if he has to risk everything by

Flirting With Danger

Available March 2005
from Avon Books

Tuesday, 2:17 A.M.

Samantha Jellicoe wondered who, precisely, had written the rule that thieves breaking into anything larger than a paper bag must always scale walls. Everyone knew it. Everyone counted on it, from prisons to castles to the movies to theme parks to the impressive east Florida estate sprawling before her. Stone walls, electric fences, cameras, motion detectors, security guards, all for the purpose of preventing an enterprising lawbreaker from climbing over the walls into the sanctity of private space beyond.

She looked from the stone wall in front of her to the wrought-iron double gate at the front of sprawling Solano Dorado House and gave a small smile. Some lawbreakers were more enterprising than others. So much for the rules.

Drawing in a slow breath to steady her heartbeat, she unslung the weapon from her shoulder, sank deeper into the shadows outside the gate, aimed at the camera mounted atop the fifteen-foot-high stone wall to the left of it, and fired. With a small puff of air, a paint ball splatted hard against the side of the casing, tilting it crazily up toward the treetops and streaking the lens with white paint. An owl, disturbed by the motion, hooted and launched from a branch of the overhanging sycamore, one wing passing right in front of the redirected camera.

Nice touch, she thought, slinging the paint gun back over her shoulder. Her horoscope had said that today would be her lucky day. Normally she didn't put much stock in astrology, but ten percent of one and a half million for an evening's work seemed lucky enough to qualify. She scooted forward, sliding a pair of long-handled mirrors into place on either side of the heavy gates to deflect the sensors into themselves. That done, it only took a second to bypass the circuitry in the control box and shove one of the gates open far enough for her to slip through.

She'd spent all day memorizing the location of the remainder of the cameras and the three motion detectors she needed to pass, and in two minutes she'd crossed through the trees and landscaped garden to sink into a crouch at the base of a red stone staircase. Thanks to blueprints and schematics, she knew the location of every window and door, and the make and model of every lock and wiring connection. What the drawings hadn't done was tell her color and scope, and she took a second while she caught her breath to admire the sprawl of decadence.

Solano Dorado had been built in the 1920s before the stock market crash, and each successive owner had added rooms and floors—and increasingly sophisticated security. Its current incarnation was probably the most attractive so far, all whitewashed and red-tile-roofed and massive, surrounded by palms and old sycamores, with a hockey-rink-sized fishpond in the front. At the back of the house where she crouched, two tennis courts lay beyond an Olympic-sized swimming pool. The actual tidal pools at the edge of the actual ocean gurgled and sighed only a hundred yards away, but that was for public consumption.

The estate was private and protected, and created to suit the whims of man rather than nature. After eighty years of tasteful modifications and expansion, it was now the house of someone with a massive pocketbook and an equally massive ego. Someone whose horoscope read the opposite of hers and who happened to be out of the country at the moment.

Doors and window casings would be wired to within an inch of their lives, but sometimes the old, simple tricks were best. As *Star Trek*'s Mr. Scott had once said, the more elaborate the plumbing, the easier it was to plug up the drain. With a check of her watch to confirm her timing, she pulled out a roll of gray duct tape. Samantha taped down a rough, three-foot circle low on the patio window, then pulled a suction cup and glass cutter from her pack. The glass was thick and heavy, the pop and squeak when she jerked the cut round piece free louder than she would have liked. Wincing, she set the circle into the flower bed and returned to the opening she'd made.

Swiftly she ran down the list of anyone who might have heard the glass separate. Not the security guard downstairs in the video bank, but at least two more guards patrolled the inside of the house while the owner wasn't in residence. She waited a moment, listening, then, with a deep breath and the customary adrenaline flowing into her system, she slipped inside.

Two more pieces of duct tape kept the curtains in place over the hole. No sense in revealing her exit to the first guard who wandered by. Next came the stairs, a genuine Picasso hanging from the wall at the first landing. Sam passed it with barely a glance. Another would be hanging in an upstairs conference room, both wired with sensors and worth millions. She knew about them already, and tempting as they were, they weren't the reason she was there.

Samantha paused at the third-floor landing, crouching on the stairs and leaning around to view the dim, long, gallery hall. Even as she reflected that she'd seen lesser collections of arms and armament in museums, she checked for any sign of movement or sensors newer than her blueprints and scowled at the number of shadowed places a guard could be standing, where she'd never see anything until she was right on top of him.

Her target was in the middle of the hallway, through a door on the left. Sam didn't bother glancing at her watch again; she knew how long she'd been in the house, and how much longer she was likely to have before an outside patrol discovered either the hole in the glass patio door or the small mirrors at the front gate. With another deep, silent breath she pushed off.

Keeping low, she made for the nearest of the motionless knights, pausing in its shadow to listen again before she slipped forward once more. It was going to be close; she needed to be through that side door before the next patrol came by. And because of the razor-sharp timing this was her favorite part—not so much gadgetry as pure nerves and skill. Anyone could purchase the former, but the latter was what separated the women from the girls.

Ten feet from her destination she stopped short. A thin, dim glint of moonlight ran straight across the hallway, two feet above the floor and three inches from her left leg. A wire. No one ran a wire across the middle of a hallway. It was stupid, not to mention primitive and dangerous to the residents. Of course no one was *in* residence, but surely the security guards would occasionally forget the damned thing and either fall on their faces or set off the alarms— or both.

Scowling, she edged closer to the wall to see how the idiotic thing was anchored. What she should do was step over it, get what she'd come for, and leave, but its presence was just so . . . wrong. High-tech security everywhere, and here a damned steel wire.

A damned copper wire, she amended, looking closer. Wire set into small, flat black panels on either wall, stretched tight and not precisely parallel to the floor. Close, but not exactly. Yes, the house's owner was famously fanatical about his privacy, but trip wires seemed a bit much. Nor had she seen any clue that he was less than fastidious about the mansion's craftsmanship. Her frown deepened.

"Freeze!"

Sam froze, crouched behind the wire. *Shit.* The guard was early. Thirty feet in front of her, on the far side of the door, a shadow stepped out from between two gleaming silver knights.

"Don't move a muscle!"

"I'm not," she said calmly. He belonged there; she didn't. And he had a big gun held not quite steadily in both hands. "I'm not armed," she continued in the same cool voice, eyeing the shaking weapon and silently urging him not to panic.

"What's that over your shoulder, then?" he snapped, edging closer. A drip of sweat slid down his forehead.

Be calm; make him feel calm. She knew how to work this—she'd done it before. "It's a paint gun."

"Put it down. And the bag over your other shoulder."

At least he hadn't already begun squeezing off rounds in her direction. Young, but with some training, thank God. She hated amateurs. Sam put her things on the floor, easing them onto the tasteful Persian carpet runner. "You don't have anything to worry about. We're on the same team."

"Like hell." Freeing his left hand from the butt of the pistol, he reached for his shoulder. "Clark? I have an intruder. Third floor, gallery."

"No shit?" came over the radio.

"No shit. Dispatch police."

Taking a heartbeat to be grateful that the owner liked his privacy enough to keep cameras out of the main house, Sam produced a loud, suffering sigh. "That really isn't necessary. Your boss hired me, to test security."

"Like I've never heard that before," he retorted, his sarcasm blistering even in the cool darkness. "No one told me, so you can tell it to the cops. Stand up."

Slowly she straightened, keeping her hands well away from her sides as her adrenaline pumped up another notch. Just in case, she took one long step back, away from the wire. "If you knew about it, it wouldn't be a test. Come on, I could have had the Picasso downstairs, or the Matisse in the drawing room, or anything else I wanted. I was supposed to test the central security. Turn on the lights, and I'll show you my ID."

The lights went on, quick and bright enough to make her jump. *What the hell?* There wasn't any of that voice command shit in here—and the guard looked startled, too, the gun twitching alarmingly. "Easy there," she urged smoothly. She bent her knees a little, getting ready to run.

His blinking gaze, though, was beyond her shoulder, toward the stairs. "Mr. Addison. I found—"

"So I see."

Sam fought the surge of annoyance, and the damned curiosity to see the rich and rarely photographed. If she got out of there, which was beginning to look dicey, she was absolutely going to kill Stoney. *No one in residence, my ass*. "Richard Addison, I presume," she muttered over her shoulder, relaxing her stance again.

"I thought he hired you," the guard said, more confident now beneath the overhead lights and with backup.

"Not him," she returned, deciding to keep up the game. "The security firm. Myerson-Schmidt. *Your* boss."

"Doubtful," the low voice murmured from closer behind, just loud enough for her to hear. For a rich guy, he moved pretty quietly. "She's not armed, Prentiss," Addison continued at a more normal level, cultured and slightly faded Brit in his voice. "Lower your weapon before someone gets hurt, and we'll sort this out downstairs."

Prentiss hesitated, then holstered his pistol. "Yes, sir."

"Now, why don't we have a look at you, Miss . . ."

"Smith," she supplied.

"How unexpected."

Sam wasn't listening. She was watching Prentiss snap the holster closed over his gun, watching him stride forward, obviously pleased to be able to show off for the big boss. Watching him not even glance down. "Stop!" she ordered, abrupt panic making the command shrill and tight.

"Like h—"

"Jesus." Sam whipped around, angling for the stairs and plowing at a dead run into Addison, registering no more than a glimpse of bare chest, startled gray eyes, and tousled black hair as she took him down to the floor with her. With a pop and flash at her back the hallway exploded. Heat slammed into her even pressed against Addison on the floor. The house shook, glass shattering. Drawing in its breath, the gallery roared even more thunderously, and the lights went out again.

Roses are red, violets are blue,
but these books are much more fun than flowers!
Coming to you in February from Avon Romance . . .

Something About Emmaline by Elizabeth Boyle

An Avon Romantic Treasure

Alexander Denford, Baron Sedgwick is a gentleman much envied for his indulgent and oft-absent wife, Emmaline—who is in fact a mere figment meant to keep the *ton* mamas at bay. But one day Alexander starts receiving bills from London for ball gowns in his imaginary bride's name, and he realizes a real Emmaline is about to present herself, whether he likes it or not!

Hidden Secrets by Cait London

An Avon Contemporary Romance

A missing boy, an unsolved murder, the feeling of impending danger. Marlo cannot figure out how they are connected—until she finds and develops an old roll of film that unlocks the past. But as she gets closer to the truth of the missing boy, she must choose between two men for protection. And if she makes one wrong move, it will be her last . . .

In the Night by Kathryn Smith

An Avon Romance

A life of crime is not what Wynthrope Ryland wanted for himself, but he will do what he must—if only to protect his dearest brother, North. Moira Tyndale, a stately viscountess, is to be the victim of this ill-timed theft, but she is also the one woman who can tempt him . . . or perhaps, somehow, set his wrongs to rights.

Stealing Sophie by Sarah Gabriel

An Avon Romance

Connor MacPherson, a Highland laird turned outlaw, must find a bride—or steal one. Intending to snatch infamously wanton Kate MacCarran, he mistakenly abducts her sister, Sophie—recently returned from a French convent. Quickly wedded, passionately bedded, Sophie cannot escape, and cannot be rescued—but perhaps this is not such a bad thing after all!

REL 0105